Ten Beach Road

Wendy Wax

BERKLEY BOOKS, NEW YORK

THE BERKLEY PUBLISHING GROUP
Published by the Penguin Group
Penguin Group (USA) Inc.
375 Hudson Street, New York, New York 10014, USA
Penguin Group (Canada), 90 Eglinton Avenue East, Suite 700, Toronto, Ontario M4P 2Y3, Canada
(a division of Pearson Penguin Canada Inc.)
Penguin Books Ltd., 80 Strand, London WC2R 0RL, England
Penguin Group Ireland, 25 St. Stephen's Green, Dublin 2, Ireland (a division of Penguin Books Ltd.)
Penguin Group (Australia), 250 Camberwell Road, Camberwell, Victoria 3124, Australia
(a division of Pearson Australia Group Pty. Ltd.)
Penguin Books India Pvt. Ltd., 11 Community Centre, Panchsheel Park, New Delhi—110 017, India
Penguin Group (NZ), 67 Apollo Drive, Rosedale, Auckland 0632, New Zealand
(a division of Pearson New Zealand Ltd.)
Penguin Books (South Africa) (Pty.) Ltd., 24 Sturdee Avenue, Rosebank, Johannesburg 2196,
South Africa

Penguin Books Ltd., Registered Offices: 80 Strand, London WC2R 0RL, England

This book is an original publication of The Berkley Publishing Group.

This is a work of fiction. Names, characters, places, and incidents either are the product of the author's imagination or are used fictitiously, and any resemblance to actual persons, living or dead, business establishments, events, or locales is entirely coincidental. The publisher does not have any control over and does not assume any responsibility for author or third-party websites or their content.

PRINTING HISTORY
Berkley trade paperback edition / May 2011

Library of Congress Cataloging-in-Publication Data

Wax, Wendy.
    Ten Beach Road / Wendy Wax.
        p.   cm.
    ISBN 978-0-425-24086-1
    1. Female friendship—Fiction.   2. Dwellings—Conservation and restoration—Fiction.   I. Title.
    PS3623.A893T46   2011
    813'.6—dc22   2010054159

PRINTED IN THE UNITED STATES OF AMERICA

10   9   8   7   6   5   4   3   2   1

PRAISE FOR

Magnolia Wednesdays

"Wax, the author of *The Accidental Bestseller*, writes with breezy wit and keen insight into family relations."
—*The Atlanta Journal-Constitution*

"An honest, realistic story of family, love, and priorities, with genuine characters."
—*Booklist*

"Bittersweet . . . Vivian's an easy protagonist to love; she's plucky, resourceful, and witty."
—*Publishers Weekly*

"Atlanta-based novelist Wendy Wax spins yet another captivating tale of life and love in this wonderfully entertaining book."
—*Southern Seasons Magazine*

The Accidental Bestseller

"A little bit *Sex and the City* with a dash of *The First Wives Club*."
—*Sacramento Book Review*

"A warm, triumphant tale of female friendship and the lessons learned when life doesn't turn out as planned . . . Sure to appeal."
—*Library Journal*

"A wise and witty foray into the hearts of four amazing women . . . A beautiful book." —Karen White, author of *On Folly Beach*

"A terrific story brimming with wit, warmth, and good humor. I loved it!" —Jane Porter, author of *She's Gone Country*

"A wry, revealing tell-all about friendship and surviving the world of publishing."
—Haywood Smith, *New York Times* bestselling author

"Entertaining . . . Provides a lot of insight into the book business, collected, no doubt, from Wax's own experiences."
—*St. Petersburg Times*

Titles by Wendy Wax

7 DAYS AND 7 NIGHTS
LEAVE IT TO CLEAVAGE
HOSTILE MAKEOVER
SINGLE IN SUBURBIA
THE ACCIDENTAL BESTSELLER
MAGNOLIA WEDNESDAYS
TEN BEACH ROAD

My life is like a stroll on the beach . . .
as near to the edge as I can go.

—THOREAU

Prologue

MARCH 2009
WALL STREET WEEKLY

Malcolm Dyer Joins Bernie Madoff
on Most Hated List

NEW YORK—Federal investigators raided the offices of Malcolm Dyer, head of Synergy Investments, in New York City this morning. Dyer is suspected of conducting an elaborate Ponzi scheme, similar to that employed by Mr. Madoff, and of bilking some three hundred clients of more than three hundred million dollars. Investors, who believed their money was being put in bank-secured CDs with double-digit yields, were, in fact, funding Mr. Dyer's lavish lifestyle, which included a private jet, a seventy-eight-foot motor yacht, and homes in Westchester, Palm Springs, Palm Beach, Florida's Gulf Coast, and the Caribbean island where the alleged securitizing bank was allegedly located.

For at least five years, investors did receive the promised returns, which were apparently paid out of successive investors' deposits, rather than the nonexistent CDs. When clients, faced with a faltering economy and plummeting stock prices, requested their principal back, the scheme was uncovered.

Although investigators have seized records and frozen all of Mr. Dyer's known accounts and assets, the majority of the missing money is assumed to be offshore. Dyer's whereabouts are unknown.

———————————

One

Though she was careful not to show it, Madeline Singer did not fall apart when her youngest child left for college. In the Atlanta suburb where she lived, women wilted all around her. Tears fell. Antidepressants were prescribed.

Her friends, lost and adrift, no longer recognized themselves without children to care for. A collective amnesia descended, wiping out all the memories of teenaged angst and acts of hostility that had preceded their children's departures, much as the remembered pain of childbirth had been washed away once the newborn was placed in their arms.

Madeline kept waiting for the emptiness of her nest to smite her. She loved her children and had loved being a stay-at-home mother, but while she waited for the crushing blow, she took care of all the things that she'd never found time for while Kyra and Andrew were still at home. Throughout that fall while her friends went for therapy, shared long liquid lunches, and did furtive drive-bys and drop-ins to the high school where they'd logged so many volunteer hours, Madeline happily responded to her children's phone calls and texts, but she also put twenty years' worth of pictures into photo albums. Then she cleaned out the basement storage unit and each successive floor of their house, purging and sorting until the clutter that had always threatened to consume them was finally and completely vanquished.

After that she threw herself into the holidays and the mad rush of shopping and cooking and entertaining, trying her best not to let the free-falling economy dampen the family festivities. Andrew came home from Vanderbilt and Kyra, fresh out of Berkeley's film school and two months into her first feature film shoot, arrived in the first flush of adulthood and once again became the center of the known universe.

Pushing aside daydreams of the projects she'd undertake once they were gone again, Madeline fed her children and their friends, made herself available when their friends weren't, and didn't even react to the fact that she was barely an appendage to their lives. Steve, who loved the trappings of a family Christmas with the ferocity of an only child, seemed worried and distracted, but when she raised the subject he found a way to change or avoid it.

While basting the turkey on Christmas Day, Madeline realized that she was more than ready for her husband to go back to the office and for her children to go back to their new lives so that she could finally begin her own.

On this first day of March, the house was once again blissfully quiet. There was no television. No music. No video game gunfire or crack of a bat. No texts coming in or going out with a ding. No refrigerator opening or closing. No one—not one person—asking what was for dinner, when their laundry would be done, or whether she had a spare twenty.

Standing in the center of Kyra's vacant bedroom, Madeline inhaled the quiet, held it in her lungs, and let it soak into her skin. Her nest was not only empty, it was totally and completely organized. It was time for her "new" life to begin.

Not for the first time, she admitted something might be wrong with her. Because the silence that so alarmed her friends sent a tingle of anticipation up her spine. It made her want to dance with joy. Go hang gliding. Cure cancer. Learn how to knit. Write the Great American Novel. Or do absolutely nothing for a really long time.

Her life could be whatever she decided to make of it.

Throwing open the windows to allow the scents of an early spring to fill the room, Madeline mentally converted the space into the study/craft room she'd always dreamed of. She'd put a wall of shelves for her books and knickknacks here. A combination desk and worktable there. Maybe a club chair and ottoman for reading in the corner near the window.

Madeline entertained herself for a time measuring the windows for a cornice that she might just make herself. This afternoon she could go to the fabric store and see what looked interesting. Maybe she'd hit some of her favorite antique stores and see about a worktable and a club chair that she could re-cover.

For lunch she made a quick sandwich and then sat down at the kitchen table to read through the *Atlanta Journal-Constitution*, Steve's *Wall Street Journal*, and the local weekly. She was in the middle of a story about yet another financial advisor who'd absconded with his unsuspecting clients' money when the phone rang—an especially shrill sound in the cocoon of silence in which she was wrapped.

"Mrs. Singer?" The voice was female, clipped, but not unfriendly. "This is St. Joseph's calling."

Madeline's grip on the phone tightened; she braced for a full-body blow. "A Mrs. Clyde Singer was brought in about thirty minutes ago. She was suffering from smoke inhalation and a gash on her forehead. We found this number listed as emergency contact on the file from her last visit."

"Smoke inhalation?" Madeline hovered near her chair, trying to get her thoughts in order. "Is she all right?"

"She's resting now, but she's been through quite a lot, poor thing. There was a kitchen fire."

"Oh, my God." Madeline turned and raced upstairs, carrying the phone with her. Last month her mother-in-law had fallen in the bathroom and been lucky not to break anything. At eighty-seven, living alone had become increasingly

difficult and dangerous, but Edna Singer had refused to consider giving up her home and Steve had been unwilling to
push his mother on it. Madeline got the room number and a
last assurance that the patient looked a bit beat up but would
be fine. "It'll probably take me about twenty-five minutes to
get there."

Exchanging her shorts for a pair of slacks and slipping
her feet into loafers, she called Steve's cell phone as she clattered down the front stairs. After leaving a voice mail with
the pertinent details, Madeline headed for the garage, stopping only long enough to look up Steve's office number, which
she so rarely called she hadn't even programmed it into her
cell phone. Adrienne Byrne, who'd sat in front of Steve's corner office at the investment firm for the last fifteen years,
answered. "Adrienne?" Madeline said as the garage door rumbled open. "It's Madeline. Can you put me through to Steve?"

There was a silence on the other end as Madeline yanked
open the car door.

"Hello?" Madeline said. "I hate to be short, but it's an
emergency. Edna is at St. Joseph's again and I need Steve to
meet me there."

Madeline slid behind the steering wheel, wedged the
phone between her ear and shoulder, and put the minivan
in reverse.

"Did you try his cell phone?" Adrienne's tone was uncharacteristically tentative.

"Yes." Maddie began to back down the driveway, her
mind swirling with details. How badly damaged was Edna's
kitchen? Should she have Steve go to the hospital while she
checked the house? "It went right to voice mail. Isn't he in the
office? Do you know how to reach him?"

There was another odd pause and then Adrienne said,
"Steve doesn't work here anymore."

Madeline's foot found the brake of its own accord. The car
jerked to a stop. "I'm sorry? Where did you say he was?"

"I don't know where he is, Madeline," the secretary said
slowly. "Steve doesn't work here anymore."

Madeline sat in the cul-de-sac, trying to absorb the words she'd just heard.

"I haven't seen Steve since he was laid off. That was at the beginning of September. About six months ago."

Madeline drove to the hospital and then had no idea how she got there. Nothing registered, not the street signs or the lights or the bazillion other cars that must have flown by on Highway 400 or the artery off it that led to the hospital parking lot. The entire way she grappled with what Adrienne had told her and Steve had not. Laid off six months ago? Not working? Unemployed?

At the information desk, she signed in and made her way down the hall to Edna's room. There were people there and noise. A gurney rolled by. A maintenance worker mopped up a distant corner of the hallway. She sensed movement and activity, but the images and sounds were fleeting. Nothing could compete with the dialogue going on in her head. If Steve didn't have a job, where did he go every day after he put on his suit and strolled out the door with his briefcase? More important, why hadn't he told her?

In the doorway to her mother-in-law's room, Madeline paused to gather herself. Edna looked like she'd been in a fight. A bandage covered more than half of her forehead. Her lip was split and her cheekbone was bruised. The eye above it looked puffy.

"Gee," Madeline said, "I'd like to see the other guy."

"The other guy is the kitchen table and the tile floor." Edna jutted out her chin. "Where's Steve?"

Good question. "I don't know. But I left him a message that you were here."

Edna's chin quivered. They both knew Madeline was a poor substitute for Edna's only child. "What happened?" Madeline asked. "How did the fire start?"

Edna dropped her gaze. Her fingers, which had become as knobby and spare as the rest of her, clutched the sheet tighter.

"I don't know. I was cooking . . . something. And then I . . . something must have gone wrong with the stove. Where's Steve?"

"I'm here, Mama." Steve swept into the room and moved swiftly to the bed, where he took one of his mother's hands in his. "Lord, you gave me a scare. Are you all right?"

"Yes, of course," Edna said, her trembling lips turning up into a brave smile. Edna Singer tolerated her daughter-in-law, and seemed to enjoy her grandchildren, but she worshipped the son who, at the age of twelve, had become all she had left when his father died.

Madeline watched her husband soothe his mother and tell her that everything would be all right, but it was like watching a stranger. They'd known each other for thirty years and been married for twenty-five of them. They had two children, a home, a life. And he had failed to mention that he wasn't working?

She looked up and realized that they were waiting for her to say something.

"I just told Mama that when I leave here I'll check her house and make sure it's secure. And that tomorrow when she's released, she needs to come stay with us so we can keep an eye out for her and fuss over her for a while."

Madeline nodded. Really, she couldn't think of any words besides, "Where have you been going every day? How could you not tell me you lost your job?" and the all-encompassing, "What in the world is going on?"

Madeline stepped closer, appalled at how natural Steve sounded. She wanted to reach up and grab him by the shoulders and give him a good shake. "Will you be able to get away from the office?" she asked. "If it's a problem, I could pick your mama up."

"Nope," he said all casual, as if he weren't lying once again. "There's nothing pressing on the calendar."

Madeline grasped the bed rail to steady herself as Steve fussed over his mother. She felt brittle, like Edna's bones; one wrong move and she might snap. As she studied her husband, she tried to understand how the person she thought she knew best could be so unfathomable. He had lied to her. Every day when he got up with his alarm, showered and dressed, went through the same old morning routine, and left the house as if he were going to the job he didn't have had been one more lie.

The question, of course, was, why? Why not just tell her, why not share the loss of this job like she'd assumed they'd shared everything else for the last quarter of a century?

Her hand shook. Dropping it to her side, she told herself not to panic and definitely not to assume the worst, though she couldn't actually think of a good or positive explanation for Steve having kept this little bombshell to himself.

Once again she noticed a silence and felt Steve's gaze on her. She looked into the wide-set gray eyes that she'd always considered so warm and open, the full lips that were bent upward and stretched so easily into a smile. For the first time she noticed a web of fine lines radiating out from those eyes and grooves, like parentheses, bracketing the lips. A deep furrow ran the width of his forehead. When had all these signs of worry appeared, and how had she missed them?

"So, I'll stay with Mama for a while," Steve said, dismissing her. "Then I'll run by her house to make sure it's locked up and maybe pick up some things she'll want at our house."

Madeline wanted to drag him out into the hall and demand the truth, but the image of hissing out her hurt and anger in the hospital hallway held the words in check.

"Okay." Madeline stepped forward to drop a dutiful kiss on her mother-in-law's paper-thin cheek, keeping the bed between herself and Steve, certain that if he touched her she would, in fact, snap. "You get some rest now and feel better."

On the way out of the hospital she focused on her breathing. "Just stay calm," she instructed herself. "When he gets home you'll tell him that you know he lost his job and ask for an explanation. He must have a good reason for not telling you. And surely he has some kind of plan. Just ask for the truth. That's all. Everything will be okay as long as you know what's going on and you're in it together."

This sounded eminently reasonable. For the time being she needed to push the hurt and sense of betrayal aside. They were not paupers—Steve was an investment advisor and had built a large cushion over the years for just such an eventuality. They could survive this. And Steve was highly qualified and well respected. Maybe he'd just needed some time off and now he could start looking for a new position. Trafalgar Partners wasn't the only investment firm in Atlanta.

She'd agreed to "for better or for worse." She was no hothouse flower who couldn't deal with reality. Once again, her hurt and anger rose up in her throat, nearly choking her, and once again she shoved it back.

As she drove the minivan through the crush of afternoon traffic, Madeline contemplated the best way to handle the situation; she even thought about what wine might complement this sort of conversation and what she might serve for dinner. She'd just tell him that she loved him and that she would stand by him no matter what. As long as he respected her enough to tell her the complete and unvarnished truth.

It was only later that she would remember that the truth did not always set you free. And that you had to be careful what you wished for, because you might actually get it.

Two

Steve didn't get home until six P.M. Madeline was in the kitchen adding strips of grilled chicken to a large Caesar salad and had already opened and sampled a bottle of red Zinfandel when she heard the automatic garage door open. She'd decided not to blurt out what she knew, had vowed to act normal and work her way calmly up to the subject. But now that Steve was here, Madeline could actually feel drops of sweat popping out on her forehead and an unwelcome burst of heat flushing her skin. For once this was not a result of her whacked-out hormones. How in the world had Steve managed to do this for a half a year?

"How did Edna's house look?" she asked carefully.

Steve sighed and took a long swallow of his wine. "The kitchen's a nightmare. Between the fire and the water from the fire hoses, the inside is practically gutted." He looked up at her. "It's a miracle she came out as unscathed as she did. You don't mind if she moves in with us?"

"No, of course not." For once, Edna's antipathy felt insignificant. "She can stay as long as she needs to or until we can get her kitchen put back together." After all these years,

Madeline could wait another month or so to start her "new life." Steve had worked construction summers through high school and college and would know what had to be done at his mother's. Madeline could help supervise the renovation of the kitchen herself if necessary, and maybe Steve would have a new job by the time Edna moved back into her own home.

"I don't mean temporarily," Steve said, though he kind of mumbled it into his wineglass. "She can't live on her own anymore. I've been putting off the inevitable, but now that you don't have the kids to deal with I thought . . ."

"You want your mother to move in with us . . . forever?" The cheese grater slipped out of her hand and clattered on the granite countertop. The square of Parmesan landed at her feet, but she made no move to pick it up.

"She's eighty-seven, Madeline. Unfortunately, I don't think forever is going to be all that long."

But it would feel like it. "Your mother doesn't like me, Steve. She never has."

"That's not true."

"We've been married for twenty-five years, I see her at least twice a week, we eat dinner with her most Sundays, and she still calls me Melinda half the time." This was no slip of the tongue or mental gaffe. Melinda had been Steve's high school girlfriend.

"She just likes to yank your chain a little bit. She doesn't mean anything by it."

"Do you know what she gave me for Christmas this year?"

Steve pinched a crouton from the salad. "It was a book, wasn't it?"

"It was called *Extreme Makeover, Personal Edition: How to Reface Your 'Cabinets' and Shore Up Your Sagging Structure*."

"It was not."

"Yes," Madeline said. "It was."

Steve frowned as always, unable to accept that the mother who loved him so fiercely had so little affection for his wife. But how could she worry about this now when Steve's lies and lack of job loomed over them? She bent to retrieve the

Parmesan, which had been left there far too long to invoke the three-second rule. She carried it to the trash while she struggled to tamp down her emotions so that she could broach the subject of his unemployment with some semblance of calm.

Steve was refilling their glasses when she returned to the counter with her shoulders squared. It was clear he wasn't planning to let her in on his not-so-little secret. She wondered if he'd told his mother.

"I spoke to Adrienne today," Madeline said.

He went still much like an animal scenting danger might.

"I called your office trying to reach you after I heard from the hospital. She told me you don't work there anymore. That you haven't worked there for six months." She swallowed and tears pricked her eyelids even though she'd promised herself she wouldn't cry. "Is that true?" she asked. "Could that possibly be true?"

The air went out of him. Not slowly like a punctured tire, but fast like a balloon spurting out its helium. His shoulders stooped as he shrank in front of her, practically folding in on himself. Any hope that he might deny it or laugh at Adrienne's poor attempt at humor disappeared.

"Yes."

She waited for the explanation, but he just sat on the barstool with all the air knocked out of him, staring helplessly at her.

"But what happened? Why were you let go? Why didn't you tell me?" The pain and hurt thickened her voice and it was hard to see through the blur of tears. Steve actually looked like he might cry himself, which did nothing to reduce the soft swell of panic. Why was he just looking at her like that; why didn't he just tell her? "I need to know, Steve. I don't understand how you could keep a secret like this from me. It's my life, too."

He took a deep breath, let it out. "The institutional accounts I was handling were actually being funneled to Synergy Investments. Malcolm Dyer's firm."

It was Madeline's turn to go still. She was not a financial

person, but even she had heard of the now-notorious Malcolm Dyer, whom the press had labeled a "mini-Madoff."

"I should have known there was something off," Steve said. "But the fund was performing so well. The returns were so . . . high, and they stayed that way for over five years." He swallowed. "It's hard to walk away from that kind of profit. I missed all the signs." His voice was etched with a grim disbelief. "It was a classic Ponzi scheme. And I had no idea."

He swallowed again. She watched his Adam's apple move up and down.

"They closed down our whole division in September, but by cooperating with the government investigators, Trafalgar managed to keep it out of the papers while they regrouped. There was some hope that if the feds could get their hands on the stolen funds that they might be able to return at least a portion to our clients. A lot of them are nonprofits and charities."

A part of her wanted to reach out and offer comfort, but the anger coursing through her wouldn't allow it. For twenty-five years they'd told each other everything—or so she'd thought. "I can't believe you think so little of me that you'd dress and go through that kind of pretense every day rather than tell me the truth." She drained her wineglass, hoping to slow the thoughts tumbling through her head, maybe sop up the sense of betrayal. "How could you do that?"

Steve shook his head. "I don't know, Mad. I just felt so guilty and so stupid. And I didn't want to worry you or the kids. I figured I'd find something else and once I did—when there was no cause for panic—I'd tell you."

Steve looked her in the eye then. His were filled with defeat. "Only I couldn't find another job. Half the investment firms in the country have folded and the rest have cut back. Nobody's hiring. Especially not at my salary level. Or my age." His tone turned grim. "I've spent every single day of the last six months looking for a job. I've followed up every lead, worked every contact I have. But, of course, my reputation's shot to hell. And I don't seem to be employable."

They contemplated each other for what seemed like an eternity. Madeline felt as if their life had been turned at an angle that rendered it completely unrecognizable.

"And that's not the worst of it." Steve dropped his gaze. He ran a hand through his hair and scrubbed at his face. As body language went it was the equivalent of the pilot of your plane running through the aisle shouting, "Tighten your seat belts. We're going down!"

For the briefest of moments, Madeline wanted to beg him not to tell her. She wanted to stand up, run out of the room and out the front door, where whatever he was about to say couldn't reach her.

"I, um . . ." He paused, then slowly met her gaze. "Our money's gone, too." He said it so quietly that at first she thought she might have misheard.

"What?"

"I said, our money's gone."

"Which money are you talking about?" she asked just as quietly. As if softening the volume might somehow soften the blow.

"All of it."

There was a silence so thick that Madeline imagined any words she was able to form would come out swaddled in cotton. Gary Coleman's trademark response, "What you talkin' 'bout, Willis?" streaked through her mind, comic intonation and all, and she wished she could utter it. So that Steve might throw back his head and laugh. Which would be far superior to the way he was hanging his head and staring at his hands.

"How is that possible?" Her voice was a whisper now, coated in disbelief.

He met her gaze. "We were getting such a great return from the fund, that I put our money in." He paused. "Every penny we didn't need to live on went to Synergy."

"But I thought most of our money was in bank CDs," Madeline said. "Aren't they practically risk free?"

"Yes, real bank CDs are secured by the bank. Nonexistent CDs backed by a nonexistent offshore bank? Not so much."

Madeline felt as if she'd ended up in a train wreck despite the fact that she'd never set foot on a train or even gone to the station. The twisted metal of their future lay strewn across the tracks.

"I invested my mother's money in the same fund."

"Is there anything left?" Madeline thought her heart might actually stop beating. She could hear herself gasping for breath, but no air seemed to be entering her lungs.

"Just this." He pulled a crumpled piece of paper from his pocket, smoothed it out, and laid it on the cocktail table in front of her. "The feds are looking for Dyer. In the meantime, he's been judged guilty in a civil suit; apparently if you don't show up, you're found guilty. I filed a claim against Dyer's seized assets." He shoved the paper toward her. "This came yesterday. In addition to our house and what's left of my mother's house we now have a third ownership in a beachfront 'mansion' in Florida. In some booming metropolis called Pass-a-Grille."

Madeline didn't know where Steve slept or even if he did, and she was too numb to get up and find out. She spent most of the night tossing and turning on her side of their bed, realigning her pillow every few minutes as if simply finding the optimal position would grant her admission to oblivion. Several times she heard Steve moving around downstairs. At one point the family room TV snapped on.

Sometime after three A.M. she finally managed to drift off but slept fitfully, bombarded by disturbing dreams. One involved her mother-in-law in a pointy black hat pedaling a bicycle across a tornado-tossed sky. The *Wizard of Oz* theme played out all night. Steve appeared as the Scarecrow, and then as both the Cowardly Lion and a heavily rusted Tin Man. The worst scene featured Malcolm Dyer as the unscrupulous Wizard caught behind his curtain with Glinda the apparently not-so-good witch giggling in his lap.

Not surprisingly, Madeline awoke groggy and out of sorts.

Steve's revelations stole back into her consciousness to command center stage, and she buried her face in her pillow and cried. When the bedroom door opened and Steve padded into the room, Madeline squeezed her eyes shut and feigned sleep. While he showered and dressed in the bathroom she lay staring up into the ceiling. Although she felt him hesitate beside the bed, she kept her eyes shut and her breathing regular. She didn't get up until she was certain Steve was gone.

By the time he returned with his mother, Madeline had put away the sheet and pillow Steve had left on the couch, tidied up the guest room and bath, and put on a pot of soup. Determined to make things look as normal as possible in front of her mother-in-law, she kept a smile on her face and her conversation casual. But pretending her world had not been shaken to its core required an Oscar-worthy performance.

"You seem a bit quiet, Melinda," Edna said as Madeline tucked her into the guest room bed and aimed the remote at the television. Madeline willed herself to ignore the insult; it hardly rated in comparison to Steve's revelations. "I'm sorry to be imposing on you. I wouldn't have come if Steven hadn't insisted."

"We're happy to have you," Madeline said, straightening as the hosts of HGTV's *Hammer and Nail* appeared on-screen and wishing this were true. She handed the remote to her mother-in-law, who was already focusing on the remodeling show. "But it would make me even happier if you stopped calling me Melinda."

Edna's gaze left the TV. Shock that Madeline had commented on the dig flared briefly in Edna's eyes.

"I hate to think your mind has really slipped so much that you can't remember your daughter-in-law's name," Madeline said. "Maybe we should do some cognitive testing. We never did go for that follow-up with the neurologist."

Edna snorted. "They're all just looking for any excuse to take away a person's rights. First it's the car. Then they don't think you can live by yourself." She strove for her usual belligerence but Madeline heard the note of fear underneath and chastised herself for putting it there. Her own fear was like a living, breathing thing. "There's nothing golden about the golden years from what I can tell so far."

"No," Madeline agreed, reminding herself that her mother-in-law's jabs were a very minor thing. "Getting older is definitely not for sissies." But then neither, it seemed, was marriage.

Three

Madeline spent the weekend alternately grilling Steve about his plans to regain their financial footing and trying to figure out what she might do to produce income after twenty-five years as a full-time wife and mother. The answer to both of these questions appeared to be "nothing."

She read through each and every want ad, but cleaning, cooking, and carpooling with heavy doses of prodding and organizing didn't seem to qualify her for any of them. At a time when highly skilled and experienced people were out of work, her chances of finding a decent paying job ranged from "not anytime soon" to "not in this lifetime."

By Sunday night she was exhausted from practicing "Would you like fries with that?" and pretending for Edna's benefit that everything was as it should be. On Monday Steve, whose strength of will had been the first thing she fell in love with and whom she'd always considered a veritable "rock," began to crumble. It seemed that now that he'd confessed, Steve felt free to wallow in his despair. For the first time he didn't dress or leave, but assumed what became

a favored position on the family room couch with the TV
remote clutched loosely in one hand.

For most of the day he watched whatever sports he could
find. Once she was mobile again, Edna waited on him and
clucked over him, complaining that Trafalgar didn't know
what they were doing and predicting that other investment
firms would be beating down her son's door to get him. Madeline assumed Edna had been given the abridged version of
Steve's departure from his previous employer and no version
of their, and her, dire financial situation.

Madeline waited for her husband to contact the insurance
company to begin filing Edna's claim, but this didn't happen. Nor did he seem inclined to resume his job hunt or any
networking activities. But he *was* working on memorizing
the daytime television schedule and had devised a system for
predicting who would be eliminated from *American Idol* and
Dancing with the Stars. Both he and Edna had proven they
were smarter than a fifth grader.

Madeline's hurt and anger didn't dissipate with time. Both
emotions coursed through her, mingling with her fear and
panic so that her heart thudded heavily in her chest. Unable
to move or motivate Steve, Madeline dug through the file
cabinet in their home office until she found Edna's homeowner's policy and bank statements as well as their own and
spent several days poring over them. Confronting the reality of their situation in black and white made her feel even
worse, which hardly seemed possible.

In fact, she began to feel very much like the Little Red
Hen, from the nursery tale, as she made an appointment to
meet the claims adjustor at Edna's house and then went in
to talk to their account person at the bank. She opened the
bills that poured in, made note of them, then placed them in
an ever-growing pile on the corner of Steve's desk. No matter
how often or how urgently she badgered him he refused to so
much as look at one. When she dragged him to a psychiatrist
for a session that they no longer had insurance to pay for, he
refused to speak.

They'd been limping along this way for a number of weeks when Madeline came home from the grocery store where she'd maxed out her third and next-to-last credit card, and found her daughter sitting at the kitchen table, eating a sandwich. Two large suitcases stood in a corner. It was April first. "Kyra?"

"Hi, Mom." Kyra stood and gave her a hug. "I saw Grandma in the other room with Dad. I hope my room's still available."

"Of course," Madeline said. "But what's going on? I thought you were shooting in Seattle through May."

"I'm not on the shoot anymore."

Madeline waited for the shout of "April Fools'!" Kyra had talked nonstop about the movie and the incredible cast and crew all through the holidays. It was a once-in-a-lifetime opportunity and a complete career builder. "But I thought . . ."

"And, um, I have another . . . small surprise."

"Do I need to sit for this?" Maddie thought maybe running and hiding would be better based on the look on her daughter's face, but she held her tongue.

"Probably."

Madeline sank down in the chair next to Kyra's. Her daughter sat, too. She looked gaunt and her eyes were puffy. "So, how do you feel about . . . grandma?"

"Well, she's not too much extra work. And she and your father do keep each other company." And she had cut back on the Melinda thing.

"No, I mean how do you feel about becoming one?"

"Please tell me this is an April Fools' thing."

Kyra shook her head while Madeline looked around for the hidden camera. "I've got it. You're shooting a new reality show. And I bet it's called *Torture Your Parent?*"

Kyra's jaw tightened and her chin jutted forward. "No, the torture part's just an unexpected perk, I guess. I'm pregnant, Mom. And apparently having sex with an actor on a major motion picture set is okay; until his wife shows up and throws her weight around."

Once again, Madeline wished she had misheard. "Oh, Kyra, honey. How could you let this happen?"

"Thanks for the enthusiasm and support." Kyra's voice was tight.

"Kyra, that's not fair. You have to admit this is a bit of a bombshell. And it's not the first one that's exploded here lately."

Her daughter's face flushed with disappointment and absolutely zero interest in any problem other than her own. "Oh, God, everything was so great. And now it's all such a mess."

"I know the feeling." Madeline contemplated her daughter. Long and lanky with a mass of dark curls and her father's wide-set gray eyes, she was more striking than beautiful. Her flair for the dramatic had become evident in the crib and had not diminished with age.

"Who's the baby's father and . . ." Madeline paused, unsure how to proceed. "What role is he planning to play in this?"

Kyra hesitated.

"Just tell me, Kyra." Madeline could not take another family member withholding critical information. "I love you, and I'll do my best not to judge."

"It's Daniel's. Daniel . . ."

"Daniel Deranian?" She named the megastar of the film Kyra had been working on. "But he's . . ."

"Married to Tonja Kay."

Madeline nodded. Tonja Kay was a huge name in her own right. Together they were one of Hollywood's premier power couples; only a couple of rungs beneath Brad and Angelina. "And he's . . ."

"Older than me?"

"I think that's a slight understatement. He's a good decade older than you. And he's got a horrible reputation with women. Why . . ."

"So much for not judging." Kyra folded her arms across her chest.

"Honey, I'm just saying I don't think you have any idea how completely having a baby will change your life. You're only twenty-three. There's so much still ahead of you. You know you don't have to actually . . ."

"Yes, I do," Kyra said. "I know what my options are. And I'm having Daniel's baby."

"And how does Daniel feel about this?" She felt silly calling a Hollywood megastar by his first name. As if she'd ever seen him anywhere besides the pages of a magazine or on a theater screen.

Kyra shifted uncomfortably in her chair. "I don't know. I never got to tell him."

"Oh, Kyra."

"He told me he loved me, Mom. He's not like you think. Or the way they describe him in the tabloids." Kyra folded her hands in front of her and then stared at them as if there might be some answer hidden between her fingers. "Everything was great. But then Tonja showed up on the set, and the next thing I knew I was off the picture." She looked up, her gray eyes cloudy with hurt. "When I knocked on Daniel's trailer door later, his assistant told me he wasn't available. And that was it.

"I didn't think it was the sort of news I should be texting or emailing."

"Oh, sweetie." Madeline reached for her daughter and drew her close. What right did some Hollywood Romeo have ruining her daughter's life and then blowing her off? How could her baby have a baby? And how in the world were they going to pay for a pregnancy and support another child right now?

"Is it okay if I stay for a . . . while?" Kyra asked as she pulled back. "I'd already sublet my apartment because I thought I'd be on location all spring. And I don't really have anywhere else to go." She bit her lip, worrying it, just as she had as a child when she was trying to hold back tears. Madeline felt like crying, too. She'd thought she was all cried out, but apparently tears came in an unlimited supply. She felt them pricking against her eyelids, trying to get free.

"Of course you can stay here. You and the baby." Madeline

closed her eyes briefly, hardly able to believe Kyra was going
to be a mother. "For as long as you need or want to."

As Madeline watched helplessly, Kyra grabbed her suitcases, dragged them to the back stairs, and then began to
bump them up to her room. Which was apparently not going
to become a study/craft room anytime soon.

By the middle of April Madeline knew that her sky was
definitely falling. Edna's claim had still not been paid and
living with her had reinforced the fact that Edna could not
live alone. Nor could she afford to live in any sort of senior
residence even if they were able to repair and sell her house in
this horrible real estate market, and even if she'd been willing to go to one.

Steve was still in free fall and could not be begged,
cajoled, or shamed into doing anything remotely helpful. He
insisted he was just waiting for the economy to turn around,
but Madeline had the feeling he'd simply decided he didn't
feel like working anymore. She carried the crumpled paper
with the address of the beachfront property and the names of
the other two owners and sat down next to him on the couch,
placing the paper in his lap. "We need to go look at this
and find out what it's worth. It's basically our only remaining
asset besides this house."

He needed a shave and although he lay around far too
much, often with his eyes closed, he didn't look at all rested.
"There is no market for real estate, Madeline. And I seriously
doubt that a 'mansion' on a Podunk beach that we've never
heard of would be worth anything if there were." His mother
sat nearby, leafing through a newspaper. She and Edna had
never had anything approaching a heart-to-heart, but Madeline had stopped trying to pretend weeks ago that everything was all right.

"But the market is going to recover, Steve. We can't just
sit here and lose everything. We have to at least try to save
ourselves."

"You have no idea what it's like out there." His tone was as weary and defeated as his eyes. "I've been the breadwinner for twenty-five years, Madeline, and I just can't stomach going out after another loaf." He picked up the letter and handed it back to her. "I'm sorry, but I can't." He raised the remote and turned the volume back up.

"Edna?" It was her knowledge of just how close the sky was to falling that made Madeline turn to her mother-in-law. Edna shrugged her increasingly frail shoulders. "I think Steven needs this little break," she said as if they were talking about an hour nap and not a complete abdication of responsibility. "We'll all just have to give him some more time." She leaned over and patted her son on the shoulder. When Madeline left the room they were both once again focused on the television screen, where a contestant was scrambling to identify the last word of the winning phrase on *Wheel of Fortune*.

In the kitchen, Madeline poured herself a glass of wine; she'd slashed their household budget as far as possible, and so it was a single glass of Two Buck Chuck from Trader Joe's that she carried out onto the deck instead of a Kendall Jackson. She sipped it sparingly while she stared out over the deck railing and up the rise of the heavily wooded backyard. The pine trees stirred slightly in the early evening breeze, and she breathed in the soft scent of the camellia bush that had begun to bloom on the side of the house. She searched the sky, hoping to find at least a smidgen of serenity, but the reality of their situation made that impossible.

Bill collectors had begun calling, and she could barely afford the store brands at the grocery store. She'd delivered the last of her lightly worn clothing to the Designer Consigner shop yesterday.

Inside the phone rang and a few moments later the back door opened. Kyra stepped out onto the deck in a spill of light. "It's Andrew, Mom. He wants to talk to you." She covered the handset as she handed it to Madeline.

Madeline took the phone from her daughter and finished the last swallow of wine before lifting the receiver to her ear.

"Hi, sweetie," she said, brutally aware that her youngest was the only family member who seemed to be where he was supposed to be, doing what he was supposed to do. "How'd that Lit exam go?"

"Not so good."

"Oh?" She settled back in her chair and propped her feet up on the railing. Compared to all the truly horrible things that had happened lately, one bad test score hardly seemed worth getting worked up about. "Well, I'm sure if you study harder for the next one, you'll be back on track. You just need to buckle down now. You've always been a great student."

"No, Mom, it's too late for that."

She drew a deep breath, less worried now about serenity than not exploding.

"How can it be too late? You've got another month left and a final exam still to take." She fingered the stem of her wineglass and looked at it with real longing, but there was not even a fraction of a drop left.

"I've got a fifty in that class." There was a brief pause. "And a sixty-five in History. I may be able to pass, but my academic scholarship's finished."

Madeline heard the words, she processed them, but she simply couldn't believe them.

"If I take them again this summer and get a B or better, I could get my GPA up where it needs to be by the end of next fall and re-qualify."

Madeline reminded herself to remain calm, but it was a tall order. "You knew what you had to do to maintain that scholarship," she said. "And the work is certainly not too difficult for you. How did this happen?" She had asked this question far too many times lately. And never once gotten a good answer.

"I guess I just got a little lazy," he admitted sheepishly, as if he'd forgotten something insignificant like returning a library book on time. "If you just send me the tuition money for summer session, I'll . . ."

"No."

"What?" Clearly it had never occurred to him that his request might be refused.

Madeline couldn't remember the last time they'd said no to Andrew, which just might be the problem. "No," she said, careful not to raise her voice. "No." She stood and paced the deck, knowing that there was no other answer she could give. "No scholarship, no Vanderbilt."

"Aw, Mom, that's not . . ."

"That's the way it is. You'll do everything you can to get those grades up and then you can come home and spend the summer working to earn next year's tuition. Next year is on you."

"But I can't afford private school tuition. There's no way I can . . ."

"Neither can we," she said. "Not anymore. If you can't make enough to go back, you'll have to apply in state."

"But . . ."

"There are no buts, Andrew. That's just the way it is."

"Put me on with Dad then," Andrew said. "He'll send me the money."

"Your father's not available." This was the understatement of the century. "And he's put me in charge of our finances." This was far too true. "So I wouldn't waste any time lobbying. Especially when you need to be spending that time studying."

She said good-bye then, and for the first time in pretty much forever she didn't feel at all guilty about saying no. She was in charge of their finances, by default perhaps, but nonetheless in charge. And she would have to figure out what to do next.

Treating herself to one last glass of wine, she carried it into the office and sat down at the desk. Pulling the crumpled letter from her pocket, she spread it out in front of her and reread it carefully. On the computer, she did a Google search of Pass-a-Grille and saw that it was a tiny comma-shaped spit of land that curved out into the Gulf of Mexico about midway down the west coast of Florida.

Then she Googled the names of the two other owners
and discovered that one of them, Avery Lawford, was a host
of *Hammer and Nail*—the remodeling show on HGTV that
Edna liked to watch. The other was Nicole Grant, who was
listed as founder and owner of Heart Inc., an elite matchmaking service with offices in New York and Los Angeles. Her
résumé listed at least fifty marriages to her credit as well as a
bestselling book on dating dos and don'ts.

Madeline spent another thirty minutes looking at both
women and another fifteen trying to find a photo of the house
they owned, but although she found its location, she was
unable to get a clear look at it on Google Earth.

She could tell she had nothing in common with these
women other than being taken by Malcolm Dyer. They were
younger and far more glamorous, and she sincerely doubted
that either of them was as desperate financially as she was.
But surely they'd at least want to take a look at their asset?
Or better yet, maybe one of them would like to buy out her
share? Either way would give her a shot at covering their
most pressing expenses until Malcolm Dyer was found and
the remainder of their money returned.

"Please, God," she thought as she dialed the first number.
"Please let them catch him soon. And please don't make these
women too difficult to deal with.

"Oh, and while you're at it," Madeline Singer, who was
now channeling not only the Little Red Hen but Chicken
Little asked, "could you please keep the rest of the sky in
place for a while?"

Four

Working with your ex-husband was almost as much fun as a double root canal. Without anesthesia. Doing it in front of television cameras was four impacted wisdom teeth thrown in.

Avery Lawford stood between her ex-husband, Trent, and a Sub-Zero refrigerator on the studio set of a partially remodeled kitchen. Behind them the key grip adjusted their backlights. Arranged in a loose triangle in front of them, three cameramen ran through their moves. Trent leaned against a nearby counter, reading through his lines on the teleprompter while their makeup woman, Dorothy, carefully mopped his brow and applied a fresh dusting of powder. Avery got a quick pouf of her shoulder-length blonde hair and a smear of gloss on her already heavily painted lips.

"When we're back in, we're going to get a close-up of Avery smiling and motioning to the corner cabinet that Trent just installed. Dottie, spray her hair some more so that it can't fall forward. It's hiding her, um, profile." This was Jonathan the director's euphemism for cleavage, which always seemed to get more close-ups than the rest of her.

"Camera one, I want you to stay with Trent. Camera two, you're going to start tight as he explains the installation and then pull out to a two shot. Three, you're tight on Avery. I'll cut to a shot of her looking up at him impressed."

Avery flushed with anger and bit back a retort as the hair person did as instructed and the wardrobe mistress tugged on the back of Avery's fuchsia sweater, which had to be a full size too small, so that the deep V dipped even lower.

When they'd sold the first season of *Hammer and Nail* to HGTV, she and Trent had been cohosts in the truest sense of the word. Married for three years at the time, she'd been designing single family homes for the Bradley Group, an architectural firm in the Nashville area. Trent was sales manager for a well-known cabinet manufacturer and dabbled at designing custom furniture on the side. On a whim, they'd documented their own home remodel and then turned the footage into a demo for a weekly do-it-yourself show.

For the first three seasons their on-camera time and billing had been pretty equal. But then the network had hired a new program director who'd wasted no time turning Trent into the main spokesperson and "expert." Avery became his "assistant." Over the last twelve months, during which their marriage had deteriorated and then limped to an end, her role had shrunk even further until she was little more than the Vanna White of the remodeling set.

"Stand by. We're on in ten." The floor director held up both hands and then began the countdown. When only an index finger remained, she pointed it at Trent. The light on his close-up camera glowed red.

Trent flashed an easy smile directly into the camera's boxy lens. Sliding the hammer back into his tool belt, he read the lines on the teleprompter that explained how he'd affixed the cabinet to the wall. The light on Avery's camera blinked on and she turned her gaze to Trent's face.

Just over six feet tall with broad shoulders, strong, even features, and a Cary Grant–like cleft in his chin, Trent Lawford was just as good-looking now as he was the day he'd first called on the Bradley Group. She'd been attracted to his air of calm confidence infused with ambition and swept along by his easy charm. It was only later after the yearlong courtship and the planning of their wedding followed by the excitement of buying and remodeling their first home that she'd begun to realize still waters did not necessarily run deep. And the air of confidence masked a deep-seated need for attention.

One day she'd realized that her frantic treading of those too-still waters was barely keeping them afloat. Her father's death had stripped away all patience for pretense.

"Cut." The director's voice rang out on set. "Avery, you can't roll your eyes like that when you're in the shot. You're supposed to be pointing and smiling. And nodding in agreement."

Avery sighed. She'd done so much nodding lately she felt like a bobblehead doll.

Trent raised an eyebrow in her direction. His lips twisted into a bit of a smirk. He'd been shocked when she'd first questioned the direction, or lack thereof, of their marriage. Given the number of women who'd pursued him over the years, it had clearly never occurred to him that any woman, especially his wife, might question her luck in landing him. In Trent's estimation, if neither party was lying or cheating, there was no problem and certainly no reason to put the relationship under a microscope. His shock had turned to anger when, in the wake of her father's unexpected death, she'd pulled out not only a microscope but a dissection kit. By the time it was over, the dissatisfaction had been all his; the fault all hers.

"Let's try it again," Jonathan said.

Trent smiled into the camera and removed the hammer from his tool belt to start the second take. Over the top of the three cameras Avery spotted Victoria Crosshaven, the network's program director, watching intently. Somewhere in her early fifties, Victoria had a good fifteen years on both Avery and Trent, but she was still beautiful in a knife-edged, well-preserved way.

The red light on the center camera flashed on as the floor director lowered her hand once again. Trent slid the hammer into his tool belt and delivered his lines. This time Avery flashed her most admiring smile, batted her eyelashes, then pointed happily at the cabinet, even though she could see that he'd hung it more than a little off center.

"Cut! That's the look!" Jonathan's voice boomed through the intercom. "Let's break for lunch. I want everybody back in exactly one hour."

The set began to empty as Victoria Crosshaven strode past the cameras to where Avery and Trent still stood. James, their producer, followed.

"You were great," Victoria said to Trent. "You are golden on camera. And I'm going to make sure everyone knows it."

She motioned James closer. "I thought we might add a viewer mail section for the next season. Maybe Trent could answer questions about architectural design and home styles."

"That's a great idea," James said. "We've had viewers asking for something like that." He shifted his weight uncomfortably. "But Avery is actually the degreed architect. Maybe we should have her handle that segment."

There was a brief but potent silence. Avery stepped into it, forcing her way into Victoria's line of sight. James put a warning hand on Avery's shoulder.

"I'll give it some thought," the network exec said without an ounce of sincerity. She looked Avery up and down. "Great sweater." Her smile was dismissive as she hooked her arm through Trent's and led him off the set.

Avery spent most of their lunch break fuming. "The whole idea for *Hammer and Nail* was mine," she pointed out to James. "I'm the one who pitched it. And I'm the one who sold it to the network. And now I've been reduced to smiling and pointing like I don't have an architectural degree or a thought in my head. I grew up on my dad's construction sites. I redesigned Barbie's Dream House and the interior of her Motorhome when I was eight." She took a sip of ice water but could barely swallow it. "Can Victoria just do whatever the hell she wants?"

"Yes," James said with complete certainty.

Avery touched a hand to the poufy blonde do. "I feel like a Dolly Parton imitator." She shoved her plate away. "It's so humiliating."

She saw agreement in James's eyes along with something else she couldn't identify.

"All I know is I'm not signing any contract that doesn't give me equal billing and promotion." She glanced down at the sweater that would have been too tight on a B cup, let alone her D. "And I think a wardrobe clause might be in order."

"That's assuming there is another contract." James cleared his throat. "Are you certain your agent is still representing both your interests?"

Avery shook her head. "We've been negotiating since before the divorce became final. Trent says we should leave well enough alone, but I'm really fed up with so many things."

"It's not Trent's contract I'm worried about," James said.

"Oh?"

"Seriously, Avery. You're no longer a package deal and the network knows it. Not to mention that Victoria clearly has the hots for Trent. And he's not exactly fighting her off."

"No, he isn't, is he?" Avery picked up her fork, then set it back down. She had no appetite for the Cobb salad staring up at her. Trent had always been attractive to women. She didn't think he'd actually started sleeping with any of his admirers until they'd separated, but he was highly susceptible to admiration and flattery. For such a good-looking guy he was surprisingly needy. She pushed her plate away and set her napkin on the table as she forced herself to accept the truth. Trent might not actively throw Avery under a bus, but he wouldn't necessarily throw himself in front of her and pull her out from beneath the wheels, either.

In the end she felt as if the bus had mowed her down, then

backed over her a couple of times just to make sure all signs of life had been squashed out of her. Less than two weeks after her lunch with James, Avery was, in fact, dropped from *Hammer and Nail*, which would now be hosted by HGTV hottie Trent Lawford. James and Jonathan and the rest of the crew took her out for a very dispirited good-bye dinner the evening after her departure "to seek other opportunities" was announced. This time Avery didn't even bother to order food, concentrating instead on the pitchers of margaritas that James kept coming. Neither Trent nor Victoria Crosshaven attended. Avery went home with her former coworkers' best wishes and the makings of a hangover.

Now as she sat in the condo that she'd once shared with Trent, Avery realized that she no longer had a real reason to be in Nashville. Her closest friends were scattered around the country and kept in touch via phone and Internet. Those friends she'd made at the Bradley Group and with Trent seemed uncertain which of them to claim. After five years on television, the idea of going back into architecture held limited appeal.

In her rattiest bathrobe, she channel surfed and ate junk food even though a few extra pounds were something a five-foot-three person could not afford. Her nails were ragged and her roots had begun to show. She clutched a picture of her father and herself in hard hats on one of his construction sites. She figured she must have been about ten at the time, based on her Farrah Fawcett shag and the absence of breasts—just a couple of years before her mother had left them. Looking at the loving smile on his face and the sturdy arm around her shoulder, Avery felt the potato chip she'd been munching go gooey in her mouth. Her vision blurred.

Her dad had died just over a year ago. He'd dropped dead of a heart attack on a construction site. One minute, according to his longtime partner, Jeff Hardin, he was arguing with a drywaller; the next he was toes up on the unfinished subfloor. Avery had done her best to feel grateful that he hadn't

suffered and had died doing what he'd loved most. She'd
gotten through his funeral by picturing him in a contractor's version of heaven with the smell of sawdust in his nostrils and a tool belt slung around his hips. Numb from the
loss of the person who'd loved her most, Avery sleepwalked
through her divorce. Despite her attorney's advice she'd asked
for little. She'd been the one who'd wanted out. Besides, she
had a decent salary from *Hammer and Nail*. And from the
day her mother deserted them, her father had made it clear
that everything he had would go to his daughter. After his
death, his attorneys had confirmed this, assuring her his
estate was significant and it was a simple matter of probating
the will.

So while Avery was somewhat embarrassed by how
pathetic she felt, the truth was she could afford to wallow a
bit. It was all right to take a little time getting her bearings.
It wasn't as if she was going to be out on the street.

She was lying on the couch, clutching the photo and the
bag of potato chips to her chest, when the phone rang. The
sound seemed shrill and unaccountably loud. The bag of
chips rustled as she reached across it for the phone.

"Avery?" It was Blake Harrison, her father's attorney.

She sat up on the couch, ignoring the crunch of potato
chips inside the bag.

"Um-hmm?" She swallowed the last of a soggy potato
chip and wiped her free hand on her robe.

"Are you okay?"

"Yes." She stood and walked to the window. "I'm fine."

"Well, we finally have some news about your father's estate."

"That's good." She couldn't really whip up any enthusiasm
for the subject. It had dragged out so long now, it hardly
seemed real. She would have traded every potential penny to
have her father back.

"Well, not exactly."

Her gaze stalled on the car in the next driveway. She
watched it back out slowly, saw her neighbor's garage door go

back down. "What's going on?" she asked. "I thought it was just a matter of paperwork. 'Dotting the i's,' I think you said. 'Crossing the t's.' "

"Yes, well, that's what we thought. But there's been a bit of a wrinkle." There was a pause. Avery stared out at the budding tulip tree. The condo's front yard was small, about the size of a walk-in closet, but pretty much everything in it was in bloom. "We'd like you to come down to Tampa so we can, um, explain things in person."

Avery hadn't studied the law. Nor had she dealt with lawyers any more than she needed to, but it didn't take a rocket scientist to know that "wrinkle" was not a word you wanted crossing your attorney's lips. She reminded herself that her father had used the firm of Harrison and Hargood since before she was born and had complete faith in them. She looked down at the ancient bathrobe. Her slippers were scuffed, the fake fur matted. "This isn't really a good time for me to travel. I don't think . . ."

"Avery, I wouldn't be suggesting a meeting if I didn't think it was absolutely imperative. We need to talk about this in person."

"Blake, I'm not coming unless you tell me what's going on."

There was another pause. Avery could feel him weighing the alternatives, trying to figure out how to couch whatever it was in the best possible light.

"Just spit it out. Really. I need to know what's going on."

"Well, there's a reason it's taken so long to get your father's estate out of probate."

She waited.

"And it's not good, not good at all."

"I'm getting that part," Avery said. "Just tell me the rest. I can't take another cloud hanging over me."

"Your father's estate was sizeable. He left you over two million dollars. Two point two to be exact."

This didn't sound bad. In fact, it was far more than she'd expected. She didn't have expensive tastes or particularly bad habits. She could . . .

"Unfortunately, every penny of it was invested with Malcolm Dyer. You may have read about the Ponzi scheme he perpetrated and the, um, fact that he disappeared with most of his clients' assets."

"He took all of my father's money? All two point two million?"

"He took a lot more than that. Over three hundred million at last count."

"But they're looking for him, right? They're going to make him give it back?"

"Oh, they're looking. But so far he's the invisible man. It's possible that the majority of the money is so far offshore it'll never be found."

"You're telling me there's nothing left?" The numbness was starting to dissipate now. How dare this crook do that to her father. What right did he have to steal what it had taken her father a lifetime to accumulate? She couldn't even let herself think where that left her.

"There is one asset. It's a beachfront, um, well, it just says 'mansion.' According to the letter we just received it's located out on the tip of Pass-a-Grille." He named the beach just thirty minutes southwest of Tampa that she'd played on as a child.

"I have a beachfront mansion on Pass-a-Grille?"

"Well, actually, you own a third of the alleged beachfront mansion. We had filed a claim and we now have a letter from the trustee assigned to award and distribute Dyer's seized assets. We haven't had a chance to send anyone out there yet."

"Which third?" she asked dully. Maybe the roof was hers. "And what do you mean by 'alleged'?"

"I can't really answer any of that. But there are two other co-owners. Two other investors who were taken by Malcolm Dyer. How soon can you get here?"

Avery looked down at her food-stained robe and the bag of crushed potato chips on the floor. She didn't have a job or anyone to check in with. Of course, she no longer had an income or, apparently, an inheritance.

"Well, it doesn't look like I can afford a last-minute airline ticket or a rental car." What little she had in the bank wasn't going to last long. "I guess I'll be driving. Why don't we say the day after tomorrow?"

Five

Nicole Grant, dating guru and founder of Heart Inc., sat at a prime table on a two-story deck overlooking the Pacific Ocean. The restaurant was one of thirty owned by her new client Darios Thomolopolus, who had made his first fortune in shipping and was currently amassing another under the brand of Darios T, which included the thirty Mediterranean restaurants spread across America and a packaged food division that had brought Greek cuisine to grocery freezer cases everywhere.

Darios Thomolopolus was seventy-five years old. In addition to his massive fortune, he possessed a full head of salt-and-pepper hair, thick, expressive eyebrows, and bold, if slightly bloated, features.

A widower with little patience for dating, Darios was in the market for a new wife. And this time he wanted a tall blonde with large breasts, long legs, and what Nicole understood to be a brain large enough to handle herself in social situations but not so large as to question anything her future husband might say or do.

"And she cannot be a day over thirty-five," he said adamantly. "I have noticed that after that the fruit becomes . . . less firm."

Nicole nodded and made a note on her legal pad. *Sell-by date—35.* She'd been in the matchmaking business for more than a decade, had a presence in New York and Los Angeles, and had a long string of successful and high-profile matches to her credit. She appeared often on the morning and noon talk-show circuit and had published one book of dating advice.

Despite all of this, she was still occasionally surprised by the laundry list of requirements and features each client demanded. Though these people negotiated every day in their business lives, they were unwilling to compromise in any real way when it came to their personal requirements. Long legs, big breasts, and moderate brain size were nothing compared to some of the things Nikki had been asked to deliver.

She herself was a decade beyond Thomolopolus's expiration date and nothing about her was as "fresh" or as firm as it had once been. The Tina Turner song "What's Love Got to Do with It" played in her head, but it had been years since she'd heard a client gush about falling in love. Which was probably a good thing. Because after two failed marriages of her own, Nicole could still deliver a laundry list of attributes, including brain size and personality; "happily ever after" was much harder to sell and deliver.

Her BlackBerry signaled an incoming message from her office, and Nicole frowned as she glanced down. Her assistant, Anita, knew not to interrupt when she was with a client. The message said simply, *Call me.*

Nicole took one last bite of the gooey sweet baklava Darios had ordered for dessert and a final sip of mud-thick espresso.

"So then, you make me a list or send me the pictures?" Darios asked as their meeting drew to a close. "And I choose who I am interested to go out with?"

Another bing from her BlackBerry. *Landlord here. Wants to talk to you.*

"Yes." Nicole pulled her gaze from the text message and dabbed at the corner of her mouth with her napkin. She pulled on the jacket of her vintage three-piece Chado Ralph Rucci pantsuit and stood. "It'll take me a few days to put together a potential list. Then we meet again to go over it. After that I can start setting up appointments for you to meet the women we select." She made a point of being very involved in the process; no point letting the client think she wasn't earning her hefty fees.

"Good," Darios said. "Remember—only fresh and firm. Nothing too long on the vine."

"Of course." Nicole pushed aside the feeling that she was standing at the open-air market haggling over produce. The truth was there were plenty of women who would fit Darios's requirements and not be at all put off by having to meet them. Darios's immense wealth and lavish lifestyle would more than compensate for the fact that Darios himself was much closer to a prune than a plum. He handed her a sealed envelope with the first half of her fee and walked her through the restaurant to the exit.

From her car, Nicole called her office but got a recording that the number was no longer in service. She speed dialed Anita's cell. "What's going on?"

"I don't know. The phone's been disconnected. The New York office, too." Her assistant dropped her voice. "The landlord's sitting in the lobby. He says your last check bounced and he's not leaving without a cashier's check or money order."

Nicole's stomach clenched, and it had nothing to do with the moussaka Darios had chosen for their first course. She made her living by traveling in the right circles and attracted wealthy clients because she looked like she was one of them. Having one's office phone shut off and the office padlocked were not business builders.

Unbidden, snapshots from her childhood flashed through Nicole's brain. Their family belongings piled out on the curb after yet another eviction. Watching the ancient station wagon being towed down the street. Trying to shield her younger brother from the other kids' taunts about their patched clothing and obvious home haircuts.

They'd made a vow that they'd never feel any of these things again. And they'd stuck to it. Both of them had been successful; if not personally, then at least financially. But she'd learned the hard way that earning money and holding on to it were very different things.

"I'm depositing Thomolopolus's check right now. When I get in I'll take care of everything, and we'll . . . regroup."

Nicole hung up. Even though she knew it was useless, she once again tried every number she'd ever had for her investment advisor. But none of them was in service. She had last heard from Malcolm Dyer a year ago just before his name had made headlines around the globe.

At the bank she confronted just how grim her situation was. She made good fees for her matchmaking services, and she still received sporadic royalties from her book. She'd created real wealth over the last ten years, stockpiling a sizeable nest egg she'd been proud of and had let herself count on.

But she'd invested virtually every penny of it in a fund run by the person she'd trusted most in the world. All of her operating expenses had been paid from the interest on that investment.

Nicole willed herself to calm down as she left the bank and drove toward her office. She had to think, had to figure out what to do. It took money to keep up the kind of appearances that were necessary to keep her business going. And at the moment she had none. There was little comfort in knowing she wasn't the only one who'd lost everything to Malcolm Dyer.

Nicole parked in the building's parking garage and went into the ladies' room in the lobby, where she locked herself in a stall and vomited up her lunch. Leaning on the edge of the sink, she stared into the mirror as she blotted her mouth and face with a damp paper towel. Even the pale yellow of her vintage suit was too bright for the white, ravaged face and desperate eyes that stared back.

With great care, she added blush to her cheeks and applied a fresh coat of lipstick. Just as her mother used to do when the landlord came to collect. As if that had ever made one whit of difference.

But as she rode the elevator up to the twenty-first floor and strode into the tastefully appointed lobby of her West Coast office, she not only had to deal with the dismantling of everything she had built, she had to face the fact that the person who'd stolen her hard-earned savings was not some faceless stranger. The person who had taken her money and trampled her dreams was someone she had not only trusted but loved and done her best to protect. Malcolm Dyer was her brother.

Nicole had spent much of the fall and all of the winter completing her pending assignments, closing both her offices and satisfying the most insistent of her creditors. By March word of her financial difficulties had spread on both coasts and the flow of clients diminished to a trickle. In the middle of the month, she attended the wedding of Darios Thomolopolus to a genuine Georgia peach who'd decided that cruising the Mediterranean and sleeping with an older man beat teaching Pilates and coaching beauty contestants. Nicole wore one of her few remaining vintage gowns to the affair and used Thomolopolus's final fee to pay the month's rent on her New York apartment.

When she received the letter informing her that her claim against Malcolm's seized assets had resulted in partial ownership in a beachfront mansion, the glimmer of hope it produced told her just how hopeless her life had become. Still, owning even a third of something at this point was . . . something.

She actually laughed when Madeline Singer called, hoping to sell Nicole her third; she barely had enough to get to Florida to look at their "asset" and wasn't sure how she'd manage to stay there long enough to take care of the paperwork and put it up for sale.

She was no longer laughing when the FBI showed up on

her doorstep, yet again, demanding to know where her little brother—and the three hundred million–plus dollars he'd stolen—had gone.

"Do I look like I know where three hundred million dollars is?" Nicole glanced around the stripped-down interior of her apartment. She'd sold off every piece of artwork she'd collected that had any monetary value, the best of her antiques, and every stitch of vintage clothing she'd been able to authenticate.

Special Agent Giraldi stared back at her from behind piercing eyes that were more black than brown. He had a strong nose and even stronger chin. If he possessed a sense of humor, he had yet to display it.

"I've told you, I don't know where he is. And I am not harboring someone who would steal from his own flesh and blood."

"So you're not worried about the other investors." Agent Giraldi's voice was carefully controlled, just like his movements.

"I didn't say that. But I'm worried about me first. I still can't believe my own brother stole every penny I had." Especially one she'd mothered when their own mother no longer could.

He nodded, conceding the insult added to injury. "All the more reason why you should help us put him behind bars and return the money to its rightful owners." He was much too large for the settee on which he sat. Nicole hoped he was as uncomfortable as she was.

"Look, I don't even have a working telephone number for Malcolm. And he certainly hasn't been in touch with me." She wasn't sure how much longer she could sit still. She folded her hands in her lap to keep them from shaking.

"And if I could provide you with a way of getting in touch with him, would you help us bring him in?" the agent asked.

Nicole stood, wanting to bring this conversation to an end. She was furious with Malcolm and hurt in a way she could never make this man understand. And yes, she damned well wanted her money back. But did she want to get involved with the FBI? Did she want to be the one who went out and dragged her brother back to justice? She didn't even want anyone knowing he *was* her brother. Every day she reminded herself of how much worse things would be if they'd had the same last name or traveled in the same circles.

Giraldi narrowed his dark eyes, and she had a horrible feeling that he knew exactly what she was thinking. He rose. "You don't owe him your loyalty, you know. He didn't feel any for you when he took all your money."

Nicole looked the FBI agent in the eye even though she had to look up to do so. He was right, of course. But Malcolm had been more like her child than her brother, and he was a product of their environment just as she was. When they'd vowed to succeed at any cost, it hadn't occurred to her that that cost would be levied on others. Or that for Malcolm, "others" would include her.

They locked gazes for a long moment. Nicole was the first to look away. "I'll think about it," she said, escorting him to the door. Which was exactly what she'd said to him the last two times he'd asked.

"Well, I wouldn't think about it too long. The longer it takes us to find him, the less chance we have of recovering the missing money."

He handed her his card, just as he had every time he'd called on her. This time he scribbled his cell phone number on the back. "Call me if you hear from him. Or if you think of anything that might help us track him down."

"Right." She opened the door and waited for him to leave, both of them aware that she hadn't actually committed.

But this time after he'd gone she didn't throw the card away.

Six

It took Madeline just under eight hours to drive from Atlanta to Tampa. Although she'd brought along a book on tape, she spent most of the trip worrying. Steve's depression and abdication, Kyra's pregnancy and refusal to talk about her baby's celebrity father, her mother-in-law's growing frailty, Andrew's belligerence—all of these things fed the panic that churned inside her. The fact that pretty much everything was riding on producing some sort of income from her third of this "property," and that she'd have to deal with two complete strangers to produce that income, just made her stomach churn faster.

She got to Tampa late in the evening and checked into a motel just off the interstate, where the worrying, churning, and burgeoning hope that all of their financial problems were about to be solved kept her tossing and turning through the night. In the morning, she climbed back in the minivan and drove onto the Howard Franklin Bridge, the center of three bridges spanning Tampa Bay, and got her first stunning view of sunlight sparkling on water. It was a beautiful May morning, and as she lowered her window to draw a deep breath of warm moist air into her lungs, she wished she could draw the sunshine in with it.

Following her GPS, she passed the rounded dome of Tropicana Field and continued south toward Sarasota/Bradenton, ultimately exiting onto the Pinellas Bayway. Condominium buildings whooshed by on either side of the causeway, each with its slice of waterfront or golf course, most of them with names that attested to the state's early Spanish influences: Fort DeSoto, Tierra Verde, Isla del Sol. Over the bridge's concrete balustrade, she spied hand-shaped neighborhoods with fingers of land that poked out into the blue green water of Boca Ciega Bay. They were far too symmetrical to have been formed by nature but were beautiful nonetheless.

Slowing for a traffic light she came face-to-face with what looked like a huge pink wedding cake with white icing trim. Massively built, it stretched for several blocks, its bright pink stucco walls broken by lines of arched windows edged in white and topped by cupolas and bell towers. It loomed over the narrow two-laned Gulf Boulevard, allowing only small glimpses of the white sandy beach and the Gulf of Mexico behind it.

At her GPS's urging, she headed south, where a sign welcomed her to the Historic District of Pass-a-Grille. There the road narrowed further, sandwiched between the bay-front homes, which ranged from small and untouched to huge and newly constructed, and the labyrinth of small streets and homes that fronted the Gulf. The call of seagulls broke through the everyday sounds as the sun continued its ascent, growing brighter and more insistent. The breeze was more subtle, barely stirring the fronds of the palm trees that seemed to be everywhere, lightly flavored with salt and warmth.

Soon her GPS, which was starting to sound a bit bossy given the palm trees and all, directed her onto the aptly named Gulf Way, and she got her first full-on look at the Gulf of Mexico and the wide white sand beach that bounded it. Drawing in another deep breath of salt-tinged air, Madeline promised herself a long walk on the beach and a swim in the Gulf. Just as soon as she saw her "mansion" and discovered, at last, just how much her share of it was worth.

The blocks were short and the avenues, which stretched from the bay to the Gulf were barely longer. Despite the tattoo of her heart, which seemed to speed up as she drew closer, Madeline drove slowly, trying to take it all in and because it didn't seem the sort of place you were supposed to hurry through.

Moments later she'd reached the tip of the island. A sign dangled from a wrought-iron post. The first line of gold scripted letters read Bella Flora. The second line contained the address: Ten Beach Road.

A thrill snaked up Madeline's spine. A house with a name was almost always more valuable than one without, wasn't it?

A low concrete wall wrapped around the property, barely containing an explosion of jungle-sized greenery. Assorted palms and massive bushes, some long dead, others flowering madly, shot up above the wall and blocked most of the first story from view. Above the unruly mass and between the curving trunks of the taller palms, she could make out large expanses of pale pink stucco, a second floor lined with windows, and a multi-angled red tile roof.

Her heart beat faster at its heft and weight. Her gaze was drawn from the house to the long brick drive just beyond it where a bright blue Mini Cooper was already parked. Madeline pulled in behind it, eager to see which of her "partners" it belonged to; even more eager to tour their asset.

As Madeline parked, a figure emerged from the driver's seat of the Mini Cooper. She was petite with pale white skin, delicate, almost doll-like features, and a bust that belonged on a much larger frame. A fringe of blonde hair hung over one eyebrow and angled to her shoulders. She wore white jeans and a long-sleeved gray and white T-shirt that deepened the gray of her eyes. Though her hair wasn't "poufed" like it was on TV, Madeline recognized her right away. Madeline was out of the van and moving forward as the blonde straightened. "Avery Lawford?"

The blonde froze beside her car and Madeline blushed. "My mother-in-law is a big fan of *Hammer and Nail*. I've seen you on TV."

"Oh." That was all. As if she thought Madeline were going to ask for an autograph or was some sort of do-it-yourself groupie. "I'm Madeline Singer. I'm one of your, um, partners in the, uh, house." She couldn't quite bring herself to say the word "mansion" aloud, though she'd loved the sound of it in her head.

Extending her hand, she noticed how much smaller Avery Lawford appeared in person than on television. The top of her head, without the big Dolly Parton hairdo, barely reached Madeline's shoulder.

The blonde smiled and her shoulders relaxed. "Nice to meet you," she said as she withdrew her hand. "I was a little worried that 'mansion' was just a Realtor's marketing term. But it looks . . . significant."

Madeline nodded her agreement even as she tried to tamp down the hope burgeoning inside her. It was dangerous to have all of her eggs in this one basket; she'd already discovered just how easily those eggs could break. She shifted uncomfortably, feeling large and clumsy beside the smaller, younger woman, unsure of what to say, knowing she needed to be careful not to reveal how crucial the sale of this house was to her.

The discomfort she felt with Avery Lawford was nothing compared to what she felt when their third partner arrived a few moments later in a classic green Jaguar convertible, from which she emerged like a celebrity being handed onto the red carpet.

Madeline and Avery exchanged glances but said nothing as Nicole Grant approached.

Everything about the tall, willowy redhead screamed "big city" and "not from around here." Her hair was pulled back in a careless yet elegant way, and her high cheekbones were set in an almost artistically angled face. The bio Madeline had read online put her in her midforties, but she looked a hell of a lot closer to Avery's age than Madeline's. Madeline regretted her white capris and cap-sleeved T-shirt. The multi-striped sandals and bag that she'd thought tied everything so nicely together shouted "Payless shoe store."

The breeze stirred the short skirt of the dating guru's halter sundress, which was undoubtedly designer and possibly vintage.

Madeline smoothed a hand down the side of her capris and wished she'd worn Spanx or at least splurged on a pedicure. "Welcome to Bella Flora," she said as the redhead drew nearer. "I'm Madeline."

"Avery Lawford."

"Nicole Grant."

They were contemplating each other warily when a Cadillac drew up to the curb. An elderly gentleman climbed out and walked toward them as briskly as the cane he leaned on would allow.

"Hello, ladies. Welcome to Pass-a-Grille," John Franklin said after the introductions had been made. "I'm thrilled to see that Bella Flora has owners as lovely as she is."

The Realtor had a ruff of white hair around an otherwise bald scalp and a long face dominated by the droopy brown eyes of a basset hound. But he appeared freshly shaven and turned out in a short-sleeved button-down shirt and khakis—which, Madeline reflected, could very well be the beach equivalent of a three-piece suit.

He turned to motion toward the house and they turned with him. The pale pink façade was almost completely obscured by the walled jungle in front of it. All she could make out at the end of the driveway was an outbuilding of some sort in an even paler pink.

"This property is one of the best known and most historically significant on Pass-a-Grille. It was built for the Eugene Price family back in the 1920s right around the same time as the Don CeSar—the big pink hotel you passed on the way here."

He looked at them as if this should mean something. Madeline smiled, but she didn't think any of them really cared who had built it or lived in it. They just wanted to know how much money they could get for it.

"The Prices were related to Henry Plant, who built Plant Hall and is credited with bringing the railroad down as far as Tampa. A very prominent family. The house remained in the Price family for over sixty years. In 1978 a distant relative named Sam Paulding inherited it and spent a great deal of time and money on it. That work stopped when Sam Paulding died unexpectedly in 1990. It's changed hands a number of times since then."

Nicole looked pointedly down at her watch. When the Realtor paused briefly to take a breath, she asked, "Do you think we could go ahead and take a look?"

Madeline winced at the impatience that underscored her tone.

"Why, of course. Of course."

They moved through the opening in the low wall and followed the path through a veritable forest of palm trees and overgrown shrubbery. The courtyard felt overcrowded and out of control, as if man had simply given up and allowed nature to have its way. "Anyone happen to have a machete in their purse?" Nicole asked, pushing a low lying palm frond out of her face.

Avery smiled. "It is a bit overgrown, but I bet it was gorgeous back in the day."

"Oh, yes," Franklin said. "Most of the garden is original to the house. There are plants here that were put in when the house was built and are still thriving."

"Taking over the world is more like it," Nicole muttered as Madeline did the math. Apparently the house, like John Franklin and much of the local population, was over eighty years old.

"It just needs a little attention," he continued. "Maybe a little pruning. My wife is president of the garden club and she says . . ."

Nicole sighed as the Realtor nattered on, but this time she didn't interrupt.

"And look at this fountain," he continued as they pushed their way through a stand of big leafed plants and stepped around a group of pointy-edged cactus-like things. It was a weathered concrete basin shaped like an upside down urn. A frieze of dolphins had been carved into its sides.

"It's beautiful," Madeline said.

"It's classic Art Deco," Avery added enthusiastically, but all of them were already looking over the top of the fountain to the house itself. Madeline's pulse skittered in her veins as she considered it.

The brick walkway opened to a series of steps, which led to a wooden double door framed in a rectangle of carved stone. Two-storied wings fanned outward on each side, stretching almost the width of the property before folding backward in an inverted U. The pink stucco was faded and splotchy like an old woman who'd had an ill-advised love affair with the sun but had nonetheless moisturized faithfully. The first floor was lined with full-length arched windows; those upstairs were square or rectangular and framed by stone and wrought-iron balconies. The tile roof angled and straightened in numerous directions. Above the roof line two chimneys and a bell tower rose up toward the sky.

"This is a great example of Mediterranean Revival architecture," Avery said. "The style was hugely popular in Florida and California in the twenties and early thirties. I actually did my thesis on the style's greatest architects in college."

Franklin smiled his approval. "Yes, it was a style that was not only elegant but functional for the climate and the times. The walls are a foot thick and the profusion of windows and balconies provide cross ventilation, which was critical in those days before air-conditioning. And inside those foot-thick walls is hollow tile construction reinforced with steel. It was built to last, and it has."

Madeline knew John Franklin was giving them a sales pitch, but nonetheless her excitement continued to build. For the last three months she'd been clinging by her fingertips, praying for a miracle; now it looked like at least some of her prayers had been answered.

She and Avery and Nicole crowded around John Franklin, the anticipation written on all of their faces as they walked up the steps. *It's a mansion,* she reminded herself as Franklin fit the key into the front lock and jiggled it to engage the old brass lock. *With a brick drive and a walled courtyard and a name.*

The heavy door creaked open and he stepped back with a courtly bow to allow them to enter. "There we go," he said.

Madeline felt an embarrassing urge to close her eyes and hold her breath as the three of them stepped over the threshold together. She managed to resist the first but apparently none of them did that well with the second. Because they'd hardly set foot in the foyer when there was a loud whoosh of released breath. Which was, unfortunately, accompanied by what sounded like the frantic flapping of wings.

Seven

"Look out!"

The bird dipped so low over their heads that Nicole could feel the air its wings displaced as it flew past them, just missed John Franklin, and shot out the open front door. Inhaling in surprise, the smell that assaulted Nicole's nose made her want to bail out with the bird.

She took another breath because there was no alternative and drew in a lungful of heavy air that smelled like a bathing suit that had been rolled up wet, stuffed in a suitcase, and then forgotten.

"Oh, my God!" Madeline pinched her nose shut with her fingers. Her brown eyes were large with panic.

Nicole cleared her throat. Avery did the same beside her. The Realtor stepped into the center of the foyer, which was large and square, and somehow managed to breathe normally. "It's been closed up for quite a while," was his only concession to the stench. "Let me open a couple of windows and let some fresh air in."

None of them answered, but Madeline and Avery were wearing the same kicked-in-the-gut look that Nicole felt on her own face. They hadn't made it past the foyer and already it was clear that the old lady had a lot more wrong with her than blotchy skin.

Above them hung a rusted iron chandelier choked with dust and trailing cobwebs. Beneath their feet the wood floors were scratched and scuffed and stained with lighter spots where furniture must have once stood. A wooden staircase angled up to the second floor, gap-toothed with missing spindles, its surface chipped and peeling. The once-white walls were speckled with yellow age spots and amoeba-shaped stains.

John Franklin took a spot beneath the chandelier and began pointing out the home's features as if they weren't all gasping for breath while trying not to breathe, and beginning to feel like even bigger victims than they'd been when they arrived.

According to their "tour guide," the central hallway stretching to the back of the house was a classic Mediterranean Revival feature as were the wide arched openings that ran along both sides. It all sounded quite lovely except that the whole place smelled like that rolled-up bathing suit—dank and sodden. Despite the open front door, the large fixed glass on the landing, and the vast number of uncovered windows, the bright sunlight outside seemed no match for the accumulated layers of dirt and grime.

Madeline, the hausfrau in the white capris, ran a hand over a squared knob of the banister and came away with a palm full of dust and grit, which she stared at woefully.

"What a shame," Avery, whom she'd mentally christened the little blonde with the big bust, said. "I don't know how anyone, even Malcolm Dyer, could neglect a house like this."

Nicole wondered if Malcolm had ever actually set foot here or had simply purchased it to add to his investment portfolio. He'd started buying up estates and properties shortly after he'd made his first million—a milestone they'd celebrated together and of which Nicole had been exceedingly proud. For children who'd been evicted from as many places as they

had, owning anything was huge. Owning homes as large and
larger than this had been a validation of just how far her little
brother had managed to come.

"Yes, it's a fine old home," the Realtor said as if their surprise had been of joy. "And as you'll see a large portion of it
has been renovated. It just needs a little tender loving care."

"More like hospitalization," Nicole said. "Or a team of
paramedics."

Relentlessly positive, John Franklin led them through
the downstairs with its large rectangular rooms and ceilings
beamed with Florida cypress, pointing out the architectural
details with great delight. They toured the formal living
room with fireplace, the study/library, the salon, the formal
dining room, a lounge with an elaborately tiled bar, Moorish decor, and torn leather banquettes, then speed-walked
through a kitchen that had clearly been modernized in a
blaze of Formica—sometime in the 1970s.

He gestured toward an open-air loggia that stretched
between the kitchen and the waterfront salon. The French
doors that spanned the back of the house would have
undoubtedly provided a fabulous view if they hadn't been
quite so caked with grime and salt. Nicole tried to make out
the detached garage and pool and beyond that the narrow
pass, where the bay and Gulf met, but it was like being inside
a somewhat murky aquarium; everything outside the glass
was vague and out of focus.

Franklin continued his monologue as he led them through
another archway and up the back stairs, but Nicole was too
numb to process anything besides the fact that this house
was in no condition to be listed for sale. Her partners' faces
reflected the same mixture of horror and disappointment.

Upstairs was more of the same. They found the escaped
birds' nest in a corner of the master bedroom just beneath
one of many grime-stained windows that were either missing panes or didn't quite close. The room had been enlarged
at some point, and with its dressing area and master bath
filled with funky green tile and ancient fixtures, it took up

the whole west side of the upper floor. But the plaster had fallen off a sodden section of the ceiling, where shards of daylight and blue sky could be seen, and lay in clumps on the floor, which was covered in a moldy pile of green shag carpet undoubtedly installed at the same time as the kitchen.

They saw three more bedrooms and two more funkily-tiled bathrooms as Franklin expounded on the damned Florida cypress, the tile and woodwork, the stone accents, the house's symmetry and generous proportions. The 1920s hardware, dull and scratched though it was, might have been the crown jewels. At least in his eyes the broken window-panes, dripping sinks, flaking chrome, and peeling wallpapers, along with the other countless signs of age and neglect, simply didn't exist.

"They just don't build houses like this anymore," John Franklin said as he led them back into the master bedroom. "Not at any price."

"You've got to be kidding." Nicole crossed her arms and looked the Realtor in the eye. She'd spent close to a year hiding her fear and desperation. Now she felt as if she'd crawled on her belly through the scorching sands of some desert only to discover that the oasis shimmering in the distance was a pile of camel dung.

"It does have great bones," Avery Lawford said. "And I can see they've tried to renovate within the original footprint of the house, but . . ."

"Maybe it just needs a facelift to get it ready for sale?" Madeline asked hopefully.

Nicole snorted. "This house needs serious reconstructive surgery." She could feel her anger mounting. She didn't even have enough money for a Lifestyle Lift. Not for herself, and not for this house. Full-blown plastic surgery was out of the question.

"If we put up a sign and sold it 'as is' what could we get for it?" she asked.

Franklin shook his head. "I wouldn't do it. You'd get maybe a million, which would be like giving it away."

They looked at each other. A million sounded like a lot until you deducted the sales commission and divided it in thirds. She might end up with enough to spend the summer in the Hamptons trolling for clients, but only if it sold quickly, like in the next twenty-four hours.

"Come on," Franklin said. "Let me show you why you don't want to do that. You have a significant ace up your sleeve. I really should have started there."

He put a key into a deadbolt lock on one of the master bedroom's French doors, manhandled it open, then led them out onto the balcony. A peeling wrought-iron stair wound down to the patio below, but no one looked straight down. They all looked out over the barrel roof of the loggia, past the cracked and empty pool and out over the seawall, their gazes inexorably drawn to the house's true reason for being.

"Wow."

"Oh, my . . ."

"Good God!"

They stared in wonder out over the very tip of the tip of the barrier island and watched the bay and Gulf meet head-on in a choppy dance of whitecaps and sea swell. The water slapped into itself, swirling and eddying. They were surrounded by water on three sides, the house at their back. To the west a jetty angled out toward the shipping channels and, presumably, the distant shores of Mexico. On the east lay Boca Ciega Bay. But in front of them in this slim comma of water, the vastness of the Gulf funneled into the more intimate confines of the bay. Beyond the pass, small mounds of land poked haphazardly out of the water, seemingly uninhabited but for the birds using them as landing strips.

It was an intensely personal experience. Like having all of nature—sky and sea and everything that lived in either—performing for your own enjoyment.

"Now *this*," Nicole said, "is worth serious money. But the house . . ." She didn't even turn to look at it. "Maybe we should just knock it down." Her hands fisted at her sides. Given all she'd been through, all she'd lost, she could probably pull the place down with her bare hands and call it therapy.

The little blonde tensed beside her and Madeline gave a small gasp of surprise as Nicole turned from the view to meet John Franklin's eye. "There can't be many pieces of property available with a better view or situation."

"Well, no, there aren't," he conceded. "But you can't just raze a home of this significance. It's on the National Register as a designated property."

"So we're not allowed by law to demolish it?" Avery asked with what Nicole thought sounded like relief.

The Realtor looked distinctly uncomfortable. His ears turned a bright red. "I don't see how, in good conscience, you could do that."

"Conscience aside," Madeline asked, her tone tentative, "could we?"

There was a protracted silence while Franklin apparently tried to come up with a stronger argument. Finally, he sighed and shifted his weight on the cane. "Unfortunately, we don't actually have the power to prohibit that." He brightened. "But there are some powerful tax and financial incentives to restore rather than tear down. And you gain an exemption from the FEMA fifty percent rule, which would allow you to put as much money as you wanted into the restoration."

Nicole thought about just how much she could afford to put into this house. That amount was zero. "But we could tear it down and just list the lot?" Nicole asked, thinking at the moment she was, in fact, desperate enough to rip the structure apart with her bare hands.

"Well, you'd have to come before the preservation board and we, um, I mean *they* would most likely impose a ninety-day waiting period in which you would be asked to hear reasons for choosing to restore or renovate. I think the community would do everything it could to stop the loss of such a significant property."

"Such as?" Nicole pressed.

Franklin removed a white handkerchief and mopped his brow while Avery and Madeline looked on. In the end he didn't answer her question, but said, "Even in this economy there is a market for well-restored, or even renovated, historic homes. I have a Realtor in my office who specializes in that and has a list of potential clients across the country. I believe that's how we originally found Mr. Dyer."

"Gee, and look how well that turned out," Nicole said.

John Franklin cleared his throat; the wattle of extra skin that surrounded it shook. "Shall we?" Despite the cane and his age, he motioned them down the circular stair that led to the back courtyard, then followed carefully behind. He must have realized walking back through the house might send them running for the wrecking ball.

The exterior damage was worse back where the house met the elements head-on. Chunks of pale pink stucco and pieces of red roof tiles lay dashed against the concrete pool deck and surrounding bricked courtyard.

A drainpipe hung down the corner of the east wing and tapped rhythmically against the dented and chipped stucco, the tune dictated by the breeze. But it was harder to focus on the signs of neglect when you were surrounded by water that sparkled so brilliantly under such a cloudless blue sky.

"We've had sales of several renovated Mediterranean Revivals in the last year, none of them anywhere close to your property in size or relevance. And every one of them sold for several million dollars."

Clearly, John Franklin was not yet ready to roll over and play dead. Nor had he forgotten how to sell. "You've got one hundred fifty feet of prime waterfront, far more than any of the others."

"So how much do you think we could get just for the land?" Nicole asked. She felt like a dog with a bone in its mouth; one she couldn't quite bring herself to drop or bury.

"Probably about three million," Franklin conceded, turning his hound-dog eyes on the three of them. "But as an active member of the Gulf Beaches Historical Society and president of the preservation board, I have to say it would be criminal."

There was a silence broken only by the caw of a seagull and the high whine of a wave runner speeding along the seawall's edge. They were all smiling over the three million, their collective relief palpable. Nicole could taste it; her share would go a long way toward getting her life back on track in every way possible.

Franklin led them around the west side of the house and pointed out the path that led to the jetty, with its concrete fishing pier, and also forked to the beach, which really did stretch as far as the eye could see. Just a few steps from the front of their property, a sidewalk began. It was separated from the beach it paralleled by a barrier of sea oat–topped sand dunes.

At the Cadillac, Franklin stopped and reached in his pocket to pull out three keys, which he pressed into their palms. "Don't be fooled by the dirt and grime," he said, making eye contact with each of them in turn. "You need to wait out the summer anyway—nothing significant will sell until fall. And you'll get far more if you use that time to finish the house properly. A well-done renovation in harmony with the house would allow us to ask for and get a full five million."

He had their complete attention then and he knew it. John Franklin might be in his eighties, but he not only still knew how to sell, he knew how to make an exit. He handed them each his card and left them standing on the driveway, his stooped shoulders squared and his spine so straight Nicole wondered if the cane had been some sort of a prop rather than a necessity.

Eight

They stood in the driveway, holding their keys and John Franklin's business cards, clearly unsure of how to proceed. All of them bore physical evidence of Bella Flora's neglect.

"This is both better and worse than I was expecting," Avery said.

"Yes," Madeline agreed. "The good news is we could each walk away with over a million dollars." She swiped at what looked like a bit of cobweb on her cheek and left a smear of dirt in its place. "The bad news is we have no idea what it would cost to pull it down or finish it."

"Or how long it would take to do either of those things and then sell it," Nicole said. A streak of dirt marred one bare shoulder.

Their smiles dimmed a bit as they considered the fact that no one was going to hand them even one dollar tomorrow.

Avery looked at her partners, knowing she must look equally smudged and wondering if their thoughts and feelings were as disjointed as hers. "My father's former partner, Jeff Hardin, has been building in Tampa for the last fifty years," she said. "He offered to come by this afternoon to take a look. Why don't we ask him to give us a quote on demolition and some sort of ballpark of what it might take to get it in good enough shape to put on the market?"

"That sounds great," Madeline said, skimming a nervous hand down the side of her white capris. "I don't really see how we can make a decision without educating ourselves first."

Nicole nodded, her green eyes veiled. "Sure. What time are you expecting him?

"Two o'clock."

They agreed to meet back at the house and then, like boxers retreating to their respective corners, they dispersed. Nicole slid into the Jag, tied a scarf around her head, and drove off. Madeline locked her purse in the trunk of her car and with a wave of good-bye, took the path that led to the beach. Avery, who had no appetite and couldn't think of anywhere she actually wanted to go, wandered out to the back of the house and plopped down on the seawall.

The day was warm and the sun high in the bright blue sky. Boats packed with people motored by at a sedate pace, picking up speed as they left the pass for open water. Gulls circled lazily overhead or dive-bombed for food; others had staked out the fishing pier waiting for man-made opportunities. When she was little she'd sometimes come with her parents to Pass-a-Grille for a day on the beach. They'd cart their things onto the sand and set up near the Don CeSar. There her mother would arrange herself artfully beneath a large striped beach umbrella and lose herself in the latest movie and design magazines, while she and her father designed and built elaborate sand castles with turrets and moats and carefully drizzled decoration. There'd been the occasional fancy Sunday brunch at the newly restored Don, as the locals called it, and once a whole weekend there with her parents. Avery closed her eyes, trying to view that weekend from an adult perspective, but all she could remember was how much her ten-year-old self had loved jumping in the big kidney-shaped pool, and her shouts of "look at me!" and "watch this!" that only her father had obeyed. Two years later her mother had left—unaccountably enough for Hollywood, where she'd ultimately become one of a handful of well-known interior designers to the stars.

After that it had been just her and her father and the Hardin family, who had done their best to include them in their ranks. She narrowed her gaze, straining to see the swell of Shell Key on the opposite side of the pass, where they'd come on the Hardins' boat on those rare Saturdays when her dad and Jeff Hardin hadn't been needed at some construction site or another. Avery sighed, remembering how they'd anchor off the island to swim and sunbathe and how she and her father would escape into their castle-building all the while trying not to be jealous of the completeness of the Hardin family.

Chase Hardin had been a whole other wrinkle—teasing her and calling her squirt and generally treating her like he did his younger sister despite the brief but painful crush Avery had developed for him as she'd entered her teens.

Over the years, her father had kept her posted. Sybil was married and living in D.C. Like Avery, Chase had started on an architectural degree, but then his mother had died and he'd left school to work with their dads after his father's first heart attack. Chase had married and had two children. Three or four years ago he'd lost his wife to cancer. The last time Avery had seen him had been at her father's funeral, where he'd pulled her aside to give her a gruff hug and then straightened her horribly wobbly spine by calling her "Squirt."

Odd that Bella Flora had been sitting here, waiting, all that time. Rising from the seawall, she turned to study the house whose fate now lay partly in her hands. She considered the long run of window and glass, the solid stonework and fanciful wrought iron, the faded and pockmarked pink stucco with its chipped white trim. It was all that remained of what her father had left her, his legacy, though he had never intended it that way.

Avery let herself into the house and stood listening as it creaked and settled around her. The musty dampness still permeated the air and Avery recognized it for what it was;

the smell of loneliness. Her footsteps echoed in the vast emptiness as she threw open doors and windows—those that would budge—to take advantage of the cross ventilation the house had been designed to capture. It took her full weight and a good bit of determination to unstick the exterior kitchen door, and when she'd finally wrestled it open, she was rewarded with a warm breeze on her cheek and a doorknob in her hand.

Avery opened her palm to inspect the egg-shaped knob, which was scuffed and scratched from decades of use, the brass aged to a deep patina. Setting it carefully on the kitchen counter, she went out to her car and rooted around in the trunk until she found her tool belt. On the way back into the house, she strapped it low on her hips and buckled it on the hole she'd notched in it. Not needing to look, she reached down for the Phillips screwdriver and used it to reattach the knob. She had just slipped the screwdriver back into its slot when she heard footsteps in the hallway followed by Jeff Hardin's "Anybody home?"

Hurrying down the central hall, Avery bypassed Chase Hardin with a smile to walk into his father's open arms, where she stayed for a few long comforting moments before turning to face her onetime crush. He was forty and it looked good on him. His dark hair was cropped close to his head, his shoulders were broad and well muscled, and his skin was tanned from a lifetime in the sun.

He looked her up and down. "Glad to see you got rid of that silly pink tool belt you used to wear."

"I was seven," she said. "Everything I owned was pink then. Besides, my father gave it to me. I'm not sure I even took it off in the bath."

"Well, I recognize *that* tool belt," Jeff Hardin said with his slow smile. "Your daddy never left home without it."

Avery nodded at the truth of his statement; she could barely picture her father without it slung on his hips. Her mother had not been charmed by this and complained that he would have strapped it on over his tuxedo if she'd let him.

Not that he'd been a fan of the formal affairs Dierdre dragged him to or the formal wear required to attend them.

Avery had spotted the expensive tuxedo balled up in the garbage shortly after her mother had deserted them. It hadn't taken her father long to shed the physical reminders she'd left behind; the memories had proven much harder to dispel.

"So this is what was left of your father's estate?" Jeff Hardin shook his head.

"Actually only a third of this," Avery said. "I have two partners. They'll be back any minute."

"I told your dad those returns were too good to be true." He shook his head again. "That Malcolm Dyer should be taken out and shot."

"They'll have to find him first," Avery said. "And, frankly, I think shooting is way too good for him. I'd like to see him torn limb from limb and then staked out on an anthill in the hot sun to die."

Chase gave her a look. "You've gotten awfully blood-thirsty." He had his father's smile but his bright blue eyes were shadowed.

"That man stole everything my father spent his life working for. And he left me with a third of a house that has definitely seen better days." She looked at her father's former partner. "Thanks so much for coming. Where do you want to start, up or down?"

"That's up to Chase," his father said. "Your dad and I always built new, and I can give you a ballpark on demolition. But Chase, here, he has a real passion for older homes. He's done some right fine renovation and restoration work and can tell you what's what a lot better than me."

Avery barely suppressed a groan. Leaving Jeff to his own devices, she followed Chase upstairs as he began his inspection, making notes on his legal pad as he went.

In the master bedroom she stood in the corner where the balcony's French doors met the longer window wall. "I figure this was probably a sleeping porch that was enclosed when they redid the master bedroom," she said, interested to see if he'd agree. "And this dressing area with the 'his' and 'hers' closets were probably once a separate bedroom."

He looked at her more closely but barely grunted, "Could be."

"These windows all look original—which I guess is why they're not closing properly. We found a bird's nest over here"—she pointed to the twigs and grass that remained—"and I'm not looking forward to discovering what other animals might be in residence."

Again no comment, just note taking.

"I noticed all the windows on the front of the house are replacements, but it looks like they never got to the back or the western side. I figure most of them will need to be reglazed." She waited pointedly for a response.

"Won't know till I look." He shrugged and made more notes.

"I'm betting there are hardwoods under this shag." She scrunched up her nose at both the smell and the color.

"Like I said, I won't know until I look." He barely looked at her; his tone was equally dismissive.

In the master bath, she took in the two wall-hung sinks with their tapered steel legs and flaking chrome fixtures. The steady drip had worn a stain in each rectangle of porcelain. Every possible surface had been tiled in some shade of green and every inch of what felt like miles of grout screamed for cleaning and resealing.

It was a mess, but she loved the look and feel of it. Almost the only true memories of time alone with her mother were of junking and trolling for treasure in the antique stores in the older parts of Tampa. Anything remotely Deco had pulled her like a magnet and apparently still did.

"Did you see this?" She pointed up toward the slightly arched ceiling at the faded pastel tones of a fanciful underwater scene that matched the etching on the shower door. "It looks hand painted, but it's hard to see the detail. The polyurethane has really yellowed."

He did stop writing long enough to look up. "Yep," he said. "Could be."

Her eyes slitted in irritation. Chase had never been overly effusive, but she couldn't remember him displaying this much attitude. Then again, they hadn't spent any real time around each other since they'd been kids, and they'd never been in anything resembling a professional relationship. Which struck her now as a very fortunate thing.

The noncommittal responses continued as they finished the upstairs bedrooms and baths. She followed him up into the attic uninvited and flicked on her own flashlight, their beams looked like lopsided headlights as they flashed against the walls and framework. By the time they'd inspected the back and front stairs and covered every inch of the first floor, he was barely even grunting and she was seething.

He was thorough, she'd give him that. He practically crawled up into both fireplaces, took his time analyzing the plumbing and the electrical, and explored the pipes of the original steam heat system as well as the more recently installed central air-conditioning. Then he walked the perimeter of the house, checking out what seemed like every inch of the foundation and running his hands, well, lovingly up the heavily stuccoed walls. But for all he said to her he might as well have been alone. In fact, it seemed pretty clear to Avery that he wished he was.

In the driveway, she found Nicole and Madeline already talking with Jeff Hardin. After the briefest of hellos, Chase went to pull a ladder off his truck, leaving Avery to trail after him as he carried it to the side of the house, put it in position, and climbed up on the barrel-tile roof to look at the damage above the master bedroom. He didn't invite her to join him, nor did he offer any details about what he'd found when he came back down with several broken pieces of tile in one hand.

"How big an area are we looking at?" she asked impatiently and when he didn't respond, "I'm assuming it's just a patch job."

No response.

"Can we match the original tiles?"

"Probably." His tone was grudging, though she thought she detected a small flicker of surprise in his eyes.

"What is it with you?" she finally demanded as he set the tiles carefully out of the way and began to fold up the ladder. "I played on the same construction sites as a child that you did. And I have a BArch degree from USC hanging on my wall. Not to mention four years on *Hammer and Nail*. I doubt there's anything you're scribbling on that damned yellow pad that I'm incapable of understanding."

"Is that right?" he asked as he settled the ladder under one arm. "I thought maybe that degree was mail order or something. Because all I ever saw you do on that show was point and gesture with the occasional flutter of your eyelashes and a sigh of admiration."

He turned his back on her and carried the ladder to the truck, taking his time getting it positioned. By the time he'd ambled back to the rest of them, Avery's jaw was clenched so tightly she doubted she could produce much more than a grunt herself. It was turning out be a monosyllabic kind of day.

"Well?" she ground out when he made no move to share his thoughts.

Madeline and Nicole leaned in closer to hear.

"Well," he said, folding his arms across his chest. "What do you think, Dad? Ten to fifteen thousand for demolition?"

Jeff Hardin nodded. "Yep."

"But you'd be absolutely crazy to tear this house down," Chase said.

"Because . . . ?" Avery prompted, trying to hold on to her temper and knowing that Madeline and Nicole would need an explanation.

"Because it's one of the finest examples of Mediterranean Revival you're going to find here on the west coast of Florida. There's one Addison Mizner up on Park Street, but it's more Palladian villa than true Mediterranean Revival. Because there are a handful of Schooley's in Pasadena and in the northeast section of St. Pete, but this house is fabulous.

And its tie to the Don CeSar, the fact that it was built right around the same time, makes it even more important than it would be on its own." He aimed all of this at her in the tone of a teacher speaking to a not particularly bright pupil.

Avery's hands fisted on her hips just above her tool belt. He was lucky she wasn't packing anything more deadly than a nail gun.

Jeff Hardin laid a hand on his son's shoulder. "Everyone's not out to save old houses like you are, Chase, and we promised to present both sides."

"There is no other side. This house is way too beautiful to be torn down. Period."

When no one immediately protested, Chase continued. "Right now the dirt and grime is covering up a lot of incredible workmanship. But the plumbing is in relatively good shape—Robby, our plumber, could take care of those leaks and go over it more thoroughly. The electrical has already been updated—probably in the seventies when the kitchen was redone. That's probably when the central air went in, too. It's going to need a full overhaul, but the original steam heat system is a really cool feature, though I don't really have anyone down here with the experience to work on it. The roof needs work, but not a complete replacement." The condescension he'd shown Avery had given way to a passion that lit his eyes in a way that his smile hadn't. It was the same kind of passion her father had brought to the homes he built, the very same passion that had made Avery want to be an architect. "The wood is all Florida cypress, which was originally hugely expensive but was put in because bugs don't like it and it lasts forever. Why, a little—"

"Promise me you are *not* going to say 'a little tender loving care,' " Nicole interrupted.

"No, it needs more than that," he conceded. "But it's not like you'd be starting from scratch. There's just no question that this work can and should be done. What did the Realtor tell you—a couple million more if the renovation is complete?"

"Yes," Avery said, drawn to his enthusiasm but still chafing at his air of superiority. "But completing the house would cost a lot more than the fifteen thousand it would cost to pull it down."

Madeline nodded. The brunette had been worrying her lip between her teeth through most of Chase's impassioned plea. "We came here to put this house on the market, not to sink a ton of money into remodeling it."

"Damn straight," Nicole said, her green eyes fierce.

Avery admired a lot of things about this house. If she'd had the money, she might have enjoyed nursing it back to life. She was even willing to concede that Chase Hardin seemed to know what he was talking about. But his complete dismissal of her made agreeing with him pretty much impossible. So did her lack of money.

"Look," Avery said. "The house is great. I've always admired Mediterranean Revival style and this *is* a fabulous example of it. But none of us live here or, as far as I know, have plans to. We just want to sell our communal asset as quickly as possible." She kept her tone chilly, but Chase Hardin didn't seem to notice.

"You don't want to put this house on the market right now," Chase said, his voice ringing with certainty. "Not in this economy and not at this time of year." He didn't even refer to the teardown as an option. "It's already May. In another few weeks summer will be here full blast. You know, the hot, muggy, close-to-hundred-degree days when just moving requires maximum effort. That is not the time to try to get a wealthy northerner to invest in property here. Maybe in Maine. Or the North Carolina mountains. Not here."

So far Chase Hardin and John Franklin were on the same page, but their agendas were not necessarily hers.

"What would it cost to get the house ready enough to put on the market for a high-end buyer?" Madeline asked softly.

"Well, it would depend," he said.

"Here it comes," Nicole said. "Brace yourselves, ladies."

Avery braced; she sensed Madeline doing the same.

Chase Hardin turned to his father. "Well, first of all I assume we're talking wholesale prices for materials and labor. New construction is a long way from anything resembling a full recovery, so our regular suppliers are hurting and ready to deal and our subs will kill to work at all."

His father nodded agreement. "That's true."

Chase hesitated, still thinking, then said, "And I would be willing to waive any fees as contractor in return for a share of the profits when the house is sold."

It was a bold offer. Avery sensed Nicole and Madeline trying to size him up as they weighed it. All three of them had lost more than they should have to a skilled swindler; no one wanted to travel that road again.

"You still haven't told us how much we'd have to come up with to cover the out-of-pocket expenses," Avery said. "No matter how bad the construction industry is, your suppliers and subs, not to mention the skilled artisans we're going to have to call on occasion, aren't going to give us materials or work for free."

"Completely true," Jeff Hardin agreed again.

"All right," Chase said. "Let me think."

They watched him for a few long moments, none of them talking as he studied the house, lost in thought. In the silence Avery told herself to just calm down and hear what the man had to say. However condescending and annoying he was, he was Jeff's son and he was connected in the construction industry here in ways she wasn't. He had experience they could benefit from.

An odd smile tugged at his lips and she was struck by how handsome he was when he wasn't scowling. "Okay," he finally said. "What if I cover those out-of-pocket expenses and keep receipts, and I get paid back at closing, right off the top?"

"So we'd have no up-front expense?" Nicole asked. "You'd serve as contractor for a percentage of the sale price and get reimbursed for documented hard costs out of the proceeds?"

"Yes." He nodded. "It's a clear win-win."

"But that still could be a huge chunk of money," Avery said, liking the idea but not wanting to leap too quickly. "Even with the hard costs at wholesale, it'll take a ton of man hours to get this house ready."

The odd smile turned evil. "Or woman hours," Chase said. "You all could save yourselves a boatload of money by investing a little sweat equity."

"Sweat equity?" Madeline asked as if trying the term on for size.

Nicole's elegant nose wrinkled at the word "sweat." "We're already investing the house. That's our 'equity' in the deal."

"But the house isn't worth all that much in its present condition," Chase said. "You need me to help realize its true value."

Jeff Hardin shook his head and smothered a smile. Avery didn't like the look of amusement that had stolen into his son's eyes.

"There's a lot of . . . grunt work that's going to have to be done," Chase said. "Work that I could teach almost anyone to do. Even a trained monkey."

"Chase," Jeff Hardin said. "That's not . . ."

"Some of us monkeys have more training and hands-on experience than others," Avery said, her body as stiff with anger as her tone.

"That may be," he replied, the monosyllables ancient history now that he seemed to think he had the upper hand. "But my monkeys won't be pointing and gesturing for a camera, they'll be working." He snagged Avery's gaze. "Plus it's going to be way too hot this summer for tight sweaters. Especially without air-conditioning."

Avery could actually feel her blood beginning to boil in her veins. Her skin flushed from the heat of it. She opened her mouth, closed it, momentarily speechless in her fury.

"So to summarize," Chase said, breaking eye contact with Avery to include the others in his gaze. "I'm willing to serve as general contractor at no charge. I'll pay my usual contractor's rate for all necessary materials and skilled labor. When the house sells I get reimbursed for my documented expenditures and then receive an agreed-upon percentage of your net profits. I'm thinking maybe two percent."

He flashed a wolfish smile and shrugged. "I'll guarantee the house will be ready to go on the market by Labor Day. And all you have to do in return is spend the summer doing what I tell you to."

Nine

"Of all the nerve!" Avery huffed as the three of them crossed Beach Road and walked up the sidewalk toward the Hurricane, a restaurant that had evidently been a Pass-a-Grille staple since her childhood and which afforded both alcohol and a front-row seat for the oncoming sunset. "I have *never* been so intentionally offended! I mean, what unmitigated gall!" The busty little blonde really had her panties in a twist.

Nicole wanted to laugh. The hunky contractor had only tweaked the woman's ego a bit. She'd like to see Avery Lawford's reaction to a baby brother, one you'd raised and protected like your own, who stole everything you had. The urge to laugh died as she accepted that blow to the heart. Looking for a distraction, Nicole turned her attention back to her surroundings. The blocks were short and at each corner a glance to the right provided a view of the bay. Newly constructed homes sat next to fifties-era cinder-block motels with the occasional bungalow thrown in.

"I can't believe he dismissed me like that!" Avery continued to complain, but with each block they covered the volume and level of outrage decreased.

Eighth Avenue consisted of a couple of restaurants, a post office, an ice cream place, a handful of small shops and galleries, and a bar. Another pier, this one white clapboard, jutted out into the bay.

"That must have been 'Main Street,'" Nicole said. "I've never seen such a mishmash of stuff."

"I think it's quaint and kind of charming," Madeline said with complete sincerity. Nicole bit back the retort that sprang to her lips. Based on the rapt expression on Madeline Singer's face, compared to suburbia this place was freakin' Utopia.

The Hurricane, which seemed like an unlucky name for a low-lying place pretty much surrounded by water, took up most of the block between Eighth and Ninth Avenues. Its motif, unlike everything around it, was Cape Cod, with gray clapboard sides and Victorian trim. They took the last available table on the patio facing the beach and sat shoulder to shoulder at Madeline's insistence so that they could watch the sunset, which was apparently what all the people streaming onto the beach were planning to do.

"He actually called us monkeys!" Avery muttered as they made room for each other on the concrete bench. "And expects us to be his grunts!" She shook her head, but agreed to a Frozen Mango Daiquiri when the waitress informed them it was a house specialty. It got quiet as they all took first sips of their drinks and helped themselves to the peel-and-eat shrimp they'd decided to share.

They talked as strangers do, sharing snippets and brief histories, putting the best light on things. Nicole noted their hesitations and evasions, storing them for future consideration, though Nicole doubted their stories were anywhere near as airbrushed as hers.

It was clear that the only things they had in common were being screwed by Malcolm—a topic Nicole was not looking forward to rehashing—and their shares in Bella Flora, a topic they all seemed reluctant to broach. She wiped the warm buttery garlic from her fingers and ordered another round of drinks as Madeline oohed and ahhed over the pinkening sky and the sun's final dramatic exit. Even Nicole, who had watched the sun set over the Pacific, thought it an impressive display, though she found herself unwilling to admit it.

Avery's outrage finally sputtered out somewhere in the middle of her second daiquiri. Nicole went for a third, savoring the thick sweetness of mango and soothed by its welcome wallop. The other two had slices of key lime pie.

"So, what do you think?" Madeline asked, putting her fork down on her now-clean plate. "Do we tear down, or take Chase Hardin up on his offer?"

There was a silence as Nicole and Avery tried to hide their surprise that the housewife had taken the initiative. Nicole drained the last sweet sip from her glass and waited to see what would happen.

"Are you willing to spend the summer being his . . . grunts?" Avery asked.

"Well, we wouldn't actually be grunting for him. We'd be grunting for us," Madeline said with only a slight quiver in her voice. "To up the asking price by two million dollars."

"Could you really spend the next four months here?" Avery asked. "Don't you have a family or something you need to get back to?"

Madeline shifted uncomfortably in her seat and Nicole took note. Through necessity she'd learned to read faces and assess "tells," but she wasn't sure whether Madeline's discomfort was caused by the current conversation or what was going on back in the burbs.

"Well, I know you all probably have to get back to your careers and all," Madeline said. "But I might be able to work things out if we, um, decided that staying and working on the house was the right thing to do."

Now it was the little blonde's turn to look uncomfortable.

Ahhh, Nicole thought. *We're all hiding . . . something.* But then if there was anything she'd learned over the years spent re-creating her life and herself, it was that nothing and no one was exactly what they seemed.

Nicole needed the money from the sale of their house as

soon as possible. The fastest way to get it was to tear the house down and list the land with the most aggressive high-end Realtors they could find, maybe the Yes Girls whose signs she'd seen on the way into town. Except of course that she didn't even have her share of the fifteen thousand it would take to demolish and had no idea whether her partners did, either. Nor did she know how long it might take to sell the land; the arguments against a summer listing sounded valid, but, of course, there was no actual guarantee that Bella Flora would sell quickly once it was renovated. It was all a great big crap shoot. But when it came to gambling, Nicole had always believed in shooting for the biggest prize.

"There are a lot of places I'd rather spend the summer," Nicole said. "But I could probably swing a couple of months here if it's going to add another couple of million to the asking price."

Avery shifted in her seat again as Nicole and Madeline turned her way and waited expectantly.

"Well?" Nicole asked the blonde. "You're probably in a better position to assess the house's potential than we are. What do you think?"

"I think I'm completely pissed off at Chase's attitude," Avery said, brushing a blonde bang out of her eye, her tone rising in indignation. "I mean, who is he to talk to me that way?" She drew a deep breath and let it out before continuing. "But I'm not really comfortable with pulling that house down, especially not just as a knee-jerk to his condescension." She looked out over the beach, which was barely visible beneath the sliver of moon that hung in the dark sky above it. "It is a great specimen," she continued, "and five million is better than two million any day. I also think he's right that it's the wrong time of year to put it on the market."

This time she looked down at the pie crumbs on her plate before raising her gaze to meet theirs. Her gray eyes were clouded. "And the show is on hiatus over the summer anyway." Her jaw tightened. "So I could make myself available if we decided to accept Chase's offer."

They paid their bill and ambled back toward Beach Road. It was a Thursday night, not even nine P.M., and there was hardly a car on the road. Nicole looked at the empty streets as they passed under streetlights and listened to the dead quiet. She'd never be able to troll for wealthy clients here or make the society column—assuming there was one. On the other hand she wouldn't be tempted to shop or spend money. Nor would she need to put on her usual dog-and-pony show. If they lived in the house while they worked on it, she'd hardly have any expenses at all.

Out of the corner of her eye she studied her partners once again. Could she spend an entire summer living and working with women with whom she had so little in common? Did she really have a choice?

"I noticed a vacancy sign earlier at those rental cottages next door," Madeline said as they stopped in front of Bella Flora. Its pale pink walls were shadowed, its windows dark. "Why don't we sleep on it and meet up for breakfast tomorrow morning to vote?"

They agreed, leaving their cars in the drive and walking to the Paradise Inn's tiny office. Tomorrow morning the fate of their beachfront mansion and their summer would be sealed.

Somewhere around three A.M. Madeline gave up trying to sleep and simply lay in bed waiting for daylight. She watched the sunrise over Boca Ciega Bay through the parted curtains of the cottage window. With hours left before they were to meet, she washed her face, brushed her teeth, and dressed. Tucking her cell phone into her pocket, Madeline headed toward the beach.

Lingering in front of Ten Beach Road, Madeline watched the house emerge from shadow as the morning sun began its ascent and deepened the pale gray sky to a robin's egg blue. The house was battered and bruised. It had been buffeted by sand and wind and time. Worn down. Neglected. But did that mean it should be torn down and carted away?

In a perfect world, this house should be showered with love, carefully restored, and sold to someone who would appreciate it. But she had reason to know this was not a perfect world. And rather than fretting over Bella Flora's fall from glory, she should be calculating its monetary value. Could they really finish the house under Chase Hardin's direction? And if they did somehow manage this by Labor Day, how long would it take to find a buyer?

It was a gamble all around, filled with uncertainties; one she'd be taking with two total strangers who had their own goals and agendas she knew nothing about. And who were not, by all appearances, anywhere near as desperate as she was. She thought about Avery Lawford's television series and her career as an architect, Nicole Grant's classic car and vintage clothes, not to mention her high-profile matchmaking business.

Would it be better to simply tear the house down and hope the land would sell quickly? But where would she come up with the five thousand dollars for her share of the demolition? She didn't even know how they were going to hang on financially without having to dig into what little they had left.

Madeline followed the sandy path that led to the jetty and forked to the beach. At the end of the concrete pier a handful of fishermen were already baiting hooks and casting their lines. The seabird population loitered with intent—the more patient pelicans hunkered on boulders and pilings waiting to see what might be caught and tossed their way while their less patient relatives skimmed low over the water and dive-bombed at will. Sleek white herons perfectly balanced on one pick-up-stick leg arched S-shaped necks and stared out to sea.

The beach itself was postcard perfect, the sugar white sand so pristine she felt almost guilty marring it. Removing her sandals, she stepped gingerly onto the cushion of night-cooled sand. Dangling her sandals between the fingers of one hand, she began to walk along the water's edge, her bare toes sinking into the damp sand and enjoying the feel of the water playing over them.

For a while she just walked, the Gulf sparkling blue green on her left, the breeze coming off it so light its surface barely rippled. Schools of needlelike fish darted in the shallows, turning on a dime and moving with military precision. Ahead of her the beach stretched in a gentle curve well past the Don CeSar. On her right, beyond the clumps of seaweed deposited at high tide, wooden walkways arched over the dunes to the sidewalk, protecting them and the wildlife that sought refuge there.

Seagulls flew overhead, gliding and diving while a flock of smaller birds raced here and there on impossibly fragile legs. As she passed the Paradise Grille, where they'd agreed to meet for breakfast, the flow of people increased. Some stopped to search for treasures in the sand while others moved at a faster pace, but no one intruded with more than a smile or a nod.

As she walked Madeline's gaze scanned from the Gulf, across the beach, and up to the homes and condos—many of them large and clearly expensive—that bracketed the beach on her right.

She drew in soothing lungfuls of the warm, salt-tinged air and lost herself in the gentle rhythm of the water as it advanced and retreated. Everything slowed, her heartbeat, the swirl of her thoughts, the pitch of the panic that had consumed her since Steve's confessions. She wished he were here with her now to share in the decisions that had to be made. The "old" Steve wouldn't have been intimidated by Nicole or in awe of Avery. But then if Steve were himself, these decisions wouldn't feel so much like brain surgery, and she wouldn't be so horribly afraid that the wrong choice would put her family's future at even greater risk.

Before she could stop herself she hit the speed dial for home and lifted the cell phone to her ear; the ringing was harsh and discordant against the wash of gentle sounds around her.

"Singer residence." Her mother-in-law's voice was not the one she'd been hoping to hear.

"Edna? It's Madeline. Is Steve there?"

"Oh." Madeline could picture the pinched lips that had produced the word. "He's . . . resting."

Madeline couldn't stop the thought "from what?" that popped into her head. Ashamed, she drew in another breath of beach air and expelled it slowly. "Could you get him on the phone for me, please? I need to speak to him."

"But he's . . ."

"Edna, I have to speak to him. Now." Madeline tried to focus on the feel of the sand beneath her feet and the warmth of the sun on her back. She did not want to think about the fact that her mother-in-law had started screening her son's calls.

"Well!" Edna huffed. A few moments later Madeline heard the murmur of voices and then the blare of the television as Steve came on the phone.

"Hi," he said, and she wondered how one word could convey such defeat. "Have you seen the house yet?"

"Yes. Yesterday," she said. "It's, um, it is, um, actually a really interesting house. And large—about eight thousand square feet. It was built in the twenties."

"And?"

"And it's beautiful. Well, it was beautiful," she amended. "And apparently it's a great architectural specimen. The style is called Mediterranean Revival."

There was a small sound of surprise. "Really? That's great." It was the most enthusiastic she'd heard him in far too long. "How much can we get for it?"

"Well, that kind of depends on what we decide to do to it."

"Do to it?" Wariness crept back into his tone. "I thought we were just going to sell it and take our third."

Madeline stared out over the Gulf, processing his use of the word "we." In the distance a person dangled from a brightly colored parasail tethered to a speedboat by a long umbilical cord.

"Yes, well, it's not quite that simple. It needs work before it can be put up for sale. A good bit of work."

"Jesus," he said. "I should have known anything to do with Dyer would be bullshit."

"The house is valuable," she said. "And so is the land," she interrupted, hating how quickly the enthusiasm had leached from his voice. "'As is' the house is worth about a million, but this apparently isn't a good time to list it. The land itself is worth three million—it's one hundred fifty feet of prime waterfront, but we'd each have to put in five thousand dollars to have the house torn down, and again, it's not a great time to list the property. Or we can stay and spend the next three to four months getting it ready under the supervision of a contractor that Avery Lawford knows. He's willing to get paid out of the proceeds from the sale."

There was a silence, and in it Madeline had this wild hope that the old decisive Steve was going to choose one of the options and offer to take over. She waited, almost breathless, for this to happen.

When he finally spoke he said, "We don't have an extra five thousand dollars." As if she had somehow managed to remain ignorant of this fact. "And we don't have any extra months to wait around for a return."

"I know," Madeline said, though what she really wanted to say was, "Ya think?" "That's why I thought maybe you could come down and help, so that we could work on the house together. It might be good for us, for you."

Again there was a silence.

"It's beautiful here, Steve," Madeline said. "And at least we'd be doing something constructive to get everything back on track. Andrew could come down when the semester's over—that's only a few weeks from now. The more people working, the faster we could get it ready."

"Jesus, Maddie," he said, and she could picture him running a hand through his hair. She wondered if that hair had been washed recently, if he'd showered and shaved. Before she'd left he'd barely bothered to dress. "We can't all go traipsing down there to work on a house that we may or may not ever see anything out of."

Did he have something more pressing to do? Was he perhaps out every day pounding the pavement looking for a job? "Why not?" she asked.

"My mother . . ."

"Your mother and Kyra can look after each other. Or they can come down and help." She did not want to think about her daughter's problems right now. Or her mother-in-law.

When he didn't answer she said, "Steve, I need you. I need you to be a part of this." She hesitated, hating the pleading tone in her voice, hating that she had to beg him to do the right thing. "Our marriage needs you to be a part of this."

There was another silence. Through the receiver she could hear his mother's voice sharp with concern. "What's wrong? Are you all right, Steven?"

"I can't, Maddie," he said so quietly she had to press the phone tighter to her ear to hear him. "I'm sorry. I just . . . I just can't do it. Not right now."

"Steve, no, don't hang up. I . . ."

The line went dead before she could finish. He hadn't even done her the courtesy of allowing her to finish begging.

Slowly, she turned and headed back down the beach, but the pleasure she'd felt in her surroundings had evaporated. Picking up her pace, she concentrated on putting one foot in front of the other as the smarter seabirds scurried out of her way.

At the Paradise Grille Madeline, Avery, and Nicole ordered breakfast at the counter and then sat at a table that overlooked the beach, sipping coffees as they waited for their food. Nicole had once again slicked back her deep red hair and was dressed in the kind of expensive resort wear more appropriate to a high-end cruise ship than a picnic table. Avery wore an HGTV T-shirt and a pair of cutoffs, clearly unworried about her public image.

It took two cups of coffee apiece and the delivery of their meals to loosen their tongues. Eating and talking were made more difficult by the defensive posture required to protect their breakfasts from marauding seagulls.

"All right," Avery said, still hunched over her plate after shooing off one of the bolder birds. "I guess we need to go ahead and see where everyone stands. All in favor of tearing down and selling the lot say 'aye.'"

They contemplated each other carefully, assessing what, Madeline didn't know, but she felt her pulse quicken. What would happen if they couldn't agree? Before her conversation with Steve, Madeline might have gone for the option if she'd had the nerve to ask one of the others to loan her the five thousand. Now she couldn't even imagine going home and watching Edna enable Steve while he deteriorated further. She felt once again like that Little Red Hen with a good deal of Chicken Little thrown in, because she could no longer pretend that any day now Steve was once again going to be . . . Steve. There was simply no question that her whole sky had finally fallen in.

Nicole sat very still; her patrician features might have been sculpted from marble. They continued to watch each other as carefully as the seagulls watched their uneaten food. After a protracted silence, Avery continued. "All in favor of working on the house and paying Chase back out of the proceeds from the sale say 'aye.'"

Madeline noticed that Avery didn't use the words "trained monkey" or "grunt" as she laid out the option, though the motion itself did seem to be passing through heavily gritted teeth.

Almost in unison all three of them said, "Aye." It took a moment for the reality of that to sink all the way in. Then Nicole picked up Avery's cell phone from the table and handed it to her. Practically choking on the words, Avery told Chase Hardin that they accepted his terms. She also accepted his father's offer of some mattresses and odds and ends of furniture from a model home they'd recently sold. Chase would bring the things with him when he came to discuss their job the next morning.

Avery ended the call and put down her phone as they all registered the fact that their gruntdom was now a mere twenty-four hours away. Nicole closed her eyes briefly before offering a rueful smile. 'Oh, boy," she said, "a whole summer here on the very tip of the back of beyond. Let the good times roll."

Ten

They lingered over final cups of coffee trying, Nicole thought, to absorb the reality of their decision.

Getting up to throw out the paper goods and stack her tray on the counter, Madeline asked, "Are we really doing this?"

"Looks like it," Nicole said as the three of them turned onto the sidewalk that paralleled the beach and headed back toward the house. "What are we going to do the rest of the day, work on our grunts?"

"I'm sure once we're dealing with Chase the grunting will come naturally," Avery replied as they passed Eighth Avenue.

"The first thing we have to do is get the house ready for habitation," Madeline said.

"That's going to take way more than a day," Nicole pointed out, not at all looking forward to it.

"I mean ready enough to start sleeping there tomorrow night," Madeline corrected. "If that's still the plan?"

Nicole would have liked to stay in a hotel, preferably the Don CeSar and not the Cottage Inn, while they worked on the house, but she could barely afford another night in the old cottage with its ancient chenille bedspread and blonde fifties furniture. "Unless someone has a better one." God, she'd love to hear a better plan; one that didn't include all the unpleasant tasks that lay ahead.

They walked in silence for the next few minutes, mulling this over, but no one offered an alternative to the coming months of slave labor. An aging hippie pedaled by on a bicycle, offering a noncommittal wave, but car and pedestrian traffic was light. The long row of parking spaces fronting the beach were mostly unoccupied.

They all looked ahead rather than at each other, waiting for that first glimpse of Bella Flora. But when the multi-angled red roof line and upper story appeared over the unkempt front garden, the view, now that the rose-colored glasses had been ripped from their eyes, was not particularly reassuring.

"We can do this," Avery said. "All we have to do is get a couple of bedrooms and a bath ready. The master's unusable until we get the roof and ceiling repaired and that moldy carpet up."

"Let's make it all three of the other bedrooms," Nicole said. "Camping out in that house is unappealing enough. I'm not planning on sharing."

"And we're going to want to use the kitchen," Madeline added, her gaze skimming over the house rather than meeting theirs. "So we don't have to run out to eat all the time."

Nicole almost laughed at how careful they all were to sidestep the subject of finances. But would any of them be sleeping on a mattress on the floor if they didn't have to?

"It *is* a great house," Avery said, but it sounded to Nicole as if the blonde were trying to convince herself. "It would have been criminal to tear it down."

Madeline wore a look of resignation. Nicole felt too much anger and fear to be fully resigned, but the decision had been made. There was nothing to be gained in second-guessing it. "So I assume the first thing we need is cleaning supplies," she said without enthusiasm.

"Yes. In massive quantities," Avery agreed. "If we get started this morning, we should be able to be ready for the mattresses and all tomorrow. But I'm sure we're going to spend weeks cleaning. That house has been pretty much unoccupied for years."

"Then we need to go to one of the warehouse clubs," Madeline said, leading the way to the brick drive. "I'm sure there must be one in the area."

Nicole stared at her blankly. "A warehouse . . . club?"

"You know," she said. "Like Sam's Club or Costco, where you get a membership so you can buy big quantities of things for less."

"I've never really needed anything in a big enough quantity to join one," Avery said. "Do they have cleaning supplies?"

"A whole section." Madeline said this as if this were a good thing. "Industrial and commercial strength, which we are definitely going to need. They cater to small business."

Nicole couldn't think of a single thing to add to this conversation. She'd spent most of her life working so that she wouldn't need to go to a place like that and cleaning supplies were pretty much the last thing she wanted to spend the last of her money on. But Madeline peered at them as if they were odd life-forms from some alien planet. Or spies from a foreign country who'd failed the slang test at some military checkpoint.

In the driveway, Madeline pulled her car keys from the pocket of her capris. "We'll take my car. I've got the most cargo space." She clicked her remote key and the locks sprang open. "We can look up the address for the nearest Sam's Club or Costco on my GPS."

Nicole and Avery made no move toward the minivan. Nicole took in its shape and size, its golden beige–ness. She'd never actually been in one before and wasn't wild about getting in one now.

"What's wrong?" Madeline asked, reaching for the door handle. "Do you need to get something out of the house?"

"No."

"Well, go ahead and get in then." She motioned Nicole to the passenger seat as she climbed in behind the steering wheel. With the click of another button the rear door behind Madeline's seat slid open for Avery.

Nicole walked slowly around to the passenger door, pulled it open, and peered in. It had leather seats and all kinds of gadgetry, but it was about as stylish as a school bus. "Maybe I should just meet you all there," she said. "Wherever 'there' is."

Avery laughed. Madeline just patted the empty seat. "Come on. I'm pretty sure that just sitting inside a minivan won't turn you into a suburban housewife."

Avery laughed again. "Relax, Nicole. If you want, I'm sure Madeline will leave you off a couple of blocks away so no one will know how you got there."

Madeline speared Nicole with a look. "We've got bigger fish to fry than our personal images," she said. "And we're running out of time." She patted the seat once again. "Your secret's safe with me." Turning to the backseat, she asked, "What about you, Avery? Will you feel the need to let people know that *the* Nicole Grant rode in a minivan and value shopped in a membership club?"

Avery pretended to think. "I don't know. It's pretty explosive information, but I think I can keep it to myself."

"Very funny." Nicole climbed into the passenger seat and pulled the door closed, pointedly ignoring Avery's laughter and Madeline's triumphant smile as she backed the beige behemoth down the driveway. "But I have a bad feeling this is just the first in a long line of new experiences that I could have gone the rest of my lifetime without."

Like the rest of the day, the hour and a half they spent in Sam's Club turned out to be better and worse than Nicole had feared. On the plus side, no one recognized her or even noticed her for that matter. Largely, she suspected, because most of them seemed to be even older than the Realtor, John Franklin, and seemed focused on navigating their unwieldy flatbeds through the aisles or speed pushing their walkers from sample table to sample table. When she finally accepted the fact that there was not a potential client in sight and absolutely no chance of running into a former one, she began to relax and even kept her complaints to a minimum as Madeline masterminded their acquisition of every cleaning product and tool known to man.

"Load the brooms and mops in Nicole's cart," she said when the flatbed Avery was pushing was piled high with industrial-sized drums of Pine-Sol and Clorox as well as anything else that could be sprayed or wiped. "And let's get another box of large trash bags and one of the outdoor kind. And a couple of those Rubbermaid garbage cans. Even if we have a Dumpster, we're still going to have to get things to it. Oh, and what about those folding beach chairs?" Madeline asked as they wheeled by a display of cheap aluminum chairs with multicolored mesh straps. "We can use them out back and take them down to the beach if we want."

Nicole kept her groan to herself as the chairs were balanced on top of the flatbed. Madeline then focused on filling up her own basket with more food and drink than Nicole would normally consume in a month. "I'm used to shopping for four, including a teenage boy," Madeline said when Avery questioned the huge quantities of everything she chose. "We definitely need at least a case of Diet Coke to start and one of bottled water." She eyed the mixed case of cheap wines she'd chosen. "Maybe we should get a bottle or two of the better wines for celebratory situations."

As if. "You mean something intended for more than its numbing qualities?" Nicole asked.

"Yes, exactly." Madeline smiled, ignoring or simply not noticing Nicole's sarcasm. "Will you choose a couple?" And then to Avery, "Can you squeeze a few of those rotisserie chickens in the basket? We're going to want to eat in as much as possible to try to keep expenses down."

Now there was a real day brightener, Nicole thought as they pushed their bounty toward the front of the store. A summer full of cheap food, folding chairs, and home-cooked meals. Those good times were so going to roll.

As they neared the checkout lanes, Madeline waved them to a stop in the ladies' clothing aisle—strategically located just past the automotive section—where Avery and Madeline selected some of the ugliest shorts and T-shirts Nicole had ever seen.

"Do you have anything you can work in?" Avery asked with a glance at Nicole's cream-colored capris and body-sculpted T. "Cleaning is a pretty dirty business." Her look said she doubted Nicole had any experience with this. "And the grunt work is bound to be even filthier."

"I have running clothes with me," Nicole replied. "I'm sure I'll be fine."

Avery shrugged, but Madeline held up a pair of plaid seersucker shorts and a poorly cut sleeveless T-shirt with a striped umbrella on it. Nikki shuddered.

"Are you sure?" Avery asked with a smirk. "I think that would really round out your wardrobe."

"It's unlikely anything nice is going to survive the summer," Madeline pointed out. "You really should have some things that don't matter."

"Don't worry about me," Nicole said, suppressing another shudder. She'd spent a lifetime making sure she'd never have to wear cheap ill-fitting clothing again. She was not about to start now.

Assorted paper goods were added to the tower of stuff. By the time they'd made it through the checkout line and anted up their thirds, Nicole was far too numb to object to the foot long hot dog and giant fountain drink that Madeline proposed for lunch. They ate them in a few hungry bites then carried their drinks with them to the van, which they loaded under Madeline's expert supervision; it seemed efficient cargo area filling was yet another suburban skill at which Madeline Singer excelled.

In the parking lot, where cars seemed to move and zip around far faster and with even more deadly intent than they did on the street, Nicole contemplated her partners and reflected on just how far out of her comfort zone their little shopping venture had yanked her. Still, she joined in on the three-way high five at all they'd managed to purchase for just a hundred dollars apiece. When it was time to climb back into the minivan for the trip back to the beach, she only flinched slightly.

An eternity later, they hobbled out to the backyard just as the sky was beginning to pinken. Bedraggled, they dropped into the beach chairs with a scrape of aluminum against concrete.

"I don't think I've ever been this dirty in my entire life." Madeline plopped a family-sized container of hummus and triangles of pita bread on the upside down packing box that their Sam's purchases had been carried in.

"Me, neither." Avery dropped a bag of Cheez Doodles beside it and swiped the back of her forearm across her forehead, managing to add another streak of dirt to her face.

Nicole set an opened bottle of Chardonnay on the pool deck next to her bare feet and handed a plastic cup to each of them. "If there was an inch of water in this pool, I'd be in it." Nicole slumped in her chair. "I think we should make it a top priority."

"We barely have a working bathroom," Avery pointed out. "It took me forever to clean the shower and the tub up in the hall. There's pretty much no water pressure. I'd rather have a shower than a swim in a pool."

"I want both," Nicole said, lifting the cup to her lips. "It's not an either/or sort of thing."

"Well, it is here." Avery took a long sip of her wine as the sun slipped farther toward the Gulf. "Everything's not going to get done at once, but I will talk to Chase about the schedule and how things should be prioritized."

Madeline looked ruefully down at herself. Together they could have posed for the illustration of "something the cat dragged in"—even Nicole in her high-end running clothes and her hair pulled back in a glittery clasp. This was only day one; she could hardly imagine what they'd look like after the long, hot summer that lay ahead.

Her arms were so tired that it took real effort to lift even the small plastic cup, but she nonetheless touched it to the others. "Cheers!" she said, and they nodded and repeated the toast. "Will you be able to run your business from here?" she asked Nicole as they contemplated the sinking sun.

Nicole's cup stopped midway to her lips. In the pass, a boat planed off and gathered speed as it entered the Gulf. "Sure," she finally said. "Have laptop and cell phone, will matchmake." She turned her gaze from the boat that was now disappearing from view to focus on Madeline. "How about you?" Nicole asked. "Can you really leave home for the whole summer?"

Madeline finished the last drops of wine and set her glass on the makeshift cocktail table. "You make it sound like going to camp," she said in what could only be described as a wistful tone. "I was hoping my husband, Steve, would come down and help for a while."

"Oh, is he retired?" Avery asked.

Madeline felt her cheeks flush. Nicole raised an eyebrow and poured them all another glassful.

"Not exactly," Madeline admitted. "He was a financial planner who made the mistake of putting all his clients' money in Malcolm Dyer's fund. Along with his family's."

Her teeth worried at her bottom lip. She hadn't meant to say so much. Or sound quite so pathetic.

"He stole my father's entire estate," Avery said. "Everything he'd built over a lifetime of hard work went into that thief's pocket." She grimaced and shoved her sunglasses back up on top of her head. "I still can't believe it. Anything short of being drawn and quartered would be far too good for him."

Madeline saw Nicole shiver slightly. "Are you cold?" The sun had not yet set, but its warmth had diminished.

"No." Nicole turned her attention to the boat traffic in the pass. A Jet Ski swooped close to the seawall, its plume of seawater peacocking behind it. The rider was big shouldered and solid with jet black hair and heavily muscled arms. Nicole watched idly at first, presumably because he was male and attractive, but straightened in surprise as the rider locked gazes and offered a mock salute before revving his engine and zooming away.

"Do you know that guy?" Madeline asked Nicole, surprised. "He waved at you."

"No," Nicole said. "I don't think he was actually waving at me. He . . ."

"Yes, he was," Madeline insisted. "He acted like he knew you."

"That guy was definitely hunky," Avery said. "And he was definitely eyeing Nicole."

"He must have thought I was someone else." Nicole took a sliver of pita and chewed it intently before changing the topic. "So, how many kids do you have?" she asked Madeline.

"Two," Madeline said, unsure how much information to share. "My son's struggling a bit at school; he's in his freshman year at Vanderbilt," she said. "And my daughter, well, right before I left she lost her job—she's a filmmaker—and she came home unexpectedly to live." She cleared her throat as if that might somehow stop this bad news dump. "That was right after my mother-in-law moved in."

"Good Lord," Nicole said. She lifted the bottle, eyed the little that was left, and poured the remaining drops into Madeline's glass. "No wonder you want to go away to camp." She smiled with what looked like real sympathy. "Drink up, girl. I'd run away from home, too, if I had to deal with all of that."

They sat in silence for a few minutes, sipping their wine, as the sun grew larger and brighter. A warm breeze blew gently off the Gulf, stirring the palms and riffling their hair.

"Maybe you should get your daughter to come down and shoot some 'before' video for us," Avery suggested. "That's actually what led to *Hammer and Nail*." She furrowed her brow. "I had no idea what was coming down the pike when I shot that first ten minutes."

Madeline considered the small blonde. "My mother-in-law

seemed to think it was your husband's show, that he got you on it."

"A lot of people came to believe that," Avery said, her tone wry. "Including my ex-husband. But the idea was mine. I'm the one who sold it, and us, to the network."

They fell silent as the sun burned with a new intensity, shimmering almost white, then turning a golden red that tinged the Gulf as it sank smoothly beneath it.

"God, that was beautiful," Madeline breathed as they all continued to stare out over the Gulf, unable to tear their gazes from the sky and the last painted remnants of daylight. "It makes me feel like anything is possible."

No one responded, and she supposed she should be grateful that no one trampled on her flight of fancy. The show was over, but Madeline could still feel its power. It moved her in a way her fear and even her resolution and Little Red Henness had not. She raised her now-empty glass to Avery and Nicole. "I propose that we all make a sunset toast. That we each name one good thing that happened today."

"Good grief," Nicole said. "Look around you." She motioned with her empty plastic glass at the neglected house that hunkered behind them, the cracked and empty pool, the detached garage with its broken windows and listing door. "Is your middle name Pollyanna?"

Madeline flushed at the comment, but she didn't retract her suggestion. "I'm not saying we should pretend everything's perfect," she said. "I'm just saying that no matter how bad it is it would be better to dwell on the even slightly positive than the overwhelmingly negative."

"You're serious, aren't you?" Avery asked. They all still held their empty glasses aloft. "How good a thing does it have to be?"

"That's up to you," Madeline said. "I'm not interested in judging; there will be no 'good enough' police."

"Well, *that's* a good thing," Nicole snorted.

"All right, hold on a sec," Madeline said. She went into the kitchen and retrieved a second bottle of wine from the fridge, grateful that John Franklin had had the power turned on. As she refilled their glasses, she searched for a positive. Nicole was right, it wasn't an easy task.

"Okay." She raised her now-full glass and waited for the others to do the same. "I think it's good that three complete strangers were able to reach an agreement and commit to a course of action."

They touched glasses and took a sip. Madeline nodded at Avery. "Your turn."

"Hmmmm, let me think." She looked out over the seawall at the gathering darkness as the three of them sat in a spill of light from the loggia. A few moments later she raised her glass. "I think it's good that this house is not going to be torn down. It deserves a facelift and a new life."

They clinked and drank and turned their gazes to Nicole. Madeline could hardly wait to hear what she would say.

Nicole looked back at the house, then at them. A small smile played around her lips, and Madeline wondered if she was going to tell them to stuff the happy crap or simply refuse to participate. But she raised her glass in their directions and with only a small sigh of resignation said, "It's a good thing no one saw me in that minivan. I can't imagine how I'd ever live it down."

Eleven

They checked out of the Cottage Inn and moved their things to Bella Flora first thing the next morning. There wasn't much to move, since no one except Nicole had come prepared for more than a couple of days' stay. They stood around in the kitchen waiting for the pot of coffee Maddie put on to brew and eyeing the open box of doughnuts she'd set out on the speckled counter.

Avery had a steaming cup of coffee, heavily creamed and sugared just like she liked it, ready to lift to her lips when Chase Hardin strode into the kitchen without so much as a knock or a shouted hello.

"Good morning, ladies," he boomed.

"Coffee?" Madeline offered, in full mother-hen mode.

"No, thanks. We don't have time." He grinned as he reached over to remove the mug from Avery's hands. She'd barely had one sip.

"Hey!" She reached for the cup of caffeine she so desperately needed, but he just put it down on the opposite side of the counter.

"Come on. I want to have the furniture off the truck

before the roofer and the plumber get here. They're stopping by to take a look before they head to other jobs."

He herded them outside without waiting for a response. Avery normally drew energy from her morning caffeine, but it appeared anger was an equally strong stimulant. "I assumed we'd go over the plans together and come up with a workable schedule before we solicited quotes."

He stopped short at the lowered tailgate, and they all plowed into each other at the abrupt halt. Avery felt like one of the Three Stooges.

"Don't worry your pretty little head about it, squirt," he said as they untangled themselves.

"I know you didn't actually say that." Avery fisted her hands on her hips.

He stared down at her, his blue eyes bright with amusement. "'Fraid so."

"I assumed we'd be collaborating on this project," she said. "Especially in the start-up phase. You can't just go off half-cocked. I expect to see the list of what you intend to do to the house so we can agree on how to prioritize it."

Chase folded his arms across his considerable chest and looked down at her. Way down. Avery had never hated being so short quite so much.

"My list," he said carefully, "is right here." He tapped his forehead. "Where it's supposed to be. And I don't really need help prioritizing it."

"You've got to be kidding," she sputtered.

"And I never go off half . . . cocked," he said, somehow managing to turn his retort into an insult and a double entendre at the same time. "There's only one boss on any job and at any site. The minute you let someone else audition for top dog the time schedule and the quality level go all to hell. I'm the contractor on this job, and a co-owner. We don't have time for design by committee." He shrugged his broad shoulders. "Besides, you have no real-world experience that I'm aware of, and I don't have the time or the inclination to educate you."

He snagged her gaze with his. "By the end of the summer you'll be back smiling and nodding into a television camera. Maybe you should stick to what you do best and let me do the same."

Avery could barely respond; she wasn't going to until she saw the satisfied glint steal into Chase Hardin's eyes. As if he'd nipped some little problem—namely her—in the bud and could now get on with more important matters.

"Good grief," she said. "You look like a normal person, but inside you're a complete Neanderthal." She pressed a finger up against his broad Cro-Magnon chest and the faded T-shirt that strained across it. "How many Mediterranean Revivals have you renovated or restored?" she asked. "Did you write your thesis on Addison Mizner and his transformation of Palm Beach?"

He dropped his gaze to her finger, then raised it to her eyes. "No, I didn't get to write a thesis on Mizner or anyone else. I've learned construction the good old-fashioned way, with my hands and my heart. I've learned how to listen to what the house wants and figure out what it needs. And that's not something they teach at college or put in books."

Avery dropped her finger as he turned to pull the first mattress off the truck. Motioning Avery and Madeline closer, he positioned the double mattress so they could get ahold of it. "Here, why don't you be in charge of this?"

Her stab of regret at taunting him fled, replaced with a flash of indignation, but she couldn't let go of her end of the mattress without dropping it on the asphalt. "Of all the nerve," she began, but he was already sliding the end of the other mattress toward Nicole and then walking backward balancing most of it so Nicole just had to hold on and follow his lead.

Avery and Madeline didn't fare anywhere near as well or move anywhere near as fast as the "boss" and his helper. The discrepancy in their sizes, which left the mattress tilted at a precarious angle, didn't help, and of course finding a good way to hold on to and support a mattress was like trying to hold on to Jell-O. Avery landed on top of it twice, almost fell down the stairs while bumping it up them, and was finally forced to push-pull it through the upstairs hallway in order to get it to her room.

"Thank God you insisted on mopping the floors up here so many times," she said to Madeline as they both collapsed on the mattress to catch their breaths. Chase walked by whistling as he carried the third mattress up on his own and deposited it in the next room before poking his head into her open doorway. "I hope you're not planning to slack off so soon," he said. "Dad sent a nightstand and lamp for each of you. And there's a table and chairs for the kitchen." He walked in and offered Madeline a hand up then turned to Avery. "Come on, Vanna. Up and at 'em."

She ignored the proffered hand and clambered up on her own. With his laughter ringing in her ears, she huffed down the back stairs and into the kitchen, where she drank her now-tepid coffee down in one angry gulp.

"We need a microwave," she said to Madeline, who'd followed her down. "To warm up coffee." She poured herself a second cup and took a long, soothing sip. "And a gun would be good," Avery said. "In case I need to blow his brains out."

Madeline laughed. "I think we've got enough on our hands without having to defend you against a charge of manslaughter."

"Vanna?" Chase's voice floated down the center hallway. "Where do you want these chairs?"

Avery closed her eyes and tried to think soothing thoughts, but really, what was the use? "If he calls me Vanna one more time, I'll be able to plead insanity." Avery turned a grim smile on Madeline. "What do you think about the chairs? Do we want them here in the kitchen? Or shall I just tell him to shove them up his ass?"

Robby the plumber arrived after Avery's second cup of coffee. He was somewhere in his midtwenties with a chunky build, a moon face full of freckles, and the carrot red hair that went with them. His big brown eyes were friendly and calflike.

"Hello, ma'am," he said when she stepped around Chase to introduce herself and shake his warm, doughy hand. "You've got a great house here. I look forward to working on it." He smiled shyly.

He was sweet and his glance was admiring, but he was awfully young. "Have you ever . . ." she began.

"Robby's family has been working for Hardin-Morgan Construction since before Robby was born," Chase said. "He worked with his father on a number of renovations in northeast St. Pete so he has some experience with cast-iron pipes and older plumbing systems."

Robby smiled. Chase gave her a curt nod. She was not invited to accompany them on their tour of the house and its bathrooms and water lines. As they left the kitchen she poured herself another cup of coffee and sank into a chair at the kitchen table, where Madeline was making a list on a legal pad. Without comment, she reached over and slid the box of doughnuts toward Avery.

"He acts like he's being generous when he gives me any information at all." She selected a chocolate-covered doughnut and practically inhaled it. "He's completely maddening."

"But you do feel like he knows what he's doing?" Madeline asked, her brow creasing.

"Oh, probably." The admission was grudging. "But I'm not going to spend an entire summer being treated like I have no brain or experience." She ate half of the second doughnut before she realized what she was doing. "Great. Day one and he's already driving me to eat." She stood and dropped the rest of the doughnut in the garbage. When the next truck pulled into the drive, she strode toward the front door, determined to be included.

Enrico Dante, the roof man, could have been anywhere between fifty and seventy. He was small and wizened, like a grape that had been left a bit too long on the vine. When he swept off his baseball cap in greeting, he revealed a head as smooth and round as a cue ball.

"Buon giorno, signorina," he said in a marked Italian accent. "It is a pleasure to meet you. I understand we will do some work on the roof tiles, yes?"

"Well, possibly. We'll have to see whether . . ."

Before she could finish, Chase was there and stepping forward to engulf Enrico in a bear hug. *"Buon giorno, mi amico. Come stai?"*

They conversed easily in Italian for several moments, apparently happy as clams to see each other. Avery stiffened when Chase ruffled her hair and said something in Italian that made both men laugh.

"You know," she began, trying desperately to hold on to her temper. "I don't appreciate—"

Once again Chase cut her off. "Before you ask for Enrico's credentials I'll tell you that his grandfather was one of your hero Addison Mizner's favored artisans. He and his brothers came over from Italy to work for him and they did the roofs of many of the best known homes in Palm Beach. No one is more qualified to assess what needs to be done to Bella Flora's roof."

Enrico bowed and smiled at her. Chase shot her an insolent wink as he threw an arm around Enrico's shoulder and left her standing in the foyer while they retrieved a ladder from Enrico's truck and carried it around to the back of the house.

Avery wanted to climb that ladder and see the damage for herself. She wanted to hear Enrico's take on what would be needed and get some idea of time and cost, but once again Chase had cut her out. Just as Trent had. She stood in the foyer staring out through the open front door as this sank all the way in. Was she going to just sit back and be dismissed again? Was she going to let someone else relegate her to pointing and gesturing?

Only if she allowed herself to be.

Avery slammed the front door shut. Turning, she strode

down the central hallway and out the rear French doors to
the covered loggia. She saw the ladder perched against the
west end of the house. Refusing to second-guess herself, she
climbed quickly up the ladder and stepped carefully onto a
flat expanse of roof. Enrico and Chase crouched a few feet
away on a sharply angled gable.

She stepped closer and up onto the angled section so that
she could peer over their shoulders. "This is where the old
sleeping porch was joined to the master, isn't it?" she asked.

Chase started in surprise and for a second she thought
he was going to tumble backward and take her with him.
"What are you doing up here?"

Enrico put a steadying hand on Chase's shoulder and the
moment passed. The roofer stood easily, as sure-footed as a
mountain goat. Chase didn't look quite as comfortable, but
then he was considerably larger than Enrico and had to tread
more carefully.

"I wanted to see what the problem was," Avery said. "It's
where the roof segments are joined, isn't it?" she asked Enrico.
"That's always the weakest spot."

"Yes, signorina," Enrico said with an approving smile as he
beckoned her closer.

Avery moved next to him and peered down into the master
bedroom. "That bird probably fell in the first time," she said.
"And then decided to build its nest there." She looked beyond
the roof and out over the Gulf of Mexico for a moment; the
angled section of barrel tiles like a red arrow pointing toward
the postcard picture view. "Can we get tiles that match?"

"Yes," Enrico said. "I have a resource for this, but it will
take several weeks to get them. We'll put a tarp for now to
keep the elements and animals out. Then I will spend about
a week repairing the wood battens and mudding so that I can
affix the tiles when they arrive."

She didn't press for figures. Enrico was a professional
and Chase's ownership should ensure that he would watch
the expenditures carefully; she wasn't looking to throw her

weight around, she just needed to know and approve of what was going on.

"Great. Thanks." She smiled her appreciation at the roofer and then climbed down the ladder satisfied.

Reminding herself that she could only be cut out if she allowed herself to be, she went to find Robby and ask his take on the scope of what he'd need to do. His answers weren't exactly what she would have liked to hear—they were going to be down to the kitchen and one bathroom for the foreseeable future as he shut off everything below the main waterline, but he answered her questions clearly and easily and he didn't speak down to her like Chase did. In fact, he seemed exceedingly eager to please.

An hour later, she stood in the driveway watching all three trucks disappear. Chase had not seen fit to share any information with her, but she didn't need him to. He could be as big a jerk as he wanted as long as she didn't allow it to stop her from finding out what she needed to know. Avery smiled, glad they had Bella Flora to themselves again and even gladder that she now had a plan of attack, a way to deal with the infuriating Chase Hardin. She and Chase could have their own version of "don't ask, don't tell."

By the end of the day, Madeline felt like she had when Kyra was four and Andrew just born and she'd first discovered what the word "exhausted" actually meant. Avery had braved the mass of junk crammed in the detached four-car garage and retrieved two ladders and what looked like an assortment of antique tools. The ladders had allowed them to reach crown moldings and the salon's coffered ceiling and almost all of the hanging light fixtures, which put Madeline up close and personal with more cobwebs and their occupants, both living and dead, than she ever wanted to see again.

Nicole, who had been assigned to re-mop all of the upstairs

floors, had not yet made it to the front stairs when they broke around one o'clock for lunch.

"I'm going to be dusting, wiping, and mopping in my sleep tonight," Madeline groaned as she carried the pitcher of sun tea she'd made to the kitchen table and swiped at a cobweb that hung down over her forehead.

"I wouldn't care what I was dreaming if I was actually asleep." Nicole reached for the bag of chips. "To think I wasted all that money on a personal trainer when I could have turned my biceps into quivering masses of jelly pushing a mop."

"I know what you mean," Avery said. "I can hardly move my arms and I've only taped up about a tenth of a percent of the missing and broken window panes." She bit into her sandwich. "I had no idea I was so out of shape."

After a brief negotiation, they gave themselves twenty minutes before forcing themselves and each other back to work. By the end of the day, Madeline would have given everything she owned—not that that was much of anything at this point—for a filled pool to dive into.

For the last half hour before quitting time, they worked in the back, righting and scrubbing bird droppings from the concrete picnic table and its half-moon benches and sweeping, bagging, and carting away the rubble from the pool deck. There was plenty of groaning and complaining as their overworked and stunned muscles and joints protested the abuse, but the day was warm and balmy and the sun sparkled off the blue green water like diamonds strewn across the slight swells.

At six thirty P.M. they quit and by tacit agreement gathered to watch the sunset. Nicole brought out the plastic glasses and a chilled bottle of pinot grigio. Avery followed with a plate of Cheez Doodles.

"Really?" Nicole asked when she saw them.

Madeline bit back a smile at Nicole's pained expression.

"Really," Avery replied as she sank down into her aluminum beach chair and scooted it a bit to maximize her view of the sun suspended over the water. "If you need something fancier, feel free to create it."

Nicole pinched two doodles from the plate before passing their hors d'oeuvres to Madeline. "I may just have to do that," she said.

"And I'm going to add a blender to our acquisition list," Madeline said as the sun began its descent, leaching the color out of the sky and turning it to the palest blue gray. "Sunsets like this practically demand a frozen drink, maybe even with an umbrella in it."

They watched the remainder of the show in silence. When the final wisps of pink had disappeared completely, Madeline offered her "one good thing." "I think we've made real inroads in the fight against dirt and grime. And I think Bella Flora is grateful." She smiled at Nicole.

"All right." Nicole nodded and thought for a moment. "I'm not sure if this is a good thing or not, but I'm beginning to *like* the 'eau de chemical' scent Bella Flora's wearing. At least compared to the smells it's starting to mask."

Madeline nodded and she and Nicole turned to Avery, whose fingers and lips were now coated a distinct Cheez Doodle orange.

"Well, I have two good things today." Avery's tongue swiped around her lips, presumably in an effort to get the last of the cheese. "Number one—we're short on bathrooms but there's a whole Gulf right there just waiting to be soaked in, if anyone wants to go for a swim with me." She hesitated briefly before smiling broadly. "And despite some very real temptation, I did not buy a weapon or try to do Chase Hardin in."

Twelve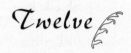

Nicole woke up stiff the next morning, her body no longer used to actual physical labor or to sleeping without benefit of bed frame or box spring. During her childhood a mattress was not a thing to be taken for granted, but over the years since she'd left home and created a new life for herself she'd grown accustomed to creature comforts and was, in fact, immensely comforted by them.

Sunlight streamed in through the uncovered windows and fanned across her face. Through the window she could see a clear blue sky with only a hint of pulled-cotton clouds. Her cell phone lay next to her attached to the charger that she'd plugged into the closest outlet. Her Louis Vuitton suitcase sat on the floor, its cover propped up against the wall. The house settled around her, its old joints creaking.

Her gaze flitted around the empty space that would be hers for the summer. She didn't have furniture or a TV or a single piece of art on the wall, but she did have her own room and bathroom, unusable though it was at the moment. A Sam's Club towel and washcloth sat on her nightstand. This was what her life had come to.

Her smile faded as she thought about why and who was responsible for her reduced circumstances, and she closed her eyes briefly against the sunlight and the truth. Six years older than Malcolm, she'd done her best to shield him from the grimmer realities of their childhood—the years when their father, who'd begun as a harbor pilot, had bounced from menial job to more menial job, up and down the eastern seaboard. When he died while working as a day laborer on the docks in Jacksonville, the bouncing stopped. And so did the small trickle of money it had produced. Nicole had been thirteen and Malcolm seven when they'd moved into the dreary duplex that was all their mother could afford on her earnings as a hotel maid. They'd clung to that hovel by their fingertips, their mother working a second job nights at a bar, Nicole trying to fill in the gaps in mothering.

Even as a child, Malcolm was bright with startling good looks and far more than his fair share of charm. He wielded these assets instinctively at first and then, as he grew older, with a fierce intent. She'd been alternately proud of and worried about him. When he made a wrong choice or cut some corner, Nicole had stepped in to protect him, understanding as no one else could the desperate need to overcome their circumstances. She simply couldn't bear to see him punished for trying to build a new life or for believing her when she told him that he could be anything and anyone he chose to be.

It had never occurred to her that he'd one day aspire to being a thief.

Though she knew it was futile, Nicole pulled her phone close and began to scroll through her address book until she'd called every number she'd ever had for Malcolm, each one representing another step up the ladder of success he'd so determinedly climbed.

Just like they were the last time she'd tried, all of them were no longer in service or had been disconnected. If Malcolm was using a phone, it wasn't one he'd ever shared with her or apparently intended to.

With a sigh, Nicole climbed off her mattress and carried

her running clothes through the doorway and down the two steps to the private bath. It was decidedly funky with raspberry tiled walls and a delicate, if still filthy, cut-glass chandelier hanging from the raspberry tile ceiling. The sink was a wall-hung rectangle of once creamy white porcelain. Wishing she could simply turn on the pockmarked chrome handles and wash her face and brush her teeth, she squinted into the ancient mirror with its etched flower border, but the glass was so cloudy she could barely make out the details of her face. With a sigh, she wriggled into the spandex and pulled her hair into a ponytail.

For the briefest of moments she allowed herself to imagine just heading down to the beach "as is," but Nicole, who had relied every bit as strenuously on her God-given assets as Malcolm had, carried her makeup bag to the hall bath, also an ode to 1920s tile, and spent the next fifteen minutes applying her "armor."

Treading gently so as not to wake the others, Nicole left through the side kitchen door and did her stretching on the pool deck, where she could enjoy the view and the early morning sun on her face and skin.

She took the path from the house, bypassing the jetty, where a lone fisherman baited his hook. The pelican and seabird audience had already claimed their spots; perhaps these were the early birds that hoped to catch the worm? Once on the beach she began a slow jog, sticking to the hard-packed sand just beyond the tide line. Her shoes crunched rhythmically on the nights' deposit of broken shell; the warm breeze teased her hair and caressed her cheeks.

Just beyond the Paradise Grille the beach widened. A bit later the larger Gulf-front homes began. An old man on a bench up near a clump of sea oats watched her progress, his tobacco-colored skin attesting to years probably spent on that very bench.

Behind her the crunch of shell announced the presence of another runner and Nicole checked her speed slightly to let them pass. Instead the bulky shadow of the other runner melded with and then blotted out her own. Nicole glanced to her right and saw that it was Agent Giraldi, who'd matched his pace to hers so that they were, for all intents and purposes, running together.

"What are you doing here?" she asked, turning her gaze back to the beach in front of her as they ran.

"Just out for a little run," he said beside her. "Beautiful morning, isn't it?"

Nicole kept her tone nonchalant. "It was."

She could feel him smile, but he didn't comment. Nor did he leave.

She sneaked a peek out of the corner of her eye to take a second look at the bare chest that triangled down to the trim waist and well-defined abs. A plain white T-shirt, which he had taken off and stuck in the waistband of his navy running shorts, bounced against one muscled thigh as he ran. Apparently the FBI still had certain physical requirements. His beak of a nose looked sunburned and his cheekbones carried early morning stubble. His eyes were hidden behind a pair of sunglasses that did not look like government issue.

"So what are you doing in Florida, Agent Giraldi?"

"Same thing I was doing in New York, Ms. Grant," he replied conversationally.

At the Don CeSar, the pool boys were setting up chairs and chaises while others carried cushions down to the wooden chaises lined up on the beach. A volleyball net bobbed slightly in the breeze. The thatched hut advertising parasail rides and Jet Ski rentals appeared open for business. Maybe she'd come down here later and have a drink by the pool and pretend she was in civilization.

"Pass-a-Grille's not exactly your usual kind of stomping grounds," Agent Giraldi observed as he ran easily beside her.

A stitch began to pull at her side and she was feeling just the tiniest bit winded, but the agent hadn't sounded at all out of breath, so Nicole was careful not to let him see it. Without comment, she turned and began to run back the way she'd come. Agent Giraldi stuck by her side, not missing a step.

"I'm not here to stomp," she replied though she'd intended to remain silent in hopes that he'd simply jog off and leave her alone. "And I don't really appreciate being followed."

They ran in silence for a few minutes, but Nicole was too aware of Giraldi to enjoy her surroundings.

"Your brother was photographed leaving a bank in the Cayman Islands last week," he said. "Yesterday we caught a glimpse of him on a yacht registered to a dummy corporation in Panama."

She managed not to respond, but it wasn't easy. The stitch in her side was getting bigger; it was getting harder to keep her breathing silent.

"Your brother is living the high life, Ms. Grant. While you're sleeping on a mattress in an empty house, which you are currently scrubbing like a maid."

She knew he was just trying to goad her into action, but that didn't make it any easier to take. She didn't need any-one else rubbing her nose in her unfortunate situation—especially not this bare-chested baboon. "Where I sleep is my own business," she bit out. "And I hope to hell the govern-ment's best shot at finding Malcolm isn't pinned on peering in his sister's window. What were you before you joined the agency, Giraldi? A Peeping Tom?"

His features hardened slightly, which was pretty amaz-ing since they'd already appeared carved from stone. But his voice gave nothing away. "We're close to nailing down his location," Giraldi said. "And once we do we're going to want you to make contact with him."

Nicole didn't respond because there was nothing to say. And because she now needed to breathe through her mouth as well as her nose.

"We know you pretty much raised him, that you put him through college after your mother died, and that you helped fund his first start-up. Frankly, I'm having a hard time believ-ing that he stole everything you have and that you couldn't reach him if you really wanted to."

That made two of them.

"In fact, the more I learn the more I have to wonder if this"—he gestured as he ran, presumably encompassing her, the house, the beach—"isn't some elaborate ruse. That you're just pretending poverty and an inability to reach him until we give up looking for him and you two can meet up and share the loot."

Nicole kept her gaze straight ahead and tried to breathe through her nose. "I have sold most of my favorite clothes right off my back, Agent Giraldi—and they didn't come from Target. That is not something I would do if it weren't completely necessary." Nicole refused to look at him. "You clearly have a very rich fantasy life," she said, careful not to huff or puff though her lungs couldn't seem to get all the air they wanted. "Perhaps you should consider writing novels."

He still didn't sound the least bit winded, and she suspected if she actually looked at him, he wouldn't have broken a sweat, either. She could feel the sheen of perspiration forming on her forehead and beneath the allegedly moisture-wicking spandex.

"You're the one living in fantasyland if you think we're ever going to stop watching long enough to let you make contact with him without us knowing."

"Well, I hope you've got the patience of Job and a good supply of sunscreen, Agent Giraldi," she replied sweetly, "because I have no way of contacting him and I'm not in on any scheme."

They passed the Paradise Grille, which was now teeming with customers who sat at the picnic tables sipping coffee and protecting their breakfasts from the seagulls. A few more yards and the jetty would be in sight.

Several women followed the bare-chested agent with their eyes. Her own chest felt like it was going to explode. Had she protected her little brother too much? Had she allowed him to grow up without suffering enough consequences? Had she been so intent on creating a better life for herself and convincing Malcolm he could do the same that she'd failed to teach him right from wrong?

"Oh, I'm a patient man, Ms. Grant," Giraldi said when they finally reached the jetty and she slowed to a walk, though she did not fall to her knees or even bend at the waist and gasp for breath as she would have liked to. "Patience is just part of my job description."

He flashed a toothpaste-ad smile. "If you have a change of heart or manage to locate your conscience, give me a wave. I'll be the one lolling around on the beach while you're working your ass off."

One more smile and he was heading to the boardwalk. The sun that had sweat trickling down between her breasts and soaking her back just made his broad shoulders look a little bit more bronzed.

Avery lay in bed, make that on her mattress, half dozing long after Nicole left. She'd been up on and off all night listening to the rustlings in the attic and the unmistakable scurrying sounds that were made by little rodent feet. She heard Madeline get up and go into the bathroom across the hall and then the creak of the back stair that led to the kitchen.

The rolled-up bathing suit smell had not yet been completely vanquished, but a steady stream of fresh air and large quantities of the cleaning products Nicole had deemed "perfume-like" had rendered it somewhat less gut-wrenching. Soon the smell of coffee stole up the stairs and tickled her nose, displacing a few more of the less pleasant aromas.

Despite the fact that she was lying on the floor and pretty much broke, the house itself thrilled her. Situated at the southeast corner of the house, across the hall from the master and overlooking the pass and the bay, Avery's room was spacious, with beautifully textured walls that had once been a ripe shade of peach. The wrought-iron curtain rods were faded and peeling, but they looked to be Art Deco with an arrow at one end and circles of flaking gold leaf banding the other. With a final stretch and yawn, Avery got up, then walked through the dressing area with its wall of listing closet doors. Though dull and scratched, a fabulous old brass heat register sat beneath an oversized window through which shards of sunlight penetrated pockets of grime.

Her bathroom had a honeycombed black-and-white-tile floor with a border laid in a cube-like stair-stepping pattern. The walls were covered in white tiles with black and pink accents. The old tiles were inconsistent, not perfectly matched like they would have been if they'd been manufactured today. The glass niches and the beautifully angled trim took her back to the hours spent in antique stores as a child following in her mother's perfumed wake. There Deirdre Morgan would negotiate with the shop owners on her clients' or her own behalf. And while her items were written up or wrapped, she would walk Avery through the shop, pointing things out, explaining each piece's distinguishing features. "This is Art Nouveau," she might say, running a hand down a leg or over a curve of inlaid wood. "And this is Queen Anne. Or Mission style. Or . . ."

As Avery got older, her mother would simply point to a piece or a detail and wait for Avery to classify it properly. Avery had learned to recognize a huge range of styles and periods in an effort to please her mother, but her own interest had always been piqued by the clean lines and rounded shapes of Art Deco. Even now Avery found it difficult to pass a piece of furniture or a lamp or a figurine of this period without being drawn to it or wanting to own it. Her mother had fled; Avery's love of all things Deco had not.

After pulling on an old pair of shorts and an even older *Hammer and Nail* T-shirt, Avery washed her face and brushed her teeth in the hall bath, then followed her nose to the kitchen. There she helped herself to a cup of coffee, sugared and creamed it, then pulled a granola bar out of the huge box of them they'd purchased at Sam's.

"Morning," Avery said as she plopped down in a kitchen chair next to Madeline, who was busy clipping coupons and articles from the Sunday paper. She peered at them more closely; one was a book review for a new release titled *Life*

After Layoff. Beside it lay an article with the headline, "You Are *Not* Your Job." A stamped envelope addressed to Steve Singer sat near Madeline's elbow.

"Good morning," Madeline said, folding the articles and sliding them out of sight. Methodically, she began to file the coupons in an alphabetical file folder. "How'd you sleep?"

"Okay." Avery finished off the granola bar in a few quick bites and went back for another cup of coffee. "But I haven't slept that close to the floor since my college drinking days. It's not exactly conducive to deep sleeping."

"No, it sure isn't," Madeline agreed. "I woke up today feeling like a hundred and ten, which is more than twice as bad as I'm supposed to feel."

"I hope I look as good as you when I hit fifty," Avery said, meaning it. Madeline Singer didn't have Nicole's flashy good looks or killer vintage wardrobe, but she was attractive in a well-groomed, I-care-about-but-am-not-obsessed-about-myself way. As far as Avery was concerned, she looked and acted like a mother was supposed to.

"Thanks. But I have to confess I'm kind of glad the mirrors in this house are so cloudy. Fifty-two can be hard to look at straight on." She smiled. "I would, however, like to see more clearly through the windows on the back of the house. Do we have time today to wash them?"

"Yep," Avery said. "These first few weeks are all about getting rid of as many layers of dirt as possible. Then we should be able to move on to stripping and refinishing and re-glazing and . . . well, there's not much in this house that doesn't need something." She sighed and looked around her. "And then there are the rooms that need practically everything."

"What are we going to do about this kitchen?" Madeline brought the coffeepot over and topped off Avery's cup.

"I don't know," Avery said as they contemplated the room together. "I like what they did with the space; this area was probably originally a butler's pantry and the way they integrated these older cabinets into the plan is cool." She pointed toward the run of painted wood glass-fronted cabinetry on the opposite wall. "But it needs to be updated with top-of-the-line appliances and countertops and all."

Footsteps sounded out on the loggia.

"The Realtor said Dyer got a great buy because so much work had to be done, but he must have been too busy stealing to do the renovation."

They looked up to see Nicole in the kitchen doorway. She wore what had to be designer running clothes and shoes and though those clothes were wet from exertion and her skin glowed with perspiration, her makeup was still intact. She had an odd, almost wary, look on her face.

"What did I miss?" she asked, pulling a bottled water out of the fridge and raising it to her lips.

"Just talking about the kitchen," Avery said, watching her. "And working up the energy to start washing windows."

Nicole closed her eyes briefly and grimaced, but she didn't stop drinking.

"Yeah, we're all really looking forward to that," Avery said. "And I thought maybe we should take a look at the 'jungle' while we're working outside and see if we can figure out what needs to be trimmed or removed." She carried her empty coffee cup to the sink. "Do either of you garden?"

"No." Nicole finally lowered the bottle; it was almost empty.

"I once got lawn of the month in our neighborhood, but that was because the real winner got disqualified for secret watering during the drought." Madeline poured the last of the coffee into her cup and turned off the coffeemaker. "Maybe we should call John Franklin and see if he meant it when he said his wife and her garden club might be willing to help." She said this somewhat tentatively.

"Good idea," Nicole said.

"You're a genius," Avery added. "I have no desire to do any grunt work that someone else might be willing to do."

Madeline flushed at the compliment, clearly pleased. "It's the first rule of committee management. I learned it when I was room mom for Kyra's kindergarten class. You can kill yourself doing everything or you can delegate."

"Sounds good to me," Avery said. Then deciding to try Madeline's technique on for size, she turned to Nicole. "Would you be willing to call John Franklin and see if his wife and her garden club are actually willing to tackle the lawn and garden?"

"Sure," the redhead said as she tossed the now-empty water bottle into the recycling bin Madeline had set up. "I've talked people into all kinds of things in the name of love; I'm sure I can get a couple of garden ladies to come over here for a little weed pulling and frond plucking."

Thirteen

The days passed in an endless blur of floor mopping, window washing, baseboard wiping, and cobweb removing. Despite Robby the plumber's constant presence they still had only one working bathroom, which required varying degrees of patience and bladder control and, at times, negotiation. Nicole had worked hard all of her life, but it had been almost two decades since that work had been physical. Pilates and jogging had not prepared her body for what was required of it now. Nor was she comfortable with the outward physical manifestations of hard labor; each jagged nail, each gash and scrape and bruise felt like a personal insult. She continued to put on makeup each morning, but she was pathetically grateful that the bathroom mirror was murky and that there were so few shiny surfaces in which she'd be forced to confront her reflection. Coming up with that "one good thing" during their group sunsets was already a challenge and the most grueling grunt work had not even begun.

It was a sign of just how radically her life had changed that Nicole was actually looking forward to going to the grocery store with Madeline. Until she realized that Madeline intended for them to go in the minivan.

Nicole jangled her keys to get Madeline's attention and motioned toward the Jag. "Why don't we take my car? It's not like we're planning to buy those huge cartons of . . . everything."

Madeline stopped where she was and gave Nicole what she was beginning to think of as the "mother look."

"My car does have a trunk, you know," Nicole pointed out, trying not to sound too eager. "And we could put the top down."

"It's just easier with the van," Madeline said, clicking the dratted doors open. "Why don't we save your car for a fun ride somewhere?" She said this as one might when negotiating with a child, then slid into the driver's seat and waited for Nicole to get in beside her. If she offered an ice cream on the way back, Nicole was going to give her some serious shit.

They drove off the beach to a Home Depot, where they wandered the aisles with a list from Avery in hand, finally finding the brass and chrome polish and extra tools she'd asked for. At the grocery store, Madeline wheeled the cart, pulled coupons from her alphabetized holder, and checked things off the list as Nicole retrieved them. All around them people twice their ages pushed mostly empty carts, which held them upright, or motored by on store-provided scooters. Many of those people stared at her outright.

Nicole stared back, taking in their age spots and wrinkles; the thin hair through which their scalps showed; the cloudy eyes that glimmered briefly with interest as they passed.

In New York you saw the occasional older person hobbling by on a cane or being pushed in a wheelchair, but they were easily overlooked in the jostle of the crowds. In L.A., she encountered very few older people—at least none who looked or admitted to anything near their actual age. She assumed the really elderly were holed up somewhere or had been tucked away by their families. By L.A. standards she was already well over the hill, but her persona as dating guru and matchmaker had kept her on the party circuit. Her income had allowed her to stave off the more obvious signs of aging, which were so prominently displayed here. Nicole shuddered slightly. If they didn't get Bella Flora finished and off their hands, she'd have to live with whatever Mother Nature decided to do to her.

In the freezer section she paused to watch a wispy-haired woman bent nearly double over her cane traverse the aisle. The woman paused for a moment to catch her breath. Before she hobbled on, she threw Nicole a pitying glance.

Turning quickly, Nicole caught a fleeting glimpse of wild hair and a dirt streaked face reflected off the freezer case. Aghast, she stared at the image while Madeline, who must have just realized that she was no longer beside her, turned and rolled the cart back to her side.

Nicole reached out toward the reflection. The mirror image reached back.

"Please tell me that isn't me," Nicole whispered, unable to tear her gaze away from the train wreck of red dust-streaked hair and dirt-smeared face. The black spandex running clothes were stained and bedraggled. "I did *not* go out looking like that."

Madeline winced. "We were just running out to do some errands . . ." Her clothes were equally dirty, but at least her hair was up in a banana clip.

"Well, it may be okay for you," Nicole said. "But I don't go out into the world like this. Not ever."

"Thanks." Madeline's tone was dry. "But it's just a grocery store. And it's pretty much filled with strangers. Not really enough to get all fixed up for."

"But I . . ." Nicole pulled herself up as a guy with a beer belly stuffed into a stained Hawaiian shirt went by. Next came a woman in a snap-fronted housecoat.

Madeline was right. So a few elderly people felt sorry for her. So she could scare children. It was not the end of the world. Pretty soon they'd be back at Bella Flora where nobody cared what she looked like as long as she pulled her weight. And they never found out she was Malcolm's sister. "Can we go now?"

Madeline looked at her list and then inside the basket, rifling through her coupons one last time. "Yes, we're good." She tucked the list into her purse and wheeled the cart toward the checkout. There they unloaded and pushed the cart toward the bagger. "But you need to stop worrying about your appearance. Even with the dirt accents and the wind-blown hair thing, you're a very attractive woman."

Partly mollified, Nicole pulled out her wallet and waited for the cashier, who might have been pushing ninety, to finish scanning their items. His name tag read Horace and his pace was too slow to be termed glacial. When he'd finally scanned and passed all their items down to the bagger and punched in Madeline's coupon codes, he asked, "Do you want your senior discount with that?"

Nicole blinked. "I'm sorry," she said, certain she'd misunderstood. "What did you say?"

"I asked if you wanted your senior discount. It'll save you five percent on your total bill."

Nicole couldn't seem to catch her breath. The blood bubbled in her veins, looking for an escape hatch. Madeline blanched beside her.

"Do I *look* like I should get a senior discount?" Nicole asked.

The cashier shrugged his bony shoulders. "Don't get mad, now. I'm supposed to ask," he said.

Nicole's hands clamped on to the side of the checkout stand, which she figured was better than around Horace's scrawny neck. "But you can't possibly ask everyone. How old do you have to be to get the senior discount, Horace?" she asked.

"Fifty-five." It was Horace's turn to blink. "But if you aren't . . ."

"Oh, my God!" She leaned closer prepared to choke the life out of him. The man actually thought she was fifty-five. "This is not happening!"

Madeline took Nicole by the arm to restrain her, then paid the now-trembling Horace. "Come on, Nicole," she said in her mother tone as she maneuvered Nicole and the cart out of the store. "He just needs new glasses. Or maybe cataract surgery."

The next thing Nicole knew they were in the parking lot heading toward the minivan. She felt vaguely grateful to Madeline for getting her out of there before she hurt Horace or humiliated herself completely. She was even more grateful that Madeline didn't crack a smile.

Madeline fought back the smile as she helped Nicole into the van and tossed the groceries in the back.

On Pasadena Avenue Nicole stared mutely out the window, her face arranged in the oddest expression. She didn't say a word when Madeline's cell phone rang.

Madeline pulled her cell phone out of her purse. Caller ID simply said Home.

"Hello," she said as Nicole continued to stare out the window.

"Mom?" Kyra sounded closer to three than twenty-three. There was a pronounced quiver in her voice. Madeline's heart did the flip-flop it always did when one of her children was in distress.

"What is it, Kyra?" Madeline asked. "Are you all right?"

Nicole turned at that, pulled momentarily from her misery.

"Daniel's publicist called me today," Kyra said.

"His publicist?" Stopped at a red light, Madeline watched an old man in madras shorts and navy blue ankle socks hobble across the street.

Kyra sniffed. "He called to tell me that if I heard from the media in any way that I wasn't supposed to say anything but 'no comment'; that I was just an assistant on the movie Daniel's making and that we only knew each other to say hello on set."

The car behind Madeline honked. She accelerated slowly, surprised to see that a motorized wheelchair on the sidewalk was moving faster than the cars in front of her. "Why would anyone be calling you, Kyra? I thought you said no one knew"—she glanced over at Nicole, who had her head back against the headrest and her eyes closed, but who seemed to be listening—"anything."

"Because Tonja did some interview with *People* magazine and said that there are always rumors about infidelity on movie sets, sometimes even between big stars and unimportant gofers, but that she and Daniel were in it for the long haul." There was another loud sniff. "And that they were thinking about going to Haiti to adopt a couple of those poor, parentless children."

Madeline drove over the Corey Causeway and turned onto Gulf Boulevard. Nicole's eyes stayed closed.

"And what does 'D' say about that?"

Kyra's voice got wobblier and more pitiful. "I don't know. He hasn't called me. I don't really understand why."

"Awww, honey," Madeline said. "I'm sure . . ." She stopped, not actually sure of anything, least of all whether a megastar like Daniel Deranian might actually feel anything other than lust for a young girl like Kyra.

"And I can't take it here another minute, Mom. Daddy just lies on the couch all day and lets Grandma take care of him. It's awful. How long are you going to be gone?"

Madeline drove down Gulf Boulevard, staying in the right lane so she could enjoy the flashes of beach between hotels, comforted by the sway of the palms and the slower pace with which everything, including traffic, seemed to move.

"It looks like I could be here most of the summer, Ky. We're trying to finish the renovation by Labor Day so that we can put it up for sale right afterward."

Kyra didn't speak, but Madeline could feel her misery reaching out though the airwaves. She didn't know if there was any long-term solution other than to hunker down and do what needed to be done, but she couldn't break this connection with her daughter without offering . . . something.

Nicole's eyes fluttered open and she turned her gaze out

the passenger window; Madeline had the sense she was trying
to give her privacy, but it wasn't like she could leave the car.
Or stop listening. Avery's suggestion about making a video of
the house came to mind and Madeline said, "Why don't you
come down here and help us, Kyra? It's beautiful and quiet.
You could kind of regroup and figure out how to proceed."
Just like Madeline, who felt as if she'd run away from home.
"Avery asked if you'd shoot some 'before' video for us anyway."

"Who's Avery?"

"One of the other owners. She's half of the on-camera team
on an HGTV show called *Hammer and Nail*."

"The one Grandma watches all the time?"

"That's the one," Madeline said. "She's really nice. And
Nicole, our other partner, is . . ." She looked up as Nicole
stopped pretending she wasn't listening in. Their eyes met.
"Nicole is interesting. She's a professional matchmaker, but
just a wee bit touchy about her age."

Nicole returned her gaze out the window, but a small
smile hovered on her lips. Madeline smiled, too, as she
thought about the dynamics at Camp Bella Flora.

"If you don't mind a mattress on the floor, there's plenty
of room."

"But what would I do there?" Kyra asked.

"I don't know, Kyra." Madeline didn't have the energy to
expend on persuasion. "What are you doing there?"

"Good point," her daughter said.

"I'm pretty sure your dad has some frequent flier miles
left over that you could use. Text me and let me know when
you're coming and I'll meet you at the Tampa airport."

They passed the Don CeSar, which she'd already begun
simply to think of as "the castle," and continued past the war-
ren of tiny streets until she could make the turn onto Gulf
Way. The sea oats swayed atop their dunes and she knew the
carpet of white sand was still warming under the afternoon
sun.

"Do it, Kyra. We could use your help, and I think you'll
like it here."

She shot a look at Nicole, who nodded in assent. Surely this was the last place anybody in the media would come looking for Kyra or anybody else.

That evening the breeze off the water was warm but soothing; the fronds of the palm trees stirred gently. Avery sat staring out over the pass. She had a big slash of dirt across one cheek and pieces of cobwebs stuck in her hair. Madeline thought they looked like a matched set.

Tonight's hors d'oeuvres was Ted Peter's smoked fish spread on crackers with hot sauce on the side. They weren't exactly homemade, but everyone but Avery considered them a step up from Cheez Doodles. The drink of the evening was rum and Coke.

"I had one celebrity, who shall remain nameless," Nicole said when pumped for stories about her high-profile clients, "who wouldn't consider dating anyone who'd ever eaten a green M&M. And another who was such a militant vegan that he wouldn't go out with anyone who'd eaten meat in the last year and a half." She reached for her drink and took a small sip. "Do you have any idea how hard it is to verify those things?" Nicole asked. "Almost as difficult as who is and who isn't a natural blonde."

"Wow," Avery said, a drink in her hand, her gaze out over the Gulf. "And that matters because . . ."

"That client wanted children with blonde hair and blue eyes. And he was afraid that if the woman he planned to marry wasn't a real blonde, it might not happen."

"Eeew," Avery said. "It sounds awfully Aryan. Maybe you should have fixed him up with a test tube so that he could clone himself." She set her drink down and reached for the hot sauce. "How did you come up with a definitive answer?"

Nicole smiled. "Well, it turned out the woman and I had the same hairdresser. And since only your hairdresser knows for sure . . ."

"Very sneaky," Madeline said, "but effective. Hairdressers

are the repositories of all kinds of personal information. Just like cleaning people. Did you deal with a lot of celebrities?" she asked as casually as she could.

"Yes," Nicole said. "But the celebrities weren't any flakier or more demanding than the really wealthy CEOs and trust funders. The more money, the more demands. That's the way it generally works."

Madeline settled as comfortably as she could in her beach chair; the neon-colored straps had started to mold to her bottom. "Did you ever run across Daniel Deranian?" she asked in what she hoped was a nonchalant tone.

"Now there's a good-looking man," Nicole said, relaxing back in her chair. "I ran into him a few times out in L.A. on the party circuit; he definitely didn't need my matchmaking services." She smiled ruefully. "But that wife of his, Tonja, now that woman is a piece of work." Nicole shook her head. "And that is not a compliment."

"In what way?" Madeline asked, hoping it was something as trivial as an M&M color bias.

"The woman is like a steamroller," Nikki said. "If you get in her way, she'll just knock you down and squash you flat."

So much for the M&M'S.

They fell silent for a while, watching the sunset and sipping their drinks. Madeline spent the time trying to imagine Kyra in Daniel Deranian and Tonja Kay's world and failing miserably. Nicole, yes; Kyra, no. Shifting again in search of a more comfortable position, Madeline turned to Avery. "We could use a little more furniture," she said. "Could you ask Chase if his father has anything else stashed in storage?"

"Sorry," Avery said. "But I am *not* asking Chase Hardin for anything I don't have to." She turned to Nicole. "You're the persuader. Will you give him a call?"

"Sure," Nicole said, standing. "But right now I'm going to have a shower; the one I shouldn't have gone out into the world without."

"Poor Nicole," Avery teased. "That cashier must have been legally blind. You don't look a day over fifty-four."

"Thanks so much." Nicole's tone was dry. "After my shower, I'm going in search of Wi-Fi. If I can't pick it up in any of the hotel parking lots, I'm going to take my laptop to that cybercafe I saw." She picked up the remains of her rum and Coke. "And just for that comment you are definitely not invited."

Avery slapped at a mosquito. "I'll consider myself rebuked."

Madeline picked up what was left of the crackers and spread. Avery grabbed the bottle of hot sauce as they prepared to go inside.

"You know, if we're going to be here until September, we might want to think about putting in cable so we can at least hook up a TV and access the Internet," Madeline said. "I can see what kind of rate they've got if we bundle both services."

"Good idea," Avery said and once again Madeline felt herself flush with pleasure. Which made her realize just how long it had been since her family had complimented her or even noticed the things she did to make their lives run more smoothly.

"Before we go in, I want to share a good thing," Madeline said, raising her glass to the others. "I spoke to my daughter earlier and I think she's going to come down and help us out for a while."

They clinked their glasses, or perhaps "click" was the better word for the sound of plastic on plastic.

"That's great," Avery said. "The more grunts the better."

Madeline aimed a look at Nicole, who gave her one back.

"I don't know," Nicole said. "This was not a particularly great day; there aren't a whole lot of good moments to choose from."

"It doesn't have to be great," Avery said.

"And you only need one good thing," Madeline agreed. "There must have been at least one."

Nicole shook her head, but Madeline could see she was thinking.

"All right," Nicole finally said. "I guess it's a good thing I didn't perform cataract surgery on the cashier in the middle of the grocery store like I wanted to."

There was laughter as they clinked their glasses again. "A very good thing," Madeline said as they turned to Avery.

"Let me see." Avery paused, her head cocked. "All right, the good thing is that we're just about done with the preliminary cleaning."

A cheer went up.

"I'll drink to that," Nicole said.

"Me, too!" Madeline clinked and drank the rest of her rum and Coke then raised her empty glass up into the air.

"The bad thing," Avery said once the cheers had faded away, "is that Chase Hardin will be on site full time as of tomorrow. It's time to kick this job into higher gear."

Fourteen

Avery awoke to the gnashing of gears and the rattle of a big truck. These were followed by shouts and the sound of a huge metal object landing on an even harder surface. She jumped up and peered out. Directly beneath her window stood Chase Hardin and a newly delivered Dumpster. Racing out her door to the bathroom, Avery skidded to a stop behind Nicole, who was already dressed. Avery was still wearing Trent's castoff T-shirt that she slept in and could tell by the look on Nicole's face that she must have an especially virulent case of bed head.

"I just need to use the toilet and then wash my face. Can I jump in there ahead of you?"

"That's all I'm doing, Avery," Nicole said. "That's all any of us ever have time to do." She tapped her foot impatiently. "But go ahead. Chase is here. And I wouldn't want you to have to do combat on a full bladder."

"Thanks." Avery stepped forward and rapped lightly on the door.

"Just a sec," Madeline called from the bathroom. Outside the truck drove off in another grinding of gears. Others arrived. There was a clatter of metal and more shouts.

The doorbell rang, which was apparently just a courtesy because less than a heartbeat later footsteps echoed in the foyer.

"Vanna?" Chase's voice carried up the stairs. "Time to rise and shine!"

"A little warning would have been nice," Avery grumbled.

"No kidding. And given the look on your face, you might want to take an extra thirty seconds to brush your teeth," Nicole said. "Just in case you have to get in Chase's face."

"Ha," Avery said. "I should stay just the way I am so he can see what this stupid plumbing schedule of his is doing to us. But then that's probably part of his fiendish plan."

"Don't worry, it's kind of hard to miss the ramifications." Nicole looked Avery up and down, which was when Avery realized how not dressed she was.

"Be right back!" In her room she pawed through her suitcase and the pile beside it until she found a pair of cutoffs and wiggled into them. She got back just as Madeline vacated the bathroom.

"I'm in desperate need . . ." Avery began.

Madeline smiled. "I'll have a pot ready by the time you come down."

Avery drew a deep breath as she sailed into the bathroom and raced through what barely qualified as a "toilet." Chase was already in the kitchen drinking a cup of coffee when she got there. An opened box of glazed doughnuts sat on the kitchen table. Madeline put a cup of coffee in her hand.

Chase looked her over, starting with her bare feet and working up her bare legs past the sleep shirt to the hair that she couldn't remember combing. "Gee, I didn't mean to pull you out of bed," he said.

Avery raised her hand and turned the palm toward him. "What?"

"We try not to talk to her more than necessary until she's finished her first cup," Madeline explained as she picked up the box of doughnuts and held it out to Avery.

Avery took a doughnut and bit into it, sighing with

pleasure as the warm sugar melted in her mouth and mingled with the coffee. She drained the cup and held it out to Madeline for more, finishing off the doughnut in a few quick bites.

Chase cleared his throat. "Hello?"

Fortified, and now fully awake, Avery turned to face him and was immediately irritated by his freshly shaved face and still-damp hair. He was too attractive under the best of circumstances but the fact that he was showered and groomed struck her as grossly unfair.

"The scaffolding is being unloaded and as you probably heard, the Dumpster's in place," he said. "That means it's time to start getting rid of anything we're not keeping. And that includes . . ."

"The wallpapers in the downstairs and upstairs baths, the carpet in the master, the ruined baseboards in the salon and the kitchen, and probably most of what's in the garage," Avery finished.

A gratifying look of surprise flitted across his face. "Um, yeah," he said.

"And I'm assuming it must be about time for Enrico to come back and finish up the roof," she commented as if they were having an actual conversation.

"Yeah. He'll be here in a couple days."

"So we're expecting him on . . . ?"

"Um, Thursday. First thing."

"Good. Now about the bathroom situation," Avery began. "Why don't we . . ."

"There's nothing to discuss," Chase said. "I need Robby to go through the entire system thoroughly and that takes time. If you want him done faster, I suggest you stop feeding and mothering him." He shot Madeline a look that sent her off to wipe the far end of the counter.

"But . . ." Avery began.

"No, no buts," Chase said. "We don't really have time for buts."

She closed her eyes briefly, searching for inner strength. She didn't understand his attitude or the obvious chip on his shoulder he brought to every conversation they had. Opening her eyes, she stared into his vibrant blue ones and saw just how eager he was to put her in her place. She told herself not to engage, but this was so much easier thought than done.

"I'd like to discuss who's going to do what when it's time to move into the next phase," she said. "For instance, I think Madeline should do the re-glazing—she's the most patient and detail oriented. When we get the doors down, I can teach Nicole how to do the stripping and I can refinish. That way . . ."

"You're getting ahead of yourself, Van," he said, cutting her off. "All you have to do for the next three or four days is remove all the excess, haul it out from wherever it is, and throw it in the Dumpster. That's it. Finito. I've got protective gear out in the truck, and I'll be here while the scaffolding goes up. You can do all the smiling and posing you want, but I'll worry about what comes next and who will do it. Because that's my job." He watched her carefully, but she had no idea what he was looking for.

"Seriously, Chase, that's just . . ."

". . . The way it is, Vanna." Once again he looked her up and down, but more slowly this time, making her aware that she had pretty much just crawled out of bed and didn't have on anything resembling underclothes. "Don't worry your . . ."

"Don't," she said, presenting her palm once again. "I don't know if you have something against me in particular or you're this big an asshole with everyone, but one more word and this grunt will be out of here."

"Tsk-tsk," he said in mock despair. "The going hasn't even gotten tough yet, Van. And you're already thinking about bailing out?"

Avery narrowed her gaze at him. He looked so damned pleased with himself that all she could think of was wiping the smug smile off his arrogant face.

"The only thing that's tough here is dealing with you," she snapped. "And I don't have a clue why. But I suggest you start thinking a little longer before you address me by anything other than my name. And just so we're clear," she said with her own most taunting smile, "the only pointing and gesturing I'm planning to do this summer is this."

She watched his face carefully as she raised her hand. But this time she didn't bother showing him her palm. She simply gave him the finger.

The removal phase sucked. After three days of prying thirty-year-old wallpaper from the even older walls it clung to, prying up baseboards that had been attached even longer, and sorting and then shlepping what had to be two tons of old shit out of the detached garage while wearing masks and gloves to avoid the toxic side effects of mold and mildew, Nicole had had enough. And that was before the three of them had spent close to three hours pulling up the sodden, moldy carpet and pad in the master bedroom and wrestling it down the stairs and out to the Dumpster.

Robby and several other of the subs who now streamed in and out of the house offered to help with the carpet, but Avery refused at almost the same instant Chase asked them to get back to the work they were being paid for. The two of them hadn't spoken directly to each other since the last Vanna incident, but the amount of glaring and nonverbal communication between them was deafening.

Enrico and his helper tromped around overhead calling up and down to each other while a crew of six assembled and placed scaffolding around Bella Flora. Chase had set up a sawhorse and a pile of two-by-fours out on the pool deck and was cutting long strips of wood for new baseboards. The house was like some big patient told to open up and say "ahhhh." One who'd been expecting a hygienist's cleaning and ended up with double root canals.

Nicole had already heard more carpentry and construction noises over the past days than she'd expected, or wanted, to hear in a lifetime. Bottom line, it was well past lunchtime and Nicole wanted out. Without asking or discussing, Nicole ran upstairs to shower, put on her favorite vintage Dior sundress, and jumped in her car. In a word, she bailed.

Even though she knew she shouldn't spend the money, she parked at the Don CeSar and walked through the lobby, breathing in the once-familiar scent of expensive beachside hotel, and exited through the back doors to the pool area, where she took a table overlooking the beach. It took her a few minutes of deep breathing and staring out over the bathing-suited crowd to regain her equilibrium. When the waiter appeared she ordered a glass of Chardonnay and a Nicoise salad. When the wine arrived she sipped it slowly, focusing on the sun glinting off the Gulf, the breeze riffling the palms, and the gentle touch of both on her skin. Soothed, she took her time enjoying her salad, then splurged on a small piece of key lime pie.

When she'd finished, she dabbed the napkin at the corners of her mouth, then reapplied her lipstick. In no hurry to return to "camp," she ordered a last glass of Chardonnay. Knowing she'd stretched her budget and could soon be back on Cheez Doodles, she savored it. If she were filling out her tax form right now, she'd file the receipt under "mental health."

When her phone rang she considered letting it go to voice mail; no news had begun to feel like good news, but there was always the small chance it might be business of some kind. When she saw her assistant, or rather her former assistant's cell phone number on caller ID, she answered and raised the phone to her ear.

"Nicole?" Anita's voice was hesitant when Nicole answered. "I wanted to say thanks for setting up that interview with the Date Doctor. It won't be remotely the same as working for you, but she's offered me a position." There was a brief pause in which Nicole allowed herself to miss the young woman she'd trained to run her back office. She'd become a miracle of efficiency and had devoted herself to making Nicole's life run smoothly. Lord knew Nicole could use a little "smooth" in her life right now.

"That's great," she said, meaning it. "She's lucky to have you."

"Listen, Nicole," Anita said, her voice lowered. "I'm not sure where you are, but I wanted to let you know that I heard from the, um, FBI." She paused as if to let this sink in. Nicole wished it were coming as a surprise.

"They wanted information about your bank deposits. They asked me if there had been any unusual deposits or more frequent transactions." Anita paused. "I told them no. That you'd always been really diligent about your bookkeeping and that I was sure you'd show them your books if they wanted to see them." Another pause. "I hope you're doing okay." It was a statement and a question.

"Thanks, Anita," Nicole said. "I'm fine." The lie tripped off her tongue automatically; if there was anything Nicole had learned over the years of reinventing herself, it was that perception could be far more important than reality. No one, not even those who seemed to be on your side, needed to see your vulnerability.

"Anything else I should know?" Nicole asked at the same moment she spotted Agent Giraldi crossing the pool deck and heading toward a nearby chaise. Nicole wasn't the only woman who'd noticed him or watched as he spread a towel on the chaise and then pulled his T-shirt over his head in one smooth, unhurried move. In fact, there was what might have been a faint collective sigh as he rubbed lotion across his chest and over his abdomen.

"There was a strange email on your old AOL account, too." Anita said. Nicole was listening but her gaze remained riveted on Agent Giraldi. Was parading around in front of her without his shirt a part of his surveillance, too, or just a byproduct of it?

"Does that mean anything to you, Nicole?"

"Hmmm?" She watched Giraldi settle onto the chaise, pillow the back of his head in his hands, and cross one ankle carelessly over the other. Despite the sunglasses, she could feel him watching her. He probably had a damned black belt in lip reading.

"I said there was a weird email on your old account," Anita repeated. "All it said was, *Sing it, Gloria.*" Anita paused again. "Does that mean anything to you?"

Nicole turned so that the FBI agent's only view was of her back, though she was painfully aware that if she said anything incriminating here he wouldn't have to read her lips to know it. Anyone who'd ever read a mystery novel or watched television knew that cell phones were about as secure as Swiss cheese. Not that she was planning to say anything he would want to hear.

Still, the message was a bit of a shock. "That *is* weird," she said in as casual a tone as she could muster, because to disavow the weirdness of such a message would, in fact, be completely weird. "When did that email come in?"

"Late last night," Anita said. "About midnight."

Which was when Nicole had been tossing and turning on her mattress in the echo-y house, trying not to hear the pitter-patter of little rodent feet in the attic above her; a noise she had, fortunately, not heard since her childhood and had hoped never to hear again.

"Hmm, I can't imagine what that would mean," she said, though of course she could. "Who did it come from?"

"I don't know. I think it came from some kind of blind address. I wasn't able to reply in any way."

"Hmmm," Nicole said one more time for good measure. "Well, it must be spam or something. I don't even know anybody named Gloria—except for that woman we fixed up once with Terrence Sim."

"I don't know," Anita said. "I just wanted to see if it meant anything to you or not."

Nicole felt Agent Giraldi's gaze on her back and was careful not to tense her shoulders or give any clue that anything of importance was being discussed. It was possible he had an advanced belt in body language, too. "Thanks, Anita. You can go ahead and delete it. I'm sure if it's actually meant for me, whoever it is will make another attempt to get in touch."

They said good-bye and, still striving for casual, Nicole took a last sip of wine and signaled her waiter for the bill. When she'd paid it she stood, and with a small nod at the sunbathing FBI agent, she walked past the pool and back through the Don, too busy thinking to even breathe in the heady scent.

Sing it, Gloria was a definite reference to Gloria Gaynor's "I Will Survive," which had served as her and her younger brother's personal anthem. It had been a promise of sorts that things would somehow work out.

As she left the hotel and walked across Gulf Boulevard toward her car, she tried to think what the point of the message was and if another would follow. The only thing she knew for sure was that after all the months of trying unsuccessfully to reach him, for some unknown reason Malcolm had finally tried to reach her.

Fifteen

When Madeline left for Tampa International Airport the next morning to pick up Kyra, Bella Flora was almost completely encased in scaffolding and footsteps thudded on the roof overhead. Four trucks, including Chase's and Robby the plumber's, were lined up along the front garden wall. The house bulged with people and reverberated with the noise they produced—in stark contrast to the gently swaying palms and the folks strolling the sidewalks and along the water's edge.

It was a gorgeous weekday. The lush greens teemed with golfers and cars puttered in and out of the condo communities and strip malls that lined the Bayway. The population as a whole was significantly older, and unlike in Atlanta, no one seemed in a particular hurry to get wherever they were going. Madeline eased up on the gas pedal and resisted the urge to tailgate or rush around the large Cadillac in front of her. According to her GPS's stated arrival, she had plenty of time to get there.

As she drove she thought about the dynamic at Bella Flora and tried to picture her daughter, make that her pregnant unmarried daughter, thrown into the mix. After a short wait in the Tampa airport's cell phone lot, a far more civilized alternative to the constant circling required at Hartsfield-Jackson in Atlanta, she pulled up to the Delta arrivals to find Kyra already waiting. A suitcase and a collection of equipment bags sat at her feet.

"It's okay, I've got it." Kyra accepted Madeline's hug but shrugged off her offer of help. "I'm used to carting equipment around." Her skin was pale, and her long dark hair was pulled back in a barrette at the nape of her neck. Her eyes were hidden behind a pair of dark sunglasses.

Madeline climbed back into the driver's seat while Kyra stashed the bags in the back. In a matter of minutes they were on the Howard Franklin Bridge and heading toward St. Petersburg.

"It's pretty," Kyra said as she gazed out the window to the water. Her tone, like her smile, was brittle.

"Are you all right?" Madeline asked, though it was obvious she wasn't. "Are you still nauseous?"

Kyra turned to her then. "The morning sickness is pretty much gone, thank God. But I don't feel any of that energy that the book says is supposed to kick in after the first trimester. And before you ask, the answer is no, I still haven't heard from Daniel." She swallowed and looked away again, out over the concrete balustrade of the bridge to the sparkling blue green water of Tampa Bay. "But I'm sure I will."

Madeline would have liked to agree, but she had no idea what the celebrity's feelings or intentions might be, or if he even had any. The things Nicole had said about his wife, Tonja Kay, did not bode well. Maybe Daniel Deranian's publicist knew what he was talking about.

"I, um, haven't mentioned your pregnancy to Avery or Nicole," Madeline said. "And maybe it's not a bad idea to keep Daniel's name to yourself until you've had a chance to talk with him."

Kyra's hands stilled in her lap. Her face was ashen as she turned to look at Madeline. "You're embarrassed, aren't you? You don't think I'll ever hear from him."

"No, Kyra, it's not that. I just . . ."

"Well, I'm not ashamed of being pregnant," Kyra said quietly. "And I'm definitely not ashamed that Daniel and I are in love." Her eyes shone with unshed tears. "You'll see," she said, sounding like a desperate child. "I won't say anything for now if that's what you want, but you'll see how important the baby and I are to him when he comes to get us."

Madeline couldn't think of a thing to say to this, so she remained silent. Not far from St. Petersburg's downtown, they shared a bowl of black beans and rice and a pressed Cuban sandwich at a tiny Cuban restaurant. Without her sunglasses, Kyra's eyes reflected an unhappiness that smote Madeline's heart; the dark circles beneath them attested to her sleepless nights. The last bites of Cuban bread stuck in Madeline's throat. She wished she could wave a magic wand that would produce her daughter's hoped-for "happily ever after," but the days when a word from her or a kiss on a skinned knee could make it all better were long gone.

The thrift store she'd found online was just a few blocks away and was filled with interesting accessories and old bits and pieces of furniture that Madeline imagined had been shed over the years as the elderly population continually downsized. In the housewares section she picked up a blender, pots and pans, a decent cast-iron skillet, and a set of utensils. Eight place settings of surprisingly fine china and silver along with an equal number of water glasses and wine goblets brought the total to just over fifty dollars.

In the furniture department, Madeline pulled out a full-sized futon in a bright floral print. "This would be a lot better for you than sharing my mattress, Ky. What do you think?"

Kyra pulled a face. "I think we should go to a real store. Don't they have any here?"

"We can get a lot more here for a lot less," Madeline said, waving to the sales clerk to carry the futon up front for them. "And that's pretty important right now."

On the way to the cash register they passed a display of old Halloween decorations. Madeline's gaze was drawn to a

life-sized Frankenstein with big blocky feet and the bolts
sticking out of its neck. It hung from a tall shelf by its own
frayed noose. Madeline headed right for it. "Here, help me
pull this down."

"I had no idea a stuffed Frankenstein could be so cheap,"
Kyra said once they'd gotten it down and laid it across their
cart. "Or that you'd become so . . . thrifty."

Kyra's tone made it clear this was not a compliment and
Madeline realized that in her effort to give her children all
she could, she'd done them a disservice. No life was without
its bumps, and even in the best times, money wasn't something that simply flowed from a faucet.

"I knew the thrift stores in the Atlanta area intimately
when you were small and your father was trying to build
clientele," Madeline said. "I'd forgotten how satisfying it is to
wring as much as possible out of each dollar. At this point, it
may be my most valuable skill."

Kyra made no comment.

They checked out and carried their purchases to the van,
an employee following with the futon. "It makes me realize
how much I've taken for granted. How much I didn't teach
you and Andrew." She blew a stray bang out of her eyes. "I
wish I'd known how much pressure your dad was under. I
wish he'd told me what was going on. If he hadn't felt like
he was facing everything alone he might not have . . . reacted
so badly."

She looked Kyra in the eye and she knew her own were
filled with regret. "We're all facing challenges and changes
that we never imagined," she said. "But if he'd said something, I might have been able to help, you know?"

Madeline saw the color drain out of Nicole's face when she
walked into Bella Flora later that afternoon and got her first
sight of the Frankenstein dummy dangling from the top
landing. Madeline had scrawled the name Malcolm Dyer in
big black letters across a sheet of paper and pinned it to the

oversized chest. Avery had helped her affix it to the upper baluster. Kyra had her video camera out and was getting some shots.

"I knew the minute I saw that monster with a noose around his neck that the time had come to hang Malcolm Dyer in effigy," Madeline said, still surprised at how compelled she'd felt to drag the dummy home with her.

"It would be a lot more satisfying to see him hanging in the flesh," Nicole said curtly, but her face still looked pale.

"I know it's not quite as good as the real thing, but at least we have a visual aid for imagining him getting his just rewards," Madeline said.

"Did it come with balls?" Avery asked. "Doing a Bobbitt on it might make me feel a little better."

"Have you always been this bloodthirsty?" Madeline asked as Avery made a scissor snipping motion. "I don't really have a baseline to work from."

Kyra smiled behind the camera, the first real smile of the day. Perhaps despite her earlier protestations, she'd like to do a little snipping of some famous balls herself.

"Nicole, this is my daughter, Kyra," Madeline said. "She's shooting our 'before' video and is going to stay on awhile to help."

Kyra lifted her face from the camera's eyepiece to say hello. "Hey, why don't all three of you go up on the landing and pose with the dummy?"

Nicole looked like she wanted to refuse, but Madeline swept her up the stairs beside her, not giving her the chance. They mugged for the video camera and then for stills, flexing their muscles and aiming gunslinger looks at their Frankensteinian Malcolm Dyer.

"That's good," Kyra said. "Move in a little closer. Mom, turn to your left just a bit."

They did as instructed and when Kyra said she'd gotten enough, they moved apart.

"Welcome to Camp Bella Flora," Nicole said as they filed back downstairs. "And gruntdom."

"Ditto," Avery said. "It's great to have an extra pair of hands even if it does bring us to four females in one bathroom."

There was a collective groan.

"Someone needs to have a talk with Robby. I bet Madeline could turn him with a batch of brownies," Nicole said.

Madeline shook her head. "Chase is not going to let that boy be bought." She turned to Kyra. "Robby is the plumber. Chase is the contractor."

"And he's not likely to let you forget it," Avery said to Kyra. "I told him your mom would be the best choice to reglaze the windows."

"Really?" Kyra's surprise was evident.

"Yep," Avery replied. "She's got the most patience and is the most detail oriented."

Madeline had to laugh. "I'm not sure if that's a compliment or you're calling me anal."

"Hard to say," Nicole drawled. "It's a pretty fine line."

Kyra smiled. "This should be interesting. I always liked sleepaway camp."

"The activities are a little different here," Nicole said. "In fact, we spent the last two weeks cleaning. And the counselors are a little on the demanding side."

"I'm sure Kyra will survive," Madeline said, slipping her arm around her daughter's shoulders. "I'm going to give her the grand tour. Then how about we meet out back in time for the show?"

"The show?" Kyra asked.

"Yes," Madeline said. "The sunset's pretty spectacular here."

Nicole offered to make something tropical in the blender. Avery lobbied for Cheez Doodles and when she was shot down, volunteered to put together a plate of crackers with cheese and salami. Madeline promised to put together a big salad that they could eat out at the concrete picnic table after sunset if the mosquitoes weren't too bad.

"The cable should be hooked up pretty soon," Madeline said as she and Kyra prepared to begin their tour.

"Great," Kyra said. "Where's the TV?"

Avery, Nicole and Madeline exchanged glances. "Well, we don't actually have one of those yet," Madeline admitted.

"No TV?" It was clear the concept was far beyond Kyra's wildest imaginings.

"But I'm sure we will soon," Madeline said.

"Right," said Avery. "We'll just get your mom to put it on the list."

Madeline smiled at her partners. "And then we'll get Nicole to talk someone into giving it to us."

Chase arrived the next afternoon bearing gifts and children.

His sons, Josh and Jason, were fifteen and thirteen, with their father's bright blue eyes and dark hair. Already well on their way to matching his six-foot-plus height, they towered over Avery when they were re-introduced. Standing in the midst of the three of them made her feel like a Lilliputian—an irritated Lilliputian.

"Boys, you remember Vanna, don't you?"

She went on tiptoe to peck them on both cheeks. "I know you're too intelligent to even think about calling me that. I can tell just from looking at you that you're way smarter than your father."

The boys were also more well mannered and far sweeter than their father and seemed glad to be at the beach even if it meant being polite and carting furniture around. She was very glad of their muscle as they unloaded Chase's truck and put the furniture where she directed.

A Naugahyde sofa and two chairs with ottomans were set up in the salon across from a TV on a stand. A coffee table and a somewhat rickety end table came off the truck next and were followed by a floor and table lamp. The mismatched furniture was dwarfed by and far too informal for the room with its coffered cypress ceiling and its row of arched windows, but at the moment Avery would have been glad for packing boxes to sit on. After weeks of perching on the kitchen chairs or on a beach chair out back, the cast-off furnishings made a small portion of the house habitable and gave at least the illusion of a home.

Four more chairs appeared and were added to the kitchen table and an old wicker sofa and chair were deposited on the loggia. When they were done Chase gave the boys permission to take their football out on the beach until he was ready to leave. They left jostling each other as they went.

"Nice kids," Avery said. "They must have gotten it from their mother."

"Yeah."

She saw the flash of pain in his eyes and realized what she'd said. "I'm sorry, Chase," she began to apologize. "I wasn't thinking."

"Not a problem," he said and then surprised her by continuing. "They are a lot like Dawn. They've got her smile and her laid-back attitude." He shook his head. "Anyway, sometimes I just kind of forget she's gone, you know?" He looked away, clearly embarrassed at the admission, and Avery wondered whether she would miss Trent the way Chase missed Dawn if he'd been taken from her rather than simply disappointing her. She realized with some surprise how seldom she actually thought about Trent other than the occasional flash of remembered hurt or anger.

"Look," she said, "I don't really understand why we're always at odds about everything. But I really hope you paid attention when I told you that Madeline should do the reglazing. She's—"

"I've got it under control." He cut her off yet again, any softness she thought she'd seen in his face gone. "There's no need for you to worry your . . ."

"Good God," Avery said. "Let's just leave my 'pretty little head' out of it, okay?" She drew in a deep and disappointed breath. "I'm not worried, Chase," she said. "And I have no interest in arguing with you again. But I'll tell you one thing. If you're not here Monday morning with a smile on your face prepared to teach Madeline how to re-glaze the windows, I will."

Sixteen

They used the weekend to remove the last clingy bits of wall-paper and paste and the stray bits and pieces of debris and carted away what Avery promised were the last armfuls of use-less "stuff" from the detached garage. By Saturday Madeline could have made the trek to and from the Dumpster with her eyes closed and sometimes did; she imagined their footprints indelibly etched into the brick of the drive. As they hauled and sweated together the formalities began to slip away. Madeline began to respond to "Maddie" and even "Mad" as she did at home. Nicole, who appeared particularly bedraggled, looked less and less like a "Nicole" by the hour. The first time Maddie called her "Nikki" she'd looked up quickly prepared to apologize, but Nicole was busy trying to get a glob of wall-paper paste out of her hair and didn't seem to notice.

At sunset Kyra sat on a kitchen chair that Avery dragged out for her. Maddie tensed briefly when Nicole offered Kyra one of the frozen margaritas she'd whipped up, but Kyra opted for a glass of iced tea, which she sipped as she watched not just the show but them in much the same way Jane Goodall must have watched her apes.

Madeline noticed that her daughter's presence altered their group's dynamic; they all thought a bit more before they spoke, and Maddie sensed a bit of editing taking place. The conversation stalled out completely when Kyra pulled out her video camera and began to shoot not only the red ball of the sun, but Bella Flora and them bathed in its glowing light. It was only when the sun had finally set and the tequila in Nicole's frozen margaritas kicked all the way in, that their conversation resumed.

Madeline watched her daughter out of the corner of her eye, wishing that for just a moment she could see her as these strangers might, but it was almost impossible to see beyond the child Kyra had been and the troubles she now faced. In the lengthening dusk they raised their glasses in a final sunset toast and searched their weary brains for a good thing to share.

Though she normally went last, Nicole was the first to raise her glass. "Frankly, the only thing that feels really good right now is the buzz from the margaritas." She stared out over the Gulf, apparently thinking. "Which I guess leads me to how good it is that Maddie bought that blender."

Madeline laughed. "My pleasure." She turned to Kyra and found herself looking into the camera lens. Gently, she pushed it away. "We have a sunset tradition of coming up with one good thing that happened during the day. But I'm not sure those things are always suitable for public consumption."

She returned Kyra's automatic eye roll with a small shake of her head.

"Your mother invented it," Avery said, her voice slightly slurred. "And coming up with even one thing can be a real . . . difficult." She paused and downed the last drop from her glass. "So that's my good thing tonight, too." She raised her empty glass and they clinked. "Let's hear it for the blender." She thought again. "And a weekend without the organ grinder."

"That's Chase," Maddie whispered to Kyra. "They're having a little communication problem."

"Ha!" Avery said, staring down into her empty glass. "That's a gross understatement."

They fell quiet for a moment waiting for Maddie to share her good thing so that they could go inside and either make more margaritas or eat something that would blot up the ones they'd already consumed.

Maddie raised her glass with its tiny bit of pale green slush in the bottom and smiled, motioning for Kyra to raise her glass of iced tea along with theirs. "I'm really happy that Kyra was able to join us in our mission to bring Bella Flora back to life. We may have our occasional differences of opinion . . ." She paused to make eye contact with Kyra. "But she's always been one of the very greatest things in my life."

Chase showed up Monday morning, walked all four of them over to a ground-floor window that had two broken panes, positioned Madeline next to him, and began to demonstrate the re-glazing process as if he'd intended to do so all along.

"First you scrape off the old paint and the glazing compound," Chase said as they huddled together, watching him demonstrate how to work the putty knife in the thin opening of the mullion.

Midway through the explanation, Nicole's eyes began to glaze over, Kyra retreated behind her video camera, and Avery's faith in her choice of Maddie for the job was confirmed.

Amazingly, he neither rushed nor cajoled as he not only demonstrated each step of the process on the pane next to Maddie but watched carefully as she performed the process on her own.

"Then we take out the broken pane and pull out the points." He showed Madeline how to use the needle-nosed pliers to remove the paint-caked diamonds of wood that held each corner of the glass in place. "Then when you've scraped the rest of the old paint and compound out, you set the glass in place."

Maddie's fingers moved awkwardly in the latex gloves

and sweat popped out on her brow, but Chase talked in the same kind of tone that a cowboy might use to gentle a horse. If he hadn't called Avery Vanna the moment he arrived and then ignored her completely, Avery would have thought some kinder, gentler spirit had taken possession of Chase's body.

For twenty-five more minutes, he demonstrated and led Madeline through the delicate and tedious procedure of affixing the glass with the "points," which were too small for easy handling in latex-covered fingers and often hit the ground and had to be retrieved. Avery didn't have the heart to mention how common a problem that was or how frustrating it could be when you were up on a ladder or scaffold.

Maddie grimaced as she pressed a point down at one corner of the new square of glass. They all watched it crack. "Shit!" she said.

Nicole reached for a work towel and lifted a corner to dab at Madeline's sweat-soaked forehead like a nurse mopping the brow of an operating room surgeon. "You're doing great, Maddie. I would have been cramming those pieces of glass into position whether they wanted to go or not."

Kyra moved in for a close-up of the broken glass as Chase helped Madeline remove it, then once again demonstrated the best way to slip it in between the rabbets. They all held their breath while she worked and broke out into smiles when she got it into position without mishap.

"Phew." Maddie wiped her forehead with the back of one gloved hand. "My eyes are crossed from concentrating so hard." She looked pleased.

"You did good," Chase said as he showed her how to roll the glazing compound into a very thin, snakelike piece and press it around the edges. "That's the last step out here. We go inside next to straighten the seams and seal the pane."

"Gee, there's more?" Nicole asked. "And here I was afraid the fun was over already."

Madeline peeled off the gloves and held them out to Nikki. "I won't be at all offended if you'd like to share this job."

"Thank you," Nicole said pushing the offering away.

"You're too kind. But I'd rather poke out my eye with a sharp stick."

Kyra laughed behind her camera.

Avery tried to hold back her own smile and failed. "I hear you," she said. "Unfortunately, pretty much everything from here on out belongs in the category of tedious and tortuous."

Chase smiled at that. He'd been mercifully noncombative and Avery intended to keep it that way. So rather than discuss or ask permission, she took Nicole by the arm and said, "I'm going to leave Madeline and Kyra with you, Chase. Nicole and I are going to start taking down the interior doors so we can strip and refinish them."

"Wait," Nicole said as Avery led her away. "I want to get a sharp stick and have it ready. Just in case."

Later that week, Nicole finished her morning run on the beach with relief and walked across Beach Road, past Bella Flora, which still sat quietly in the early morning light, its driveway and front curb not yet littered with trucks or workmen. Stripping the doors, which meant leaning over them all day while she wiped the stripper on and off, was indeed stick-in-the-eye-worthy, not to mention backache inducing, as was sleeping on a mattress every night. Each morning when she got up, straightening felt like a major accomplishment. She needed her morning run to work out the kinks.

Trying to bring her breathing back to normal, she continued to the sidewalk that hugged the bay and walked it at a leisurely pace. The neighborhood woke up around her, the occasional car passing on her left, the even more occasional boat puttering by on her right. Ahead she saw signs of life on the whitewashed wooden fishing pier. On the opposite corner of Eighth Avenue folks were already lined up for breakfast at the Seahorse Restaurant. The smells of frying bacon and freshly brewed coffee carried on the breeze.

Nicole stopped to lean against the concrete wall that bordered the sidewalk. Closing her eyes, she breathed in the smells along with the salty tang of the air and listened to the insistent caw of a lone gull. If it got any more exciting here she'd be asleep. When she opened them, she saw Kyra Singer approaching from the opposite direction.

The girl's dark hair hung down her back in a careless braid and she hadn't bothered to put on makeup, but even a close inspection proved the girl didn't really need it. She had that clean, fresh-faced appeal that only those under thirty took for granted. Her eyes were a clear gray and she seemed practically bursting with rosy good health. Her legs were long and lean and her bust swelled against the tight T-shirt with its logo for some film production company.

"Hi." Nikki nodded and the girl stopped and leaned against the concrete railing beside her.

"'Morning."

"No video camera?"

"Nope, just out for a stroll." Kyra smiled.

"I was beginning to think it was surgically attached." So it had seemed yesterday morning when the girl had panned it down the line as they waited for the bathroom.

Kyra opened her hands, palms out. "Nope." She smiled. "Not even Velcro'd."

"I think I speak for all of us when I say that's a good thing. I may have to use it at sunset."

"You all are strangely camera shy," Kyra said.

Things were bad enough without documented proof that she'd been reduced to performing manual labor. "How many women do you know who like to be filmed while sweat is pouring down their faces? Or standing in line to use a bathroom?"

"Point taken." Kyra tucked a stray piece of hair behind her ear and smoothed a hand over her stomach. "Are you ready for another day in the salt mines?"

"No," Nikki said. "The only thing that's keeping me going at the moment is that I figure if your mother can survive that re-glazing business, I can strip a few hundred doors."

Over Kyra's shoulder Nikki noticed a van approaching.

She'd noted the name of the cable company painted on its side and had begun to turn back to Kyra when the van's horn beeped twice. Feeling the workmen's assessing gaze on them, her own gaze narrowed at their nerve. Which was when she recognized the dark good looks of the man in the passenger seat. Agent Giraldi saluted her with an annoying tip of his cap as the van drove by and made the turn onto Beach Road.

"Cable company," she said with a grimace that she could tell from Kyra's expression was out of place. "I, uh, think I'll head back to the house to make sure they, um, put the outlet in the right place." Not waiting for a reply, Nikki turned and strode after the van, ready to head the agent off at the pass. Kyra fell in beside her. If she thought it strange that they were racewalking back toward the house, she didn't comment.

Giraldi was already out of the van with a coil of cable over one broad shoulder and a work order in the other hand by the time she reached Bella Flora. Unable to accost him in front of Kyra, she followed him and his partner inside and waited while Madeline led his colleague toward the salon and their lone television. Kyra shot Nikki one questioning look and followed them.

Giraldi stood staring up at the effigy that dangled from the upper landing. "Not a bad likeness," he said softly. "Although I'm sure your brother is wearing a better suit and more expensive shoes. When we went into his home on Long Island I found twenty pair of Italian loafers—all handmade." He shook his head. "He has a real thing for the Italian designers." He turned to her, his eyes probing hers. "Just like his sister."

She glanced over her shoulder to make sure no one could hear them, but she didn't respond to the jibe.

"I guess growing up poor gives some people a craving for expensive things," he continued. "Maybe it makes them think they're entitled to those things, even if they have to steal to get them. But stealing is stealing. And thieves deserve to be punished."

She ignored this, too. "What do you think you're doing here? Are you planning to bug the house?" She kept her voice low, afraid that Kyra would come back with her camera rolling.

An upstairs door opened and closed and bare feet sounded on the floor above, but she didn't know whose. "We've got rats and roaches. Oh, yes, and birds. We've also got dust, dirt, and a kind of caked-on salty grime that I've never encountered before. What are a few listening devices?" Her laugh held no humor. "I told you I haven't been able to reach Malcolm, and he certainly hasn't reached me." Not a lie exactly since his email attempt had been unsuccessful and unclear.

"And how do you think your 'partners' would react if they knew you were related to Dyer?"

The answer of course was badly. In fact, she suspected she'd be hanging right next to the dummy, in person, at this very moment if they had any idea. But she knew it was better to brazen it out; she'd be damned if she'd let him see her fear. "Do you want to tell them?" she hissed as Madeline came down the hallway toward them. "Or shall I?"

"Tell me what?" Madeline glanced at Giraldi, seeing, no doubt, nothing more than an extremely good-looking cable installer.

Nicole was careful to keep her breathing normal and her face expressionless as she waited for him to "out" her. But he turned to Madeline and said, "We weren't sure if you wanted another outlet upstairs. The one will be enough to network your computers off of, but we didn't know whether you wanted outlets in the bedrooms."

"I don't think so," Madeline said. "Do you, Nicole?"

Nicole wondered if Giraldi's partner had finished planting bugs in the salon and wherever else he could reach. Unless, of course, he was a real cable guy and not a pretender. Then she had a brief but visceral vision of Agent Giraldi poking through her belongings. Where would he plant anything in that room? Under the mattress on the floor? In the lone lamp? The drawer of the single nightstand?

"No," Nikki said firmly. "We're not going to be here that

long." She glared at Giraldi, who nodded and smiled like an actual cable guy might.

His partner came out to join them, apparently done in the salon, and he and Giraldi went outside and around to the back of the house, stringing the cable as if they were nothing more than the installers they were pretending to be.

She waited with Madeline out on the front steps, tapping her foot with impatience, spoiling for a fight. And that was before all the other trucks started pulling up to the front curb like spacecraft returning to the mother ship.

Chase Hardin pulled in with his father. Behind them came Robby and Enrico, a pool man, the AC guy, and a truck delivering lumber. When there was barely a spare inch left to angle in, John Franklin's boat of a Cadillac floated in and nudged one fender toward the curb. The Realtor caned his way around to the passenger side and opened the door, handing out a large woman with short salt-and-pepper hair. She was Franklin's height, but looked to outweigh him by a good fifteen pounds— a St. Bernard to his hound dog. As they made their way toward the house, the woman carved a path through the chaos of cars and equipment for the less hearty Realtor to follow.

Avery joined them on the front steps, her hair up in a ponytail, a fine layer of sawdust coating her hair and face. She wore the old tool belt at a jaunty angle, or maybe that was the only way it would stay up. When she spotted the Hardins, Nicole felt her tense slightly, then watched as she arranged her lips into a smile and swaggered out to greet them.

John Franklin worked his cane prodigiously but still trailed behind as he and his companion made their way up the drive and toward the garden gate. The woman wore pastel-colored madras walking shorts that pulled unflatteringly across her stomach and thighs and a sleeveless button-down blouse in a bright lemon yellow. Her arms were heavy but well muscled. Her skin was tanned from the sun.

Giraldi walked toward them from the opposite direction while his partner headed for the truck.

"I'm just going to assume you've bugged the whole damned house," Nikki said under her breath as he handed her the work order for her signature. "So you might as well not bother listening."

"Thanks for the warning."

"And if our television reception's bad, I'm going to call the company and report you."

Giraldi smiled and handed her the same card he'd handed her before. The "company" listed didn't have the word "cable" anywhere in it. "Both my boss and I would love to hear from you."

She turned to go in the house, but he put an arm out to stop her. "I've got something for you," he said. "Walk out to the truck with me and I'll get it."

"Fine." She strode past him toward the driveway, nodding to John Franklin and the woman as they passed, aimed like vectors now toward Madeline. At the cable company van, Giraldi slid open the back door and Nicole peered inside half expecting to see agents with headphones and listening devices like she'd seen on TV. But it was just the inside of an empty van. He reached inside and pulled out what looked like clothing.

"What is it?"

Giraldi held up a bright blue T-shirt with the words "Convenient Cable" scrawled across it, then flipped it to show her the cable company logo on the back. "A small parting gift for you," he said.

"I already have clothes."

"You're overdressed for your surroundings, Ms. Grant," he replied. "If you're going to work on this house and blend in, you're going to have to start dressing like the natives."

She snatched the T-shirt from him and wadded it into a ball.

"I took the liberty of getting you these, too." He unfolded a pair of gray knit short shorts with "I (heart) Pass-a-Grille" stamped across the seat in large pink letters.

She'd never seen anything less her. "You shouldn't have."

"You really shouldn't be stripping those doors in designer

clothes. I hate to see you ruin them." He winked at her before he turned to open the passenger-side door. "You need to have something left to wear when it's time to go get your brother and bring him in."

Nikki stood in the driveway, clutching what looked like a wad of fabric to her chest. There was something odd about the intensity with which she watched the cable truck drive away, but Madeline dismissed the thought as she stepped down into the garden to meet John Franklin and the woman clearing a path before him.

"Hello, Ms. Singer." The Realtor was slightly out of breath unlike the sturdy woman beside him. "I want to introduce you to my bride, Renée. Renée, this is Madeline Singer."

"It's Maddie," Madeline said, extending her hand. "Thank you for coming."

"Oh, I've been dying to get my hands on these grounds for a good long time." Renée Franklin's handshake was firm and decisive, just shy of bone crushing. "Everything is so overgrown and out of control." She shook her head. "A garden is like a child, Miz Singer. It needs a firm hand and constant attention." Her eyes glittered with an almost religious fervor. Her accent was vaguely southern as if it had been acquired slowly over time. "Why, this level of neglect is almost criminal."

"Now, now, dear. Don't get yourself worked up." John Franklin gently patted his wife's formidable shoulder, the adoration in his eyes so stark it made Madeline's stomach hurt. Her own husband was getting harder and harder to reach. Steve had pretty much stopped answering his cell phone, and far too many of her attempts to reach him on the house phone had been deflected by Edna.

Renée Franklin raised her arms in supplication. "Oh, just look at those poor birds-of-paradise. You can barely see them or the frangipani. And the bougainvillea and confederate jasmine! They're magnificent, but they really need to be trained up over those balconies."

She circled the fountain as she exclaimed and pointed. Facing the house, she gestured toward two huge, straggly-looking plants that flanked the front steps. "Those are triple hibiscus. There'll be three blooms in different colors. But they're so leggy." She clutched her heart as if she were wounded. "Oh, I wish I'd brought my pruning shears."

If Renée Franklin were a ship, she would be a Coast Guard cutter—solid and certain, slicing through the waves without a moment's hesitation. They followed her out of the front garden and around the side of the house as best they could. Her husband, who managed surprisingly well with his cane, responded eagerly and lovingly. Maddie, who enjoyed spring in Atlanta mostly as a pleased observer, simply nodded when it seemed appropriate, but understood little.

On the western side of the house the amount of fine white sand far outweighed the grass and was overgrown with sandspurs and creeping cacti; definitely not a barefoot zone. Renée Franklin gestured dismissively toward a low-lying green plant. "That Sprengerle needs to be removed." She turned for a moment to address Madeline. "It's actually a weed"—she whispered this word as if it were somehow dirty—"and as you can see, highly invasive. It must be ripped out by the roots. Up north they put it in pots! Imagine!"

In the back the palm trees were plentiful, and apparently each palm had a name. Renée exclaimed over cabbage palms with petticoats of dry brown fronds that hung beneath them, and proclaimed the multi-trunked reclinada "quite valuable." She led them toward a huge tree she referred to as a sea grape, its leaves dark green and rounded, that hung in a huge mass over a portion of the seawall.

Together they turned back toward the house. The buzz of saws and the pounding of hammers rang in the air and ricocheted off the thick stucco walls, the concrete pool deck, and the courtyard that surrounded it.

"There's so much to be done," Renée said, clearly relishing this fact. "But the grounds will be breathtaking once again."

"And the house, too," John Franklin agreed. "I'm so pleased to see it finally getting the attention it deserves."

Madeline searched out the throng for her partners. Avery and Chase were squared off in front of each other again, their faces contorted in anger, their hands next to their tool belts as if they were holsters. The senior Hardin had a hand on each of their shoulders, trying to placate them. Nicole stood nearby downing a glass of tea, clearly in no hurry to start on the door stretched across a nearby sawhorse. Maddie knew the feeling. She was starting on a bank of upper windows today, and although she didn't fumble quite as much as she had at the beginning of the week, each pane still took far too long. By the end of each day her whole body screamed in protest.

At the opposite corner of the gash of concrete that was the pool, Kyra stood, feet planted, her video camera aimed at Avery and Chase, apparently capturing their argument. As Maddie studied her daughter, the camera swung in her direction. For the first time that morning Maddie became aware of what she probably looked like. She hadn't showered or worried about makeup because she got so dirty and sweaty every day that starting out clean felt practically sacrilegious. One hand stole up to smooth her hair, which was when she remembered that she'd never even combed it before clamping it up on top of her head.

Seventeen

By the end of the next day the way Maddie looked was once again the absolute last thing on her mind. Her shrieking muscles were making so much noise nothing else could sink in.

"Oh, my God." She looked up the front stairs wondering if she could possibly make it up them and if she did, whether she could force herself back down again. She began to inch her way upward, her hand clutching the banister, but each step produced groans of inner protest. She was apparently far too old to spend close to six hours hunched in an untenable position. The number of times she'd climbed up and down the scaffolding did not bear thinking about.

With Herculean effort and complete concentration, she made it up another step. She knew better than to look up or count how many stairs remained.

"Mom," Kyra called from behind. "Turn around and give me a smile."

"No." Both movements were far beyond her current capabilities. She managed to contain the groan as she took the next step. "You better not have that camera pointed at me right now," she said as she completed one more step, then took another. This time the groan refused to be contained.

"Are you all right?" Kyra's voice was, mercifully, farther behind her than it had been.

Madeline took another step. Then one more. She spied the landing just ahead and used what little arm strength remained to hoist herself up to it.

"Mom?"

The landing achieved, she stood beside the dangling effigy of Malcolm Dyer and braced her weight on the banister, careful not to move too suddenly; her sole mission aside from reaching the top, and ultimately the shower, was not to jar her back.

Kyra stood at the bottom, her camera angled upward.

"No, I'm not okay," Maddie said. "And if you actually shot footage of my Mount Everest climb, I suggest you delete it now."

Kyra laughed, but she did lower the camera. "You don't look so good."

"I'm stunned to hear that," Maddie said. "No, I'm too tired to be stunned."

"Aren't you going to do your sunset toast?" Kyra asked innocently. "Don't you want to make sure everybody shares their 'one good thing'?"

Madeline bit back a whimper. "No. Anyone who feels thankful today will have to announce it on their own." She paused, gathering her strength to tackle the rest of the upward journey. "You're in charge of dinner tonight, Ky," she said as she hoisted her weight up another step. "Don't wait for me to eat. I'm going to take a hot shower and then I'm going to lie down. And I'm not planning to come out anytime soon."

Avery sat slumped in the oversized chair, munching on a slice of pizza, when Maddie finally hobbled into the salon in her robe and fuzzy slippers and lowered herself into a corner of the sofa.

"Are you okay?" Avery asked as she watched Madeline

try to get comfortable. "Today felt especially long to me. My back is very pissed off at what it was put through."

"I think I'll survive," Maddie said. She looked at the slice of pizza in Avery's hand. "Is there any pizza left?"

"Here, Mom." Kyra reached into the box on the coffee table, slid a slice onto a napkin and handed it to Maddie. "Do you want something to drink?"

"That would be great." Maddie nodded her thanks.

"You should know that your daughter not only managed to place the order online, she found a coupon for it," Nicole said.

"Like mother, like daughter," Avery said with a smile.

Kyra shrugged. "I didn't realize coupon clipping was an inherited trait. Can you believe they actually have an early bird discount here for pizza delivery?"

"I'm just glad there's no senior citizen discount," Nicole said. She and Maddie exchanged a glance.

The salon was dark, lit only by the flicker of the ancient TV. With its coffered ceiling, floor-to-ceiling arched windows, and cast-stone fireplace surround, the room was meant for more elegant evenings. But all of them, even the uber-sophisticated Nicole, were far too tired to care.

Unable to decide or agree on what to watch, they put the remote in the hands of the youngest member of the group, and Kyra wielded it freely. Avery didn't think she was the only one of them glad to see something other than the video camera in her hands.

Through a full-length window she saw the light in the detached garage go off, and she tensed slightly, waiting to hear the sound of Chase's truck starting up and leaving. Instead she heard the creak of the outside kitchen door as it opened, then clicked shut. This was followed by the refrigerator door and heavy footsteps crossing the hall. Avery sighed when Chase Hardin appeared in the doorway. Even in the flickering light she could see that his face and T-shirt were streaked with dirt and his jeans had what looked like a new rip in the knee. He held an open beer in one hand.

"You look a little tired, Boss," Nicole said. "Something get the better of you?"

"Well, it turns out the pipes passing under the former garage have nothing to do with the pool and everything to do with the main house's original steam heat system. I hit two of them when I was digging and they're going to have to be replaced by somebody who's actually worked on a steam heat system. Which we're unlikely to find down here."

Avery sat up and shot him a look. She'd not only warned him that the system might pass under the detached garage but offered to help. He'd told her not to worry, that he'd be fine.

"I guess everything wasn't so fine after all," she observed but got no response. Big surprise there.

"Hey, look, there's Avery!" Kyra said, pointing at the TV screen with the remote.

It was an episode of *Hammer and Nail*, and the camera was focused on a tight shot of Avery's chest and then zoomed out to reveal her and Trent on set. She cringed at the vacant smile that appeared on her face.

A moment later Trent's voice filled the room. "It's a very simple matter of reattaching the shoe molding, Avery," he said in the tone one would use with a child who was unlikely to understand. "Here." He took the piece of molding and fit it into place, then gave a few gentle taps of the wood mallet.

There was a cutaway of her watching. None of the fury she'd felt at the time was reflected on her face. None of the disappointment, either. Maybe when this was all over, she should forget about architecture and consider acting.

"Jesus!" Chase swore. "How in the world does a licensed architect get talked to like that on national television?" He shook his head. "And you wonder why people don't take your input seriously?" He took a long swig of the beer and turned his gaze on Avery.

"It's just as obnoxious being talked down to off camera as on," she fired back. "The only thing that's different is the size of the audience." They glared at each other for a few long seconds and she reminded herself of her "don't ask, don't tell" vow. It worked, but she resented having to resort to subterfuge. And sometimes he simply pushed her over the edge of reason so that all her best intentions crumbled. Maybe she should change the vow to "don't ask, don't yell," she thought as Chase shrugged and turned his attention back to the screen, where Trent was explaining yet another very basic construction technique in insultingly simplistic terms.

"You really are so much more knowledgeable and competent than they portrayed you on that show," Maddie said. "That's not you at all."

"I didn't know you were an architect," Nicole said.

"Were you really married to him?" Kyra asked.

Avery nodded yes to all of them, not trusting herself to speak as the screen revealed yet another close-up of Trent's handsome face.

"Not bad." Nicole contemplated his image on the screen like an art connoisseur judging a painting on a wall. "But he looks like he knows it." They all watched as the camera moved lovingly across the planes and angles of Trent's face. Avery had once made the mistake of counting his close-ups compared to hers; in the entire last season, the camera had rarely moved closer to her face than her bust.

"Oh, yeah, he's definitely aware of his looks." Nicole was looking at Avery now. "I'm thinking he was just a wee bit self-absorbed."

Chase snorted derisively and took another long pull on his beer. He and Trent had disliked each other pretty much on sight, not that they'd seen a lot of each other. They'd nearly come to blows at her father's funeral, though neither of them had been willing to share details.

"You can leave out the wee bit part," Avery said because there was simply no denying it, especially not with Chase, who'd actually known him, in the room. "Trent was Trent's biggest fan. And he spent a lot of time and energy recruiting people to join the fan club." Especially women who could be helpful to him. Like Avery. And more recently Victoria

Crosshaven. Avery shot Chase a look and caught him studying her. Would she have admitted Trent's shortcomings if Chase and his flagrant disapproval hadn't been there filling up the room?

"You see it all the time out in L.A.," Nikki said. "I never matched up actors with other actors. Most of them were fully occupied being in relationships with themselves."

"They're not all like that," Kyra said when Avery and Trent were replaced by a Home Depot commercial. Avery breathed a sigh of relief when the channel and topic changed.

"No?" Nicole said.

"I was on the set of *Dark Thunder* and Daniel Deranian is not—"

"Here, Ky," Maddie said, cutting her daughter off in mid-sentence. "Let me have that."

She gave her daughter a look as she held her hand out for the remote.

"I'm just saying that some of the actors weren't like that. It wasn't all about them and their . . . image." Kyra turned back to the television as her mother began to click rapidly through the channels, the images flying by at a dizzying speed. "They do have feelings, you know. They're people, too." The last was almost whispered as Madeline finally stopped changing channels.

"Oh, look," Madeline said. "Barbara Walters is interviewing Deirdre Morgan. I absolutely love her!"

Avery went still as Chase's gaze fixed on her.

"Yes, she's done the homes of some of the biggest names in Hollywood," Nikki said.

"She's been an A-list interior designer for decades."

Avery sank lower in her seat, wishing it were possible to disappear as Barbara and Deirdre ambled through the Beverly Hills estate of a Hollywood actress, recently deceased, that Deirdre Morgan had designed, alternately solemn about the loss of the one-time star and chuckling like old chums.

The salon fell silent except for Barbara's careful lisp and Deirdre Morgan's elegant tones. The musical sound of her voice brought a rash of memories hurtling back, and pretty much all of them hurt. Avery had seen her in person only a handful of times over the last twenty years. The last time had been at her father's funeral. She had no interest in repeating the experience.

"I guess this is just your night, Avery," Chase said. "You are all the hell over the television tonight. What were the chances, huh?"

Madeline, Nicole, and Kyra turned to look at her as she practically cowered in the chair cushion.

"What does that mean?" Nicole asked. "What does Deirdre Morgan have to do with Avery?"

"Nothing," Avery said. "Actually, less than nothing." She heaved her way out of the chair and stood.

"Unless you count the fact that Deirdre is Avery's mother," Chase said quietly as everyone, even the people on TV, seemed to freeze in surprise.

"No," Avery said. "No, she's not." She shot Chase a withering look and stepped away from the others, more than ready to make her escape. "She gave birth to me. That's all. She left us more than twenty years ago. As far as I'm concerned, she gave up her rights to the title then."

Posted to YouTube, 12:01 A.M., June 1

Video: *Extreme close-up dummy.*

Audio: "This is Malcolm Dyer, or at least an effigy of him. He probably doesn't really have bolts in his neck."

Video: *Zoom out to wide shot to include Avery, Nicole, and Mom.*

Audio: "These three women are just a few of the people whose money he stole. And do you know what they and their families have left?"

Video: *WS exterior Bella Flora.*

Audio: "This house. Not bad, huh? Except it's not exactly ready to move into or sell."

Music up.

Video montage of cracked pool with beach chairs beside it, hole in ceiling, missing balusters, cardboard in missing window panes, mattresses on bedroom floors, peeling wrought iron.

Music under. Sfx buzz saw, hammering, workmen shouting.

Audio: "So now they're going to have to fix it up. Which means it's loud and messy here."

Video: *Ladies work/sweat. Mom working on window. Glass cracks. Chase and Avery.*

Audio: "And even with a kind of sexy contractor-slash-slave driver, and some professional help, it's hard to believe these three can pull it off. Especially not by Labor Day."

Video: *Avery and Chase fighting/all angles.*

Audio: "At least there's entertainment. I'm going to suggest they fill in the pool and make a boxing ring instead."

Video: *Door stripping/sanding. In line for bathroom. In chairs facing sunset. Nikki toast.*

Audio: "And maybe I'll take bets on whether they can make it happen or not. Stay tuned. I'll try to keep you posted."

Music up and out.

Eighteen 🪶

The days began to lengthen, keeping pace with the rising temperatures and thickening humidity that acknowledged the approach of summer. The dismantling of Bella Flora was complete; almost everything removable had been detached from its mooring for cleaning and/or refinishing. The house was now stripped down to its barest and, Avery thought, most beautiful bones.

The thick stucco walls and hollow tile construction kept the house a good seven or eight degrees cooler inside than it was outside—something they were all thankful for now that the central air-conditioning had been pronounced dead and had not yet been replaced. Most days lunch was a quick pick-up affair from whatever Maddie, who was their most frequent and inventive grocery shopper and coupon clipper, had stocked in the refrigerator. They quit the harder manual labor by five thirty or so and took an hour to themselves to regroup before sunset.

As often as possible, they gathered to toast and watch the sunset—a show that changed nightly and never disappointed. Sometimes they lingered outside eating dinner at the concrete picnic table near the gaping wound of the pool, mosquito repellant perched nearby.

At the moment, although it was barely four P.M., Avery was more than ready to call it a day and more than relieved that Chase had decided to take the weekend off. She'd spent the day helping sandblast the wrought iron and her clothes and hair were filled with grit. The only part of her that may have benefited was her face, which had been sorely in need of a facial before she'd started and now stung from the crude, if powerful, dermabrasion.

She'd like to say she wasn't sure what had driven her to participate, but the truth was it was only Chase's automatic "no" to her offer of help that had compelled her to insist on being included. All she wanted now was a shower that would remove the grit that had found its way inside her clothes and under her skin. But first she had a task to complete.

She waited until both Chase and the rest of the workmen had left for the weekend before she went into the empty garage where Chase's circular saw was set up. Carefully, she pulled several two-by-fours from a pile and cut the blocks of wood she needed then gathered the other women to help her carry them up to the master bathroom.

They stood now in front of the sink and its old etched mirror. "I want to take the legs and fixtures to be refinished, but the sink's attached to the tile wall. I need you to help slide the piles of wood into place to support the front of the sink."

"You're going to remove the legs?" Nicole asked.

"Yep."

"Can't we just polish them and leave them alone?" Maddie looked dubious.

"They're too far gone for that," Avery said. "But they're original and they're really fabulous. I have an idea about where we might get them re-chromed, but I want to take a sample and be sure before we dismantle all the bathrooms."

"It's not like the bathrooms are usable anyway," Nikki said.

"True. But I want to make sure my idea works first." She

shoved the blocks of wood, which she'd arranged in two piles, closer to the sink. "When I remove the first leg, Maddie, I need you to shove the pile of wood into position."

"Okay." Maddie slid the stack closer as Avery pulled out her screwdriver and dropped down under the wide rectangle of porcelain. The tile floor turned gritty as the sand poured out of her clothes like some portable beach that crunched beneath her body. It took some muscle power, but she managed to unscrew the bolts on the first leg. Kyra's feet moved in an arc around the sink, probably filming the operation. Avery tried not to think about which parts of her were visible to the camera.

"Here." With the bolt loosened, Avery removed the curved chrome leg and handed it to Nicole while supporting the sink with her other hand. "Can you slide that first pile in here, Maddie?"

"I feel like I should be wearing a trench coat," Nicole said after she'd set the leg down. "Does Chase know you're doing this?"

"No." Avery scrunched over to start on the other leg. "And contrary to his opinion, I don't actually need his permission to take care of things."

Kyra crouched close to the tile wall and aimed her lens under the sink.

"Do you really need to do that?" Avery asked, reaching out with her free hand and gently pushing the camera lens out of her face. "I'm not exactly made-up and ready for my close-up."

"Just documenting," Kyra said as she panned the camera across Avery and presumably out to Maddie and Nicole's feet.

"You know, I think you might want to reexamine your relationship with Chase," Nikki said, reaching a hand down to help Avery up. "It's pretty volatile."

"I don't have a relationship with Chase," Avery said, brushing off her bottom as best she could. Sand littered the tile floor and she knew there was a mop in her immediate future.

"We all have a relationship with Chase," Nicole said. "And it's in our best interests for it to be a smooth one."

Avery removed the handles and faucet and pulled out the drain. She was way too tired to analyze herself or Chase Hardin. "Well, you'll have to talk to him about that. The way I see it, he's too busy treating me like an imbecile to actually consider that I might have something worthwhile to contribute." She stared at Nicole for a long moment and then down at the sand-strewn floor.

Maddie slipped an arm around her shoulders. "You know, I just don't get why they never show you doing anything real on your show. It's like some kind of fifties time warp. Or something designed for the Playboy Channel."

Kyra stepped back and shot video of Avery unbuckling her tool belt. "Don't worry about the floor, Avery. You go ahead and take a shower. I'll take care of the mop up," Madeline said.

"Thanks, Maddie, I appreciate it," Avery said. "Almost as much as I'm going to appreciate having three whole days without the Big Cheese around."

Nicole stole a look at her passenger seat, still trying to figure out how Kyra Singer had ended up in it. As soon as she'd heard that Chase was taking the weekend off, she'd accepted an invitation to a former client's home in Palm Beach. She'd no more mentioned her plans than Kyra had asked for a ride.

"I have a friend who lives in West Palm. She'll pick me up anywhere you say and will drop me off wherever you are whenever you want to head back."

Nikki had wanted to say no, she didn't need her past and present lives rubbing together quite so closely, but it was hard to come up with a good reason to refuse. It was just a couple of hours in the car each way. And she could hardly say she needed the alone time to get her current story straight and her former act together. Or that one of the reasons for going was to try to find at least some bread crumb of information that might help her pick up Malcolm's trail.

In the first fifteen minutes of the drive, Kyra polished off two chocolate iced doughnuts, a large glass of milk, and a banana. Nicole made no comment; she was not the girl's mother and her daily caloric intake was not her concern. They drove over the Sunshine Skyway, which arched high over Tampa Bay. Boats cut through the blue green water, leaving frothy white wakes like airplane trails behind them. The sun looked almost golden against the pale blue of the sky.

Malcolm had always had a soft spot for Florida—as children they'd lived in several of the state's northern cities. One Thanksgiving, which had been celebrated in a tent in a panhandle campground, they'd offered thanks for the clear skies and warm temperatures. After they'd finished their meal, a feast of KFC extra crispy with two sides and a roll for each of them, the six-year-old Malcolm had vowed that one day he'd own a beachfront mansion. Apparently one of the few promises he'd kept.

Once her food was gone, Kyra stared silently out the window while the palmettos and scrub brush flashed by. As they continued along Highway 78 with its sugar-cane-field border, she turned her gaze on Nicole, who kept her own on the road.

"Could you tell which couples you matched up would stay together?" she asked.

"Sometimes."

"What was it that gave it away?" Kyra asked. "Their personalities, their backgrounds? What they did for a living?"

Nicole thought about it, something she'd tried not to do too much over the years. She'd always been afraid that it would render her too cynical to continue in the lucrative field. "Motivation."

She could tell it wasn't what Kyra had been expecting. She was a little surprised herself. "It comes down to how much both parties want to stay married. I think that has to be fairly equal, even if their reasons are different, for it to work. One person wanting it isn't enough." She knew this not only from observation but her own two disastrous marriages, failures she rarely mentioned and wished she could forget. Deep down she'd known that she'd chosen badly, an irony that haunted her, like a doctor failing to diagnose his own illness. Or a hairdresser who arrived at the salon with her own hair uncombed.

"So those reasons could be about a person's career or something and not just about how much they love the other person," Kyra said.

"Yes." Nikki looked at the girl wondering whether it was her parents' apparently strained relationship on her mind, or one of her own. "I've seen horribly mismatched couples—not by me of course—stay together if the reasons were compelling enough, while others who appeared perfect for each other couldn't make it through the first disappointment."

"Do you ever advise people to split up or try to keep them together?"

Nicole laughed. "Fortunately, my business is introducing people who meet each other's criteria, not keeping them married. I'm a matchmaker, Kyra, not a marriage counselor." At least she was before Malcolm ripped that business out from underneath her.

This was met with silence and more staring out the window, but as she'd just pointed out, Nicole wasn't a therapist. Kyra and her mother belonged in the "not my problem" category. She already had far too many problems of her own.

Still, she was curious. When they'd first met, Madeline had seemed stretched to the breaking point and Nicole recognized a loneliness in Kyra that reminded her of her own.

With each passing mile, Nicole felt less and less monkey-like. The thought of spending the entire weekend in an interior-designed guest bedroom with its own plush private bath, waited on by a well-trained staff, had her foot pressing ever more firmly on the accelerator.

"Did you ever date a married man when you were young? Er, I mean younger?"

As if she couldn't date any married man she chose right

now. Nicole sighed. "I have," she said. "But not intentionally." She looked at Kyra. "It's a bad idea from every point
of view. Even if you're able to overlook the morality of the
question, those kinds of scenarios rarely end well for anyone."
She watched Kyra's face for a reaction but didn't get much.
"A cheater is a cheater is a cheater." She'd learned this during
marriage number one. "Any man who would cheat on his
wife with you would cheat on you with someone else."

"But what if he's only staying married for business reasons? Or because his wife's publicist says it's important for
her image?" The question was so earnest it almost hurt to
hear it.

"Kyra," she said. "I don't know who you're referring to,
and I'm not sure I want to know. But that's just bullshit. It
belongs in the same category as 'my wife doesn't understand
me,' 'we don't sleep together anymore,' and 'I've never done
anything like this before.'" She gave her a stern look, hoping
to help the message sink in. "And that's especially true in
Hollywood, where most marriages *are* business deals or based
on mutual convenience. People in the movie business often
confuse fact and fantasy. It's an occupational hazard."

"But he's not . . ."

"If I were your mother," Nicole continued, "and I'm sure
we're both glad I'm not, I'd tell you to forget about him, whoever he is, and move on. Chances are if he's out on the West
Coast and you're here, he's already done that."

"That's what my mom says." Kyra drooped in her seat.
"But haven't you ever listened to your heart instead of your
head?"

Nicole hesitated. "I have," she admitted reluctantly. "And
it didn't end well." Not with either of her husbands. And
certainly not with her brother, whom she'd loved so intensely
from the moment he was born. "Listen to your mother. She
loves you and she's trying to protect you. Which is exactly
what mothers are supposed to do."

That put an end to any confidences that might have been
coming Nicole's way.

They were in the outskirts of Palm Beach County now. Nikki had left just enough time for a manicure and pedicure before she had to be at Bitsy Baynard's; there was no way she could arrive with her hands and feet looking like she'd been working on a chain gang.

She pulled the Jag into the first strip center in West Palm with a nail salon; she didn't have the time or the money to be fussy. "I'm going to run into that nail place," she said to Kyra. "Why don't you have your friend pick you up here?"

Kyra followed her into the shop, her thumbs already flying over her phone keyboard. An older Asian woman led Nicole back to a well-worn spa chair and waited for her to remove her shoes. Nikki sighed with pleasure as she sank her bare feet into the warm bubbling water and set her hands where the technician could reach them. The place was nothing like the salons that lay just over the bridge in Palm Beach, but it had been a long, grueling month and Nikki was too tired to care. She closed her eyes, eager for some pampering.

"Shit!" Kyra said.

Nicole's eyes flew open. "What? What's wrong?"

"My friend got a call for a commercial shoot in Miami this morning and she's leaving within the hour. She says she's been trying to reach me."

"Now? But . . ."

"Yeah, I know," Kyra said.

"What wrong?" the manicurist asked. "You try relax."

Right. "Can't you go with her?" Nikki asked. "Or maybe stay at her place while she's gone?"

"No," Kyra said. "She's taking the place of an assistant camera operator who got sick and she doesn't know anyone on the shoot. And I can't stay at her place; apparently her roommate got all freaked out about having a complete stranger in the condo all weekend."

There was no time for making other arrangements or putting Kyra on a bus; she doubted Palm Beach possessed anything as pedestrian as a bus station, and she didn't have time to look for one here.

The manicurist removed the remnants of Nikki's polish and began to slough the dead skin from her feet, but Nicole's brain was racing down the possible courses of action.

"You'll just have to come with me to Bitsy's," Nikki said when nothing better presented itself. "After lunch we'll figure something out."

"Bitsy?" Kyra wrinkled her nose. "Really?"

"Really. And when you're worth the kind of money Bitsy is you can be called anything you want. Like Smuckers for rich people."

"Who is she?"

Nicole sank lower in her chair and tried to relax, but all she could think about was how to explain Kyra and how much more carefully she'd have to tiptoe around the truth once they got to Bitsy's.

"She's a former client of mine. One of the few who isn't embarrassed to admit I helped her find her husband."

Kyra nodded. "Out in L.A. people pay plastic surgeons tons of money for a service and then want to pretend it never happened."

"Exactly."

"That would make you the plastic surgeon of love. The Botox of boogie. The . . ."

The nail tech giggled.

"Kyra, please," Nikki said.

"Hmmm?"

"I'd really like to enjoy this experience in silence."

"Got it."

Now if only her freaked-out brain would get the message to slow down and shut up.

An hour later they'd passed Worth Avenue and were in a residential area where the gates and walls covered increasingly large acreage and you were lucky to catch a glimpse of a roof line off in the distance. Nicole looked Kyra over briefly, wondering if she should have taken the time for the girl to have a manicure, but it had seemed somewhat pointless since it was unlikely Kyra had anything approximating an appropriate ensemble stashed in the duffel bag she'd thrown in the trunk of the car.

"Listen," she said as she slowed the Jag. "There are a few things we should discuss."

Kyra turned to Nicole. The girl was lovely in a completely unaffected way, the recipient of enough natural gifts that she didn't need to put much effort into enhancing them. "You've worked in the movie business so I'm sure you understand that sometimes, actually many times, perception is more important than reality."

They were at Bitsy's gate now. Nicole hesitated briefly before punching the intercom button. "I'm going to introduce you as the daughter of a friend. I'm not planning to offer a lot of information."

Kyra's brow furrowed. "You're not going to tell anyone that you're spending the summer on St. Pete Beach working on the house because that's all that's left of what you had invested with Malcolm Dyer?"

Nicole was careful not to wince since she could no longer afford Botox or collagen injections to repair the resulting damage. "Not exactly."

Kyra didn't respond, but she did pull out her video camera as the curved wrought-iron gate opened inward.

"No." Nicole took the camera out of Kyra's hands and placed it back down in Kyra's lap. "That's not going to work."

Nicole drove forward onto the bricked drive and up a tree-lined allée. It took several minutes before the landscaping fell away and the house appeared.

"Wow," Kyra said as the full expanse of the stuccoed Mediterranean villa came into view. "It looks like Bella Flora on steroids."

The girl was right. Nikki was no expert on architectural styles or periods, but Bitsy Baynard's home had a lot of the same features: the towers jutting upward, the multi-angled red barrel-tile roof, the massive arched windows across the front, the balconies. Rounded concrete steps led up to a long columned arcade and a massive arched wooden door. The front courtyard radiated outward from a fountain that could have fronted a royal palace.

"I can see why you stopped for the manicure and pedicure," Kyra said. "This may be the first time in my life I wouldn't have minded owning something 'designer.'"

At the front door Nicole straightened Kyra's collar. "Stand up straight; posture's very important in these circles. In conversation, just follow my lead." She looked Kyra in the eye. "And try not to react if you hear me fudge a little."

"Got it," Kyra said, her eyes telegraphing her understanding, just before the door swung open.

And then they were standing in the magnificent foyer with its glazed marine blue tile floor and sweeping double staircase. A chandelier hung from the domed ceiling high above their heads, its dropped crystals shooting off sparks of reflected sunlight. Bitsy Baynard came toward them with a smile on her long face and both sinewy arms opened wide.

She kissed Nicole soundly on both cheeks. Bitsy Baynard was no air-or-ass kisser. Nor was she thrown by the appearance of an unexpected guest.

"Come on," she said after the introductions and explanations had been made. "We're out on the patio. But I have to warn you that Lisa Hanson's already on her second martini. You either need to hurry and catch up or brace yourselves." She led them through a central hallway twice as wide as the hallway in the house on Pass-a-Grille, with wide archways leading off to massive rooms on either side. An open-air loggia opened to a patio that overlooked a large invisible-edge pool and a beautifully manicured version of a tropical paradise that stretched on and out as far as the eye could see.

Two women sat at the wrought-iron table, a pitcher of martinis between them. One was Grace Lindell, also a former client of Nikki's. The other had to be the already tipsy Lisa Hanson.

"So tell me how the season was," Nicole said once she and Kyra had been seated and the introductions made. A servant appeared to take their drink orders and after a longing look at the martini pitcher, Nicole ordered a glass of white wine. Kyra asked for orange juice.

"Oh, God, it was dismal," Lisa whined, reaching for her glass. "All anyone could talk about was that damned Malcolm Dyer and how much money he stole. We aren't even going to summer in Tuscany this year; we've had to rent out the villa. Imagine!"

"Oh, how awful!" Nicole said, careful not to give vent to even the smallest drop of sarcasm. For a brief moment she imagined Lisa's face were Nicole to describe the magnitude of her own loss. Then she could work into what it felt like to sleep on a mattress on the floor, and just how much she was looking forward to spending the entire summer performing manual labor beside two other women she would probably never have spent more than thirty seconds with in her former life.

The chilled crab and avocado salads were served, but Lisa stuck with her martinis and Grace picked at her food tentatively as if unsure why she was eating. Nicole was too busy sifting through what she could and couldn't say to fully savor the food. Bitsy watched her guests and did her best to smooth things over. Only Kyra tucked into her food with gusto.

"Did you have money with him?" Nicole asked Bitsy, unable to even call her brother by name.

"A little." Bitsy took a sip of her martini. "Fortunately, Bertrand pulled out early on the advice of our investment manager. But a lot of people here weren't so lucky."

Grace's hand shook as she set her fork down. Very carefully, she folded them in her lap.

"How about you?" Bitsy asked Nicole.

Nicole stiffened for a brief moment. Beside her, Kyra did the same.

"I didn't escape unscathed," Nikki said truthfully. "But I'm still standing." For a moment the Gloria Gaynor lyrics popped, unbidden, into her head. She shoved them out.

"And what on earth are you doing in St. Petersburg?" On Lisa's lips the name of the city might have been "back of beyond."

Nicole put her own napkin down and faced Lisa Hanson with a light smile. "Actually Kyra's mother and another friend and I are getting a home ready to put up for sale there. It belonged to Dyer and was awarded to us as partial restitution after the civil suit was adjudicated."

Kyra jumped in then, bless her. "Who designed this house, Mrs. Baynard? The house in St. Pete is smaller but very similar in style—I think my mom's, um, other friend called it Mediterranean Revival?"

"It's an Addison Mizner," Bitsy said, clearly relieved by the change in topic. "It's actually what would probably be classified as a Palladian villa, but it has a very strong Mediterranean influence. We spent close to three years restoring it."

Nicole doubted Bitsy's role had been quite as hands on or "monkey-like" as Chase Hardin was demanding. But she filed the information away for the future. One thing she'd learned in the matchmaking business was that you never knew when an introduction or a piece of information might prove useful.

"I'll be glad to give you the grand tour, but Bertie's actually the one who spearheaded the whole undertaking. I'm thrilled with how it turned out, though. It's a wonderfully livable home. Mizner is pretty much revered here; he almost single-handedly created the whole look of Palm Beach back in the twenties."

They talked architecture for a time, which led to the horrible real estate market, and once again the misfortune of many Palm Beach residents. When Kyra finished her second helping and excused herself to go to the ladies' room, Nicole pushed her plate away and began to probe with more intent.

"Who else was impacted by Malcolm Dyer?" she asked. "Is anything being done about the losses?"

"Who wasn't?" Lisa asked. "Some were awarded assets in the civil suit against him, but others haven't gotten back a dime." Her eyes glittered. "A number of investment firms went under in the process. One or two are facing charges."

"Dyer made out like a bandit here," Lisa said. "He was so

damned charming. And it didn't hurt that he kept ponies at the polo club."

Nicole might have laughed if it hadn't all been so awful. As a child Malcolm had lobbied hard for a dog, when their mother could barely feed the three of them. He'd had a gold-fish once for a week before it had gone belly up and been flushed down the apartment's finicky toilet. The picture of him owning, let alone riding, a polo pony was a difficult one to conjure. But he'd taken his gentlemanly pursuits very seri-ously. Those social contacts had afforded him an impressive set of victims.

Grace looked up from her plate then. Her eyes were bleak. "Nathan and I were pretty hard hit," she said quietly. "But Nathan can make more money. We still have assets. I think I can live without a vacation." She didn't look at Lisa when she said this, but the censure was clear.

"But Dyer didn't just steal from people who could afford it." She swallowed before going on. "I invested every penny that I'd raised for my foundation—the one that sends chil-dren in foster care to college—with him. And every penny of it is gone. What kind of monster would steal from people who have nothing?"

Tears slid down Grace Lindell's cheeks to dampen her blouse and Nicole wished for just a moment that Malcolm were there to witness the damage he'd done. Stealing from the rich was bad enough; stealing from charitable founda-tions and those in need was unconscionable. But then Mal-colm appeared to have ditched his conscience along with his scruples some time ago.

That afternoon after she'd dropped a disappointed Kyra off at a rental car agency, Nicole sat in the chaise in a nook of the guest bedroom and took out her laptop to begin an Inter-net search of every victim's name she'd been able to winnow out of Grace and every email address she'd ever had for Mal-colm. But nothing was live; everything had been shut down.

So far, Palm Beach, like every other place she'd searched

for clues about Malcolm, had turned out to be one great big dead end. But for the first time as she remembered Grace's tears and allowed herself to think about all the people Malcolm had hurt, she began to acknowledge that Malcolm needed to be found and punished. In her own way, Nicole had been as selfish as her brother. This whole tragedy was absolutely not all about her.

Still, he was her little brother. She'd loved him since he was born and done her best to raise him. Now, the last thing she could do for him was get to him before the FBI did so that she could make him admit that he'd done wrong and return the money he'd stolen. Maybe if he did those things, and was genuinely repentant, the authorities would go lighter on him.

Nineteen

"It's Sunday," Maddie groaned. "I thought we were taking the weekend off."

"We are," Avery said, despite all evidence to the contrary.

"Then why are we doing this?" Madeline motioned with the wand of the pressure washer she'd been aiming at the wall of the garage, then attempted to wipe her forehead with the back of her hand. She was a sodden mess and Avery didn't look any better.

"Because we have so much to do and so little time to do it in." Avery turned off the nozzle of her wand and sank down on the lounge chair. "And because it's way too pretty out to work inside."

Avery was right about that. Bright blue skies, sparkling blue green water, golden sun, white sandy beach. Madeline felt as if she were in an advertisement for Florida living. And if she'd been forced to pick up that putty knife or so much as touch another pane of glass, she would have run screaming from the house and never come back.

"Too bad the pool hasn't been resealed and resurfaced yet." Madeline managed to swipe at her face with the back of her

free hand and looked down into the long, deep, empty rectangle. They were already wearing bathing suits under their
T-shirts. "We could be in it right now."

"Well, we do have the estimate from the pool guy. But
it could be another month before the work gets scheduled."

Madeline dropped down on the chair, letting the wand
clatter to the concrete. Grime and water coated her skin. She
was far too tired to go inside for the glass of iced tea she
wished she were sipping right now. Her exhaustion wasn't
just physical. Earlier this morning she'd managed to get
Steve on the phone and then spent thirty grueling minutes trying, unsuccessfully, to convince him to show up for
a counseling appointment she'd scheduled for him. Maddie
sighed and turned her gaze out over the water. It was a good
thing it wasn't sunset; she'd be hard-pressed to come up with
a good thing right now.

"Nicole was smart to bail out," Maddie said. "She's probably soaking in a Jacuzzi right now." Kyra had come back
late yesterday and her description of Bitsy Baynard's estate
still rankled. "Or floating in that invisible-edge pool with an
umbrella drink in her hand."

"No doubt," Avery said.

Madeline pushed away the images of Nicole in her vintage
designer clothing schmoozing with the socialites. "Well, at
least the folks there hate Malcolm Dyer as much as we do. It's
amazing how many people he managed to dupe."

"I'd like to meet that asshole's family and ask them how
they can live with themselves," Avery agreed. "But then they're
probably too busy enjoying themselves to worry about it."

"Well, I just hope I never meet any of them," Maddie
replied. "I've never thought of myself as a violent person, but
I don't think I could be held responsible for my actions."

She dropped her head back and concentrated on the
warmth of the sun on her face. She willed herself to relax.

"Hey, Mom!" Kyra's voice floated down to her from above.
"Phone!"

Madeline opened her eyes and saw Kyra leaning over the master bedroom balcony. "It's Andrew."

Madeline stifled a groan. Conversations with Steve were infrequent and futile. Conversations with Andrew, who was now back in Atlanta for the summer and most likely the fall, were frequent. And frustrating.

"I don't think we're finished here yet." She looked hopefully at Avery. "Are we?"

Avery shook her head.

"He says he needs to talk to you now." Kyra made her way down the curl of wrought-iron steps and handed Maddie the phone, plopping down beside her. Kyra wore a pair of Soffes and a tank top that clung to her slightly rounded stomach and barely contained her burgeoning bust. It wouldn't be long before her pregnancy became noticeable.

"Hi, sweetie," Maddie said. "What do you need?"

What her son needed, it turned out, was everything from her attention to some sort of vacation. He was both whiny and angry. At the moment he sounded about five years old.

"Slow down, Andrew," she said, trying to extract the important points from his litany of woe. "What exactly are you calling me for?" He'd barely been home from school for a week and she'd already lost track of the things he thought she should take care of from five hundred miles away. If remote laundry had been possible, she had no doubt he'd expect her to be doing a load right now.

"I want to go to the beach for a week with the guys. Everyone's chipping in on a condo in Destin."

"And what did your father say when you asked him?" she asked although the answer seemed obvious.

"He wouldn't even talk to me about it." Andrew's voice was tinged with both anger and amazement. "He told me to call you."

Maddie closed her eyes against the hurt in her son's voice. The demands and belligerence were far easier to deal with; she was no longer impressed or swayed by them. "We can't afford it, Andrew. Period. If the house down here gets finished by Labor Day and sold sometime in the fall, we can get back on our feet, but for now there is no money. We all have to hold on as best we can."

There was what could only be described as a sullen silence. And then, "What's wrong with Dad? He just lies on the couch all day."

Madeline felt the sting of tears and willed them away. "He's having a hard time dealing with what's happened. He feels responsible, and he doesn't seem to be able to move forward." Just talking about it dredged up that morning's conversation and reminded her how completely alone she felt without Steve to turn to.

"Can't you come home?" he asked in a voice she hadn't heard in years.

"No." This was the truth as far as it went. The part she kept to herself was that she was relieved that she couldn't. She just couldn't deal with one more thing. "At the moment this house is our best hope. And the more hands we have working on it, the faster we can put it on the market."

There was a silence on the other end of the line, and she pictured her son not as the strapping six-footer he'd become, but as the small sweet boy who'd worshipped his father and gone so out of his way to please.

"Look, Drew, your father's going to have to find a way back to himself. I've been trying to push and pull him there, but it doesn't work that way. I'd like him to get some professional help, but I can't even get him to admit he needs it." And, of course, they'd have to come up with the money to pay for it.

"Well, it's not up to me," he said. "I don't know what to do. I just want to go to the beach like everybody else."

Part of her wanted to tell him it would be okay, that she'd somehow find the money and that things would get better soon. But everything wasn't okay and this was not the time to coddle him. Her mother-in-law's love for Steve had always felt far too fervent to Maddie. After his father's death, Steve had become the center of his mother's universe; but worship didn't necessarily build backbone. Andrew was no longer a child and she needed his help.

She stood and walked with the phone to the edge of the seawall. Though she looked out over the Gulf and breathed in the warm salt air, in her mind she saw her son holding on to his childhood as tightly as he could. She shoved the image away.

"You're an adult now, Andrew, and your family needs you. You're going to oversee the repairs at Grandma's and when her house is ready, I want you to call our neighbor Mrs. Richmond and tell her we want to list the house for sale. I'll email you the details."

"No. I'm going to the beach," he said. "I want . . ."

"What we each want doesn't matter anymore," Maddie said. "Our family's in trouble and it's up to all of us to pitch in." She felt the pinprick of tears again and she shoved those away, too. Her hurt and anger blended into a potent cocktail; she wasn't prepared to play the Little Red Hen a moment longer. She had a family and they needed to step up to the plate. "What defines us isn't how we behave when things are good, Andrew, but how we respond when they aren't."

"Where'd you get that?" he sneered. "Off a frickin' fortune cookie?" Then he hung up on her, leaving her staring out over Shell Key with no idea of what he would or wouldn't do.

Maddie walked back to the pool deck and handed the phone to Kyra.

"Is everything okay at home?" Kyra asked.

Maddie looked at her daughter with her ripening body and her gray eyes clouded with uncertainty. How had everything changed so unexpectedly? She felt as if her family had been standing on a fault line all along and only discovered it when the earth began to tremble beneath their feet.

"No," Maddie said. "Of course not. But it's as okay as it's going to be for a while."

Kyra carried the phone back inside. Madeline and Avery forced themselves to their feet, turned on the pressure washer,

and took aim at the outbuilding. Madeline watched the grime
of close to a century wash down the stucco and soak into the
ground; too bad a life couldn't be pressure washed as easily.

They worked without speaking, and after a while Maddie
lost herself in the whoosh of the spray and the hum of the
machine's motor, going back to just a year ago when everything had seemed so promising, so normal.

"Oh, my God, Maddie. Stop!" Avery grabbed her hand
and tried to redirect it even as a small hole began to appear
in the wall. "The psi is too strong to hold it in one spot like
that."

There were short beeps of what turned out to be a boat
horn, and they whirled toward the sound, sending a spray of
soapy water arcing over the seawall toward the sleek black
boat floating beside it.

"Hey!" Chase Hardin shouted as the spray hit the water
beside him, shoving the boat away from the wall and kick-
ing a spray of seawater on Chase. Josh and Jason ducked. His
father laughed out loud.

"Oh!" Madeline didn't know how to turn off the wand.

Avery grabbed Maddie's arm and the spray hit Chase in
the shoulder before she could redirect it. Avery aimed her
wand at a patch of scrub grass beyond the house, which was
quickly blasted to smithereens.

Josh and Jason stayed down. Jeff Hardin was still smiling,
but he moved out of the line of fire.

"Hey, cut it out!" Chase yelled from the boat. "Turn it off!"

Avery aimed both wands out over the seawall but away
from the boat. Her gaze stayed on Chase, who sputtered and
glared back.

"I don't know," Avery said to Maddie. "I've been dying to
wash his mouth out with soap from the first day he started
calling me Vanna. But I guess we don't want to put a hole
in him like we did the garage." She threw Maddie a hopeful
glance. "Do we?"

"We do not," Maddie said. She took the wands and waited
for Avery to turn them and the pressure washer off.

They walked, still dripping, to the edge of the seawall. The boat idled a few feet out, its side coated with soap. Chase was wiping his face with a beach towel. His T-shirt was plastered to his body. "Good shot," he said dryly. "Thanks for the wash."

"Sorry," Avery said, though she didn't sound the least bit regretful. "My hand slipped."

"Right." He rubbed his hair and dropped the sopping towel on the deck while the boys tried to mask their laughter. He nosed the boat closer.

"We came to see if you ladies would like to go out for a ride," Jeff Hardin said. "We've got a picnic. We're going to anchor off the beach over at Fort De Soto."

"Oh." Avery turned to Maddie and gave her a small shake of the head. "No," she began just as Maddie said, "That sounds great."

Avery raised an eyebrow her way, but for once Maddie didn't care. It was a beautiful day and anything that might take her mind off of their predicament and the work still to be done was way too good to pass up. "Do you have room for all three of us?" Maddie asked. "Kyra's inside."

"Sure," Jeff Hardin said. "Why don't you get her and meet us over at the Cottage Inn dock? It'll be easier to board there."

Avery turned back to the Hardins. "Look, it's really nice of you to ask, but . . ."

"What?" Chase asked. "Is there something in the monkey handbook about fraternizing with the boss?"

"You are so not the boss." Avery's chin went up a notch.

Chase folded his arms across his chest.

Good grief. Maddie felt as if she were in the middle of a Rock Hudson/Doris Day movie. "Children, children," she said in her best "mother" voice. "It's way too beautiful a day to be acting out some fifties battle of the sexes film." She took Avery by the shoulders and turned her away from Chase. "Let me just get Kyra. We'll meet you there in five minutes."

Fifteen minutes later she sat next to Avery on the bow of

Hard Case, their backs braced against the exterior wall of the cabin, her knees pulled to her chest, her bare feet flat on the deck. Warm salt air skimmed over her, whipping her T-shirt around her, as the boat sliced through the water. Occasionally she closed her eyes just to draw the fabulous feeling even deeper inside her. "God, I hate to sound like a cliché," she said, "but this really is the life."

Avery nodded. Her bikini top clung to her ample bosom, her legs, short but shapely, were stretched out in front of her and crossed at the ankles. She'd pulled her hair up into a high ponytail, but curly strands had pulled free and were streaming behind her with the wind.

"The Hardins have always had a boat," she said, raising her voice just enough to be heard over the motor and the wind. "I used to love and hate going on it."

Maddie considered Avery's profile. The childlike freshness of her face belied the strength of her features and the determined set of her chin. When you added the curves and the bust and the short stature, it made it easy to dismiss that strength. She wondered how many men had made that mistake and how many ever even attempted to look beyond the pert good looks. Based on their roles on *Hammer and Nail,* her husband hadn't. And whoever produced the show certainly hadn't bothered to present the real Avery, who was so much more than she'd seemed on TV.

"I'm getting the love part." Maddie also raised her voice, knowing that nothing could be heard behind them. "I'd like to stay here and never go back to the real world. But why the hate?"

Avery tilted her head back and closed her eyes, and Maddie wasn't sure she was going to answer.

"Did something happen between your families?"

"I think it was just the jealousy, you know?" Avery hesitated again, but Maddie waited her out.

"They seemed so complete. And my dad and I were so . . . not. I mean we loved each other and were always there for each other, you know." She opened her eyes and turned to face

Maddie. "I miss him like crazy. But I don't think either of us ever really got over being abandoned. There was always this gaping hole that we didn't know how to fill."

"Your parents were divorced?"

"Oh, yeah." Avery nodded, but turned her gaze back to the waterfront mansions that flew by, each with its yacht moored behind it. "Deirdre left when I was thirteen. Just decided she didn't want to be a wife or a mother. I guess re-covering celebrity sofas was a nobler calling." Her face was still as stone in stark contrast to her hair, which flew around it like snakes. "You know what I remember most about her leaving?"

Maddie waited.

"I got my period for the first time two days after she left. And I had to ask my dad to go to the store to get me sanitary napkins." A sad smile played at the corner of her lips. "It was so pathetic. I can't think about it to this day without picturing him in the drugstore trying to figure out what kind to buy." All these years later and Avery's voice was still thick with pain.

"Do you see her?"

"Not if I can help it." Avery wrapped her arms around herself even though the wind that blew over them was warm as a caress. "Not that she ever beat my door down or anything. We went years without a word from her. And then her work started showing up in magazines and she was the go-to designer to the stars. Every once in a while she shows up and doesn't understand why we can't start over." She drew her knees up to her chest and opened her arms to include them.

The boat slowed for a no-wake zone, and they passed Tierra Verde's sprawling condos and headed directly toward the Skyway Bridge. Maddie sat up and turned to get a glimpse of Kyra, who sat next to Jeff Hardin, her head fallen back, a small smile on her lips. No one could love you or hurt you more than your mother. And Kyra was about to tackle that trickiest of jobs on her own.

"Did she ever tell you why?" Maddie asked, turning back.

"I don't care why," Avery replied. "You can't just walk

away from your own flesh and blood and then reappear and ask for a do-over. It doesn't work that way."

They rode in silence for a time, moving into the intra-coastal waterway, the sun and water and steady roar of the boat's powerful engine as soothing as a deep-tissue massage.

Then they were picking up speed again and running along the massive bridge. They passed a large island teeming with birds and the boat made a right and slowed slightly. Jet Skis skimmed by, buzzing around the larger boats like insects around livestock.

"There's the fort!" one of the boys shouted as a long sliver of white beach appeared on their left, the ruins of a fort still standing off at one end.

The boat slowed and turned toward the beach.

"Let's pull in over there, Dad!" Jason said.

"Here, you take us in," Chase said, cutting their speed a notch further as his oldest stepped behind the wheel and rested a hand on the throttle.

Josh opened a rear compartment and pulled out a coil of rope with an anchor tied to its end. Jason slowed the boat further until they were putting slowly toward an empty stretch of beach dotted with stands of palm trees. There wasn't another human being in sight.

Chase stood between his sons watching, but not intruding, as Jason maneuvered in and aimed directly for the beach. The boat slowed further.

"It's deep enough right off the beach to pull up onto the sand," Chase explained from the other side of the windshield. Josh joined them on the bow, quickly tying the anchor line to a cleat.

At Chase's nod, Jason pulled all the way back on the throttle and cut the motor. A few moments later the bow slid up onto the beach so smoothly Maddie was surprised when the boat stopped. Josh clambered off and set the anchor up on the beach.

"Good job," Chase said as he clapped Jason on the back, then climbed up on the bow and gave a hard tug on the anchor line. "Just right, Josh."

His sons beamed at the praise while their grandfather added his own nod of approval. No "but" followed, no suggestion on how it might have been done better, how performance might be improved next time. Maddie liked that and found herself offering Chase and his father her own nod of approval as they handed her and then Kyra down with some ceremony. Avery insisted on disembarking herself and the Hardins made no comment. Jason and Chase brought up the rear, carrying blankets and a cooler.

"I feel like we're on our own desert island," Kyra said as she pulled off her T-shirt and stretched out on one end of a blanket. A tiny pouch rose above the top of her neon green bikini bottom and the tiny top rode her burgeoning breasts like triangular band aids. "I think I'm going to catch a little nap."

Maddie and Avery sank down nearby and Jeff handed around cold drinks. Idly they watched the Hardins pass around a football, then ate sandwiches from the cooler and topped them off with chips and bakery cookies. Chase offered to show them around the old fort, but Kyra was fast asleep and neither Maddie nor Avery could make themselves move.

Maddie felt the band of control she'd been holding on to for the last months loosen slightly. As the warm breeze played over her skin and the wash of waves on sand mingled with the distant buzz of boat motors, her own eyes fluttered shut and she drowsed for a time, surprisingly content.

She might have gone on this way all afternoon if Chase hadn't suggested they build a sand castle. And Avery hadn't suggested they choose up sides and turn it into a competition. And Kyra hadn't roused just in time to retrieve her video camera from the boat so that she could document what turned into the Sand Castle Edition of *Survivor*.

Twenty

Avery was smiling when they pulled up to the Cottage Inn dock at the end of the day. According to self-appointed judge and mediator Jeff Hardin, the Beach Bellas, as she and Maddie and Kyra had called themselves, had dominated the sand building competition with their version of Bella Flora. The only disappointment had been the inability to vote Chase off the island; a move that would have left her satisfied but stranded.

She'd savored her victory all the way back, glad for once that Kyra had had her video camera there to document their superior design. But mostly she'd enjoyed building the hard-packed castle walls and the memories that evoked of her father.

"Thanks," she said as she climbed off the bow and onto the dock. The sun had already set and the brilliant sky faded to pale gray as dusk hunkered down over the water. "That was fun." She resisted a last dig on Chase's loss as she reached a hand down to help Madeline and Kyra off the boat.

"Thanks again. Drive carefully," Madeline called as Chase

backed *Hard Case* away from the dock and then turned the boat for the ride back to Tampa.

"Gosh, I feel so . . . relaxed," Avery said. *And victorious.* "I kind of forgot what that felt like."

"Me, too," said Madeline. "I can't wait to take a shower and get the salt off, but I feel pleasantly tired." She shot Avery a look. "Which is completely different from physically exhausted."

Kyra smiled her agreement and repositioned her video camera bag. "That was the fiercest sand castle building competition I've ever seen," she said.

"Chase Hardin needed humbling," Avery said without a trace of regret. "And I'm glad we were the ones to do it." She smiled.

"You don't think that last victory lap around the fort was just a tad unsportsmanlike?" Madeline asked.

No, Avery did not.

They passed the Cottage Inn and their own castle came into view. "Hey," Avery said, pointing to a midsized sedan in the driveway. "That's not Nikki's car."

"No, and I don't think she's coming back until tomorrow morning anyway." Avery peered at the vehicle, but all she could tell was that the license plate wasn't local.

They huddled together in the gathering dusk. "Did we leave those lights on?" Avery asked.

"I don't think so," Madeline said.

A shadow passed in front of an upstairs window and then a light flipped on in the hallway. Madeline pulled out her cell phone. Kyra took out her camera.

"Should we call the police?" Maddie asked.

"I don't know," Avery said. "It's not exactly the dead of night and whoever's in there doesn't seem to be sneaking around. I mean they left their car right there in the driveway."

"I'd say it's one of the subs who decided to get some work done," Kyra said. "Except that car doesn't look like it belongs to a workman."

"Well, we can't stand out here cowering all evening. I'm going in." Avery took a step forward.

"Me, too," Madeline said. "But I've got nine-one-one on speed dial and I'll have my finger on the Send button."

Avery turned to look at her.

"It never hurts to be prepared. I'm not interested in being a headline in the local paper. I can just see it now—'Women Taken in Dyer Ponzi Scheme Murdered!'" Maddie shook her head. "There's no point in taking chances."

"Okay, troops," Avery said. "Let's go in the back. At least we'll have the element of surprise."

They moved forward quietly, Avery in the lead. As they snaked toward the detached garage, she picked up a two-by-four from a pile. Maddie raised her phone in front of her, her finger poised. Kyra flipped her camera on and held it at the ready.

"What are you planning to do, film them to death?" Avery asked.

Kyra shrugged. "You have your weapons of choice, I have mine."

They inched up to the kitchen door and Avery opened it, freezing at the resulting creak. When no one came pounding down the stairs brandishing a weapon, they went into the kitchen leaving the door open behind them.

"In case we need to make a speedy exit," Maddie whispered before reaching into a drawer to retrieve their lone sharp knife.

"I'll take the front stairs," Avery said. "You two take the back."

There was the creak of floor above them and a cell phone rang. They froze and reached for their phones, but it was coming from upstairs, the melody loud in the quiet of the house.

"That is *not* a ringtone of Ethel Merman singing 'There's No Business Like Show Business,'" Maddie whispered. "Is it?"

Avery shrugged, and then like a Special Forces person on television, she executed a series of hand motions meant to signal them to the back stair and herself to the front. The Singers rolled their eyes at her.

As she crept silently up the front stair, trying to avoid the known squeaks, a vaguely familiar scent tickled Avery's nose, trumping the smells of sawdust and cleaning products. She sniffed the heavy floral scent for a moment, not quite able to place it, then drew a steadying breath before climbing the rest of the way up to the second-floor landing, reaching it at just about the same time as Maddie and Kyra.

A sliver of light spilled into the hallway from the master bedroom. There was a murmur of a female voice and the occasional quick click of heels on wood. Avery inched forward and pushed the bedroom door open another crack. A mound of expensive luggage sat in the middle of the bedroom floor and an even more expensive briefcase leaned against one wall.

"Great," Maddie said, still brandishing her weapons. "Maybe someone got their hotel reservations wrong. Do you think they thought they were checking into the Don CeSar?"

Avery looked up at the ceiling and the large amoeba-like stain around the hole that had been patched. The moldy green shag carpet and most of its bad smell were gone, but the long-neglected wood floor underneath was in desperate need of attention. "Not unless they're blind and have lost their sense of smell," she said. "And I don't think there are too many homeless people with a matched set of Louis Vuitton luggage."

The click of heels drew closer and they all turned to the double doorway that led to the dressing room and master bath. Kyra raised her camera to her eye. Maddie held the knife and phone out in front of her. Despite the signs that they were not dealing with a violent intruder, her hands trembled slightly.

Feeling incredibly stupid, Avery raised the two-by-four up over her head. Just in case.

The doors flew open and the familiar smell snapped into place in her memory. A beautifully dressed and perfectly coiffed woman posed in the opening. "Darling," the woman said with a look of delight. "Trent told me what was happening, and I thought you might need my services. And now I can see that you do."

She walked forward sort of like Lauren Bacall or Bette Davis in one of those old glamorous black-and-white movies—moving shoulders and lots of hip sway.

"I hope you don't mind that I put my things in the master. It looked unoccupied." Her smile dimmed but only slightly. "But, of course, that was before I realized that the bathroom wasn't functional. And, of course, there is no bed."

Avery couldn't think of a thing to say. Slowly she lowered the piece of wood still clutched in her hand.

Kyra kept filming. She actually moved to get a wider angle of the three of them. Maddie lowered the knife and her phone, but she still looked uncertain.

"Aren't you going to introduce me, darling?"

Avery gritted her teeth. A burglar would have been preferable. As far as she was concerned even Norman Bates from the Bates Motel would have been more welcome. It already required all of her self-control to work with Chase Hardin. Throwing Deirdre into the mix was cruel and unusual punishment.

"Deirdre, this is Madeline Singer, one of my partners in the house, and her daughter, Kyra." Avery clenched her jaw in an effort to prevent all of the things that threatened to slip out as recognition dawned on their faces. "Maddie, this is Deirdre Morgan, well-known interior designer to the stars."

It was hard to believe that there were degrees of comfort when sleeping on the floor, but there were. After drinking half of their remaining bottle of red wine with her nose scrunched up so as not to actually taste it, Deirdre had passed on Maddie's offer of a blow-up bed and commandeered Avery's mattress instead along with what felt like most of the air in Avery's room.

Avery had spent the entire night trying to find a comfortable position on the twin-sized air mattress and failing miserably; she was small and didn't hang over the sides, but she was not a child. So she'd lain in the room like the slave who waited on the queen, listening to her mother's breathing while trying to figure out why Deirdre was there and how to best get rid of her. She didn't fall asleep until just before sunrise.

It was ten A.M. before she stumbled into the bathroom to splash water on her face and hurriedly brush her teeth. Male voices floated up from outside; the female voices rose from downstairs. She followed the latter into the kitchen and found Deirdre at the head of the kitchen table apparently holding court. Maddie, Kyra, Chase, and Nicole sat in a semi-circle around her.

"Ah, there she is," Deirdre cooed when Avery stepped into the kitchen. "My, you're a sleepyhead."

Avery stopped where she was. Deirdre was impeccably dressed and fully made-up as if she and not Nicole had just returned from a pampered weekend in Palm Beach. "Sleepyhead? Try, mercifully glad to have finally fallen asleep at all. It was bad enough having to give up my mattress, but the snoring? Oh, my God! It was like trying to sleep on train tracks."

Deirdre laughed, a beautiful tinkly laugh, which Kyra captured on video. "I'm so sorry to have usurped your mattress, Avery. But I do not snore. I'll get a bed delivered as soon as possible." She sounded like the Queen of frickin' England.

Avery poured a cup of coffee, using the time to tamp down her panic and irritation, and took the only empty seat next to Chase. The others looked surprised at Deirdre's apparent intention to move in, but no one voiced the slightest opposition.

Kyra lowered her video camera. "Your mother knows people who know people in Hollywood." Her voice hummed with an odd sort of excitement. "Apparently Daniel Deranian's wife, Tonja Kay, is moving into a house of her own. Without Daniel."

Maddie shot her daughter a worried look, but Kyra just lifted the camera back to her eye and smiled happily. It was the most animated Avery had seen her.

"Your mother did a walk-through a little while ago, and

she has some really great ideas for the house," Maddie said, shooting Avery a silent look of apology. The rest of them were smiling and nodding at Deirdre. Much like Avery used to do on *Hammer and Nail*.

Avery paused with the cup midway to her lips. "Really." It was not a question.

"Yes," Deirdre answered. "The bones of this house are just magnificent. Chase says much of what it needs at this point is cosmetic rather than structural and, well, that *is* my area of expertise." She smiled as if that was that and that explained everything.

"But we don't know why you would want to be involved in this . . . project," Avery replied. "I don't remember anyone here placing a call to you asking for your help. And as I do remember, you couldn't wait to get out of Florida. You couldn't shake the sand off your shoes fast enough." Ditto for her husband and child.

Chase was looking at her now; everyone else was watching Deirdre.

"Seriously," Avery asked. "What are you doing here?"

"Why, I came to help. To help you." Her voice shook and her eyes glistened. She actually looked like a mother might look. But then, she'd been in Hollywood for a very long time. They stared at each other while everyone else looked on.

"Your mother could bring a lot to this project," Chase said.

"Don't call her that."

"We could never afford the services of a topflight designer," he continued. "And to make this house attractive to the right kind of buyer, we're going to need more than just a physical renovation."

"He's right," Nicole said. "We're not in a position to turn down manna from heaven."

"She is not manna. And she is definitely not from heaven," Avery said, hating how betrayed she felt.

There was a small flare of something in Deirdre's eyes. Dare she hope it was hurt? But then Deirdre smiled and that smile was triumphant.

Avery gave her the eyebrow. And got one in return.

"Sorry," Maddie said, stifling a laugh, "but it's amazing how alike you two look. Very Marilyn Monroe—esque."

Deirdre smiled more openly. Chase laughed.

In the silence that followed, Deirdre stood and stepped away from the table. "I think it would be best to let the principals discuss my fate in private. I'm happy to help you get the house ready to show. I have contacts in the design community, and I suspect if I put my mind to it, I could provide the finishes and furnishings for this home on a level few could match. And for somewhere under wholesale."

Avery remained silent, but she could feel the others' interest.

"Why don't I step out for a few minutes so you can talk privately? Kyra, let's go take another look at the bar. I just love the Moorish touches; it has such a wonderful feel."

They filed out of the kitchen and Avery waited for Chase to leave, too. She aimed the eyebrow at him.

"What?" he asked.

"Don't you think you should step out, too?" Avery asked.

"I'm a partner now, Avery. And I'm definitely planning to vote on this. It's a no-brainer."

"As if you could make any other sort of decision."

This time it was Nicole who laughed. But Avery could tell their minds were made up. Oh, Deirdre had been sneaky with her little sales pitch and her "I'm connected in the design community" bullshit. Of course she was connected. She'd always put her work first.

"All right," Maddie said. "Let's go ahead and get this over with."

"Yes," Chase said. "Let's."

"All in favor," Nicole finished, "of having Deirdre join us to handle the design work say 'aye.'"

The three of them looked right at her as they voted in favor. Only Maddie appeared apologetic.

"All opposed."

Avery raised her hand, then lowered it. "Believe me when I tell you that Deirdre has some sort of ulterior motive," Avery said. "She may act like she's doing us a favor, that somehow we're going to get all of her . . . services for free. But we'll pay in some unpleasant way. Don't be fooled by the whole mother act. She doesn't have the experience or the instincts for it."

Posted to YouTube, 11:00 P.M., June 4

Audio: "Dueling Banjos."

Video: Castle building contest, quick cuts. Close-ups Avery and Chase arguing.

Audio: "There are a couple of type A personalities here at Camp Bella Flora and even a day off can be a little extreme. But there've been some laughs, too. Hardly any of them intentional."

Video: Mom spraying hole in garage, out-of-control pressure-washing wand aimed at boat. Mom and Avery tiptoeing in to find intruder. The morning bathroom lineup. Master bathroom chrome removal.

Audio: "The celebrity cast on this little reality show of ours keeps growing. Now on top of dating guru Nicole Grant and TV host Avery Lawford, we have Deirdre Morgan, who turns out to be Avery's mother."

Video: Deirdre and Avery glaring at each other.

Audio: "And we've got our resident hunk, Chase Hardin, too. He's not a celebrity. He just looks like one."

Video: Shots of Chase working, no shirt. Wide shot Bella Flora.

Audio: "So maybe the odds of success are increasing a little. I'm not sure. Keep those bets and posts coming. I'll let you know what happens."

Twenty-one

Maddie positioned the neon-strapped beach chairs, which now totaled five, in a semicircle around the low wicker table that she'd found at a garage sale last week and tried not to see the bargain basement furniture through Deirdre Morgan's eyes.

The designer was in the kitchen with Nicole, preparing the sunset snack. Chase was still sawing away over in the garage while Avery, who did her best to stay as far away from both of them as possible, had headed down the beach for a walk as soon as they'd knocked off for the day. Last time she'd checked, Kyra was upstairs fiddling with her video equipment.

"Come on, you all!" Maddie called. "You're going to miss the show!"

A few minutes later Nicole backed out of the kitchen door carrying a tray with a bottle of white wine and glasses. Deirdre followed with a tray of artfully arranged canapés and . . . Maddie did a double take. "That's not actually caviar, is it?"

Nicole smiled. "It so is."

Kyra came out with a tall glass of juice and her video

camera. They'd settled into their seats and poured glasses of wine by the time Avery came up from the beach. She made a face when she saw the small bowls of condiments and the fancy cocktail napkins beside them, but continued on into the kitchen without comment, coming back with a warehouse-sized bag of Cheez Doodles.

They ate and drank and watched the sun slip lower in the sky while Deirdre entertained them with stories about some of the celebrities she'd worked with. Every time Kyra asked a question Maddie caught her breath, afraid that the next name she was going to hear was Daniel Deranian's.

She knew that it wouldn't be long before Kyra's pregnancy became obvious, but there was still that small, irrational part of her that wanted to believe if they just didn't talk about it, the problem would somehow cease to exist. She frowned as she realized how closely this resembled Steve's abdication; there was no real safety dwelling in the land of denial.

Everyone fell silent as the sun brightened and glowed before beginning its slide toward the water. The whine of the saw ceased and Chase came out of the garage, mopping his face with his T-shirt. Muscles rippled beneath his darkly tanned skin; his abs could have been cut from steel. Only Avery kept her gaze on the Gulf as he walked toward them. Until his hand snaked down into her bag of Cheez Doodles.

"Hey!" she said.

"Mind if I join you?" He popped the Cheez Doodle into his mouth and munched contentedly.

"Of course not," Maddie said before Avery could object. "There's a six-pack in the fridge. I'm pretty sure it's got your name on it."

"Thanks." He reached down into Avery's bag of Cheez Doodles again and snagged a whole handful before heading inside.

"*These* don't have your name on them," she called after him, closing the bag against further encroachment. "Did you really have to invite him, Maddie?" she asked. "Between the caviar and the crowd, it's turning into a damned cocktail party. I'd rather have one of Nikki's frozen drinks."

"My, someone's grumpy this evening." Deirdre sipped her wine and reached for another canapé.

Avery tensed. Maddie put a hand on her arm to hold her back. "It's just one sunset. We have a whole summerful ahead of us."

Avery sniffed. "If he even looks like he's getting ready to call me Vanna, he's going to be wearing this bag of Doodles."

"He called you Vanna?" Deirdre smiled. "Really?"

Avery's hands tightened on the Cheez Doodle bag, making it crackle. "You know, you never said how you happened to have your summer free to join us."

Deirdre turned from the view to face her daughter. "Trent told me what was going on and I made the time because I thought you might need my help."

"Next time call me first so I can tell you no."

Chase came out with his beer and a kitchen chair. Deirdre scooted over to make room for him.

Maddie wasn't sure how much Avery enjoyed the rest of the sunset; she seemed to be fuming through most of it. When the sun had completed its disappearing act, Maddie raised her glass. After explaining their "one good thing" tradition to Deirdre and Chase, she said, "I'm grateful that I didn't break a single pane of glass today." Maddie took a small sip. "Of course, it figures I'm finally getting the hang of glazing now that the end is in sight."

"I'm grateful for tonight's caviar," Nicole said. "I'd almost forgotten how much I like it."

Maddie noticed that Kyra had her camera out and was, once again, recording them.

"Well, I'm grateful for Cheez Doodles," Avery said belligerently. "Because a life without Cheez Doodles is hardly worth living. Caviar is only fish eggs with a fancy name."

They looked at Deirdre, who hesitated slightly before saying, "I'm grateful to have this chance to be with my daughter and to work on Bella Flora. I'd gotten kind of tired of all the glitz."

Avery snorted but remained silent, and Maddie found herself wondering how both of their mother-daughter scenarios would play out over the summer. Physical togetherness was one thing; the emotional kind could be so much more elusive. Everyone turned to Chase.

"Do I get to play?"

"It's not a game," Avery said. "And no, I don't think you deserve . . ."

"I'm grateful that I'm only a bit player in the YouTube videos about the renovation someone's been posting, because they aren't the most flattering things I've ever seen," he said before she could finish.

Avery's mouth snapped shut. Kyra went very still, her camera blocking the expression on her face.

There was a long silence and it wasn't the reverent kind that sometimes fell as they watched a spectacular sunset.

"What did you say?" Nicole looked up from the toast point piled with caviar that had been on its way to her mouth.

Madeline's hand went to her hair, which she rarely bothered with anymore. She didn't have to look down to know just how bedraggled she probably appeared.

Chase's lips tilted upward. "I said someone's been posting videos to YouTube. Along with a pretty scathing commentary. The boys showed them to me. There've been two so far." He finished off his beer and tilted it toward Kyra. "I guess we should all be grateful that we've only gotten about ten thousand views. So far."

Avery arranged the master bath fixtures in a cardboard box and carefully listed the contents, then handed the pair of curved legs that had supported the sink toward Nicole. "Do you mind driving? I think your car will make a better impression than mine where we're headed."

"Okay." Nicole slung her purse over one shoulder and

cradled the sink supports in her arms. "Where exactly are we going?"

Avery cut her gaze toward Chase, who was huddled with the carpenter he'd brought in to replace the missing balusters for the front stairs. "I'd rather not say right now."

Nicole shrugged. They'd made it to the open front door and were about to slip outside when Deirdre's voice reached them from the landing. "Whom can I ask to help set up the furniture I'm having delivered today? I've organized a few pieces for the master bedroom, so that I can give you your mattress and your privacy back. I mean it's bad enough with all of us in the one bathroom."

Robby, who had poked his head out of the downstairs guest bath, retracted it much like a turtle might pull back into its shell. Chase and the carpenter looked up.

Damn. Her escape thwarted, Avery turned to face her mother. "If you're not happy with the accommodations, please feel free to check into a motel. Cottage Inn is next door. The Don is just down the road. A hotel in another city would be even better."

"Now, darling, you know I'm committed to helping you here. And I know we don't want to put in too much furniture before the upstairs floors are refinished, but there's no reason for us to double up if we don't have to." As always, Deirdre managed to make whatever she wanted sound as if it benefitted others.

"Nicole and I will be gone for most of the morning. Maddie and Kyra have an appointment. I believe Chase has to check in on another job. Unless you're planning to wander down the road looking for random muscle, that leaves you."

Deirdre's eyes widened in surprise.

"There are no supervisory positions available on this job, Deirdre. No opening for 'queen.' We're all worker bees." She was aware of Chase and the carpenter's attention shifting to the conversation. "Or as Chase prefers to put it, 'monkeys.' You wanted in on this project and you're in. Maybe you can get Chase or Robby to hang around until the furniture arrives given your advanced age and all." She let that one sink in. "Or you can do it yourself. My concern is having this house ready and on the market by Labor Day, not where or how you sleep. Or how much you might have to shlep."

Something she didn't recognize flashed across Deirdre's face before she turned and went back into the bedroom. If it had been anyone but Deirdre, Avery would have apologized. Her feelings simmered so close to the surface lately that she sometimes erupted without warning, a Mount Vesuvius of pent-up emotion.

Right now, she just wanted to get out of here before Chase noticed the box of chrome or the sink supports in Nicole's arms.

"I wondered who had stripped the chrome out of the master bath," he said before they'd made their dash to freedom. "Where in the world are you taking them?" He asked this as if she'd removed them for the hell of it and was even now planning to do something stupid with them.

She didn't want to tell him what she had in mind because he was bound to give her a hard time or laugh at her or both—responses guaranteed to set her tectonic plates in motion. "That's for me to know and for you to find out," she blurted. The only thing missing from the childish response was the singsong "nah-nah-nah-nah-nah." Never had an open doorway seemed so close and yet so far.

"The last time you said that to me you were what, ten?" Chase came closer. Presumably so that he could tower over her.

"Look," she said, reining in the automatic retort that sprang to her lips, "I've found a place I think can handle the re-chroming and I'm taking a sample there. End of discussion." She tried, once again, to clamp down on her automatic urge to argue with him, but the need to wipe the dismissive look off of his face won out. "Is there something in the contractor's handbook that says the contractor is the only one allowed to have a thought or idea?"

His eyes began to narrow. This, she now knew, precipitated increasingly terse replies.

"You know, if you toned down the sarcasm just a little, we might actually make it through a conversation without fighting." His words were clipped and angry. Some might call them terse.

"And if you didn't question every little suggestion I made and treat me like a complete imbecile in the process, sarcasm wouldn't be required," she said.

They were staring at each other in frustrated silence when Kyra came down the stairs, her video camera aimed right at them.

"Shit," Nicole said. "I'll be in the car." She took the box from Avery and balanced the chrome legs on top of it. "I can't be on YouTube right now. My lipstick's all worn off."

"Kyra, do you have to point that camera at Chase and me every time we disagree?" Avery asked, trying to hold on to her temper.

"Sorry. But it's kind of hard to find a time when you're not doing that."

"She has a point," Chase said.

"Besides, I'm just documenting the process like you all asked me to," Kyra said. "I think the exposure could help when it comes time to put Bella Flora on the market."

"All we were really looking for were before and after shots, Kyra," Avery said. "I seriously doubt our target buyer is checking out real estate on YouTube."

"Everybody watches YouTube," Kyra said.

"Well, everybody doesn't need to be yucking it up at our expense. If you're planning to keep posting, you need to drop the snarky commentary and make it a little bit more about the house and a lot less about us," Avery said. "And you," she said to Chase. "I'll let you know how the re-chroming goes."

Satisfied, she walked out through the open front door before either of them could respond. She hadn't exactly asked and he hadn't really yelled. Perhaps, Avery thought as she retrieved her portable GPS and slid into the passenger seat of Nicole's Jag, that was progress of some kind.

"I can't believe she put us on YouTube without telling us." Nikki had wound a white scarf around her auburn hair and put on an oversized pair of designer sunglasses. In the classic convertible, she might have been an old-time Hollywood starlet. "I look like shit on those videos. Inept and sweat-soaked are not the images I'm looking to project."

"No kidding." Avery sank lower in the leather seat. "I'm not exactly wild about appearing without a hair and makeup person. And frankly I've had enough of looking like a fool in front of a national audience to last a lifetime."

"Can't argue with that," Nikki said as they headed off the beach. And then, "Speaking of arguing, what's going on with you and your mother?"

"Nothing," Avery said. "And that's the way I'd like to keep it."

"You're not planning to accept her apology?" Nicole asked. The ends of the white scarf streamed behind her adding yet another whiff of glamour. As if she needed one.

"I haven't heard an apology," Avery said. "I've heard an offer to decorate. Those are not the same things."

They rode in silence for a while traveling farther inland. Retail stores and restaurants multiplied, then grew sparse again as they moved into a more industrial area. The air remained warm but was no longer salt-tinged.

"Hardly anyone gets through life without being hurt or hurting others," Nicole said, driving past a storage facility and several commercial warehouses. The Jag jounced over a railroad track.

"Yes, well, that's easy to say when you've lived the charmed life you have—running around fixing up famous rich people." Avery was on a rant now, not even pausing to let Nicole respond. "When I hear an 'I'm sorry I abandoned you and ignored you for over a decade' from Deirdre followed by an explanation that doesn't reek of total selfishness, I'll decide whether the apology should be accepted." Avery didn't want to think about how long she'd hoped for this very thing or how long ago she'd given up on it. "Maybe Hallmark will come up with a card to that effect and she can slip it under my bedroom door."

They drove in silence for a time. At the GPS's insistence, Nicole pulled into the parking lot of a former filling station. Several vintage cars sat behind a chain-link fence, but the doors to the service bay and office stood open. A rusty metal sign proclaimed that they had arrived at Alfred's Auto Body Shop. Beneath it were scrawled the words Home of the King of Chrome.

Nikki turned off the engine and contemplated the sign. "What are we doing here?"

"I hope we're going to get the bathroom fixtures re-chromed."

"Does Alfred know that?"

"Not exactly," Avery conceded as they climbed out of the Jag.

Nicole removed the scarf and dropped it in the driver's seat. "Do they even do that here?"

"I'm not sure," Avery replied. "But I don't know why they *couldn't.*"

They looked up and saw a tall gangly man with pale white skin and the name Alfred stitched across the pocket of his splotched work shirt. A shock of faded red hair fell over one eye, and he tugged at the waistband of his ancient work pants, which hung so low on his nonexistent hips that Avery couldn't help wondering how they stayed up.

The stark metallic smell of chemicals preceded him as he sauntered closer. "Nice ride," he said with admiration. "Don't see too many of those around here. It's a V12 '74 XKE, isn't it?"

"You've got a good eye." Nicole smiled at him. "And my friend and I here are hoping you have the right equipment."

"Oh, Lord, I hope so," he said fervently, and Avery knew she'd been right to ask Nikki to accompany her. "Car looks in mighty fine shape. Love that butterscotch interior. And if you don't mind my sayin' so, so do you two." His look turned quizzical. "You sure you're in the right place?"

Avery retrieved the two legs and the box of fixtures from the Jag's trunk and carried them to Alfred. "We hope so."

He stared down into the box, then reached in and pulled out a handle. "But this is bathroom stuff." He considered the multi-spoked knob before placing it back with the other parts. "I restore cars."

"But it's chrome," Avery pointed out helpfully. "Good vintage chrome. From a really cool house built in the 1920s. It should be the same process as dipping rims and bumpers, shouldn't it?"

"Well . . ." Alfred looked unconvinced. Apparently bathroom faucets didn't float his boat in quite the same way as classic car rims.

"Maybe you could show us your operation." Nicole stepped forward and linked Alfred's bony, freckled arm through hers. Avery admired the fact that she didn't wince or react to the chemical cologne that wafted off of him.

Nikki pointed at the sign that stretched over the entrance. "I'm sure the King of Chrome should be able to handle something a little out of the ordinary."

Avery followed them into the office and then into the old service station where Alfred's cologne had originated. Even though the big bay door was wide open, she still had to swallow carefully and keep her breathing shallow. Setting the cardboard box down on a workbench, she and Nicole toured the various-sized vats of solution and listened intently as the king described the stripping, dipping, and buffing process. Nikki subtly stroked his vanity while Avery asked the technical questions. When she was satisfied that he could and would re-chrome the fixtures she asked for an estimate and was careful not to blink when he named the small fortune he would charge them. Nor did she react to the fact that it could be several weeks before he'd have this first batch done.

But that might have been because their eyes were already slitted against the harsh sting of the chemicals and the whole lack-of-breathing thing. Or because Avery couldn't think of any other alternative and wasn't about to replace all this great stuff with reproductions.

Clutching a claim form and written estimate, Avery and Nicole exited into the parking lot where they drew great gulps of sunshine and air into their lungs.

"You were awesome!" Avery said when they'd left the body shop behind. "You handled the King of Chrome perfectly."

They did an exaggerated high five, and Nicole laughed freely, something Avery realized she hadn't heard before. "You're hereby elected to pick up the finished pieces and deliver the next set. If anyone can get us a better price, it's you."

Avery tilted her head back against the leather headrest, enjoying the play of sunshine and fresh air on her cheeks as she thought about Nicole's manner with Alfred. Nikki was extremely attractive, but she didn't use her looks overtly, they were just part of her package. And she didn't play the helpless female; Avery couldn't imagine anyone forcing Nikki into the Vanna role that Avery had been relegated to on *Hammer and Nail*. But she wasn't a battering ram, either. Her persuasive skills seemed to work equally well on the high-net-worth individuals who were her clients as well as the more blue-collar variety.

"How do you do it?" she asked Nicole when they'd driven through Pasadena and on to the Corey Causeway Bridge. "How do you get people to do what you want without them even realizing it?"

On Gulf Boulevard they waited while a stream of beach-goers crossed with the light. "Handling people isn't all that complicated," Nicole said. "It doesn't really matter whether they're men or women, young or old . . ." She shrugged. "Because it's not really about them."

"No?"

"No." Nicole smiled, but there was no humor in her voice, and her chin was set. Avery wished she could see behind her sunglasses, to what might be revealed in her eyes. "It's really a matter of knowing exactly what it is that you want to achieve in each situation; you can't be hoping for some vague outcome. You have to be specific. Then you simply help them think it's what they want, too."

The light turned green and Nikki eased her foot down on the accelerator. "It's all about force of will. Mind over matter," she said as the Jag sprang forward. "You just have to make sure that it's your mind, your will that dominates theirs."

"How did you learn all that?" Avery asked, surprised by the depths lurking beneath Nicole's sophisticated surface.

"The hard way," Nikki said so quietly her words were almost lost in the wind. "Out of necessity."

Avery had cause to remember this when they got back to Ten Beach Road and found large furniture boxes sticking up over the edge of the Dumpster.

"There's no way Deirdre unpacked and carried that bedroom furniture upstairs on her own, is there?" Nicole asked as they passed the Dumpster and headed up the drive.

"No. My money's on her having found some poor schmo to do it for her." They entered through the kitchen door and found Deirdre standing at the center island. A sketch pad sat in front of her, a tape measure next to it. She was studying the kitchen cabinets with a thoughtful expression on her face. "But feel free to ask," Avery said as she went to the refrigerator to retrieve two Diet Cokes.

Nicole paused beside Deirdre and took a sip of the proffered Coke before asking, "How did you get the furniture upstairs, Deirdre? You look miraculously unscathed."

Deirdre took the other Coke out of Avery's hand, despite the fact that it was already halfway up to Avery's mouth. "It was the most serendipitous thing," Deirdre said. "A nice young man who was out fishing on the back seawall helped me."

"You invited a stranger into the house?" Avery asked.

"Darling, there've been a million strangers in and out of this house already. And he was very well mannered. And exceptionally good-looking."

"Oh, well, as long as he was attractive." Avery took her Coke back and wiped the rim with her T-shirt. The lack of air-conditioning had her pressing it against her neck.

"He was broad shouldered and had dark hair and eyes. He could definitely be in movies."

An odd look passed over Nikki's face.

"Besides, he wasn't a complete stranger," Deirdre said. "He told me he'd met Nicole a number of times." She winked conspiratorially. "I think he must be interested. He asked me all kinds of questions about her."

Nikki made a strange sound; Avery couldn't have identified it, but it matched the look on her face.

"Girardi? Jenari?" Deirdre cocked her head and squinted, trying to remember. "Giraldi, that's it. Joe Giraldi," she said, pleased at having successfully plumbed her memory banks. "He said he'd be in touch."

Twenty-two

Maddie sat next to Kyra in the ob-gyn's office they'd been referred to by their GP in Atlanta, waiting for Kyra's name to be called. Kyra had come reluctantly. "I feel fine, Mom. The morning sickness is over, and I don't feel all that tired anymore."

She didn't seem to understand the importance of prenatal care or preparing for the baby's future, but then Kyra had always been more of a dreamer than a planner. As demonstrated by her apparent faith that despite all evidence to the contrary, everything would simply work itself out.

"Did you hear what Deirdre said about Tonja Kay?"

"Hmmm?" Maddie was pulling out the order forms for *American Baby* and *Parenting* magazines. She planned to stop at the bookstore and buy Kyra a copy of *What to Expect When You're Expecting* on the way home. She could still remember how eagerly she'd read each chapter and marked off each developmental milestone when she'd been pregnant with Ky and then Andrew all those years ago. "I'm sorry?"

"I said, I think it's a really positive sign that Tonja has moved out. Daniel told me he loved me and that they were only still together because their publicists insisted on it."

Maddie slipped the forms in her purse and pushed the magazines aside. "I hate for you to pin your future happiness on someone else's marriage falling apart, Kyra," Madeline said. "I don't care who they are or why they're together. Marriage is meant to be a sacred vow."

The phrase "for better or for worse" flitted through her mind. She and Steve had had a lot of "better" and only now were dealing with the "worse." Kyra was starting out backward; what sort of mother would she be if she allowed her daughter to hold on to such hollow hope? "Have you even heard from him?" She still couldn't bring herself to refer to the movie star by his first name. Her daughter had no such problem.

"No, but I'm sure that's because Daniel doesn't even know where I am. His people won't take a message." Kyra said this with absolute certainty as if it were just a matter of logistics that needed to be circumvented.

"And you don't think that means something?" Maddie asked, trying and failing to keep the incredulity out of her voice.

"It means he's not getting my messages."

"Kyra, honey. If he loved you, wouldn't he be asking if there were messages? Better yet, wouldn't he be calling you?"

Her chin quivered the tiniest bit.

"You have the same phone number, Kyra. You are completely reachable. And it's not like you're not checking your voice mail constantly." Kyra flinched at that, but Maddie was determined to make her see reason. She needed to be facing reality and preparing for the future.

"He's busy with the film. You don't know how it is for him," Kyra said. "Always surrounded by people, everything handled and intercepted. His life isn't his own and neither is his schedule."

She could feel Kyra clinging to her fantasy and rationalizations. She actually believed, or wanted to believe, that she and Daniel could be out of touch for months and somehow, suddenly and miraculously, he would appear and proclaim

his love for her and their child—a child he didn't even know
existed.

"Well, he seemed to find enough alone time to get you
pregnant. Or did his people schedule that for him?"

Kyra gasped in shock and outrage, but Madeline did not,
could not, let that stop her.

"Kyra, this is not a movie you're in. And Daniel Deranian
is not going to ride in on a white horse and carry you and
your child off into the sunset."

"Not my child," she said. "Our child. And that's only
because he doesn't know about it."

Maddie closed her eyes against Kyra's foolish certainty;
somehow she had to get through to her. "This is real life,
Ky. And it can turn hard and gritty practically overnight. If
he loved you as you seem to think he does, he'd be here with
you. Or at the very least in touch with you and making plans."

"Like Dad is for you?" It was a taunt, cruel and intentional.

Madeline flinched at the truth of it as she was intended
to. "I hope to God your father is going to come through. We
have twenty-five years of being there for each other, which
gives me real reason to believe that this will still happen."
She held Kyra's gaze with her own, refusing to let her look
away. "What do you have?" she asked quietly. "A couple of
weeks of sex with a celebrity on a movie set for which you
lost your job and now face a completely altered life as a single
mother." She paused to let her words sink in. "How many
months are you going to spend hoping the sex was good
enough to motivate him to figure out where you are? And
whatever makes you think he's going to care about or help
support your child when he didn't have enough conscience or
honor to keep his marriage vows?"

There was a dead silence as the bomb she'd dropped det-
onated. Maddie could read the direct hit in her daughter's
stunned eyes.

"Kyra Singer?" The nurse walked into the waiting room
and looked around expectantly.

Maddie gathered her purse and began to stand, but Kyra

hissed at her to stop. "No," she said as she rose. "I don't want you in there thinking your poison about Daniel and me. You can just leave if you want to. I'll find my way back to the house."

Maddie began to protest. "I only wanted to make sure you understood your situation. You can't . . ."

"Oh, I understand all right. And I'm not interested in hearing another word of it. If you are here when I come out, this conversation is over. I'll help you with the house and we'll be civil to each other. But I won't listen to any more of your opinions about Daniel." She drew a breath and squared her shoulders. "Do you understand?"

Maddie nodded. But she could barely swallow the tears that rose up to clog her throat as her daughter turned her back and followed the nurse through the doorway and down the hall. She looked at the empty seat on the other side of her and knew Kyra's words wouldn't have been half as painful if Steve had heard them, too.

Deirdre had apparently given the good-looking fisherman free access to the house; not that he would have needed her permission, given his training and the fact that the only upstairs room with a door was the lone working bathroom. The package Nikki found on her bed contained a list of charitable organizations and the amount of money each had lost to Malcolm Dyer. There were pictures, too, many of them of Malcolm entering or leaving banks in tropical-looking countries or lounging in elegant settings. He looked well dressed and well rested—not at all like someone grappling with his conscience or suffering from remorse.

Nicole looked down at her hands, already rough and chapped from working on the house. She was doing manual labor while her brother seemed to be island and bank hopping. The list Agent Giraldi had provided made it clear that Grace Lindell's foster children's charity was just one of many that Malcolm had bankrupted. Her anger had not diminished, but it was hardened by shame. Didn't he feel remorse? How could he go on about his merry way while his victims grappled with the fallout of his thievery?

Nicole pulled out her laptop and booted it up. She'd been the one who raised him after their father had died and their mother had expended all of her energies on survival. Had she somehow led him to believe that the end—triumphing over poverty, becoming financially secure—justified any means?

She typed in the address of a chat room he had once met her in years ago and when she was in she stared at the blinking cursor, thinking what she might say.

If she could just find him and talk to him face-to-face, she might have a chance at getting him to turn himself in. Or at least convince him to return the money he'd stolen.

Tentatively she typed, *Gloria not singing. Suggests flight back from outer space. Will meet craft in person.* It was a little vague, but then she had no idea what she was really proposing. Or whether Malcolm would ever see her message or act on it.

With her fingers still poised over the keyboard, she stared out the window and out over the bay, wondering where Giraldi was right now and when she might see or hear from him again. She'd been unable to discern any pattern to the agent's drop-bys and had no way of guessing how often he might be watching her without her knowledge. The sheer unpredictability of his actions was unnerving, which might—or might not—be his intent.

Nikki closed down her laptop and put the incriminating pages and photos back in the envelope. She wasn't sure how to get in touch with Malcolm or whether he might try to reach her. But maybe if the FBI thought she was willing to work with them, they'd give her some clue that would help her get to Malcolm first. What she did or said to her brother then would depend on a lot of factors. And would be no one's business but her own.

It was just before sunset and Avery could already taste the strawberry daiquiris Nicole had volunteered to make. Maddie was in charge of the hors d'oeuvres, which meant something between Deirdre's caviar and Avery's Cheez Doodles. Instead of a swim or a shower or even a walk during the transition hour, Avery had decided the time had come to talk to Chase about the detached garage and her plans for it. Her "don't ask, don't yell" strategy had yielded results and cut down on the combat, but she was tired of the subterfuge. The whole approach reeked of cowardice.

Before she could change her mind or chicken out, she crossed the loggia, which had been turned into the door-refinishing area, and strode across the pool deck to the free-standing garage where she found not only Chase but Deirdre. Great.

She nodded to Deirdre, then turned to face Chase. Without preamble she said, "I think this should be converted to a pool house."

He opened his mouth to speak, but she wasn't ready to hear his objections. "There's plenty of room to leave a two-car garage facing the drive and commit the rest of the space to a cabana-slash-guest house."

"Avery, I . . ." He began what was bound to be the same old knee-jerk objection to any idea she raised.

She simply didn't want to hear it. "Look, before you piss me off completely, why don't we just walk through the space and discuss it?" Anger, hot and heady, began to pulse in her veins. She would not let him dismiss her.

"Avery, I already . . ."

"Seriously, Chase." She was tired of sneaking around or arguing for every little thing, tired of being treated like a moron. "I get that you think I'm some little numbskull. I'm completely aware that my role on *Hammer and Nail* didn't help change that impression. That's one of the reasons I'm no longer a part of the show." She could not bring herself to admit that she'd been shoved out before she could even broach regaining her original role. Not to them.

"But . . ."

"But the fact that I'm blonde and female doesn't mean I don't have a brain."

"Amen to that," Deirdre said.

"You've known me a good part of my life and my father treated you like a son. Do you really believe he raised a ninny? Or that I got my architecture degree in a box of Cracker Jack?"

She glared at him, pretty much daring him to say yes, then continued without giving him a chance to answer. "I mean we can spend the summer arguing about every little thing that happens in this house or we can work together and do a better, more efficient job."

"Well said," Deirdre said.

The blood pumped in Avery's veins. She squared off all the way and looked up directly into his eyes. Hating, once again, how completely he towered over her.

"Avery," he said. "That's enough."

But it wasn't, not nearly. She wasn't leaving this spot until she'd convinced him that she knew what she was talking about. "I can completely see this space. And it wouldn't be horribly time intensive or expensive to convert it."

"Yes," he began. "Deirdre and I . . ."

She noticed the tape measure in Deirdre's hand and reached for one end of it, pulling it to the opposite wall. "We could put up a wall right here to separate the two spaces and a row of floor-to-ceiling windows overlooking the pass."

Deirdre continued to hold the base of the tape measure as Avery walked her end across the width of the space. "I'd put French doors opening to the pool here." She gestured to the wall closest to the pool. "It's a simple structure and I think we go clean lined but not too screamingly contemporary. Maybe a touch of the Mediterranean and a hint of Deco."

Deirdre smiled. "I've never seen a piece of furniture or a decorative piece in that style without thinking of you," she said. "You fell in love with it when you were, what, five?"

"If you're thinking of a stroll down memory lane, it's going to be a pretty brief stroll," Avery said. She let go of her end of the tape measure taking some satisfaction from the way the length of metal snapped back toward Deirdre, but she kept her focus on Chase. "I'm tired of your condescension and your . . ." She was so agitated she couldn't even find the words. "It needs to stop." Her neck craned upward and she crowded him, invading his space. Sort of like a bumblebee buzzing up against the trunk of a redwood.

He cut his gaze to Deirdre, which only incensed Avery further.

"I'm talking to you," she said. "You could at least show me the courtesy of acting like you're listening!"

"Avery," he said. "Stop."

"Why? So you can insult me again? Call me Vanna? Tell me not to worry my pretty little head about it?"

Deirdre bit back a laugh. But Avery was already in mid-eruption; she'd get to her later.

If she were taller, she would have snapped a Z in his face with a ton of attitude. She was still searching for something bad enough to call him when he gave her the palm.

"Jesus," he said. "I've been trying to tell you I already decided to convert the space. Deirdre and I were just talking about it."

Avery blinked and stepped back. She looked at Deirdre. Whom he had willingly consulted.

"Chase's thoughts on the renovation are almost identical to yours. He just wanted my input on the finishes and furniture," Deirdre said. "I'm thinking Saltillo tile with a wrought iron and cushion group and a few wood pieces. Definitely Mediterranean with a touch of Deco."

"What's wrong, Van?" Chase asked. "Cat got your tongue?"

She couldn't seem to get past the fact that he'd consulted Deirdre and not her. Or that the only reason she'd gotten what she'd wanted was because he'd already decided to do it. Or that he'd called her Van. If she'd been able to reach it, her hands would be wrapped around Chase Hardin's neck.

"You know," she said, biting out the words, trying to hold her anger at a controllable level when everything inside her was dying to spew out. "If anyone had bothered to consult me or include me in the conversation, I wouldn't have just wasted my time and energy trying to convince you to do something you'd already decided to do."

She turned to leave, but Deirdre put a hand on her shoulder to stop her. "You were dead on, Avery," Deirdre said. "You know it, I know it, and whether he wants to admit it or not, Chase knows it. Does it really matter who decided first or who consulted whom?"

Avery looked at the mother she'd given up on so long ago and at the man who'd apparently given up on her. "Maybe it shouldn't," she said, drawing herself up to her full height, insignificant as it might be. "But I'm tired of the insults. Whatever chip Chase has been carrying around on his shoulder, he needs to get rid of it. Now. I don't know what I've done to deserve his disdain, but it's affecting the job and we don't have time for that."

She gave them both a nod and prepared to leave.

"Avery, honey," Deirdre said, reaching out to her. "Don't . . ."

"Don't call me honey," Avery said, shrugging her off. "We don't know each other well enough for that." She paused, considering the woman who'd abandoned her to pursue her own dreams, never caring what she did to her daughter's. "And FYI, I'm not that wild about Art Deco anymore." It was a lie, but it was the best she could come up with. "A lot about me has changed since you left us. So don't go thinking you know the first little thing about me."

Twenty-three

It was the middle of June and the days had grown longer and steadily hotter, the moderate temperatures of May already fading into distant memory. This made their lack of air-conditioning even harder to take. The duct cleaning and rerouting that Chase had scheduled while they waited for new units contributed to the chaos. The only relief from the increasingly oppressive heat was the afternoon rain showers—some of which could be seen moving in off the Gulf and others of which simply sprinkled down without much ado, lasting for ten or fifteen minutes before stopping, like a faucet that had been turned on and then off.

They woke early both by choice and because there were no window coverings to speak of—or doors for that matter. And because there was nothing that even resembled privacy once Chase arrived at seven thirty A.M. and the daily ebb and flow of workmen began.

Maddie would spend today just as she had spent yesterday, bathed in sweat as she sat hunched over a worktable Chase had set up in the empty dining room, polishing the door knobs and hinges that she and Avery had painstakingly removed from each door. The polishing was tedious and never ending, like pretty much every other task she'd tackled so far; but unlike the re-glazing, it required little concentration. Polishing was far too mindless for someone with so many problems on her mind.

It was seven A.M., the air already hot and heavy. Nicole had left for her morning run. Someone was showering in the bathroom—Maddie assumed it was Deirdre, the only one of them who spent any real time on her appearance. There'd been a few bumps and thumps from Avery's bedroom directly overhead, but nothing that signaled a full awakening.

Maddie set down her scissors and sorted the grocery coupons, slipping them into the alphabetized holder she kept in the minivan. She spread the articles she'd clipped from the paper in front of her: "How to Find Yourself After You've Lost Your Job," "Mind Over It Doesn't Matter," "Male Depression and Its Toll on the Family," "Winning Outcomes and Positive Visualization." She slipped several in the envelope she'd already addressed to Steve but wasn't sure why she persisted in these long-distance motivational attempts.

Every day Madeline debated whether she needed to go back to Atlanta and try to light a fire under Steve personally, but it took everything she had to do what needed to be done here. She couldn't even imagine taking on Steve and Edna, who protected her son's right to wallow with the same zeal the U.S. military guarded the gold at Fort Knox.

Thinking she might slip by the gatekeeper with an early call, Madeline dialed the house phone. While it rang, she braced herself for whoever might pick up. As luck, or the lack of it, would have it, her mother-in-law answered.

"Hi, Edna," Maddie said brightly, channeling the article on favorable outcomes. "It's great to hear your voice." She tried to project the positive, but suspected she just sounded loud.

Edna's hello was very small.

"I'd like to talk to Steve," Maddie said. "Please put him on."

"He's still sleeping," Edna said. "I'll tell him you called when he gets up."

Edna's voice was low. Maddie pictured her standing guard in front of the master bedroom door or, possibly, the family room couch. "Or maybe you should try again later."

The articles on the table stared up at her accusingly. "No!" Maddie replied quickly before Edna could hang up. "Maybe you should shake his shoulder until he wakes up."

Edna gasped with indignation. "Well, I never!"

"But you should," Maddie said, tired to death of the pretense that Steve was just resting, when in fact he was hiding. "You're his mother and you need to tell him it's time to get up and start getting it back together."

"Hmmmph!" Edna said. "Why don't you come back here and tell him that yourself? Unless you're too busy vacationing at that beach house."

The injustice of it made Maddie's eyes sting. Her heart felt too large for her chest. She reached for one of the articles she'd clipped with its *Every important journey begins with that first step* intro and crumpled it into a ball.

"Edna?" Maddie said. "Put him on. Now."

"I told you, he's asleep, Melinda!" her mother-in-law replied then thumped down the phone.

Maddie's tears dried in mid-blink. The hurt, which had lain so heavy, went hot and liquid. She barely recognized the anger coursing through her; it was an emotion she rarely allowed herself. Quickly she hit the speed dial for Andrew's cell phone. "Hmmm?" Her son's voice, that misleadingly adult baritone, sounded thick with sleep.

"Andrew, it's me. Mom."

There was a long yawn and the rustle of sheets. "Um-hmmm?"

"I need to know what's going on there. Are you making progress on Grandma's house?"

Another yawn. The creak of the bed. "I'm sleeping." He yawned again. "Can you call back later?"

His words grew softer and the phone farther from his mouth.

"Andrew!" she shouted. "Don't you dare hang up!"

Unlike his grandmother, he listened. "Why can't we talk later? I . . ."

"Because I need to talk now. And you need to hear me," Maddie said, her anger building. She was down here fighting to save their lone asset, the one thing that might keep their collective heads above water, and none of them could be bothered to support her, let alone help.

"You call Mrs. Richmond and get the referrals for subcontractors and ask her to pull those comparables on Grandma's house. And you do it today." She drew a deep breath, trying to calm down, but her whole body quivered with hurt and anger.

"As soon as the house is ready for the Realtor to list, I want you and Dad to come down and help us finish here."

"Dad's not going anywhere. Not if it means getting off the couch."

Maddie flinched at the disgust and disappointment in her son's voice, but there could be no more sugarcoating or evading the reality of their situation. She could not be in this alone. "Andrew," she said. "Carry your cell phone to your dad and tell him I need to talk to him."

"He won't talk. He hardly even moves." His tone remained sullen with a hint of whine, and she had no idea whether he simply didn't want to get out of bed or couldn't face seeing his father that way.

"He doesn't have to talk at the moment," Maddie said. "I'm going to do the talking. He just has to listen." She clung to her anger; if she let the wave of helplessness swamp her, they were lost. "Hurry up, Andrew. This won't take long."

She held on while he did as she asked. She could hear the sounds of home melding with the sounds of Bella Flora: Chase and Robby's trucks pulling up out front. The whine of a wave runner motor out in the pass. Upstairs, the bathroom door slammed. The scramble of feet and a shout of irritation followed. If Robby didn't get another bathroom up and running soon, blood would be drawn. The only question was whose.

"Mom, he says he can't talk right now. Grandma says . . ."

"Andrew," she said, hating that her son had to be put in this position. "Put the phone up to your father's ear so he can hear me."

"Here, Dad," Andrew said. An unintelligible murmur from Steve followed. And then she heard him breathing.

Maddie hung on to her resolve. Steve didn't need any more pity, and he certainly didn't need even one more second of enabling. "Steve," she said clearly and forcefully. "We can't afford for you to lie around feeling sorry for yourself anymore."

There was no response.

"I get that a horrible thing has happened. I know you feel guilty about all those losses and that not having a job has thrown you. But you have to get up and help." She paused, concentrating on not letting her voice break. Crying would be pointless; if ever there was a time for tough love, it was now. "Do you hear me?"

"Yes." That was it. Nothing else.

"You need to get up off that couch and get back in our life," she said. "We need you."

The breathing stopped for a second; there was the slightest hitch before it resumed, but he didn't speak. She had no doubt Edna was hovering protectively nearby. The image of their son being forced to crouch next to his father, holding the phone in place, summoned back the anger that she needed.

"You know what?" she said, no longer weighing each word before she uttered it. "The man I married was not a quitter. He was not someone who would abandon his wife and children in an emergency." She drew a breath, forcing herself to continue, giving free rein to her hurt and anger so that there could be no doubt in his mind that she meant what she said.

"And in case you need something to think about, you can think about what I've been doing down here. I've been sleeping on a mattress on the floor and fighting complete strangers for bathroom time in the only bathroom that works. I've worked ten-hour days scrubbing and cleaning a seven-thousand-square-foot home that hasn't had a two-legged resident or a lick of attention in years. I've been on scaffolding re-glazing windows and removing doors and hardware and polishing them until my hands are numb. I've been pinching our pennies so tightly that Abraham Lincoln's face is imprinted on my fingers."

There was no response, but she could feel him listening. His breathing sounded labored in her ear.

"And you know what the worst part is?" Emotion clogged her throat and turned her voice ragged. "I sat alone at the doctor's office with our pregnant daughter who wouldn't even let me go in with her and insists on believing that Daniel Deranian is going to show up here and carry her off to happily-ever-after land." She swallowed again, but her throat burned with all the words that spewed out. "She barely talks to me anymore because I don't believe that's going to happen."

She sat for a moment staring out the window through the sheen of tears, gathering herself, waiting once more for a response that never came.

"I love you," she said, a new resolve growing inside her. "And I love the life we've shared. I've always assumed we'd be together until the end. But you need to get your shit together now and help our family get back on its feet. I'll expect you down here ready to help put the finishing touches on Bella Flora by early August. Or . . ." She barely hesitated as the ultimate ultimatum formed on her lips. "Or I'm going to file for divorce."

Both of them stopped breathing then as they absorbed the threat. But still he said nothing. Even in her shock at what she'd said, she recognized that the threat could not be an idle one. Quietly she hung up the phone.

Maddie's hands shook as she made a fresh pot of coffee, refilled the sugar bowl, and set out a new carton of nondairy creamer. The kitchen began to fill up with coffee seekers—first Chase and Robby, then Avery. Deirdre came down dressed and made-up and settled at the table with the morning cross-word puzzle. Nicole returned from her run.

Normally, Madeline enjoyed everyone congregating around the coffeepot before the workday began, but she still felt raw and uncertain in the wake of her conversation with Steve. "Please, God," she murmured to herself as she set out a bowl of fruit. "Help him get it together. Don't let me have to carry out my threat."

Kyra was the last one down. Ignoring Maddie, she set her video camera on the table then went into the refrigerator for a glass of orange juice. Maddie pushed the fruit bowl, which she kept stocked, toward her daughter, but Kyra ignored that, too.

"How'd you sleep, Ky?" In the wake of the ob-gyn visit and the whole YouTube debacle, Kyra had not been overtly nasty but maintained just enough emotional distance to let Maddie know she'd screwed up.

Kyra spent a good bit of time surfing the Internet architectural salvage sites when some knob or pull or another needed to be matched, and putting together a Bella Flora "sales piece." Maddie had made it a point not to look for her postings on YouTube, but Avery, who did, said Kyra was honoring their ban on extreme close-ups and had dialed back the sarcasm to an acceptable level.

"Fine." Kyra moved toward the table where Nicole sipped a morning smoothie.

"Look, Kyra, I'm sorry." Maddie had lost track of the number of times she'd tried to apologize; she was so tired of being made to always feel in the wrong.

"I said I slept fine." Kyra kept her back to Maddie, plopping down into a seat next to Avery, who was peeling off the wrapper from a granola bar. "What do you need me to do today?"

"I was thinking we could get more of the doors out of the way if we set up an actual assembly line. Nicole strips," Avery said, nodding Nicole's way. "I sand and repair. You apply the finish. We've got plenty of sawhorses and we can set up in the shade of the reclinada." She nodded out the window toward the triple palm to the west of the pool. The doors waiting to be refinished were stacked on the loggia. "I've got a mask you can wear and some heavy gloves."

"Sure," Kyra said at the same time Maddie said, "No, she can't."

Chase sighed as he reached for a granola bar and Maddie waited for him to object to Avery organizing his grunts, but all he said was, "I was hoping someone else had made the doughnut run. These bars are way too small." He held up the shiny wrapper with pastel script lettering. "And . . . girly."

"Feel free to eat before you come," Avery said. "But just for the record, granola bars are not gender specific." She turned to Madeline. "Why can't Kyra do the finishing?"

"Yeah, Mom." Kyra taunted. "Why not?" She threw her an angry look, but it was laced with hurt.

"Because Kyra can't work with chemicals right now." Maddie wished she could simply walk out the front door and head out to the beach, which she'd discovered was far more soothing than the "downward dog" she'd practiced in yoga. She'd hoped to keep Kyra's pregnancy to themselves for at least another few weeks; could she face this conversation on top of the ultimatum she'd launched at Steve? They all stared at her expectantly. Did she have a choice?

"Because she's pregnant," Madeline said into the questioning silence.

"Oh!" Avery and Deirdre exclaimed.

"Wow," Nicole said.

Chase reached for and unwrapped another granola bar.

"It's not a good idea to expose the baby to chemicals," Maddie said. It was her turn to stare at Kyra. "I imagine the doctor must have mentioned that."

"Congratulations," Chase said easily. But then he was not only male but the father of sons.

"Yes, I guess congratulations are in order?" Avery looked between Kyra and Maddie.

"Yeah, that's, um, really great," Nicole said. "When are you due?"

"In November," Kyra said, accepting hugs from both of them.

Maddie frowned. Where would they all be at Thanksgiving? Would this chapter be over? The house finished and sold? The money deposited and their debts paid off?

"As you can see by her expression, my mother's not too excited about the whole idea." Kyra was going for flip, but her voice wobbled.

"Oh, Kyra that's not fair. I just think . . ." Maddie began.

They all waited to hear what she thought, but the right words, if they existed, didn't come. She so didn't want to introduce Daniel Deranian's name into the conversation or mention that her daughter was living in the land of denial. "It's just that she's not married and she's so young." Maddie was no longer sure who she was trying to convince. "And she has no idea what she's in for."

Chase snorted. "No one ever does."

"No," Deirdre agreed. "It can be so overwhelming. I was twenty-one when I got married and twenty-two when Avery was born. I wasn't ready for . . . any of it."

Avery's jaw tensed. "I didn't realize there was an 'optional' clause in the parenting contract," she said. "But Deirdre always did know how to work the fine print."

"I understand that you're not wild to have me here," Deirdre said. "I freely admit I haven't been much of a mother, and certainly not the mother you deserved."

She paused, looking at her daughter.

"If you're waiting for an argument from me, you're going to be waiting a long damned time," Avery said. "I don't know why you've pushed your way into this project, but you're not going to be able to design yourself back into my life, Deirdre. It's way too late for that."

Maddie watched Avery toss salvos at her mother and wondered if they hurt Deirdre as much as Kyra's hurt her.

The designer didn't flinch, but that said more about her self-control than her feelings.

Madeline had always been Kyra and Andrew's mother first; it was how she'd thought of herself and how the rest of the world had defined her. She'd been there for her children and always would be. But did that mean she had to pretend that she was unequivocally happy that Kyra was pregnant? Did being supportive demand that she also keep silent?

"I just don't think Kyra realizes how huge a responsibility this is going to be or how completely it will change her life. And to do it all alone . . ." Maddie's voice trailed off at the enormity of it.

Kyra's face closed, her shoulders stiffened.

"Your mother's right," Nicole said quietly. "Being a single parent is one of the hardest things there is. It's huge."

"Surely the baby's father will accept responsibility?" Chase said, not sounding sure at all. He tossed the last granola wrapper in the trash and poured himself another cup of coffee. "If he doesn't understand how many people it takes to create a child, I'll be happy to explain it to him."

Maddie blinked in surprise and saw a similar expression on Avery's face.

"You all don't need to be talking about me as if I'm not here," Kyra said. "I'm here. And I'm sure the father of my child will want to be involved."

Madeline closed her eyes against Kyra's childlike certainty. She'd had the same tone in her voice at seven when she'd insisted on staying up all night to catch a glimpse of the tooth fairy. And at thirteen when she'd been convinced that the animated short she'd managed to shoot and cut together, could, in fact, be entered in the Sundance Film Festival. "Kyra, please," Maddie whispered. "It's not a good idea to mention that . . ."

Kyra got up from the table and stood where everyone could see her. "What my mother doesn't want me to tell you—or anyone—is that Daniel Deranian is the father of my child."

If anyone's attention had been about to wander, that

simple statement brought all eyes and ears back to Kyra. Nicole winced, but didn't speak.

"Daniel Deranian, the actor?" Avery asked.

Kyra nodded. "My mother's convinced that because he's a celebrity I can't possibly mean anything to him. She believes that I was a . . . convenience . . . on the set and that he has no feelings for me and certainly no honorable intentions." Her jaw tightened. "That's how much my mother thinks of me."

"I never said that," Madeline protested. "I only . . ."

"I happen to know that Daniel loves me. And I know he'll want to be a part of our lives." Kyra's hand slipped to her rounding stomach.

Madeline stole a look at the now-familiar faces around them and saw everything from surprise to the same doubt she felt. Kyra was just too young to see her situation ending in anything less than a happily ever after.

"Daniel will be on the next plane here. Or sending his private jet to pick me up." She smiled the confident smile of a foolish child. "Just as soon as I get through to him."

Madeline could hardly bear to contemplate what would happen when and if Kyra actually got through to Deranian. The man was used to people covering for and taking care of him, and he did, in fact, have a wife regardless of where she'd chosen to live.

"I'd be careful not to get on the wrong side of Tonja Kay," Nicole said. "That woman has a reputation for being even stronger in person than she is in the roles she plays."

"Well," Madeline said, drawing another angry glare from her daughter, "until that plane arrives I think it would be best if we keep this information to ourselves."

Kyra grabbed her camera and left the kitchen, clearly incensed. Maddie followed her, hoping to smooth things over, but not until she'd gotten a nod of agreement from the others. Though, of course, a nod of silence wasn't exactly binding.

But then, what was?

Twenty-four

"What was that?" Nicole leaped out of bed and raced to the window. She stared out not over the bay where the sun was still inching upward but down into the front garden where an army seemed to be massing. An army of people with white hair and really bad taste in clothing. She heard footsteps in the hall and threw open her door but knew she was too late when the bathroom door slammed shut. Avery and Madeline already stood in line. Five women and one bathroom belonged in the category of cruel and inhuman punishment. This house needed to be closed down like Gitmo.

Maddie shot her an apologetic smile.

"We let Kyra go ahead since she's pregnant," Avery said, not looking at all put out. But then she was first in line.

"Good God. I'd get pregnant myself if it would get me to the front of the bathroom line," Nikki muttered.

"I don't think you can do that yourself. Didn't we establish that the other day in the kitchen?" Deirdre came out of the master bedroom fully dressed and made-up. If Nikki hadn't personally delivered the master bathroom hardware to the King of Chrome, she would have suspected the designer of secretly convincing Robby to get her bathroom up and running. Through the closed bedroom door, Nikki could hear the whir of the window air conditioner Deirdre had had delivered and installed.

"The fact that I haven't chosen to reproduce doesn't mean I don't know how the equipment works," Nikki replied. "Or how a seed gets planted." She moved closer to the fixed window above the front door. "Speaking of which, how long have Renée Franklin and her garden ladies been here?"

The army had spread out to attack different sections of the garden. John Franklin sat on a camp chair that had been placed near the fountain, a smile on his face as he watched his wife command her battalion.

"Mrs. Franklin wanted to get started before it got too hot," Avery said. "I don't think a single one of them is under seventy-five. They'll fill in with some new plantings after the house has been pressure washed and painted."

Nicole moved down the hall to peer out the rear windows above the loggia; that was the one advantage in being last in line—she didn't need to hold on to her spot. Only her bladder. "Good God, that woman is climbing up that tree. I think she's got a . . ."

The whir of an electric saw drifted up to them followed by the crash of a limb landing on concrete. There were a few "whoo-whoo-whoos" punctuated by surprisingly vigorous arm pumps and a lot of swinging arm flesh. The saw whirred again and another limb dropped into the empty crater of concrete in the center of the back patio.

"I guess it's a good thing the pool hasn't been done yet," Deirdre said beside her.

"Right. Just like it's a good thing we only have one bathroom because it cuts down on the cleaning." Nikki narrowed her gaze on the immaculate Deirdre. "We do still only have one bathroom, right?"

Deirdre just smiled. "Of course," she said. But Nikki vowed to make sure. Avery wasn't the only one suspicious of her mother's motives. Or maybe Nikki's nose was just out of joint because Deirdre had proved even better at getting others to do her bidding than Nikki was herself.

Down below, the garden ladies continued to swarm over the property, cutting and pulling and weeding; each sure movement confirming that despite their advanced ages they were neither frail nor timid.

"Wow," Avery whispered. "Look at her go." Renée moved from group to group in a most un-Vanna-like way—a commander with a clear mission in mind. Occasionally she went back to her husband for a moment or two like a sun responding to gravitational pull. And then she was back at it, her husband's admiring gaze following her wherever she went.

Nikki saw the sheen of tears in Avery's eyes and felt the telltale prickle behind her own eyelids as she witnessed the couple's obvious connection. Good grief! She swiped at them with the back of her hand as Madeline came out of the bathroom fully dressed.

"Jesus," Madeline said. "I haven't had a period in six months. I thought I was done." She shook her head, disgusted. "It must be the stress. I'm not sure whose tampons those were, but I'll buy some to replace what I borrowed."

"No problem," Avery and Nikki said at the same time, then the three of them looked at each other.

Nikki groaned. "This is what happens when you have a group of women living in such close quarters; everybody's cycles start syncing up. I feel like I'm in the middle of Anita Diamant's *The Red Tent*."

"Don't look at me," Deirdre said. "I am *way* over that. But it may explain some of the whacked-out behavior over the last week. A pregnant girl and three PMSers? Somebody should warn Chase and his guys to tread lightly. Thank God there are no weapons in the house."

"You know how much it hurts me to agree with you," Avery said as she moved toward the now-vacant bathroom. "But you got that right."

Maddie sighed and headed for the back stairs. "I guess

I'll mix up a couple of pitchers of lemonade to hydrate the troops."

"Well, whatever you do don't piss them off," Nicole said. "Even the smallest of them seems to have major muscle and some of them have power tools."

After what felt like an eternity, Avery finally came out of the bathroom. With a nod, she went down the front stairs. The bathroom was Nikki's at last. Hers, all hers!

She raced in, locking the door behind her, and claimed the toilet. She sighed in sheer relief; the word "hallelujah" formed in her brain.

Heavy footsteps sounded outside and there was a knock on the bathroom door. "Ma'am?" The voice belonged to Robby the plumber. "I have to turn off the water! It'll only be for about an hour."

Nikki washed her hands in the sink and yanked open the door. "Oh, no, you don't," she said with a shake of her head. "I've been waiting for way too long, and I just now got in here."

"I'm sorry, ma'am." That's how young the plumber was. She was a "ma'am" in his eyes. "But . . ."

She looked him in the eye. He was very sweet, respectful, and earnest. Chase insisted he came from a long line of plumbers and knew what he was doing. At the moment none of those things mattered in the least. She reached out and grabbed a handful of Robby's T-shirt and pulled him closer. "You can't turn off the water right now, Robby. We only have one working bathroom. Which includes one sink. And one toilet. And one shower. For all five of us. And I haven't even brushed my teeth yet." Something he undoubtedly now knew given how close they were standing.

He swallowed. She actually watched the excruciatingly slow movement of his Adam's apple.

"You can't shut off the water until I'm done. I need to use this bathroom. I *will* use this bathroom."

"There's a Port-O-Let outside, Miz Grant," he said, trying not to show his fear. "You could . . ."

"No," she assured him. "I most definitely could not."

She got a tighter grip on his shirt and pulled his face up to hers. She was vaguely aware that someone had come up behind him. "You will not even think about turning off that water for the next thirty minutes. If you make one move toward the water line, I'll come and find you. And it won't be pretty."

Robby blanched; his face turned white. That was when she heard Joe Giraldi's voice. "It's not worth your life, boy," he said quietly. "You definitely don't want to stand between a desperate woman and her *toilette*." He said it in the French manner and with an annoyingly taunting smile in his voice.

A red haze formed in front of Nikki's eyes. "What are you," she asked Giraldi, never taking her eyes off the nervous plumber, "a hostage negotiator?"

"Only if I need to be." Giraldi took her hand and pried Robby's T-shirt out of it. She could feel his gaze locked on her; hers remained on Robby.

"Why don't you go on downstairs and I'll let you know when it's safe to turn off the water?" Giraldi said to Robby in the same "let's not get anyone killed" tone. "Go on," he said when the young man didn't move. "I'll give you the all-clear when it's safe."

Robby hotfooted it downstairs. Nikki and Giraldi stood face-to-face. Or in their case, face to chest. She tried not to think about how she looked or what she might smell like.

"Is he even a real plumber?" she demanded. "Or have you had some FBI trainee screwing around with our pipes? Because I think that would make what I'm thinking about justifiable homicide."

"Robby's the real deal," Giraldi said in that same calm, infuriating voice. "I'm just 'assisting' him today. If you behave yourself you may have a second bathroom up and running soon."

"You've just been playing with us, haven't you? It's some sort of bizarre bathroom deprivation technique. I bet all the guys in the trench coats and dark sunglasses got a big chuckle out of that!"

He smiled. "Maybe a few grins, but the plumbing issues are real. Definitely not our doing."

She took a deep breath trying to calm herself, but there was no real calm to be found.

"I just wanted to talk to you, and I didn't want it to look suspicious in case your brother's watching," Giraldi continued.

"Malcolm?" she asked. "You think Malcolm's close enough to see us?" She laughed somewhat hysterically even as she wondered if that could be true.

"It's unlikely," he conceded, "but possible."

"And how many different work people do you think you can pretend to be before someone else notices? You've been a cable guy, a fisherman-turned-mover, and now a plumber. How many jobs you don't know how to perform can you possibly use as cover?"

"Oh, I know how to do all those things," he said. "They just don't happen to be what I do for a living."

She leaned in to him, not because she was drawn to, but because she wanted to crowd him in the way his mere existence crowded her. She looked him right in the eyes, the dark intelligent ones, and wished he were older or far younger. Or uglier. He was way too good-looking for someone so dangerous. Agent Joe Giraldi was like her very own personal Venus flytrap.

"We know you've been trying to reach him," he said, stepping neither back nor forward.

"Then you also know he hasn't responded. And probably never will."

His look sharpened, and she wondered again if he knew about the message Malcolm had sent. Not that it had proven particularly helpful or clarified anything.

"Look, there are a lot of people at the agency who think you're in this with him."

"Does that include you?"

He looked like he didn't want to answer.

"Does it?"

She could see him considering his answer. Finally he said, "You're still a 'subject of interest,' but I think you've been duped like everybody else. I think he's an ungrateful bastard given everything you did for him. But our forensic accountant and financial analyst are tracking the money, and there's an arrest warrant at NCIC and Interpol. It's just a matter of time before we catch up with him. I'd like to see you end up on the right side of this mess."

"Is that a warning?" she asked even as she realized she was standing far too close. She was relieved when he dropped back a step and leaned against the wall.

He shrugged. "He's been spotted in Florida. He hasn't landed anywhere for long, but we have reports of him in the Keys and in the Florida panhandle. Does either of those areas mean anything to you or your brother?"

It took everything Nikki had not to react, but she couldn't help thinking of that long ago Thanksgiving.

"If you know something, you need to share it," Giraldi said. "You can't possibly think he deserves to go free after ruining so many people. That money doesn't belong to him. And the longer it takes us to catch him, the less of it there will be left."

She studied him for a long moment, trying to see past the good looks and the focused determination. Special Agent Joe Giraldi was a force to be reckoned with. As was the Federal Bureau of Investigation. It was highly unlikely she could reach Malcolm without Giraldi and his people knowing it; it seemed even less likely she could find him without their help.

Once her brother had been everything to her. Even now, as angry and disappointed in him as she was, he was the only family she had. She didn't want to set Malcolm up for capture; she wanted to get to him first so that she could convince him to turn himself in and return the money. It was far too late to prevent all the harm he'd done, the lives he'd ruined, but she desperately wanted him to do at least some semblance of the "right thing." Giraldi might never knowingly give her that chance, but he might well locate Malcolm before she could.

"I'll tell you what," she said as she looked into the agent's clear dark eyes. "Let's stop all the cloak-and-dagger stuff. You say you're handy? We can use some more hands on this job. That way you can watch for Malcolm." And she could watch him. "I for one don't expect him to show his face here, but I guess you never know."

"You want me to work on your house," he said, straightening. "With you."

"Sure, why not?" she asked. "You're here half the time anyway. As a taxpayer, I'm probably already paying your salary. And while we're working together I'll decide whether I can trust you or not."

"And then?" he asked with a look in his eyes that made her think maybe that flytrap was about to slam shut. "Then you'll help us catch your brother?"

"If you find him, I'll talk to him," she said, careful not to give away too much.

"Okay," he said easily, and she knew she wasn't the only one holding back. "You're on." He glanced down at his watch. "But you better hurry. You're down to about fifteen minutes."

She gave him a wink. "Make it the original thirty minutes, and I'll give you a few days off before you have to start."

His soft laughter followed her, floating in the hallway until the bathroom door clicked shut behind her.

The YouTube post was cut to the strains of Tchaikovsky's 1812 Overture. At each boom of the cannon the shot changed.

The morning bathroom line was punctuated by the door being yanked open and slamming shut. The sunset toasts were broken down into a sequence of shots: caviar and Cheez Doodles. Toasts and hoots of laughter. The sun rising and setting in a frenzy of animation that illustrated the passing days as well as how much progress had been made and how very much was left to be done.

The work shots were compelling: Nicole leaning over to swipe chemicals across the door stretched out in front of her. Avery sanding beside her, her face determined, her muscles defined. Both of them shot from every conceivable angle. Not a smiling point or gesture to be found.

There were shots of the trucks and the workmen and Chase from all sides; he apparently didn't have a bad one. The standoff in the pool house was there, apparently shot through the open door. The sweet-faced Robby at work was intercut with the bathroom line each morning. The swarm of the white-haired garden ladies was there, too. Throughout the three minutes of video were close-ups of Maddie's hands, mother's hands, polishing and wiping, cooking and cleaning, writing lists and clipping coupons.

Kyra, who was only seen in the occasional reflection of a shiny surface, had caught it all: the sweat and the tears, the toasts and high fives, the agonies and the ecstasies, the growing friendship and the bonds that had formed. She'd managed to demonstrate the magnitude of the task and each struggle and mistake, even more clearly than she had with her sneering commentaries.

Avery watched it twice and though they could have used hair and makeup people and quite a lot of airbrushing, she was impressed with how well Kyra had captured the essence of their efforts to renovate Bella Flora.

And she wasn't alone. The video got more than twenty thousand views and hundreds of comments. She had no idea whether a video like this could actually sell a multimillion-dollar home, but one thing was for sure: they and the house at Ten Beach Road were no longer a secret.

Twenty-five

They were already breakfasted and out back when their new recruit reported for duty. Nikki watched Giraldi carefully as he strolled toward them and then introduced him as an old friend of the family just as they'd agreed. She'd decided that his past appearances had been brief enough that no one would remember him.

Chase stuck out a hand. "Glad to have you on board, man," he said. "We can use a little more testosterone on this job." He cocked his head. "Have we met? You look familiar."

"Joe Giraldi. I have been on site a few times. I don't think we were introduced, though." Giraldi gave everyone a smile. His manner was low key and personable. Somehow he'd dialed down the hard-assed cockiness several notches; he could have been the good-looking guy next door.

"Hey," Avery said considering him more closely. "I thought you worked for the cable company."

Deirdre raised an eyebrow. "I thought he was just here on vacation fishing."

"He was helping Robby yesterday," Kyra said.

Nicole opened her mouth to explain further, but Giraldi beat her to it.

"I've been doing some odd jobs out here on the beach, and I happened to notice Nicole. Her brother's an old friend of mine. I figured Nikki would be able to help me track him down."

Nicole kept her lips pressed into a smile in order to stifle her reaction to how close to the truth he'd come. Giraldi gave them all a wink and snaked an arm around her shoulders, pulling her against his side. "I've got to tell you, I've always had the biggest crush on her." He tilted his head against hers, playing it to the hilt. "Even when we were kids and she was an 'older woman.'"

Appalled at the past he was inventing, Nikki stepped out from under his arm. "Behave yourself." She shook a finger at Giraldi. "Or I'll have to . . . warn my brother about your behavior."

He shot her a cocky smile that said, "please, be my guest." Nikki was relieved when a man who looked like Enrico but wasn't walked out onto the loggia from the house.

"I kind of hate to miss what's coming next, but Umberto, our plasterer, is here," Chase said. "Do you need me to get you all started?"

"Um, that would be a no," Avery said. "I'll get Joe and Nicole going out here and then I wanted to pull the chandelier down so that Kyra and Maddie can start cleaning the crystals. I've got a crude sort of pulley hooked up."

Kyra groaned, but Maddie barely seemed to be listening, which Nicole found decidedly un-Madeline-like.

Avery turned to Joe. "Nicole and I will be working over there." She pointed to the two doors already set up in the shade. "I know how men feel about power tools, so we'll try you out over here on the sander."

Deirdre went inside to make phone calls, presumably from her air-conditioned bedroom. Avery led Kyra and Maddie into the dining room. Nikki might have been envious of the indoor assignment except that the spot beside the reclinada palm was fabulously shady and the breeze off the Gulf not only lowered the temperature but carried the scent of the stain away with it. And then there was the view. Which got even better about twenty minutes later when Giraldi, who was working smack in the sun, peeled off his sweat-soaked T-shirt and dropped it on the ground.

Two hours later Avery put down her rag and wiped the sweat off her brow. "I think we're going to have to fire Joe."

"We're not paying him. I'm not sure firing is the right word," Nikki said.

"He's a distraction." Avery pointed to Nicole's door. "You've redone that one three times now. You can't stain uniformly when you're not even looking at what you're staining."

Nikki would have liked to argue or deny the accusation, but Avery was right. Nicole had spent far more of the morning watching the muscles ripple across Agent Giraldi's broad back and shoulders than she had her own brushstrokes.

"You're a little behind yourself," Nicole pointed out.

"I know." Avery laughed. "And I think Kyra made more trips out here than she needed to. Of course that could have been out of boredom; there's nothing more tedious than cleaning a chandelier of that size one drop crystal at a time."

"Or not."

They smiled at each other, complicit, but Nicole didn't feel at all good about how often her gaze had stolen over to check Giraldi out. She'd asked him to help partly to torture him and partly to keep an eye on him—not his rippling muscles or near-perfect butt.

During lunch, a make-your-own-sandwich affair that Maddie only halfheartedly supervised, Nikki did her best to stay far enough away from the FBI agent not to be caught staring and close enough to make sure he wasn't saying anything that might expose her as Malcolm's sister. For the most part, he talked baseball and boats and other manly topics with Chase and Robby and Umberto, who was apparently Enrico's cousin. The agent came across just as he'd presented himself, and she had to admit if she hadn't known he was there to keep her under surveillance, she never would have known. Still she didn't begin to relax until Giraldi left around two thirty, saying that he had some things he had to take care of. She blew out a breath of air, grateful to see him go with no real damage done.

She was so relieved to be rid of Giraldi that she almost didn't hear what Chase was saying as he packed up his tools an hour or so later so that he could get to one of his sons' baseball games. "Robby says the master bath will be functional at some point tomorrow, so if you've got the fixtures back it could be usable."

There was a hushed silence as they all took this in. Then came a group smile, although Maddie's seemed a bit strained. Nikki heard what might have been a celestial choir singing in her head.

"Figures it would be Deirdre's bath," Avery grumbled. "She'll be the only one here with air-conditioning and her own bathroom."

"Well, I'll share it with you," Deirdre said. "And anyone else who wants in. It'll give us a chance to get better acquainted."

"Gee, I can hardly wait," Avery deadpanned. "Will you call the King of Chrome, Nikki, and see if he's done with the master bathroom fixtures?"

"Sure." She'd find a way to send smoke signals if it would expedite the increased bathroom time.

Chase laughed. "You took the faucets to Alfred?"

"Yeah." Avery crossed her arms across her chest, which Nikki already knew was not a good sign. "What's so funny?"

"He's never been willing to look at anything that didn't belong on a car. And he's not exactly an inexpensive option."

"Well, we didn't have a problem at all, did we, Nikki?" Avery just loved one-upping Chase.

"Nope."

"In fact, he was kind of like a great big teddy bear. Wouldn't you say, Nikki?"

"Yep."

"And how much did he charge you?" Chase asked, clearly not yet willing to concede.

"Well, his original estimate was a little high," Avery admitted. "But Nicole's going to pick up the finished pieces and handle the final negotiations. We'll let you know how things shake out."

"And he'll undoubtedly be too busy drooling over Nikki and her car to put up much of a fight," Chase said. "That's so Vanna-esque."

The choir stopped in mid-hallelujah. There was another silence nowhere near as pleasant as the first as Avery squared off in front of Chase.

Avery couldn't believe he'd called her Vanna again. Even as she straightened her shoulders and angled her chin upward, she was aware of how much shorter she was than Chase. Which pissed her off even more. "What the hell is it with you?" she asked.

Robby and Umberto eased out of the kitchen and ostensibly back to work. Kyra lifted her video camera, but Maddie, who still seemed to be doing an imitation of a limp rag, took the camera from her daughter and led her out of the kitchen.

Out of the corner of her eye, Avery saw Nicole motion to Deirdre. Before Chase could open his mouth to respond, they left the kitchen with about as much subtlety as rats abandoning ship.

"I am so tired of this," Avery said when she and Chase were alone. "Tired of your judgment, tired of your automatic disapproval, tired of your damned superior attitude. No matter what I do, you find a way to belittle it. And I'd like to know why."

Chase's jaw tensed; she could see it working. For a brief moment she regretted not letting his comment slide.

"You want to know why? Then I'll tell you," he finally said. "I hate like hell that you've taken all the advantages you've been given and let them be pushed aside by the way you look and act. You have an architecture degree from Duke, for chrissakes, and you managed to get your own show on television, and what did you do with all that?" He shook his head in disgust. "You wore tight sweaters and you smiled and pointed. Your father was so proud of everything you'd achieved, and you trampled all over that."

The anger in his voice spurred her own anger even higher. Who was he to judge her? What did he know? And why on earth would her humiliation matter so much to him? "What business is this of yours?"

"When my mother died and my father had his first heart attack, I had to go into the business instead of architecture. You had every damned thing I wanted and you wasted it!"

"Well, your mother may have died, but at least she didn't leave you." Avery couldn't stop the things that came out. "She never would have left you."

She looked at his face, flushed with anger and indignation. "That's not nothing."

"You were given every opportunity and you let yourself be dismissed."

"It was beyond my control!" Avery shouted, her neck hurting from having to crick back so far. "Do you think I liked the way I was presented? Do you honestly think I agreed to any of that?"

"You sure looked perfectly happy doing it."

"Well, then you're as stupid as I looked!" she shouted.

They glared at each other. But even as she watched, the anger in his eyes became tinged with embarrassment. It was clear he hadn't meant to reveal so much.

She was surprised by all of it: That he'd been as angry as she'd been at the way she'd been portrayed. That he, more than anyone, had understood that her role on the show was far beneath her training and capabilities. That it had become nothing more than an ongoing insult.

Avery could hardly catch her breath as he continued, now in a calmer but no less biting tone.

"And I absolutely hated the way they turned that ego-ridden husband of yours into the 'expert' when he shouldn't even have been on the same stage. And I bet he never argued that it should be any other way."

Avery didn't think she'd ever felt more pathetic. "No," she said as she drew herself up and prepared to leave the room. "He never did."

She could not, would not, tell him that she hadn't chosen to leave; that even after she'd allowed herself to be turned into a laughingstock, they still didn't want her.

Twenty-six

In the late afternoon the sunbaked sand was toasty between Maddie's toes, the breeze a warm caress on her bare skin. She walked toward the pink castle walls of the Don CeSar soothed by the rhythmic wash of the tide and the erratic caws of the gulls, trying to draw the beauty of it inside, willing it to alleviate the worry and panic that she'd felt churning inside ever since she'd issued her ultimatum to Steve.

Tilting her face to the sky, she tested the smile she'd kept plastered on her lips, and knew that if she'd been a sailboat that smile would have been at half mast. A part of her would have liked to simply keep walking north from Pass-a-Grille, to St. Pete Beach, and on to Treasure Island, from one sandy beach to the next all the way up into the curve of Florida's panhandle. Instead, she turned and headed back toward Bella Flora where her responsibilities lay, hoping she could corral her thoughts and worries; had she gone too far? Was she right to bring up divorce? Was there some other way she'd missed?

Kyra was the first to accost her when she got back to the house. The others were getting ready for sunset. Kyra had her hand out.

Maddie saw her daughter staring expectantly at her, but had missed what she'd said.

"Mom?" Kyra said, clearly irritated.

"Hmmm?"

"Your keys. I'm going to a movie at the Beach Theater. Can I borrow them?"

"Oh. Sure." Maddie walked to the kitchen to retrieve them. The fact that it didn't even occur to Kyra to invite her should have hurt, but it was barely a pinprick. She was far too numb to feel the sting.

Maddie watched Kyra leave while Nikki and Avery bustled around the kitchen, getting ready for sunset. She saw the looks they sent each other and knew she wasn't behaving even remotely like herself, but then her self had never been contemplating divorce before.

"Come on, Maddie," Avery said. "I made you your own personal bowl of Cheez Doodles. And we've got those cute little cocktail hot dogs in buns you bought at Sam's Club."

The blender whirred. "Strawberry daiquiris coming right up," Nicole added. "It's just the three of us tonight." Nicole poured the first glass and set it in front of her. "Take a sip and come on. We don't want to miss the show."

Maddie took a long sip of the drink, letting the iced strawberry slide over her tongue and down her throat. Out on the pool deck she sank into her orange neon–strapped beach chair and rested her elbows on the short aluminum arms. By the time Nikki and Avery had arranged the snacks and poured their own drinks, Maddie had finished hers. She held her empty glass toward Nikki.

"Goodness, we're thirsty tonight." Nikki refilled her glass to the brim.

"That's an understatement." Maddie felt as if she could drink a Gulf full of daiquiris and still be thirsty for more.

Avery raised her glass toward the setting sun. "Well, I think we should toast having the air-conditioning up and running. And our second bathroom. Even if I do have to share it with Deirdre. Who, by the way, owns more makeup and beauty products with the word 'antiaging' on them than Nikki, which I didn't think was possible."

Nicole laughed. Maddie managed a small smile. "To the air-conditioning and the bathroom," they said. "And to Alfred, the King of Chrome."

"And to Maddie," Nikki added. "Who needs to tell us what's wrong."

In the fading light, Madeline looked out over the sea oats and the jetty. It was hot and muggy, the breeze off the Gulf thick with heat and salt. "Let's just say I'd be pretty hard-pressed to come up with one good thing tonight."

A Cheez Doodle crunched nearby and Avery lifted the bowl as if it contained an offering from the gods. Maddie had no appetite.

"Is it Kyra?" Nicole asked. "Because I think she should be grateful she has a family to turn to. I could have a talk with her if you like."

"Thanks." Maddie tried to picture what that talk would be like. "But she's just a part of it. Everything feels completely out of whack. Especially my relationship with Steve." She hadn't had a real conversation with him in so long she wasn't even sure they still had a "relationship."

"When do you think he might come down?" Avery asked. "Is it hard for him to get away?"

For a moment Maddie thought about making up some excuse, trying to change the whole sorry topic. But the concern in her partners' eyes demanded her honesty.

"No," she said. "It's hard for him to get up off the couch."

For a moment she wasn't sure if she'd actually said it out loud. A look at her partners' faces confirmed that she had.

"Is he sick?" Avery asked tentatively.

Maddie sighed. Setting her empty glass down, she wrapped her arms around herself and stared down into her lap.

"In a way," Maddie said. "He lost his job last fall and he hasn't been the same since he told me in March."

"You didn't know?"

"No." Maddie realized how bizarre it sounded. She still

couldn't believe how much Steve had kept from her. "He just kept getting dressed and leaving every day. I had no idea." Her eyes blurred with tears.

"Wow," Avery said.

"And then once he told me, once he could stop pretending, it was like he just gave up. And then his mother came to live with us." Maddie tried to sound matter of fact, but could tell she was failing miserably.

"There's a lot of that going around," Avery said. "And it's definitely not a good thing."

Now that she'd begun talking Maddie couldn't seem to stop. All of it came pouring out of her as she talked and sipped from an always-full glass; Steve's loss of job, loss of all that money, loss of himself. Edna and her enabling. Andrew. Kyra. There wasn't one thing she could think of that seemed to have a bright side.

"Maybe you should go up there and drag him to a psychiatrist or something?" Nikki asked.

"I tried that. I actually got him to one appointment and he wouldn't talk to the doctor. Two hundred and fifty dollars and he didn't say a word. I had another one scheduled for him after I came down here, but he refused to go."

She held her glass out for another drink. Somehow numb from alcohol seemed preferable to numb from despair.

"There must be something else you can try," Avery said.

"What I tried was divorce."

Two sets of eyes riveted to her own.

"The last time we talked—well, we didn't really talk; I had to have Andrew hold the phone up to Steve's ear—I told him that he needed to get it together."

"That's good," Avery said.

"And then I told him that if he wasn't down here ready to help us by the first week of August, that I was filing for divorce."

"Wow."

"Yeah." Maddie still couldn't believe it.

"Did it work?" Nicole asked.

"I don't know. I'm going to call and check in in a few days, but I may not really know for sure until he shows up." Maddie could barely see through the unshed tears. "Or doesn't."

They continued to drink, stopping only long enough for Nicole to make another pitcher of daiquiris. As they drank and talked a cocoon of comfort began to wrap itself around her. Sharing her worries seemed to dissipate them. Or maybe it was the alcohol.

"I hate to offer advice," Nicole said. "I'm really good at bringing people together, but not so good at getting and staying married. I married two men I shouldn't have and for all the wrong reasons." She shook her head, regret on her face. "I don't really have the first idea how couples stay married as long as you have. You wouldn't have made it for . . . how long has it been?"

"Twenty-five years." Just saying it made Maddie want to cry.

"You wouldn't have been together for twenty-five years if there wasn't something major still there." Her gaze shifted from Maddie's before she said, "I think you did the right thing. Even when they hurt you or behave in ways you don't understand, you can't give up on the people you love."

The cocoon became gauzier, hazier. Madeline noticed a mosquito hovering around the rim of Nicole's glass and told it to get lost.

"Well, sometimes they give up on you." Avery downed the remainder of her drink and held it out for a refill. "And it sucks big time."

"Are you talking about Deirdre?" Maddie asked. Even in the blessed fog that seemed to be enveloping her, she could not imagine how anyone could walk away from their child.

"Always," Avery said. "I can tell she thinks she can make me understand it, but there's nothing that she can say that will excuse her running out on us. Nothing."

They mulled that one over, although Maddie's brain seemed to be mulling more slowly than usual.

"But I'm actually a two-time rejectee." Avery raised her hand as if taking an oath.

"Trent?" Nicole asked.

"Not exactly. I wanted the divorce. We weren't particularly good or right for each other. But I didn't really leave *Hammer and Nail*, I was pushed out. As badly as I was portrayed on that show, I'd still be clinging to it if I'd been given the choice. We're not on hiatus. I'm off the show."

The three of them stared at each other, contemplating Avery's revelation on top of the others. Their expressions were grim.

"Shit!" Nicole said. "Look at us! We are *pathetic*!"

"I know!" Maddie said. "And we're out of daiquiris, too."

"Oh, my God," Avery said. "That's terrible. Wait here a minute while I go inside and get my violin!"

They erupted into laughter then. Maddie had no idea who laughed first; she only knew that they were doing a first-rate impression of ROTFLOL while Avery mimed playing a tiny violin and Nicole peered into the empty pitcher looking for one last drop. They were still giggling when a car pulled into the drive and a car door opened and slammed shut.

Light footsteps raced through the kitchen and out onto the loggia. Kyra practically skidded to a stop in front of them. She was breathing heavily. "Quick, we have to go inside. Some of them might be following me." She looked back over her shoulder as if she expected a horde to come around the side of the house at any moment.

Nicole stood, the empty pitcher still clutched in one hand. Avery grabbed the Cheez Doodles and hugged them to her chest. It was a good thing she hadn't already retrieved her violin, Maddie thought, then laughed at the ridiculous image.

Kyra shushed them impatiently. "What's wrong with you all?"

The three of them looked at each other and broke up again. Kyra didn't crack a smile but began herding them, much like goats, toward the kitchen door. Every time they erupted in hoots of laughter, Kyra rolled her eyes and herded a little harder. It seemed that Kyra had left her sense of humor wherever she'd been. "What happened?" Maddie asked. "And why are we whispering?"

More cars arrived. Several doors opened and slammed shut on the street. Kyra pushed them faster. When they were inside the kitchen with the door locked behind them Kyra flicked off the kitchen light so that they were standing in the dark.

This made them giggle harder.

"Shush," Kyra said like some irate kindergarten teacher. Any minute she was going to tell them to use their "inside voices."

"What is it, Kyra?" Maddie was swaying slightly on her feet. Sitting down seemed safer so she inched her way toward the outline of the kitchen table and chairs. "Who are we hiding from?"

She could make out Nicole moving toward the table, too. Avery looked kind of happy where she was.

"The photographers," Kyra whispered. "They started shouting my name and taking pictures of me when I came out of the theater." She threw another look over her shoulder and out the kitchen window. "They wanted to know where Daniel was."

"The paparazzi?" Nicole laughed out loud despite Kyra's insistent shushing. "The paparazzi are here in Pass-a-Grille?"

They laughed even harder. Great, big belly laughs that required even greater gulps of air. Right up until the first flashbulb went off just beyond the driveway and the Jet Ski zoomed in and began to idle just off the seawall.

Twenty-seven

Avery stood in the master bathroom, staring at her reflection in the oversized makeup mirror that Deirdre had affixed to the wall when the mirrors were sent out for re-silvering. She was achingly glad to have both privacy and time, but she could have lived without the magnification and illumination. She also could have lived without all of Deirdre's things spread around her, especially the scent of her heavy gardenia perfume—the one that Avery used to sneak into her missing mother's closet to smell.

Avery moved aside the bottom of the white sheet that now hung over the bathroom's garden window and peeked out toward the street where a small mob of photographers milled around hoping for a shot at Kyra but settling for anyone they could catch in their viewfinders. They'd lost almost a full day of work as they'd raced to cover the bedroom and bathroom windows and debated whether to continue to work outside where the zoom lenses had no trouble capturing them. Finally they'd decided that they couldn't keep cowering inside even in the deliciously air-conditioned cool and still meet their schedule, so for the most part they went back about their business, ignoring the shouts of "look this way" and "what's your name, luv?" But Avery wasn't the only one of them who'd gone back to wearing makeup and giving thought to what she wore.

Deirdre poked her head through the bathroom doorway, now also hung with a sheet since the bathroom and bedroom doors had been removed for refinishing. Her hair looked freshly blow-dried and her makeup artfully applied. She wore a pair of white linen pants, a glittery fuchsia T-shirt, and a cropped linen jacket as if she were off on a cruise or for lunch at the yacht club. Avery would die before saying so, but she hoped she looked half that good when she was staring down sixty.

"Can you join us in the kitchen?" Deirdre asked.

"Join who?"

"Chase and I are going to discuss the kitchen renovation. I thought you'd want to be a part of the conversation."

Avery looked at Deirdre, uncertain.

"He's never going to come out and invite your participation. He's a lot like his father; once he takes a position he doesn't really know how to back off it." Her mouth softened. "And you're a lot like yours."

Avery grimaced. "I'm surprised you can remember that far back. I'm sure there have been tons of men since my father."

"Oh, you never forget your first love." She came through the door to stand next to Avery.

"Right."

They were exactly the same height, had the same hazel gray eyes and busty build, the same flyaway blonde hair, or they would have if Deirdre's had been allowed to fly anywhere but where she intended.

"And you certainly never forget your daughter. Even if you've made the mistake of leaving her behind."

Avery closed her eyes for a moment and moved out of mirror range. "You make it sound like you forgot a lipstick or an outfit. Is that the way you remember it? Well, I don't have any fond memories of you." She wouldn't let herself. "All I remember is that you left and didn't come back."

"Avery, it wasn't about you. It was . . ."

"I don't really want to hear what it was or wasn't." She smoothed a hand down the T-shirt and capris she'd pulled on, wishing she could smooth the hurt away as easily. "We can work together and I'll be as civil as I can. But there's not going to be anything more than that. Ever."

Deirdre nodded and followed her out of the bedroom and down the back stairs where a glance out the fixed glass confirmed that several boats idled off the seawall, their occupants holding cameras with lenses long enough to shoot into the next city. Several other photographers had congregated on the path to the jetty and on the far side of the Dumpster. For all Avery knew, several could be crouching inside sifting through their garbage.

Chase stood as they entered the kitchen. Maddie was wiping the countertop. A fresh pot of coffee was brewing.

"I can't believe they're still out there," Avery said. "I feel like we're under siege."

"I know," Maddie said. "I never thought I'd say this, but I'm glad there are so many crystals on that chandelier. I'm nowhere near ready to go outside and face those cameras."

Maddie poured Chase another cup of coffee.

"Do we know how they found out about Kyra?" Chase asked.

Maddie shook her head. "Kyra says their relationship wasn't exactly a secret on set, but I didn't think anyone outside Bella Flora knew that Deranian had fathered her baby. As to how they found her here—she's been pretty vocal and visible on YouTube."

"No kidding." Avery's tone was dry.

"Hopefully they'll just get tired of waiting and go away," Chase said. "I don't know, though. They're pretty inventive. One of them put on work clothes and followed Umberto out back to the pool house—we're going to stub out a bath and kitchen area and frame the interior rooms. We all thought he was another one of Enrico's cousins until he whipped out his camera."

Maddie carried a cup of coffee into the dining room. Through the back window, Avery could see Nikki and Joe Giraldi working on the last of the interior doors under the shade of the triple palm. Not for the first time, she wondered what was going on between them; they didn't seem like lovers or even great friends, but there was something not at all casual between them.

"So." Avery joined Chase and Deirdre in the center of the kitchen. "Deirdre says we're discussing the kitchen renovation."

Chase looked between Deirdre and Avery in surprise and it was clear Deirdre hadn't warned him.

"Do you have a problem with that?" Avery asked.

"And if I did?" He snagged her gaze.

Deirdre stepped between them. "The kitchen is too important for egos to get in the way. I want to show you what I have in mind so that you can both sign off on it."

She gave Chase an eyebrow.

"Fine." His agreement was grudging.

Avery got the other eyebrow.

"Sure." Avery shrugged. "Why not?"

"Good," Deirdre said. "Because whoever did this to this house should be shot."

Avery had to agree. The kitchen could have been a set on *That '70s Show* with its speckled turquoise Formica countertops that coordinated with the boxy turquoise Frigidaire. The white twelve-by-twelve floor tiles were cracked and without character while the turquoise-and-white laminate cabinets screamed Florida almost as loudly as the white seashell knobs.

"Shot in front of a firing squad," Avery added.

"Live on HGTV," Chase said, shooting Avery a look. Avery shot one right back.

"Right," Deirdre said, taking charge. "I'm glad we're in agreement. Of course, the footprint of the kitchen has already been changed with the incorporation of the butler's pantry. And I love the original built-in along that wall." She waved an arm to encompass the space. "All we need to do is restore the kitchen's harmony to the rest of the house."

Avery and Chase nodded; they kept their gazes on Deirdre and off of each other.

"I think we should go for reclaimed wood countertops—I can get solid pieces of oak twenty-four inches wide that'll look fabulous and tie the room to the rest of the house. The floor should be real Spanish tile and I'd do the backsplash in hand-painted reclaimed tiles. I've got a great salvage person over on the East Coast."

"And the cabinets?" Avery asked, not wanting to be impressed.

Deirdre did a three-sixty, taking in the space in one final glance, though Avery suspected she'd been measuring and thinking about the kitchen since the day she'd arrived.

"I think soft green glass-fronted cabinets would be spectacular in here."

Chase nodded. "Sounds good."

It would, of course, be far more than good. It would be fabulous. "Would you put in a stainless-steel sink?" Avery asked casually.

"Absolutely." If Deirdre had been hoping for praise, she didn't show it, continuing with complete assurance. "Of course, we'll want top-of-the-line appliances. There's room for a Sub-Zero refrigerator with matching cabinetry. And I'd put a freestanding Aga stove over there." Deirdre pointed to the spot. "And we'll put in some spectacular period lighting, something iron I think, over a Biedermeier table and chairs."

Avery, who could see it all, realized she was nodding far too happily and stopped so abruptly she nearly gave herself whiplash.

"What do you think?" Dierdre asked.

"It sounds . . ." Avery paused, searching for the right word. "Fine." She threw in a casual shrug for good measure.

Deirdre's eyebrow went sky high. Chase gave her a knowing smirk; he read her far too well. But Avery didn't care. It

would be a cold day in hell before Avery handed Deirdre a
compliment no matter how well deserved.

"We need to go ahead and start the kitchen and pool
house," Deirdre said. "But I've been thinking I might pitch
the house to the designer and symphony guilds. I don't know
when they do their primary show house here, but maybe
they'd be open to an additional fund-raiser."

Avery felt a real stirring of excitement. Turning Bella
Flora into a designer show house would be a great way to
get the house furnished and decorated for almost nothing.
It would also give John Franklin a whole lot of additional
marketing opportunities.

"That's a great idea!" Chase broke into a smile. He nodded
with complete abandon. "That would be huge!"

Avery's smile was considerably smaller and her nod briefer;
she imagined a letter "H" for hypocrite scrawled across her
forehead. If anyone but Deirdre had proposed the idea, Avery
would have been bobbleheading, too.

Nicole swiped at her forehead with the back of her arm and
stuck her cell phone back in her shorts pocket. If they hadn't
had a camera-toting audience she would have lifted her sweat-
soaked cable company T-shirt and mopped her face.

"Well?" Avery asked. "What do you think?"

"I left him a message. His secretary said he'd be back in
later today. I'll do my best to convince him." "Him" was Tim
White, a former New York client who owned a company that
installed and repaired steam heating systems. Something
that didn't seem to exist in Florida.

"Great. Thanks." Avery handed her a glass of iced tea and
watched as Nicole drained it, then held the empty glass to her
neck and cheek. Maybe the *National Enquirer* would like to
run a shot of a former dating guru reduced to refinishing doors
in ninety-five-degree heat with one hundred percent humidity. "We can't really take care of the pool until we have these

steam heat pipes taken care of; they run awfully close to each other."

"I'd give everything I own and then some if that pool actually had water in it right now," Nicole said. She was so ready to take the Nestea plunge.

"Where's Giraldi?" Avery asked.

"He went down to the beach for a swim."

"Smart guy. And now's the time. In another few weeks it'll feel like bath water."

Giraldi came up the beach path still wet from his swim, his dark hair slicked back, water sluicing down his beautiful chest and muscled legs.

"Wow," Avery said, waving to him before she went back to whatever she'd been doing in the pool house.

Wow was right, Nicole thought. Even compared to the social and Hollywood elite she'd dealt with over the years, Giraldi was a standout. Too bad he was only here for Malcolm. And to expose her if necessary.

"Come over here and drip on me a little," she directed.

He obliged, not only dripping but shaking himself off like a dog.

"Ahhhh." The droplets were cool, her skin so hot she thought she heard a slight sizzle. She smiled. Maybe if she got someone from Tim's company down here she should get them to check out her personal thermostat. It seemed to run a little too hot whenever the FBI agent was near. "That feels good."

"There's a whole Gulf full of it right over there." He motioned past the gauntlet of photographers.

Staring at them staring at her, she felt like an animal on exhibit at the zoo.

"I like salt with my margaritas," she said. "Not in my bodies of water."

He smiled and one of the paps aimed a camera their way. "Hey, Nicole! Who's your friend?" he shouted.

For a fraction of a second she considered telling him who

Giraldi was and why he was there. So that if Malcolm was watching he'd know to keep his distance. Except, of course, that that would expose her to far worse than just the anger of her partners.

Giraldi shot her a look. "Those people are disgusting. They've already gotten shots of Kyra, and the story about her and Deranian is out. I don't know what the hell they're still hanging around for. But they're screwing up my surveillance."

It seemed being thwarted didn't agree with Giraldi. She knew exactly how he felt.

"Everybody here except you and Madeline are 'names' of some kind," she said. "And I guess Maddie is the mother of a 'name.' I don't think they're going anywhere until people get tired of the story. Or Daniel Deranian actually shows up."

"Do you think that could happen?" He didn't sound at all happy about the prospect.

"I don't know," Nikki said. "My experience tells me no. But Kyra seems pretty convinced."

Giraldi shook his head, but no water sprayed her way. In the few minutes they'd been talking all signs of his swim had evaporated. "Bottom line," he said. "I need them out of here. If they don't lose interest on their own, I'll have to help them along. There's no way in hell your brother's going to try to make contact with you with this crowd around."

They went back to work, Nikki hot and sticky with sweat, her hands slippery on the brush, Giraldi bare-chested and sure-handed. He couldn't have been more certain or deter-mined. And as it turned out, he couldn't have been more wrong.

That night's YouTube posting was titled "Paparazzi in Para-dise." The video, which Kyra had shot almost entirely inside Bella Flora looking out, was cut to the Jimmy Buffett song "Cheeseburger in Paradise."

There were the usual shots of the crew working on the house: Nicole and Joe side by side beneath the reclinada, stopping only long enough to study one another or to argue. Avery and Chase in the kitchen alternately glaring at each other and getting the eyebrow from Deirdre.

Umberto's putty knife caressing Bella Flora's thickly textured walls as he repaired them, Robby cutting an imaginary ribbon to the master bathroom, Maddie stoically working her way through crystal after crystal—the dunk in the ammonia and water bowl, the scrubbing, the bathing in clear water, the hand drying. The light fixture itself hung denuded of its crystals, the strength behind the shimmer. Like a peek into the secret mechanical tunnels at Disney World.

Each of the work shots was intercut with a shot of their personal paparazzi. The fat ones, the tall ones, the land and the sea ones. Each and every one of them had multiple cameras laced around his neck. Each and every one watched and waited. Occasionally one of them shouted in hope that something, anything, would finally happen.

When she viewed it, Nicole gave it only two stars, not at all happy with being caught staring at Giraldi's bare chest. Avery would have given it three except that she said she had a feeling she looked like Miss Piggy, what with the fists on her hips and the way she had to stare up at Chase when they argued.

Deirdre professed to love it. But then she was in full makeup, with her hair in place, and hadn't been caught on camera staring at anyone.

Twenty-eight

It was the Fourth of July and so far no one had cleaned, sanded, or stained a single square inch of Bella Flora. They'd slept in, dunked day-old doughnuts in freshly brewed coffee for breakfast, and then spent most of the day lounging around the house like ladies of leisure.

Outside the heat was furnace-like; the humidity clinging to the air made it thick enough to choke on. Bella Flora's castle-like walls and newly juiced air conditioners kept the engine buzz of boat traffic muted and almost made Maddie feel sorry for the paparazzi still stationed outside.

In the early afternoon Deirdre left for a cookout hosted by the president of the designers guild, whom she was courting. The rest of them made sandwiches. Now Kyra was planted on the couch with her already dog-eared copy of *What to Expect When You're Expecting*. Her video camera sat on the floor within reach.

Maddie picked up her phone and tried to reach Steve and Andrew again, but for the second time that day she got no answer. She could hear the click of fingers flying over a keyboard in the kitchen, where Nikki sat at the table searching the Internet for . . . something. For the last thirty minutes, Avery had been wandering Bella Flora with a legal pad in one hand and a pen in the other.

Kyra laid the book open on her rounding stomach. "Who do you keep calling?"

"Dad and Andrew."

"And?"

"No answer."

"Is there ever?" Kyra asked.

Maddie sighed. She'd been getting a text or two a week from Steve since she'd issued her ultimatum, but they were completely impersonal and maddeningly inconclusive: *The weather's good. The magnolia tree's blooming*, or *Andrew met the contractor at Mother's yesterday.* She wasn't sure why he bothered and at the same time reread each one over and over, looking for some sign of hope or hidden meaning.

"Do you think the fact that they're not answering could be a good thing? You know, maybe they're out at your grandmother's, working on the house," Maddie couldn't help adding.

Kyra gave her the "you're dumber than dirt" look.

"Or at the neighborhood pool."

Another look.

"You know . . . swimming."

This earned Maddie an eye roll.

Nicole wandered into the room on the tail end of their conversation. "Swimming would be good. Maybe we should go down to the Don and take a dip in the pool, have a drink, and pretend we really are on vacation."

"That's a great idea," Maddie said. "We could invite the photo crew to come with us so that they can get some good action shots when we're thrown out of the pool for not being guests."

"Well then, maybe we should be guests," Nicole replied. "We could chip in on a room and take turns napping on a mattress that's not lying on the floor. Then we could spend the whole day by the pool."

"It's a holiday weekend. I seriously doubt they have any rooms available," Maddie said. "And if I got ahold of a real bed I don't think I could make myself share it."

Avery came into the salon and plopped down on the chair. "It feels really weird not to be working. Do you think I should go out and find something to do in the pool house?"

"No!" Maddie said.

"We're trying to figure out a way to feel more on vacation, not less." This came from Nicole.

"Well, we do have the whole Gulf of Mexico at our doorstep," Maddie said. "We should have taken Chase and Jeff up on their invitation to go out in the boat to watch the fireworks. Deirdre's going to meet up with them, isn't she?"

"You all are free to go," Avery said.

"Isn't it about time you and Chase waved white flags at each other?" Nikki asked.

Avery shrugged. "It's enough we have to work together. I don't need to be around him twenty-four/seven. And I don't want to be in that small a space with Deirdre without the ability to leave. Sharing a bathroom has been tight enough."

Maddie got up and moved to the floor-to-ceiling windows. Out in the pass, family-laden boats wallowed low in the water while Jet Skis whizzed by. Photographers loitered on the path to the beach, but the jetty was packed with fishermen and out on the Gulf the bold colors of a parasail danced through the sky. "Are we really in here relaxing?" she asked. "Or are we hiding?"

"Good question." Nicole looked down at her watch then stood. "This is Independence Day. And we do have the whole day off."

"Why *are* we inside?" Avery asked. "When we don't have to be?"

"Another good question," Nikki said. "Why *should* we be stuck in here? It's the Fourth of fuckin' July!" She moved toward the kitchen. "I'm going to whip up some strawberry daiquiris to take down to the beach. We could go for a swim, toast the sunset, and watch some fireworks."

"That's it," Maddie said leaving the window. "I'm making

a batch of fried chicken. And we can bring the potato salad and coleslaw I picked up from the deli."

"I'll bring the Cheez Doodles," Avery offered. "And I'll put ice and soft drinks in the cooler."

Kyra snapped her book closed and sat up, reaching for her video camera. "I'm in. I'll find the picnic basket Mom picked up at that garage sale. The paps can take their pictures—I'll even pose for them," she said. "Maybe they'll get what they're looking for and go away."

This didn't happen. In fact, as they toted their beach chairs and their picnic down the path and onto the beach, a few of the photographers ran ahead while others trailed behind. When they'd set up down near the water they turned their backs on the intruders and did their best to enjoy themselves.

Kyra shot the photographers watching them. Then she shot the sunset and the toasts that followed. Maddie raised her to-go cup in the light of the pinkening sky and proposed the first toast. "To life, liberty, and the pursuit of happiness," she said, trying not to stumble over the words or dwell on how long it had been since she'd felt truly happy.

"To Bella Flora and the grunts who've come to love her," Nikki said.

"To Malcolm Dyer!" Avery said.

"Because?" Maddie asked, lowering her glass.

"Because if it weren't for him, we would never have met?" Avery said.

They raised their glasses and clinked and Nicole said, "I guess that makes us the silver lining."

They fell silent after that, waiting for the sky to fade to black. And then they oohed and ahhed like everyone else as the fireworks boomed and exploded, staring upward in delight until the last of the color bursts shot through the sky like oils painting on black velvet.

Nicole came out of a deep sleep to a large male hand clamped over her mouth. She tried to scream but the sound was trapped against skin. With panic skittering up her spine and her pulse thrumming in her ear, she shook her head and tried to catch her breath, but she couldn't loosen the hand's hold.

"Shhh," a familiar male voice said. "Don't scream. It's me. Malcolm."

Nikki's eyes flew open. She stopped struggling.

"Will you keep quiet?"

She nodded slowly, still trying to make out his face. When he removed his hand she turned and sat up on the mattress, reaching for the lamp.

"No, don't. It's after two A.M. The photographers are gone, but they've been great cover." He raised the camera around his neck with a pleased smile. "Maybe I'll submit some anonymous shots of Daniel Deranian's little girlfriend."

Nicole held back the grimace of distaste. She had no idea what to say nor did she know if he was aware of Agent Giraldi. Or that the FBI had been watching.

"Great house, huh?" Malcolm said. "You've done a lot with it. I never did have a chance to renovate like I planned." He smiled slightly. "I have a villa in Tuscany. And a beach house on Grand Cayman, though. This was the only fixer-upper."

Nikki thought she might gag on her anger. Despite all the mental conversations she'd had with Malcolm and all the times she'd imagined screaming her anger and disappointment and hurt at him, she could hardly form thoughts, let alone words.

Her gaze narrowed as she strained to see his features in the moonlight. His face had a grayish tint and his eyes spoke of exhaustion. He didn't look like a man with three hundred million dollars.

"I need your help," he said. "I need your help to get to the money."

The maternal instincts that had been revving up sputtered out. "You stole, Malcolm. From your clients and from me."

She stared into his eyes; even in the dark she could see his surprise. "And you're surprised that I'm angry." She studied him—her little brother, the person she'd loved most for most of her life. But she also saw Madeline and Avery and Grace's foster children. "Because you obviously never stopped and thought about the consequences of your actions." Her fury mounted. She wanted to take hold of him and shake him until he understood. As she probably should have when he was a child.

"Did you ever stop and think about any of your victims?" she asked. "You put me out of business and practically out on the street. You remember what that feels like, don't you? The vow we took to never let that happen again?"

It was his turn to nod.

"You weren't raised to steal. To survive, yes, but not at the expense of everyone else."

"I didn't mean to. I never meant to. And I'm going to give you everything back." He smiled the old cocky smile that had always helped him get whatever he wanted. "Plus interest and a lump sum for pain and suffering." That smile again.

"It's not funny, Malcolm. I've seen some of the lives you've ruined up close and personal. How did this happen?"

He took the camera off and set it on the mattress, then hugged his knees to his chest like he used to when he was a child. "I don't know," he said. "It was all legitimate at first. The investments went well and the marketing went even better. I had people who wouldn't have let me in the front door of their mansions when we were growing up fighting to invest with me. You know, the harder you make it, the more they want in?

"It was everything I ever dreamed of. I had . . . so much."

She sensed him wanting to stand and pace, but his eyes skimmed over the window and the closed bedroom door. They were both aware of the others sleeping in the house and the fact that he was wanted by the law.

Was Giraldi out there watching or listening? Did he know that Malcolm had been one of the photographers, waiting patiently in front of their noses to contact her? Was the agent really trying to gain her cooperation? Or had he simply been playing her, waiting for Malcolm to make this kind of brazen move?

"But why did you have to steal? Why not just make everybody a ton of money the good old-fashioned way?"

He sighed. "Because it's not that easy." Giving in to his restlessness, he stood, but he didn't pace. "The market sucked and then it sucked even more. And if you're not delivering better returns than everybody else, then you're nowhere. I couldn't afford to lose those clients, so I started paying off the old investors out of the new investors' capital. And then all the juggling began."

"Oh, Malcolm."

"If the economy hadn't tanked so spectacularly and sent everybody running for their money, I would never have been found out."

Nicole sighed. "But it was still a Ponzi scheme. You were stealing money that didn't belong to you." She looked into his eyes and the only remorse she saw seemed feigned for her benefit, though she suspected he was genuinely remorseful about being found out. "There's always someone else to blame, isn't there?"

Her criticism didn't seem to faze him in the least. "I can make things right for you, Nik, if you'll help me access the money. I need someone the feds don't know to get the money out of my offshore accounts." He reached a hand down to her and pulled her to her feet. "Hardly anyone knows we're related; we have different last names. You could waltz in and out without anyone looking twice."

Except, of course, Agent Joe Giraldi and his merry band. And anyone else who chose to dig deep enough.

"Malcolm, I think you should turn yourself and the money in. So many people have been hurt, wiped out. You need to do the right thing."

His look of shock was almost comical. His laughter, though quiet, was derisive. "Do the right thing? That's a great movie title, Nik. As a course of action, not so much."

"Seriously, Malcolm. You have to . . ."

"No, I really don't. And if you won't help me, I'll find someone else who'll want a cut bad enough to take the chance. But there's nobody I trust as much as you."

She'd once felt that way about him, too. Clearly that trust had been misplaced. "You'll never get away with this. Really, you need to . . ."

"You need to stop trying to mother me, Nikki, and help me get that damned money," Malcolm said. "I'm going to be moving around for a while, waiting for the heat to die down a little more. But here's where you'll be able to find me after that." He handed her a folded piece of paper. "You've got a two-day window to meet me there so that I can explain what needs to be done."

She opened the piece of paper and saw two lines of type with the name of the campground near Tallahassee where they'd spent that long-ago Thanksgiving and the date August 25, the day their mother had died. She had no idea whether he'd left this information unspoken because he knew about Giraldi or was simply being cautious.

When she looked up to tell him she could try to get him a deal if he'd just turn himself in, he was gone.

Twenty-nine

The month of July brought longer days and ever-increasing heat and humidity. The first of the no-name storms formed and dissipated in the Caribbean and walking barefoot on sand, brick, or asphalt became close to impossible. Whenever possible middays were spent working inside the thick walls of Bella Flora or the soon-to-be pool house, from which they'd emerge following the daily late afternoon rain shower.

Madeline watched Kyra's pregnancy develop in tandem with Bella Flora's renovation, her stomach and breasts growing larger as each room of the house was considered and addressed. Rotted baseboards were replaced, missing plaster cornices re-created, and the salon's coffered cypress ceiling was painstakingly cleaned and retouched so that the original coats of arms of the original workmen could once again be seen.

Enrico's younger brother Reggio came to lay the new kitchen floor, re-grout all of the bathrooms' original tile and re-point the brick drive. Deirdre had the leather banquettes in the Casbah Lounge replaced, and Avery and Nicole spent almost a week cleaning and resealing the grout in the elaborately tiled room where they moved their sunset toasts when the weather turned bad or the heat and mosquitoes became unbearable.

The bathroom mirrors were re-silvered and re-hung and King Alfred promised the last of the bathroom fixtures no later than August 1, an announcement that had been toasted unanimously as a "good thing."

In addition to the photos they took, the paparazzi generated some nasty headlines and more than one article questioning what this particular group of women were really doing camped out at Ten Beach Road. Without a quote from Daniel Deranian's wronged wife or an appearance from the actor himself, there was little monetary value in continued stalking of a woman who might or might not be carrying his child. One day late in July, Madeline walked out back and noticed that the paparazzi had vanished.

For Maddie, there was little time to contemplate the joy of becoming a grandmother when each person and element of her life seemed determined to compete for the title of "most stressful." Despite countless attempts, she still hadn't spoken directly to Steve since she'd issued her ultimatum, but Andrew claimed his father was doing "better." She felt her first stirring of real hope when Edna sniffed that Steve was "out" rather than sleeping, but she kept herself busy to the point of exhaustion because she was too afraid to bank on it.

Now she and Kyra sat in the dining room with the crystals from the master bathroom chandelier spread across the worktable before them. This was their third chandelier, and although it was significantly smaller than the dining room fixture that sparkled above them in the late afternoon sun, the process remained painstakingly tedious. Maddie had learned the hard way to take photos before disassembling and knew just how hard it could be to tell one drop crystal from another. "I can't clean another piece." Madeline sat back in her chair and stretched, her hands stiff and cracked from the harsh ammonia, wanting to be done with this job. Just like she'd probably want to be done with whatever came next. She turned to Kyra. "Do you want to go for a walk? Now that the photographers are gone, getting to the beach isn't such a hassle."

"It's still too hot," Kyra said. "I'm going to go upstairs and take a nice long nap." She yawned and stood. As she reached for her cell phone it rang, startling them both. She picked it up to look at the caller ID on the screen and gasped.

Madeline looked up. "What is it?"

"The caller ID says Deranian! Oh, my God, it's him. It's Daniel!" Kyra shot Madeline an "I told you so!" look and brought the phone to her ear with an eagerness Madeline hadn't seen since she'd arrived.

"Daniel? Daniel, oh, thank God. I told my mother you'd call." Kyra began to leave the room, undoubtedly for someplace more private, but practically skidded to a stop before she reached the archway. "Who is this?" Kyra asked. "What do you mean by that?" And then simply, "Oh."

Maddie didn't know what was being said, but she could tell it wasn't good. Kyra's body remained tightly clenched, her shoulders hunched inward. She didn't speak, or even nod, but just stared out into the hallway as if there might be some answer there.

Maddie could hardly stand it; she wanted to go to Kyra and take the phone away and demand to know what was going on. In the end she didn't have to. Kyra turned on trembling legs and brought the phone to Maddie. "It's Tonja Kay," she said quietly, the tears already pooling in her eyes. "She says she wants to talk to you."

Slowly, not understanding, Madeline took the phone and raised the receiver to her ear. "Hello?"

"Are you the fucking bitch of a whore's mother?"

Madeline blinked, certain she'd misheard. "I'm sorry?" she said tentatively.

"You should be fucking sorry!" The movie star's voice carried none of the seductive quality it did in a movie theater. It was vile and nasty and out of control. "And so should your fucking bitch of a daughter!"

"Now you just hold on a minute," Madeline said. Maddie did not approve of Kyra sleeping with a married man, nor did she feel good about the current situation, but that didn't mean she was going to stand by and let someone attack her so viciously.

"Fuck, no, I won't hold on!" Tonja Kay shouted in Madeline's ear. "You should have taught that cunt to keep her fucking hands to her fucking self! He's my husband and she has no right to him. Not any part of him! You tell her to fucking . . ."

Madeline's face was burning, but it was nothing compared to what she felt inside. One hand went to her throat as she struggled for control. "If you're as foul in person as you are on the phone, it's no wonder he's looking elsewhere!"

Kyra's eyes got big. Surprise lit her face.

"Don't you tell me how to talk, you bitch!" Tonja Kay shouted back. "If your daughter thinks she's going to get a penny out of me or Daniel, she's fucking crazy. I'm gonna make sure everybody fucking knows just how skanky that slut is!"

Madeline had been about to hang up. She'd taught her children that discretion was the better part of valor. That it was always better to take the high road. That bad language was the hallmark of a poor vocabulary. But then she'd never been spoken to this way or felt the need to defend one of her children from this kind of onslaught. Tonja Kay was vulgar, crazy, and way too full of herself for Maddie to do nothing more than hang up.

Madeline signaled for Kyra to cover her ears. In the prim tones she'd learned in Mrs. Merriweather's charm class all those years ago, she said, "I think I know a skanky slut when I hear one. And if you ever call my daughter or me names like that again, I'll be releasing the recording I just made of this conversation to the media worldwide."

There was a shocked silence on the other end. And from Kyra as well.

"Good." Madeline smiled, her tone saccharine sweet. "It sounds like we understand each other. Have a nice day."

"Wow," Kyra said as Maddie hung up and handed her the phone. "Thank you." Her face and tone reflected both shock and admiration, an interesting combination. "I don't know where that came from or who you are, but that was truly . . . impressive."

Maddie was more than a little surprised herself. But she'd never been one to miss out on a teaching moment. "There isn't a lot a mother won't do for her child, Kyra. It's sort of hardwired into our DNA." She smiled and reached out a hand to stroke Kyra's cheek. "You'll see what I mean soon enough."

Giraldi caught up with Nicole near the Don CeSar, the midpoint in her morning run, and fit his pace to hers. They ran in silence for about a half a mile while the beach woke up around them, then turned to head back toward Bella Flora. It was the prettiest time of day and the only one in which Nikki could even imagine running now that the days were hot enough to melt the skin off your bones and even the evening breezes off the Gulf felt like blasts from a furnace.

Giraldi had been out of town for a week after Malcolm's visit. Even though Nikki knew that Malcolm's was only one of a number of cases the FBI agent was working, she spent that entire week worrying that Giraldi had listened in on her conversation with Malcolm and then followed Malcolm from Bella Flora. Which meant her brother might already be in custody and his capture not yet announced. Or that Malcolm had eluded Giraldi and his financial fraud squad. Which could mean that the FBI was now waiting to see if she would lead them to her brother so that they'd know once and for all whose side she was really on. As if she knew.

Since his return, Giraldi had helped out two or three times at Bella Flora. She'd also spotted him on the beach, at the concession stand, in line at the grocery store, as she was meant to. Each time they talked he pressed her to work with the FBI and she debated whether to tell him about Malcolm's visit. She knew she should tell Giraldi about the campground and when Malcolm planned to be there. But she couldn't seem to do it. Her brother wasn't the man she'd hoped he'd become or believed him to be, but some small part of her still imagined that if she went there herself she might convince Malcolm to turn himself in before she did it for him. How could she not give her brother that one last chance to do the right thing?

Nicole kept her eyes on the beach ahead. She did not want to look at Joe Giraldi's naked chest, and she definitely didn't want to look him in the eye.

"Are you okay?" he asked as they neared the Paradise Grille and her pace began to slow. "You don't seem quite like yourself."

"I would have imagined you'd think that was a good thing." She still couldn't look at him. Pretending, putting on a show was one thing; lying was another. A distinction she'd apparently not made clear to Malcolm.

"Yeah, it should be," he said. "But I find myself wondering whether there's something I can do to help."

They came to a halt near the path to Beach Road and she bent double, trying to slow and control her breathing. She imagined the relief of telling Giraldi the truth and letting him take over. But could she live with being the one to put Malcolm in jail without giving him a last chance to redeem himself?

Nikki steeled herself to look Giraldi in the eyes, keeping hers as wide and as innocent as she knew how. She couldn't forget that Giraldi was here to do a job. And that job was not watching out for her—it was watching her.

Avery carried her cup of coffee out to the pool house the next morning, pausing briefly to scan the pass. Right now boat traffic was minimal; the bay and the Gulf appeared smooth and untouched. The fishermen were already out in their favored spots, the recreational boaters hadn't yet started motoring or sailing toward their destinations. Pelicans dove for their breakfast and perched on the rocks and pilings around the jetty while gulls careened overhead. The air was already warm and heavy. By noon it would feel as if it weighed a ton.

Inside the back half of the former garage, the musty smell had been replaced by the more comforting scents of fresh sawdust and freshly mixed plaster. The newly installed French doors that fronted the pool and the bank of windows overlooking the pass stood open to catch any breeze that stirred.

The main room had been designed as a studio apartment with the living/sleeping space overlooking both the bay and the pool. An L-shaped kitchenette lay on the opposite end with a full bath stubbed in just beyond it.

Chase stood bare-chested in the kitchen area, a measuring tape in one hand and a pencil tucked behind his ear. His chest gleamed with perspiration and his tool belt hung low on his lean hips. He looked up as she entered.

"It works," she said somewhat grudgingly. "Even keeping the two bays of the garage, it feels okay." They'd fought for their differing visions for the space with ferocity until Deirdre had finally stepped in and merged what she'd deemed the best of both of their plans. Now Avery ran a hand over one plastered wall. "Umberto's done a great job matching the texture in the big house." They walked into the small bath where the toilet and sink were already installed; tomorrow the shower would be tiled. "But I can't help noticing that Robby's moving a lot faster on the bathroom out here than he did inside."

Chase shrugged. "It's virtually new construction. Less complicated."

"Right." She walked around the room, taking it in before coming back to where Chase stood, thrilled to see the space being fleshed out. A new circuit breaker box was up and the wiring under way. The countertop and appliances would go in soon; so would the air-conditioning.

"John Franklin's really excited about this addition. He says it'll be a significant asset in marketing the property," Chase said.

"That's good news." They'd been on even more awkward footing since his tirade about her role on *Hammer and Nail* and his take on her disappointing professional life. There was just too much energy in the air when they were near each other, as if someone had added one too many sticks of dynamite and accidentally lit the fuse. "Lord knows we can use all the significant assets we can get." She felt as if they were standing too close, though a good foot separated them.

He flashed an automatic smile before he caught himself, and she couldn't help noticing how white his teeth seemed against the tan of his face.

"In a few weeks we should be ready to refinish Bella Flora's floors," she said. "I thought we might move in here while we do the work."

"You want to live in here?" he asked, incredulous. "All five of you?"

No, she didn't, but there was no room in her budget for a weeklong stay anywhere, not even the Cottage Inn. She and Nicole and Maddie never discussed how broke they were, but Nicole no longer turned up her nose at Madeline's coupon clipping, though she still steadfastly rejected any hint of a senior citizen discount and hated early bird specials. The only one in the group who might opt for a hotel was Deirdre, and that would be just fine with Avery. "Do I want to stay here?" she said. "No. But I will. And I'm pretty sure the others will, too."

She blew at a bang that had fallen down over one eye, but it fell right back down. Chase was definitely standing too close, because he didn't have to move when he reached out with one hand and tucked it behind her ear. They both frowned in surprise at the automatic gesture, but continued to stare into each other's eyes.

From outside she could hear Nicole and Joe Giraldi arguing about something. There was the whir of a saw from inside the house and an unidentifiable banging, but inside the pool house it was so quiet she could hear Chase's breathing and what she was afraid might be the beating of her heart.

His blue eyes darkened. If she wasn't reading this all wrong, he was about to . . . "You're not going to kiss me, are you?" she asked.

"Of course not," he said. His voice was gruff. "I was afraid you were going to kiss me."

"Right." That was all she could manage around the lump lodged in her throat.

They stood frozen for a long moment, gazes locked, teetering on the verge of . . . she wasn't sure what. And then although she had no idea who moved first or even that someone had, their lips were locked and his warm, firm lips were moving on hers. His strong male scent filled her nostrils. Her keen awareness of his naked chest lent an added rush and she realized with some surprise that she was kissing him back. Fervently.

"Oh, there you two are!" Deirdre's voice pierced her consciousness, and they jumped apart like two children caught playing doctor.

Avery felt her face flush with embarrassment. She also felt a rush of irritation at Deirdre's intrusion. The irritation was nothing new; the twinge of disappointment that accompanied it was.

Deirdre laughed. "If I've come at a bad time, I can come back later."

They both swore. Their gazes collided and Avery saw the same horror she felt etched in Chase's eyes. They both looked away.

"We were just discussing the space," Avery said, all too aware how lame that sounded.

"Yes, I could see that." Deirdre seemed to be smirking. Avery would have liked to see Chase's expression, but she didn't want to be caught looking at him.

"What is it?" Chase asked Deirdre. "Did you need something?"

"Actually, I've got great news," Deirdre said and then paused as if waiting for a drum roll. "The presidents of the design and symphony guild are coming for a tour. There's been a problem with their show house. They may be looking for a last-minute change of location."

Thirty

Thunder boomed outside and lightning jagged through the steel gray sky. The rain fell in sheets outside Bella Flora for two days straight, the result of a tropical storm stalled somewhere out in the Gulf.

Used to searing sunshine with only brief afternoon rain showers that fell from bright blue skies, none of them knew quite what to do. It felt odd to be so idle when so much still needed to be done. But it was too wet to move their things into the pool house and refinish the wood floors as planned. Too wet for painting or touching up. As they played cards at the kitchen table, then gathered in the salon to watch *The Money Pit* for the third time, Maddie found herself thinking, *The sun did not shine. It was too wet to play. So we sat in the house all that cold, cold, wet day.* Replace the word "cold" with "dark," Maddie thought, and it was so them. The only things missing were Thing One and Thing Two.

With a sigh, she stopped squinting out the salon windows trying to make out anything through the curtain of rain. The pool house, the seawall, the pass, and Shell Island had temporarily ceased to exist. Maddie's gaze turned to Kyra, stretched flat on the sofa except for the rise of her stomach, the bowl of popcorn propped beside her. How many thousands of times had Maddie read *The Cat in the Hat* to Kyra and Andrew? Would she read it soon to Kyra's son or daughter?

They hadn't really spoken about the horrendous call from Tonja Kay, though Maddie had the sense that it had brought them to a truce of sorts. Maddie shook her head as she remembered her own response. As memories went, both sides of that conversation were truly cringe-worthy.

Sunset was impossible to pinpoint in the downpour, but when the movie ended Deirdre called a meeting in the Casbah Lounge to discuss and toast the show house opportunity.

Nicole blended a pitcher of piña coladas while Maddie heated up a cookie sheet of Bagel Bites and mini-quiche, the most recent selections from the frozen appetizer section at Sam's Club. Avery poured her prized Cheez Doodles into a serving bowl. Then they put on exaggerated Moroccan accents and invited each other to "meet me in zee Casbah."

The 1920s-era Spanish tiles gleamed in blues and reds and yellows. They bypassed the room's two banquettes, framed by tiled columns supporting Moorish arches and set up on the tiled bar, Nikki playing bartender behind it, the others climbing up on high-backed stools.

"So," Deirdre said right off. "I propose a toast to Bella Flora, this year's Symphony Designer Show House!"

"Oh, my God! That's so great!" Madeline said. "I feel like we've just gotten that last-minute reprieve from the governor." She, Nicole, and Avery raised their piña coladas. Kyra raised her nonalcoholic version.

"That's because we have," Deirdre said. "The Designer Show House was already scheduled to open the week after Labor Day, which is perfect timing for us. And it was set for another Mediterranean Revival on Snell Isle." She named the tony northeast St. Petersburg neighborhood. "But just two weeks ago, when the designers had already finished their plans and were ready to start working on their actual rooms, the owner backed out."

"Why?" Madeline asked.

"The owner has decided to tear it down and sell the land. There's been quite an uproar."

"Can he do that?" Nicole asked.

"Apparently. I mean everyone from his neighbors to the preservation community is livid, but the owner's in debt and hasn't been able to sell the house. He can't afford to maintain it. Unless his neighbors are willing to pitch in and buy it there's not a lot they can do."

Maddie looked around the bar and thought about all that had gone into Bella Flora; what an amazing house it was. When they'd first come it was simply a project of last resort, but she was incredibly glad they hadn't torn it down.

"The show house people must have been ready to kiss your feet when you showed up with an alternative," Nicole said. "This is about as win-win as it gets."

"Yes," Deirdre agreed. "And I may have implied that we might be able to get some sort of coverage through our connections at Lifetime and HGTV." She smiled and took a sip of her drink. "It never hurts to dangle that extra carrot.

"I've invited the designers to come choose the rooms they want. Hopefully, they can adapt their original designs to fit Bella Flora. The fact that both houses are of the same period and style will be a huge help."

"How much will they take over?" Maddie asked. "I mean, what do we have left to do?"

"Design-wise, since I've already started on the kitchen and the pool house, we'll be responsible for seeing those all the way through; I'll need your help with that. And I thought someone might approach Renée Franklin and her garden club to make sure they're willing to finish the landscaping. We can offer them a credit in the program and possibly some tasteful signage."

"I'll talk to her," Nikki said. "I bet they'd like that. Will the designers finish everything else?"

"Pretty much. We'll need to get the steam heat taken care of so the pool can get done. How long do you think it'll take to get someone here?"

"I'll call Tim back in the morning," Nikki replied. "We've been playing phone tag. I won't let him say no. But we'll probably have to take care of the workmen's airfare and hotel and other expenses."

Avery had pulled out a pad and was making notes. Madeline wondered how she felt about Deirdre becoming so crucial to their effort and how easily she seemed to be able to juggle all the details; another trait she and her daughter shared.

"I figure it'll take us about a week to refinish the wood floors and any other structural things that remain. And then maybe another to help paint the exterior of the house. That would put us into the middle of August and leave us a little room for weather delays and so on. Does that seem like a workable time frame, Avery?"

She got a somewhat reluctant nod of agreement from Avery. All Maddie could think about was whether Steve would be here by then. She wanted so badly to believe he'd make it, but was horribly afraid that meant she was living beside her daughter in the land of denial.

"The designers can use that time to adapt their ideas," Deirdre continued. "But once the floors are done, we'll have to give them free access; they're going to be under a major time crunch." She paused and cocked her head toward her daughter. "I figure Avery and Chase can be in charge of scheduling and supervising our efforts." She kept her gaze on Avery, but Avery didn't respond. She did, however, seem to be blushing.

Maddie watched her stop writing, then slowly set down the pen. The blush had almost faded when Avery looked up from the pad. "Obviously we need to get started on the floors. So we'll have to make the move to the pool house as soon as the rain stops."

There was a collective groan even though they'd all known it was coming.

"It's going to be pretty cramped in there," Avery said, zeroing in on Deirdre. "Maybe you'd be happier at a hotel."

A small flush spread over Deirdre's cheeks, but Maddie

wasn't sure if it was one of hurt, anger, or embarrassment. The designer folded her hands on the bar in front of her. "I'll be fine here," she said, her tone crisp. "But thank you for your concern."

They contemplated each other and Maddie was almost glad when Kyra lifted her video camera to her eye to preserve their identical expressions. Maddie wondered, not for the first time, whether Deirdre would succeed in building something with her daughter. She wondered if she'd be able to hold on to what she'd always had with Kyra.

Deirdre looked away first and addressed the group. "With each designer doing a room, it'll really cut back on our time and expense. Of course there'll be unexpected things that crop up, but I feel far better now about hitting our Labor Day deadline."

With the high points hit, the meeting portion of their faux sunset ended. Avery popped the last Cheez Doodle into her mouth and Nicole divvied up the last of the piña coladas. Inside the lounge with its leaded glass casement windows it was somehow both exotic and cozy.

"So," Avery said after she'd wiped the last of the cheese from her lips. "What did Tonja Kay sound like on the phone?"

"Pissed off," Maddie said. "And extremely vulgar."

Kyra snorted her agreement.

"I've never heard such foul language." Maddie shuddered at the memory.

"I knew it wasn't going to be good when she asked to talk to the 'whore's mother,'" Kyra admitted.

"And you just handed the phone over?" Nicole asked.

"Well, Mom was standing right there, and I guess I was too stunned to think straight," Kyra said. Maddie felt her daughter's gaze on her; Kyra had been more than stunned, she'd been devastated that it wasn't Daniel on the line.

"But Mom gave it right back to her," Kyra said. "I didn't even realize she knew some of those words. I know I've never heard her say any of them."

They all turned to look at her. Maddie shrugged. "She

provoked me." This, of course, was an understatement. The woman's ugly attack had left her with no recourse but to defend her child.

Nicole considered Madeline and Kyra. "I hope you know how lucky you are, Kyra. Your mother's one of the most nurturing women I've ever met. And she's definitely got your back." She looked down at her glass before meeting Maddie's gaze. "That's not always the way it works."

Maddie smiled her thanks to Nikki, and figured Avery would take the opportunity to get a dig in at her own mother, but it was Deirdre who said sadly, "No, it's not."

In the silence that followed, Maddie lifted her mostly empty glass. "Well, I propose a toast to Deirdre snagging the design and symphony people! And to how close we are to completion!"

They drank.

"I'm already trying to figure out what I'm going to do with the money from the sale of Bella Flora . . . after we pay off the bills." Of course there'd be Andrew's tuition and Kyra's delivery and whatever the baby would need. Still, Maddie felt almost starry-eyed thinking about not having to pinch every penny.

"I can hardly wait to buy pretty clothes again. Hell, I can hardly wait to *wear* some," Nikki said. "Soffes and T-shirts do not count!"

"And I'm going to buy something that I can spend my time designing and remodeling," Avery said, her glass held high. "I just hope I'll have enough left over to hire my own grunts instead of being one!"

Kyra filmed all of their toasts and boasts, offering nothing of her own. But Maddie knew what she was holding out for. A healthy baby went without saying, but Maddie didn't know how likely a happily ever after could be with someone who'd chosen to marry the likes of Tonja Kay.

Sometime during the night the rain finally stopped. Maddie wasn't sure what woke her. It might have been the abrupt silence. Or maybe all the worries that kept trailing through her mind finally registered, demanding to be dealt with.

She climbed off her mattress and stood, stepping carefully around Kyra's futon. Her daughter slept on her side, her cheek pillowed in her palm, her long dark hair spilling over one slim shoulder. The sheets were tangled and Maddie bent down to gently smooth the covers around her. She slept deeply, a small smile on her lips. Maddie was glad that her dreams, at least, were happy.

Padding down the stairs, she paused on the landing to stare out the fixed glass. The backyard was pale in the moonlight, the pool house little more than a long rectangle of deeper shadow. Out on the pass, the moon was reflected on the now calm water. Shell Key was a large lump of darkness in the distance.

Downstairs she walked from room to room, listening carefully to the creaks and moans as the house settled in the silence. In the kitchen she sat at the table and reached for the laptop she'd left there. After booting it up and logging onto the Internet, she stared at the screen for a time before clicking on the link to YouTube, where she watched all of the posts so far and had to admit that although all of them had been exposed in ways they never would have chosen, Kyra had also managed to catch not only the personalities of the participants but the tone of their life together and what anyone could see was a growing friendship.

But she hadn't turned to the computer for a YouTube evaluation. Screwing up her courage, she typed in her password and waited for AOL to come up. Unwilling to continue to place calls to Steve that went unanswered, she'd sent him an email and asked Andrew to make sure his father at least saw it. She'd been putting off looking for a response, afraid there wouldn't be one. But August was upon them. She needed to know whether it was time to rejoice or to give up hope.

She double clicked on the mail icon and almost closed her eyes, afraid to look. But there was an email from Steve waiting. Holding her breath, she clicked it open, telling herself that whatever it was it was something. And that even if it was from Andrew it would be okay.

The message was short and to the point. It was written in Steve's usual style with none of the lowercase breeziness that had become so popular. Maddie licked her dry lips as she read, *Very sorry I left you holding the bag. You deserve better. Steve.*

She reread it far too many times trying to decide exactly what it meant. Was it just a straightforward apology with no promise of change? Did it signal an end or a beginning?

Maddie stared out over the dark backyard and the still water beyond and prayed that it would somehow turn out to be both.

Thirty-one

The move into the pool house didn't take long. They had little baggage, Avery thought, except for the emotional kind. Chase, Giraldi, and Robby, who was back, along with the current Dante family member, moved the rest.

Following Deirdre's direction, they crammed the couch, TV, chair, and Kyra's futon into an approximation of a living area at the end overlooking the pass. Maddie, Avery, Nicole, and Deirdre's mattresses filled in the center of the space and left just enough room to fit in three barstools at the oversized kitchen counter.

"Well," Deirdre said, having to step back into the doorway to study the space. "As design styles go I'd have to label this 'jam-packed.'"

"No kidding. When we get in bed we're going to look like sardines wedged into a tin," Nicole said.

"It does give downsizing a whole new meaning," Maddie said. "But I think it's kind of cozy."

"Claustrophobic is a better word." Kyra had her camera out and was already panning across the row of mattresses.

"No, seriously." As always Maddie seemed determined to

put the best spin on things. "It's kind of like a tree house without the tree. Or a clubhouse."

"Do you really have to shoot in here?" Nicole asked. "It's bad enough having to be the sardine. I can't stand having it broadcast all over the Internet. My reputation is already shot. I don't know how I'll ever show my face again in Palm Beach or L.A. Why don't we just keep this final humiliation to ourselves?"

"I don't know," Maddie said. "We're up to fifty thousand views, which means Bella Flora is getting some pretty broad exposure. And most of the comments have been really positive."

"Some of us don't see 'not bad for a bunch of old broads,' as particularly positive." Nicole's tone was dry. "Ditto for 'where's the button to vote people off this reality show?'"

"I thought the 'we want more of the hunky guys' comments were pretty positive," Chase said, coming to join them.

"I'm pretty sure they were referring to Giraldi and Umberto," Avery said.

Giraldi, who now stood in the open doorway, took a mock bow and struck an exaggerated muscle pose. Nicole gave Giraldi a once-over. "Don't let it go to your head."

He just smiled and flexed. Once again Avery wondered what was up with them.

"My favorite was 'almost as entertaining as Foreman vs. Frazier,'" Deirdre said. "I'm pretty sure that one was about you and Chase."

Everyone got a big yuck over that, but Avery was not amused. She didn't have the energy to argue about video and was far too busy thinking about what still had to be done and how they were going to accomplish it to get sidetracked by all the weird vibes zinging between her and Chase. Not to mention living in even closer proximity to Deirdre, who'd turned out to be not at all as expected. And far more valuable to all of them than Avery would have liked.

Today Deirdre had gotten Chase and Giraldi to mount an additional towel bar and decorative hooks in the tiny bathroom. With Maddie's help she'd organized a rolling clothing rack, a dresser, and a temporary shelving unit for their clothes, somehow managing to fit in the necessities and still make the space surprisingly stylish.

She did all this while impeccably dressed and in full makeup. But although she looked like the Design Diva the television shows and magazines had always made her out to be, she didn't actually whine, demand, or complain. She just got things done. Her determination to establish a relationship with Avery hadn't wilted under the living or working conditions. When the going had gotten tough, she'd gotten going. What she hadn't done was turned and run.

"I think we need to put a big sign outside that says, Girls Only, No Boys Allowed," Avery said.

"Yeah and we can have a secret handshake. Maybe even a password." Nicole's tone remained dry.

Avery looked up and noticed that once again Kyra was filming it all.

Broad shouldered, Chase and Joe pretty much filled the doorway. "That's all right. We don't want any of those girl cooties anyway," Chase said. "Do we, Joe?"

"I don't know, I'm thinking panty raid." Joe grinned and shot Nicole a look, which she pointedly ignored.

Avery wished she could tune out Chase as easily, but she always felt so damned . . . aware of him. Pretending to ignore someone wasn't at all the same as actually not noticing them. Still, she couldn't let her adolescent reactions or the fact that she'd been stupid enough to kiss him keep them from doing what had to be done, not when they were getting so close to the finish line.

She caught up with Chase beside the pool. "When will we be able to start on the floors?" she asked, careful not to get close enough to get caught up in all that zinging.

"The belt sander's up in the master," he replied. "I've got my floor guy scheduled to start first thing in the morning."

Avery nodded. After the initial sanding, a coat of stain would be applied, then a coat of polyurethane, which would

sit for twenty-four hours. This would be followed by a light
sanding and a last coat of poly. All in all a week to ten days
should see the floors ready for foot traffic.

"Of course both sets of stairs and the edges and thresholds
will have to be sanded by hand." Chase looked her in the eye,
and she caught herself remembering the way he'd looked at
her as he moved in for the kiss. "I figure if we put all five of
you on that, we can get the first pass done in two days and
be ready to stain."

Avery closed her eyes and groaned, though a grunt would
have been more appropriate. "Oh, God. I don't have the heart
to tell Nicole or Maddie just how tedious and backbreaking
a job that is."

"I can get my guy and his people to do the whole thing,"
Chase said easily, and she wondered if he were a better actor
than she was or simply didn't feel all that zinged between
them. "But it'll be pricey. We can cut the overhead significantly if you all handle the staining, too."

The grunt rose in her throat and Avery bit it back. Having to agree with Chase was almost painful, but he was right;
she'd much rather keep that money in their pockets. "All
right," she said finally, meeting his gaze while being careful
not to be drawn into it. "But you can do the demo and get
everybody started. You can be the slave driver that everybody
hates. I could end up banished from the clubhouse."

He nodded but didn't look away. His eyes dropped to her
lips, and she knew exactly what he was thinking about.

"And about that kiss?" she said, pulling his gaze back
up to meet hers. "I think we should pretend it didn't happen. Because of course it shouldn't have. And we don't ever
want it to happen again." She realized she was blathering and
stopped, not caring one bit for the glimmer of amusement
that had stolen into his eyes.

"Are you listening?" she asked, off kilter now as he'd no
doubt intended.

"Of course," he said smoothly. "You want to pretend that
we didn't kiss the hell out of each other in the pool house."

"Um, right." He was standing too close again, making it difficult for Avery to catch her breath. If they hadn't been outside she wouldn't have had enough air to breathe. "So what do you have to say about that?"

He shrugged. "What is there to say other than 'what kiss?'"

Madeline had thought glazing was tedious, but it had nothing on hand sanding. At first when Chase gave them each a piece of two-by-four wrapped in sandpaper and explained that they'd be using it to sand the edges up against the walls of the rooms, the thresholds, and then the balusters and front edges of both sets of stairs, she'd squinted at the small block of wood in her hand and assumed he was joking. He wasn't.

Without even a hint of a smile he'd positioned them around the upper floor and put them to work. She and Kyra started in Avery's back bedroom, away from the electric sander and the fine wood dust it kicked up. Kyra sat on her rear and attacked a small section at a time before scooting along to the next section. Her video camera sat on the floor nearby and her head bobbed to some tune playing on her earphones.

They were supposed to finish the upper floor and begin on the stairs before the end of the day. It had only been an hour and a half and her hand was starting to cramp and her shoulders ached; she'd barely made it through the L of one bedroom wall.

The loud whir of the sander in the master bedroom prohibited conversation, but it also camouflaged the muttering and the groans. Deirdre and Nicole each had a front bedroom while Avery worked her way down one side of the hallway.

When it was—thank you, God—at last time to break for lunch they hobbled downstairs and fell into kitchen chairs. Even Maddie was too tired to contemplate so much as spreading peanut butter over a slice of bread. Through one of the kitchen windows she watched Chase Hardin conferring with the steam heat guy Nicole had found them in New York.

When her neck could no longer support her head, she folded her arms on the table, laid her forehead on them and thought longingly of her mattress in the pool house, which just went to show how relative the concept of comfort could be. As she closed her eyes and tried to regroup, she did her best not to think about what Steve was or wasn't doing. She hadn't been able to speak to him since his cryptic email and had the sense he was avoiding her, but she couldn't quite bring herself to give up all hope.

If there was anything she'd learned from working on Bella Flora, it was to focus on one task at a time and refuse to be overwhelmed by the enormity of what still had to be done. She would not be Chicken Little or the Little Red Hen. She'd be that ant in the proverb who consumed the elephant one small bite at a time.

Kyra, who sat at the opposite end of the table, raised her camera to pan across their ravaged faces. Even Deirdre, who'd spent the longest in the pool house bathroom that morning, looked tired and disheveled.

"Really?" Nicole asked, apparently unable to mount a full protest. "Do you have to?"

Kyra shrugged. With her hair pulled up in a high pony-tail, the big gray eyes and the smattering of freckles across the bridge of her nose, she might have been twelve except for the rounded belly and bulging breasts. Maddie knew that Kyra still clung to the hope that her hero, Daniel, was going to swoop in and carry her off into the sunset, but since the call from Tonja Kay, they'd established a certain détente; Kyra no longer voiced her expectation, and Maddie no longer tried to break her of it.

"We're getting too many followers both on YouTube and Twitter to just disappear now," Kyra said.

"Oh, joy," Maddie thought, raising her head. She did not want to think of all of those strangers watching and commenting on their daily struggle.

The doorbell rang, and they all looked at each other, silently willing someone else to get up and answer it.

"I couldn't get up right now if it was Ed McMahon with a check for a million dollars from the Publishers Clearing House," Nicole said.

"Ed McMahon's not delivering checks anymore. He's dead," Deirdre said. "Johnny, too." She said this with regret.

"I don't care," Nicole said. "I wouldn't even get up if he came back from the other side especially to deliver it."

"Me, neither," Avery chimed in. They turned to Maddie as if she were going to get up any minute and go to the door, but she couldn't even make herself walk the five feet to the refrigerator.

Chase poked his head into the kitchen, saw them drooping around the table, and strode to the front door. Maddie couldn't imagine moving that quickly ever again.

All of them perked up when he reappeared with two pizza boxes emitting the most heavenly smell. He'd barely set them on the table when the first was thrown open and they were reaching for slices.

"Bless you," Deirdre said. "Remind me to tell your father what a good boy you are." She took a large bite and sighed with the same degree of pleasure she'd previously reserved for caviar and the other delicacies she and Nicole occasionally bought for their sunsets.

"I agree." Maddie dragged herself out of her seat and went to the fridge to retrieve the pitcher of iced tea. Kyra struggled up out of her chair and went to the cupboard for glasses. "If I weren't so busy stuffing my face I'd call him right now and tell him."

"Me, too," Nicole said between bites. "I'm going to email him as soon as I'm done eating." She licked her fingers and then beat Avery to the last piece in the first box. Kyra flipped open the second box and helped herself to a slice.

"It was very sweet of you to provide lunch today," Maddie said. Her shoulders still hurt and her back ached, but she could feel her spirits rise with each bite. She only had to make it through the rest of today and tomorrow. Chase had shown them the mop-like applicators they'd be using for the staining and sealing. Surely that would be easier than all this hand sanding. Like the ant versus the elephant, the floors were just one more bite.

Avery ate as rapidly as the rest of them, but she was eyeing Chase with suspicion. "There's no such thing as a free lunch, ladies. Especially not where Chase is concerned."

He smiled amiably but didn't deny the accusation. "I can't have you fainting from hunger," he said. "And we don't have time for hunting and gathering." He reached over to pluck a stray pepperoni from the box. "We're on a tight schedule." He walked over to the counter and carried the napkin holder to the table. "Even monkeys need a banana now and then."

Nicole gritted her teeth as she sat on the couch in the pool house and viewed that night's YouTube posting. It began with shots of the last two days' hand sanding and was cut to the theme song from the Monkees. Every other shot was a close-up of a female hand clutching a wood sanding block. The skin on those very different hands was scraped and bloody; the fingernails jagged and dirty.

In between the shots of sandpaper in motion were unforgiving close-ups of sweat-soaked faces, the set of hunched backs and shoulders. She cringed at the first glimpse of her own face furrowed in concentration, her age and discomfort clearly etched in the lines that bracketed her mouth and radiated outward from her eyes. Once again Kyra had demonstrated their monkey-like servitude, but had also managed to capture their grim determination now that the end of their labors was within sight.

Chase Hardin would undoubtedly get a good chuckle out of the video and its music track. Giraldi would probably enjoy it, too. The agent had been absent for the last four or five days, which both relieved and worried her as she continued to wrestle with whether to tell him about her conversation with Malcolm or assume that he already knew. She had no idea what her brother would think if he could see what he'd reduced them to. If he checked out Kyra's YouTube postings, would he feel guilty or care in the least? All she knew for sure was that barely three weeks remained until August 25; she was running out of time to figure out her next move.

The music changed and drew her back to the video. She heard the plaintive "we-de-de-de" and then the "a-wimawehs" of "The Lion Sleeps Tonight" covered by shots of them sleeping on their mattresses in the sardine can of the pool house, their exhaustion apparent in the sprawl of their bodies beneath the sheets. The bright yellow ball of moon hung over the pass, clearly defined in the pool house window just as it was now.

In another five or six days when the floors were done and dry, the designers would take over the interior of Bella Flora and the monkey squad would move outside to help paint the exterior of the house. Avery said they'd be done sometime the week before Labor Day. Which meant she could go meet Malcolm on the twenty-fifth without arousing suspicion if she chose to.

The video ended, and she scrolled down to read some of the comments. They now had eighty-five thousand views and a surprisingly large number of viewers who posted regularly. The odds that her clients and friends in New York and L.A. didn't know she was slaving away on this house out of desperation were small to no-way-in-hell. If she ever saw Malcolm again, she'd have to be sure to thank him for it.

Thirty-two

After a week of almost cloudless skies, it rained during the night. In the morning, they treated themselves to breakfast at the Seahorse, then walked in a light drizzle back to the house, where everyone but Avery climbed into Maddie's van for a trip down to a Sarasota design center. Avery noticed that Nicole no longer quibbled about accepting a ride in what she'd dubbed the mother-mobile, but seemed perfectly happy to give up the shotgun seat to Deirdre.

As they backed down the drive and disappeared around the corner, it hit Avery that these onetime strangers were now among the handful of people she knew best. Alone, Avery walked around the house to the backyard. On the loggia she stared out over the repaired but still empty pool. Despite the raindrops that still fell, sweat pooled between her breasts and slid down the small of her back; her T-shirt clung like a damp rag. She would have liked to take a shower and stretch out on the couch in the pool house with the air-conditioning set on "igloo"; having the space to herself for a few hours would be completely heavenly. But she had work to do.

"Onward," she muttered, throwing open the French doors

to the salon, whose wood floor needed its final coat, and inhaled a face full of chemicals. Sputtering and gasping for breath, Avery turned her back on the room that had been shut tightly against the rain, hoping that at least some of the pent-up fumes would escape.

After drawing in a few deep breaths of fresh, if humid, air she eased out of her sneakers and stepped into the room in her white socks. The wood, laid inside a basket-woven brick border, already gleamed brightly. Just one more coat, she told herself, trying to keep her breathing shallow. One more coat and a day to dry and Bella Flora would be ready for humans again, as long as they wore white socks those first few days.

Carefully, she poured the polyurethane into the pan, which she'd set in the rectangular room's far corner, and dipped the mop head into it. Gently she began to spread the protective layer, smoothing it on with the grain of the wood, spreading it as evenly as she could, as she worked her way back to the French doors.

The smell seeped into her nose with each breath, making her throat burn and her eyes water. As she squinted against the assault, she wished she'd thought to bring goggles and a mask. For a moment she imagined tears squeezing their way out and landing on the floor, possibly causing the wood to bubble. Would she be able to catch them before they landed? The thought made her smile.

She worked steadily, trying to concentrate on each stroke and each backward step, but the thoughts flitting around in her head began to flit more quickly and then began to border on the bizarre. She stumbled and used the mop handle to keep herself from falling into the still-wet polyurethane.

Outside a truck rattled onto the brick driveway. A single door opened and slammed shut. Chase materialized in her mind, contributing to an odd light-headedness. A cartoon heart drew itself before her eyes and thumped wildly, which struck her as hugely entertaining. She laughed out loud.

Still smiling, Avery took two steps back and pulled the pan of poly with her. Her lips felt larger than usual, her tongue too thick for her mouth. It slid out to smooth her dry lips, and she realized they'd automatically twisted up into a kind of loopy smile.

Chase's footsteps crunched on the gritty concrete around the pool, and she stole a peek out the window. He stood contemplating the pass as she had earlier, his expression reflective. Then he walked to where the pipes for the steam heat system still lay exposed and crouched down to inspect them. Avery giggled.

Although he couldn't have heard her, something made Chase turn toward the salon. His brow furrowed as he stood and looked her way. Avery pushed the mop back and forth a few times and giggled harder.

"Avery?" Chase's voice sounded behind her.

Startled, she turned and teetered precariously, almost falling into the section she'd just finished. His hand shot out and wrapped around her upper arm to steady her. It was warm and firm, just as his lips had been. She glanced down at the patch of floor she'd just finished and knew she was lucky her socks weren't now stuck to it. Then she turned and looked at him.

He smiled, and she burst into laughter.

"What's so funny?" He leaned close to peer directly into her eyes. "Are you all right?"

She nodded, which made her head spin wildly. This, too, made her laugh. Chase looked at her as if she'd gone batty.

"Avery?" His hold on her upper arm tightened, and he reached across her to take the mop. "How long have you been in here breathing these fumes?"

She felt her eyes get big as he put the mop down and used both arms to lift her off the floor and cradle her against his chest.

"Don't know," she said, surprised when the laughter turned to tears, unable to make sense of what was happening. "But I can't cry on the floor." She looked up urgently. "It's not good to let it get wet."

The tears slid down her cheeks, but Chase carried her out

of the room and onto the loggia before they could land. There he dropped onto the wicker sofa, still holding her against his chest with her bottom cushioned in his lap.

"Tha's nice," she said.

His chest rumbled beneath her ear, and she raised her head to look into his laughing eyes. "'S not funny," she said as the tears continued to slide down her cheeks, dampening both of their shirts. "Don't want to have to start over. Have to kill myself first." She buried her face in his dampened T-shirt, her thoughts still swirling. "Hey," she said in amazement. "You smell good."

"You are completely blotto," he said, setting his chest humming again against her ear. "That's what happens when you try to seal a floor without proper ventilation."

She wasn't sure what he was talking about, but she liked the way his arms felt around her. She especially liked the feel of his chest rumbling beneath her ear, the safe feeling that enveloped her.

"Can I kiss you?" she asked but then went ahead without waiting for an answer. His lips felt even better than she remembered. And so did his tongue when she managed to locate it.

"Avery." He pulled his mouth free but didn't let go of her. "I don't think . . ."

"Good." She breathed him in and felt him all around her. "Don't think." She brought their lips together again and kissed him more fully, pressing her bottom into his lap. He hardened underneath her. "I'm not." She moved her tongue to his ear while the rhythm of her blood whooshed in her own. "Can't think right now. Don't want to." Her mouth formed the loopy smile that it apparently preferred. For fun, she nibbled on his earlobe and repositioned herself slightly so she could rub her chest against his. "Doesn't that feel good?"

He groaned and shifted beneath her. "Jesus, Avery. You're not going to like it when you wake up and realize . . ."

She stopped the words, which made no sense to her at all, with her mouth, kissing him until he finally shut up and kissed her back like she wanted him to. Thoroughly. Deeply. Completely.

Then, although she hadn't realized it was possible to kiss all the way into oblivion, she must have figured out how to do it. Because all of a sudden, everything went dark.

"Avery?" There was that rumble under her ear again. "Ave?"

She tried to burrow into the sound. "Hmmmm?"

"Avery, you've been sleeping on my arm so long it's gone numb. Put your arms up around my neck. I'm going to carry you into the pool house and put you to bed." Her arms slid up as directed. There was movement. "That's it. Hold on."

Her arms clung to his neck as he rose, taking her with him. Her mind was a lovely blank except for the strong arms and solid wall of chest. The world had stopped spinning, but she held on anyway. The word "bed" made her feel all warm and tingly. Her nipples strained against the thin fabric of her T-shirt and there was a deep tug between her legs. If this was a dream, she wasn't anywhere near ready to wake up.

Then there was another voice. One that she knew. But it wasn't at all warm or rumbly.

In fact, it was the tone of shock in it that roused her.

"Avery?" the voice said. "Avery, what's wrong?" And then, "What in the hell are you doing to her, Hardin?"

Avery's eyes flew open. It took them a moment to adjust to the sunlight and bring the person standing in front of them into focus. Recognition hit her like a pail of ice water. The voice belonged to Trent. Trent Lawson, her ex-husband.

"Where's Trent?" Deirdre asked that evening over sunset drinks. "Is he going to join us for dinner?" She looked closely at Avery as if she knew her well enough to glean the answer just from studying her face.

The rain was finally gone, and while Avery wouldn't have

called the air refreshing, it had cooled things off a bit. Except
for the flush of heat she felt each time she remembered her
behavior that day.

"I can't believe we missed all the excitement," Madeline
said. "Did you really get high from the polyurethane?"

Avery winced. The details were mercifully sketchy, except
for the fact that she'd been clinging to Chase like a second
skin when Trent showed up out of nowhere.

"We could have saved a ton on alcohol this summer if we'd
known," Nicole added, handing her version of mango daiquiris around. "I'm pretty sure a gallon of poly is less expensive
than a gallon of good rum."

"And apparently faster acting," Avery said as she declined
the drink to stare out over the Gulf. It was difficult to decide
which part of today she didn't want to think about most.

"It's a lucky thing Chase was here. If you'd been exposed
to the fumes any longer, there could have been serious consequences," Deirdre said.

As opposed to abject humiliation. "Yes," Avery said. "I
certainly feel lucky."

"So where is Trent?" Deirdre asked again. "And what did
he want?"

Avery continued to stare out over the water. The sky had
lightened to a pale gray shot through with even paler pink
streaks. As hazy as her memory of all that had come before
still was, the conversation with Trent was excruciatingly sharp.

"He asked me to come back to *Hammer and Nail*."

There was a brief silence as they all processed this bit of
information.

"Well, I hope he apologized first for letting them treat
you the way they did on that show." The comment was from
Deirdre again. Her tone was fierce.

Avery looked at her in surprise. "I thought you were such
a big fan of Trent's. As I recall you sent me a letter of congratulations after we announced our engagement, telling
me how lucky I was to 'land him.'" She'd torn the letter up,

furious that Deirdre had presumed to comment, but had secretly agreed.

"We all make mistakes," Deirdre said. "On paper, he seemed perfect for you. But he didn't love you anywhere near as much as he seemed to love himself. I've been in Hollywood long enough to know that what you see is often not what you get. And I got Trent all wrong."

"It happens," Nicole said quietly. "Even the people you think you know the best can shit all over you. If you ever find anyone who puts you first, you need to hold on to them."

"Your father put me first, but I was too young to understand how rare that was. Or that it might never happen again." Deirdre was looking at the sunset now, too.

Avery considered the women around her. All of them looked solemn. Maddie's eyes glistened with tears. Kyra just looked wistful, but she didn't chime in with her usual comment about Daniel and their love for each other. Maybe she'd run out of excuses for why he hadn't shown up yet. Not that having your past materialize unexpectedly before your eyes felt like such a good thing at the moment.

"So?" Nicole asked. "Are you going to do it? What did you tell him?"

All of their gazes fixed on her, but she knew it was out of concern and not just idle curiosity. It was odd how important they'd become to her, how reassuring it was to know she wasn't slogging through everything alone. Well, everyone but Deirdre anyway.

She hesitated for a few moments, remembering how reluctant Chase had been to put her down and leave her with Trent. He'd bristled like a guard dog, practically growling at Trent, until she'd convinced him she was capable of talking for herself.

She smiled at them all, still surprised by how urgently Trent had tried to convince her to come back; she wished she'd had a tape recorder to play back all the things he'd promised.

"Oh, he apologized all right," Avery said. "But then he

told me he knew just how bad things were for me, how he'd heard I had pretty much nothing left, and that the show was doing great, but he really wanted to help me." She grimaced at the memory. He'd been so certain of himself. And of her.

"And?" Nicole asked the question Avery saw in all of their eyes.

Avery's smile turned even grimmer as she remembered how thick Trent had poured it on: how much he missed her; what an unappreciated asset she'd been to the show; how different it would be if she came back. His feigned sympathy had made her want to puke.

"And if I were as big an airhead as Trent and the producers of the show seem to think I am, I'd be on my way back to Nashville right now," she said.

Deirdre's eyebrow went up. She smiled. "They always underestimate us blondes."

"But I saw a recent blurb in the trades about how Victoria Crosshaven, Trent's biggest admirer, has lost interest in the show. And that there's some question about whether it'll be picked up for another season." She looked up and smiled. "And, of course, he made the mistake of mentioning the following we have on YouTube. How there's been chatter all over the Internet about Ten Beach Road. Apparently some-one's even set up a fan site for us."

Only Kyra didn't look surprised at the level of Internet interest. All of them leaned closer.

"And?" Madeline asked, clearly needing to hear her answer.

"And I thanked him for his belated concern."

Avery smiled as she remembered the shock on Trent's face at what followed. It had been so incredibly sweet. "And then I told him to go fuck himself. And I showed him to the door."

Thirty-three

On August 6 another tropical storm formed in the Caribbean and held together long enough to be given a name. While they waited for the wood floors to dry, Tropical Storm Bernard rained down upon the islands of Haiti and Jamaica. Winds blowing from the east moved it farther westward where it gathered strength and picked up speed. Intent on finishing before the Labor Day weekend, Chase stepped up the start date for exterior painting. In hopes of finishing before the band of thunderstorms preceding Bernard or any sibling storms it might spawn could reach them, they prepared to paint.

It was August 8, the end of the first week of the month, the date by which Steve was supposed to appear. Maddie opened her eyes slowly when the morning light first trickled through the blinds, hoping against hope that he'd somehow be sitting on the side of her mattress dressed and smiling and ready to help them start painting Bella Flora, like he had last night in her dreams.

All she saw was three out of her four roommates still sleeping around her and the light shining out from beneath the closed bathroom door. Swallowing back her disappointment, she put on a pot of coffee and pulled a Danish ring out of the refrigerator. As she waited for the bathroom, she gave herself a stern talking-to. The day wasn't over yet. Technically, Steve had until midnight to get here. Even a text or an email that he was on the way or planning to be would be good enough for her.

"Should we be worrying about Bernard becoming a hurricane and landing here?" Maddie asked thirty minutes later as she and Kyra and Nicole and Deirdre finished off the Danish and stepped out of the pool house. At the moment the sun was a bright cartoon-like ball of yellow, the sky a watercolor blue. It was hard to imagine a cloud, let alone a rain cloud, blocking even a portion of that picture-perfect sky. Maddie told herself not to look for one more thing to worry about even as she pulled out her cell phone and glanced at the screen. She'd had two more texts and one email since Steve's apology, but they were all oddly vague while satisfyingly upbeat. Things like: *I'm thinking about you. Wish you were here.* Or *Edna's house is coming along.* They implied that he was doing something besides lying on the couch wielding the remote, but whatever he was doing he wasn't doing it here. And so far there was no message today, vague or otherwise, about when she might expect him.

"I don't know," Nikki said. "I've dealt with power outages and terrorist threats in New York, and mudslides, forest fires, and earthquakes out in L.A. But other than living in the Florida panhandle for about ten minutes as a child, I have no personal experience with hurricanes. Maybe Avery or Chase would have a better idea."

"Probably," Maddie said as she spotted the two of them setting out paint cans and brushes in the shade of the loggia, being careful not to look at each other. Whatever had happened the day Avery succumbed to the polyurethane must have been a doozy, Maddie thought. Ever since, you could have cut the "awkward" between them with a knife.

"What do you think, Chase?" Deirdre asked when they'd

assembled on the loggia. She was expecting delivery of the kitchen cabinets today and the counter tomorrow and had been absolved of painting duty in order to finish the kitchen and coordinate the designers' installations. "Should we be worried about Bernard?"

"Nah." Chase began to parcel out the paint and pans. Avery inspected the stack of paintbrushes. There was a good two feet between them. "It's still way south of us and the most we're probably going to see is some heavy rain. There hasn't been a direct hit here since 1928."

Nicole's friend Joe arrived to help and Maddie found herself wondering, once again, why the word "friend" didn't seem to fit. Like Chase and Avery, something else crackled between them; but in their case Maddie was fairly certain it wasn't lust. Of course, given the state of her own marriage, perhaps she was no longer qualified to judge.

"But even an indirect hit could be dangerous, couldn't it?" Kyra asked from behind her camera. She'd passed from "rounded" to obviously pregnant and had begun to lead with her stomach. Worry for her daughter wriggled to the forefront of Maddie's mind. Even as she willed it away, she marveled that so many worries could fit into such a confined space; at this point they were stacked up like airplanes at Atlanta's Hartsfield-Jackson waiting for the go-ahead to land.

Chase shrugged but was careful not to do it in Avery's direction. "Hurricanes are nothing to take lightly. But Bernard isn't even hurricane strength yet and probably won't be. The odds are with us."

Maddie's stomach dropped. They were living on the very tip of a tiny spit of land that jutted out into the Gulf of Mexico. She did not want to lay odds on the possible trajectory of a hurricane that could wipe them off the face of the map. Another planeload of worry began to circle her mental airport.

"Our goal right now is to get Bella Flora painted as quickly as possible and to do whatever we can to help the designers finish their installations before Labor Day." Chase looked at all of them. "We've got just over two weeks and it's going to be tight." He pried a lid off one of the paint cans, then moved on to the next. Avery laid a paintbrush next to each pan. "Will Renée Franklin and her ladies be ready to come finish the landscaping as soon as the paint dries?"

"I've got them on standby," Nicole said. "But we're thinking late this weekend or early next week, right?"

Chase nodded, then watched surreptitiously while Avery assigned them to different sections of the exterior. The scaffolding had already been adjusted to allow them to begin cutting paint into the corners and around edges. The real painters would move in behind them to fill in the large expanses of wall.

Feeling almost like an old hand, Maddie climbed the scaffolding up to her position at the top of the arch of the westernmost salon window. The pan of paint and her brush were handed up to her. For a moment she stared out over the rooftop and down the beach, where the Don CeSar pierced the watercolor sky. Bella Flora would be done in the same flamingo pink that had been so popular in Florida in the 1920s, the limestone moldings and balustrades would be left their natural sand color, and the wrought iron would receive a fresh coat of black paint.

She sat down on the scaffolding next to her paint supplies and let her legs dangle over the side. Instead of picking up her paintbrush, she pulled her cell phone out of her pocket, wishing it were a genie's lamp and all she had to do was rub it and concentrate, maybe do an *I Dream of Jeannie* blink to make Steve appear. For an embarrassing moment she actually considered rubbing the phone—a quick just-in-case, covering-all-your-bases rub—then settled for simply staring at its screen with intent.

Nothing.

Maddie's eyes misted in disappointment, and she turned her blurry gaze back out over the Gulf as a flock of gulls glided low over the water, looking beneath the surface for their midmorning snack. For them the Gulf of Mexico was one giant drive-through.

Below and to the right on the opposite end of the scaffold, she heard Nikki and Giraldi talking, their voices rising and falling, their words indecipherable. With a sigh, Madeline set her phone down where she could reach it if a call or text came in. She was the one who'd set the deadline and issued the ultimatum; she could change that deadline if she chose or push it back in some way. It wasn't like she'd be filing for divorce one minute after midnight, if Steve didn't show up in person. She just wanted him moving forward with their life. All she needed was a decisive sign that this was happening.

But even Maddie could hear the evasion in the thought; the urge to rationalize was strong, almost impossible to resist. Was this what Edna felt before she tucked her son in in front of the television? Would any sign of hesitation undo whatever good her ultimatum might have set in motion?

Once again uncertain, Maddie reminded herself that she had no choice but to let things play out. So deciding, she reached over, repositioned her phone a few inches closer, then dipped her paintbrush in the thick pink paint, tapped off the excess, and got to work.

Nicole dabbed at the thick plaster wall where it met the wrought-iron stair leading down from the master bedroom. Giraldi stood on the stair itself. The black paint he was using sat on the step in front of him. They painted for a few minutes in silence while the sun got stronger and the breeze off the Gulf grew warmer. She hadn't seen him for over a week, though she realized that given what he did for a living, that didn't mean he hadn't been around.

"Where have you been?" she asked when what she really wanted to ask was, "Have you been chasing Malcolm? Do you know what he asked me to do?"

"Following up on a lead." He didn't say whether it had anything to do with Malcolm or was a part of some other investigation. "Did you miss me?" he asked.

"No."

"Another hope dashed." He moved down another step and dipped his brush into the black paint. "I keep thinking I'm going to grow on you."

"Unlikely," she said though the truth was if he weren't chasing her brother and trying to use her to catch him, she might have appreciated his good looks and dry sense of humor. As it was, she worried when he was around all the time and worried even more when he wasn't.

"You know, you don't have to like me to do the right thing." He looked her in the eye when he said it, and it took every bit of self control not to blanch at the very words she'd thrown at Malcolm. "You're going to have to declare yourself, Nikki. You won't be able to ride the fence much longer."

She swallowed painfully. She put down her paintbrush and opened the water bottle she'd brought up with her, buying time while she drank. *He knows*, she thought, while the cool liquid trickled down her throat. *He knows Malcolm asked me to meet him on the twenty-fifth and he's waiting for me to tell him.* She set down the water bottle and licked her still-dry lips.

But once she told him, if she told him, the course would be set, and she wouldn't be the one calling the shots. If she confirmed the time and place, Malcolm would be captured with no possibility of turning himself in. If she did what Giraldi considered the right thing, it would eliminate Malcolm's chance to do the same. They'd catch him and lock him up. But if he refused to tell them where he'd stashed the money, what would happen then? Could they make him provide access? Could they retrieve the money without his help? She had no idea what the FBI could and couldn't do or what Joe Giraldi was really capable of.

She, who had dug her way out of poverty by being ruthlessly decisive, dithered yet again while Giraldi watched her

in the same way the big brown pelicans watched the schools
of bait fish dart through the shallow water.

"If Malcolm turned himself in and gave back whatever's
left of the money he stole, would things go easier on him?"
she asked.

"Probably," he said. "It depends. I apprehend, I don't pros-
ecute." He didn't blink but continued to study her as if he
knew all the thoughts racing through her head and even what
she felt deep down in her heart. "If you think that's going to
happen or have any information at all about his whereabouts,
you need to speak up. Don't let him put you in the middle."
His dark eyes bored into hers, searching for answers, willing
her to confide in him. "You haven't been ruled out yet as
a subject of interest, Nikki," he said. "You could take a lie
detector test to rule yourself out as an accomplice. Or you
could simply agree to help us lure him in."

She looked away then, because she was actually afraid that
if she didn't, she was going to spill everything: What Malcolm wanted her to do and what she wanted from Malcolm.
How much she wanted him to redeem himself. Or maybe
she wanted Malcolm to redeem her. Maybe she just wanted
him to prove that it wasn't her parenting that allowed him to
disengage his conscience at will.

"You need to decide whose side you're on," he said. "And
soon. Before your friends here find out who you really are and
wonder why you haven't tried to help the authorities find the
person who ruined their lives."

Below there were footsteps on the pool deck. Nicole looked
down and saw Deirdre dragging the Frankenstein dummy
past the pool and toward the reclinada palm. With Chase's
help, she tied it to one of the three trunks so that it dangled
out over the grass near the seawall. Then she walked away,
leaving Malcolm's effigy swinging in the morning breeze.

Maddie fell asleep just before midnight, nodding off with
the cell phone still clutched in her hand, her mind only

partially numbed by the sunset margaritas she'd consumed. She hadn't brought up the deadline she'd given Steven and neither had the others, but she'd fallen asleep with the sound of a clock ticking off the minutes in her head.

The text came in at 12:01, though she didn't see it until the next morning. It read, *Please think of yourself as the IRS. I have to file an extension. I love you.* It had been sent from Steve's cell phone. Which could have been located anywhere. Including the family room couch.

Thirty-four

From her perch at the highest point of the scaffolding where the living room chimney met a large section of angled roof, Avery kept an eye on the activity below as the first wave of designers unloaded furnishings and accessories at tightly controlled intervals and began to set up the rooms and spaces they'd been awarded.

In the back, a long garden hose snaked across the pool deck and emptied water into the resealed and newly tiled pool. Big cardboard cartons containing outdoor furniture sat waiting to be unpacked. Any and all exposed pipes had been reburied. Renée Franklin's landscape plans, delivered just yesterday, included a bed of flowering perennials to camouflage and mark the area.

Deirdre buzzed in and out of Bella Flora, seemingly everywhere at once, managing the ebb and flow of workmen and designers with a calm efficiency that was difficult to dismiss. Even from this height and distance, Avery could tell she was reveling in her role of Queen Bee.

Baked by the sun and knocked out by the one-two punch of heat and humidity, they broke for lunch around twelve thirty, heading for the pool house, which was the only space that currently possessed both air-conditioning and seating. Kyra, now too bulky and off center to climb the scaffolding, painted what she could reach in the early mornings before the heat became unbearable and then spent the rest of the day shooting video of Bella Flora's final transformation. She was already seated at the kitchen counter when Avery and Madeline staggered in out of the heat. A half-eaten sandwich, a tall glass of milk, a jar of dill pickles, and one of the more sensational tabloids sat open on the counter in front of her. Tears streamed down her sunburned cheeks.

"I thought we agreed we weren't reading those rags any-more," Madeline said, striding to the tiny kitchen to remove the tear-stained publication.

"We agreed not to waste money on them." Kyra scrubbed at one cheek. "It was free. Someone slipped it under the door. I found it on the floor when I came in."

Maddie pulled the perennial pitcher of iced tea and the cold meats and cheeses out of the refrigerator, position-ing herself directly under the air-conditioning vent. Nicole headed straight for the bathroom, so Avery squeezed by Mad-die to wash her hands in the kitchen sink.

"What crap are they writing now?" Avery dried her hands on a paper towel and reached for the tabloid. A picture of Daniel Deranian and Tonja Kay walking arm in arm, their heads bent together, on an undisclosed beach carried the headline "Reconciled!" An incredibly unflattering profile shot of Kyra standing alone and pregnant on the sand-strewn path to the jetty had been inset beside it with the caption, "Already Forgotten?"

Maddie took the stool next to Kyra and the still-open tabloid from Avery as Nikki came out of the bathroom and began to assemble a sandwich. A ringtone sounded and they all checked their phones. As the distinctive notes of "There's No Business Like Show Business" played out, Avery followed the melody to Deirdre's mattress, where she ran a hand over the sheets. Finally locating the cell phone under the pillow, she answered, knowing that Deirdre was expecting a call from a salvage house. "Hello?"

"Glad I caught you, Dee. I've been calling all morning." The voice was female and rushed. She clearly thought she was talking to Deirdre.

Avery opened her mouth to explain but didn't get a chance as the voice continued in the same rush. "I just wanted to congratulate you on all the publicity you're getting down there. When you told me about Deranian's little girlfriend, I knew it was a gift from the PR gods. And those YouTube posts with you leading the charge are pure gold!" There was a delighted chuckle. "We're in a perfect position to negotiate with that moron at Lifetime. I still can't believe they dropped you. And to think they thought you were too old to pull the demographic. Ha! Wait until they see how often your name is popping up now on the Internet." The woman was on a roll. "Those young designers don't know shit and they don't have the A-listers you do. Tonja remembers that freebie you did for her when she was stinking up the box office a couple of years ago. There are a lot of celebrities who still want to work with you."

At the bar, Madeline flipped the pages of the tabloid. Nicole slid her plate to the empty spot at the bar and climbed onto the stool. Kyra munched on a pickle; the tears still streaming. But the everyday realities seemed almost surreal to Avery as Deirdre's true motives and manipulations became clear.

"Dee?" The woman behind the voice finally seemed to realize she was the only one talking. "Deirdre? Are you there?"

"Sorry. You've got the wrong number." Avery hung up. Even as disappointment spiked through her, she chided herself for expecting anything else. Deirdre could spout all the bullshit she wanted about making amends and trying to reconnect. For Deirdre it was "business as usual," and as usual the business that mattered most to Deirdre was Deirdre.

There was a sharp intake of breath at the counter.

"Oh, my God!" Madeline said. "There are pictures and paragraphs about all of us."

Nicole went still at the counter. Kyra sniffed and swiped at her nose with the back of her hand.

"I'm the over-the-hill desperate housewife," Madeline said, wrinkling her nose and turning the page. The irritation in her voice grew. "With the pregnant, celebrity-obsessed daughter."

Madeline skimmed the article with her forefinger. "Avery's the former airheaded HGTV star who was booted out in favor of her ex-husband." She winced and shot a sympathetic glance at Avery. "Deirdre's apparently our savior."

Avery closed her eyes against the added insult. When she opened them, Kyra had lifted her video camera to shoot their reactions.

"But I don't see anything about . . ." Maddie's voice trailed off as she creased the paper at the fold and brought it closer to her face. The room grew quiet with an uncomfortable anticipation. All eyes, and the lens of the video camera, were now on Maddie.

"The most surprising member of the cast at Ten Beach Road is celebrity matchmaker and dating guru Nicole Grant," Madeline read out loud. She looked up briefly at Nikki, who'd gone so still Avery wasn't sure she was breathing. "They've got a whole list of your highest-profile matches and marriages." Maddie looked down again and went back to reading. She looked at Nicole, then back down at the paper again. Her voice tripped over the next lines. ". . . Who in yet another bizarre twist also happens to be financial bad guy Malcolm Dyer's older sister."

Madeline stopped reading. There was a silence so massive a caravan of semitrucks could have driven through it.

Avery moved to the counter, Deirdre's offenses already fading in the light of this revelation. Her gaze, like Madeline's and Kyra's, was now fixed on Nikki.

"Is that true? Are you really Malcolm Dyer's sister?" Kyra asked.

"Well . . ." Nicole began.

"Are you or aren't you?" Avery asked.

Nikki's gaze darted between the three of them, quick and furtive, like a fly trying to assess from which direction the fly swatter might come.

"Answer the question!" It was Maddie, usually the peacemaker, who refused to let her off the hook.

"Yes." Nicole nodded, her expression numb. "Malcolm's my brother, but . . ."

"No," Maddie said. "There can't be any buts about that."

"What the hell are you doing here?" Avery asked, trying to make sense of it. "Did he send you to gloat?"

"Or is he hoping you'll help him find some way to screw us out of Bella Flora, too?" Maddie asked. The horror and disbelief all of them were feeling were starkly etched across her face.

"No!" Nikki said. "I'm a victim like you are. He stole every penny I had invested with him. He didn't leave me with anything."

"Right." Avery wasn't buying it. "You expect us to believe that your own brother stole all your money?"

Nikki nodded. Her voice, when she spoke, sounded like something torn from her throat. "It's true. If I had more than two hundred dollars to my name I wouldn't be sleeping on a mattress and slaving on this godforsaken house."

It was a sign of just how agitated they were that they let her get away with the slur to Bella Flora.

"There must have been some mistake. Were you estranged? Didn't he realize . . . ?" Maddie seemed to be struggling to make sense of it, but Avery didn't want to understand it. There was no explanation that could justify Nicole's dishonesty.

"I raised him." Nicole slumped in her seat, her voice barely a whisper. "Badly, it would seem. But for all intents and purposes, I was his mother. There was no mistake."

Another silence fell. Kyra lowered the camera and switched it off. Nicole looked at all of them in turn, her face a glut of emotion. Avery saw shock, hurt, anger, disappointment, and ultimately an odd sort of resignation. But Avery didn't care how Nicole felt. She could barely stand to look at her.

"You just stood there when we hung him in effigy," Maddie said, shaking her head in disbelief. "And you never said a word. Not once in all the thousands of times we discussed and cursed Malcolm Dyer did you mention that you were related to him." She folded her arms across her chest as if warding off cold. "I feel so betrayed. How could you?"

What Avery felt was ill. Their closeness, the sense that they were in the trenches together, was all one great big lie. "I can't work beside you. And I sure as hell am not going to sleep next to you."

Nicole didn't respond, and she didn't look surprised.

Avery turned to Madeline. "I need for her to leave," Avery said. "Now."

"But she's an owner," Maddie said. "Can we just tell her to go?"

"She can have her third when we finish and sell," Avery said. "We're not trying to *steal* from *her*." She took the time to emphasize the pertinent words. "But every time I look at her I'm going to know that she's Malcolm Dyer's sister and that she's been lying about it from the moment we met her."

"I didn't lie," Nikki said. "I just couldn't tell you."

Maddie shook her head one final time. Her brown eyes were dark with hurt and anger. Leaving Nicole sitting alone at the counter, she and Kyra came to stand on either side of Avery.

"We're almost done anyway." Maddie's voice shook, but her tone was resolute. "I'm sure if you leave an address with John Franklin, he'll make sure you get your share at closing."

The three of them left the pool house and went back to work without further conversation or a backward glance.

It took Nicole less than fifteen minutes to gather her things and stuff them into the trunk of the Jag. Chase called out after her, asking where she thought she was going, obviously

assuming she was trying to duck out of work. Only Joe
Giraldi actually tried to stop her, striding out to the car just
as she slid behind the wheel and bending double to lean in
through the driver's side window. "Where are you going?" he
asked. "What's happened?"

"As if you don't know!"

Nicole revved the gas pedal with her foot and sent the grit
under the wheels flying. "It was a nice touch, planting the
story in that tabloid as if some scuzzy reporter was the one
who figured out my connection to Malcolm," she said. "Did
you arrange for the paparazzi, too?"

He looked surprised but quickly masked it. "That wasn't
us. I told you you were running out of time. Anybody bothering to dig would have figured it out. We didn't want you to
be found out."

"I don't really care what you wanted, Agent Giraldi. And
I sure as hell don't care what my alleged partners think.
All these months we've spent together, all of this 'pulling
together because we're in the same boat' crap! And as soon as
they hear I'm related to Malcolm, I'm the scum of the earth."

She pushed at his hands, wanting only to back down the
drive and leave the house along with everyone and everything inside it, behind her. After all these years of going it
alone, she'd bought into the hype, had actually felt as if she
and Maddie and Avery had formed some sort of bond. She
could hardly believe how stupid she'd been. Or how much
the rejection hurt.

She'd been right to teach Malcolm that each man had to
be for himself. As soon as you started worrying about others
your chances of success shrank down to nothing.

"Nikki, look. It doesn't have to be like this. Just work
with us and I can explain that . . ."

"Leave me alone!" she shouted. "I don't need you running
interference when you're just trying to get me to do your
dirty work."

She shoved at his hands again and slammed the gearshift
into reverse. "And you better stay out of my way. If I see your

face even for a second, you'll be sorry." She hated how child-like and impotent she sounded. Without another word she smashed her foot down on the accelerator, not even caring whether she ran over his feet or ripped his stupid arms out of their sockets as she backed down the brick driveway for what she assumed would be the very last time.

Nonetheless, Nicole watched Giraldi watch her leave in the Jag's rearview mirror until he and Bella Flora grew small and disappeared from view. She actually cried all the way over the Corey Causeway Bridge into St. Petersburg and on a large section of Interstate 275. But by the time she reached Tampa she knew where she was headed. And exactly what she had to do.

Thirty-five

The house was still packed with frantic designers and Maddie and Avery's shock over Nicole's true identity was still fresh when Chase called a halt to the day's painting. Maddie and Avery had simmered with anger and righteous indignation for most of the afternoon, calling up instance after instance when Nicole could and should have told them the truth, expending far more time and energy piecing together the clues they'd somehow missed than perfecting their brushstrokes.

In the pool house, Maddie found Kyra on the couch fiddling with her editing equipment, a wan smile on her face. The tabloid article lay crumpled but still legible beside her.

When it was time to prepare for sunset, Maddie foraged in the refrigerator for a bottle of white wine and a beer for Chase, uwilling to try to follow in Nikki's frozen-drink footsteps. With Kyra's help she arranged snacks on a tray and carried them out to the pool.

"Everything feels so weird," Kyra said, taking in the sparkling pool and the new wrought-iron patio furniture artfully arranged around it. Massive clay containers with a 1920s feel dotted the resurfaced pool deck, waiting for Renée Franklin and her gardening crew to fill them. The concrete picnic table with its mosaic top had been moved to the small porch on the west side of the house. There was no sign of their neon-colored beach chairs.

"I know," Maddie said, setting veggies and dip and a bowl of Cheez Doodles in the center of the large round table. The new furniture was the least of it.

Kyra set down the wine and glasses, then went back inside for Chase's beer and her own iced tea. "I can't believe how much we can fit on this table." As opposed to the packing box they'd begun with and the garage-sale find that had replaced it.

"It's Brown Jordan," Deirdre said coming out of the house with Chase. "It's one of their newest groupings. Top of the line."

Avery came out of the pool house showered and changed. Deirdre flashed her daughter a smile that froze on her lips when Avery looked right through her.

Nicole would have had no problem adjusting to the high-end furniture, Maddie thought as they hovered around the table not quite able to claim it as their own. She would have done more than adjust; she would have loved it. Maddie kept this thought to herself but suspected from the angry, yet baffled expressions on the others' faces that she wasn't the only one thinking of Nicole at that moment.

"Ahhh." Chase reached for the lone cold beer and lifted it to his lips with a grateful sigh, then drained half of it in one long, thirsty gulp. "I needed that." He looked around the pool area. "It's been a pretty bizarre day," he said. "Not to mention that we've lost a high percentage of our work force." He took another sip of beer. "Giraldi's gone, too. It kind of makes you wonder if that guy was who or what he claimed to be."

"There's an awful lot of that going around." Avery aimed a pointed glance at Deirdre as Maddie poured her a glass of wine and positioned it and the bowl of Cheez Doodles within easy reach.

"Well, despite all the turmoil, it's great to see things

finally coming together," Chase said. "With any luck Tropical Storm Bernard will fall apart before that band of thunderstorms gets this far. We probably only need another three to four days on the exterior." He took another long sip.

Maddie didn't know if he was actually unaware of the way Avery was looking at Deirdre or simply hoping to sidestep any further confrontations. Either way, Chase was out of luck.

"Speaking of 'not what they seem,'" Avery said. "Why don't you tell everybody why you're really here, Deirdre," Avery said.

Deirdre blinked. One eyebrow arched up in surprise.

"You know," Avery continued. "You can start with how you were dropped by Lifetime and pushed aside by younger designers. Then you can explain what a boost this whole experience has been for your sagging career. And while you're at it, maybe you can fill Kyra and Maddie in on how well you actually know Tonja Kay. Which you could use to segue into how the press found out Kyra was here and carrying Daniel Deranian's baby."

Kyra gasped. Chase stopped fingering his beer bottle. Maddie looked at the designer, not wanting to believe she'd intentionally exposed them, especially Kyra, to all that negative scrutiny. "Is that true?" Maddie asked. "Did you tell Tonja Kay and the press about Kyra?"

"Oh, no," Deirdre began, but Maddie didn't know if it was a denial or dismay.

"I happened to answer your phone today, *Dee*," Avery said, cutting her mother off. "I don't know if it was your agent or your publicist who called, but she was practically creaming in her pants over how you managed to use Bella Flora—and us—to resurrect your dead career. Apparently some things never change."

"It wasn't like that," Deirdre said. Her shoulders were stiff, her hands had fisted in her lap. "I had no idea it would get so out of hand."

The whole thing felt like some kind of train wreck, especially on top of the revelations about Nicole. Maddie wasn't sure what was supposed to happen next, but if Avery's accusations were true, Deirdre was not going to get off scot-free.

"You voted Nicole off the job," Maddie said. "Maybe Deirdre needs to go, too."

"This is *not* the Beach Road version of *Survivor*," Chase said, making a small stab at humor.

Nobody laughed.

"Maybe it should be," Maddie said, drawing in a breath, trying to stay calm. She had an almost overwhelming urge to reach over and wrap her hands around the designer's neck.

Deirdre remained quiet, her expression uncharacteristically uncertain, her eyes on Avery.

"Believe me, I'd like nothing better than to send Deirdre on her way," Avery said. "But at the moment she adds value. She brought the design community here and she's the face they know." She shrugged, but her smile was forced and Maddie had no doubt that what Avery felt inside bore no resemblance to her matter-of-fact tone. "Much as it pains me, I think we're just going to have to use her. Like she's been using us."

Beside her, Kyra simmered silently. Despite her anger, Maddie wasn't sure whom she pitied more: Deirdre, who seemed to have once again sacrificed her relationship with her daughter to her own needs. Or Avery, who had to once again feel abandoned and deceived.

Slipping her arm around Kyra's shoulders, Maddie hugged her own daughter close. "I don't understand you at all, Deirdre, but I'm putting you on notice right now. If you set those paparazzi on us intentionally and exposed my daughter to all of that nastiness, you better cut those ties right now. And you sure as hell better make sure nothing like that happens here again. Do you understand?" Maddie glared at the designer with all the menace she was feeling and none of the pity. If Maddie had been a Mafia don, Deirdre would already be wearing cement overshoes and standing at the bottom of the pool.

"I need a nod or some kind of acknowledgment, Deirdre,"

she said. "Because I may not understand your relationship with
your own daughter, but you are *not* going to mess around with
mine."

After a long uncomfortable moment, Deirdre nodded.
"None of what happened was intentional. I'm sorry everyone,
and especially Kyra, got caught up in it." She excused herself
to go check on something in the house. As they watched her
go, Chase lifted a finger like an imaginary gun to his lips and
blew on the barrel before reholstering it. He gave Maddie an
approving nod, then stood and followed Deirdre inside.

"Wow," Avery said to Maddie. "I don't think I've ever
actually heard her apologize before."

"Yeah," Kyra said with a puzzled smile. "My mom is full
of surprises. I'm starting to wonder if I ever really knew her
at all."

Avery slid into her car and backed down the driveway. With
no destination in mind, she aimed the Mini Cooper straight
up the beach, keeping the Gulf on her left as she drove north
from one beach community to the next, trying to absorb
Nicole's betrayal and Deirdre's disappointing predictability.

In the Greek fishing village of Tarpon Springs, she
stopped at a tiny taverna near the sponge docks, where she
wolfed down a Greek salad and gyro and acknowledged that
she couldn't keep driving indefinitely. By the time she headed
back down the beach toward Bella Flora, the streets were
almost completely deserted. It was close to eleven o'clock
when she pulled back onto the brick drive and saw that
Chase's truck was still there.

Still searching for some sense of calm and craving solitude,
she let herself into the main house and stood for a moment
in the foyer, inhaling the "new" Bella Flora, which smelled of
fresh wood and paint and wallpaper paste with just a hint of
"eau de polyurethane." It was a far cry from the musty neglect
that had smacked them in the face on that first day.

A slash of light fell across the front stairs from the upper landing and Avery trod quietly across the gleaming wood floor, sticking to the protective runners that had been put down, not wanting to talk to Chase or think about Nicole. Unwilling to deal with Deirdre.

Above her head the iron chandelier hung clean and cobweb free, its hammered finish rippling in the moonlight. To her left the study stood empty except for a row of shelves waiting to be affixed to the wall and a tightly rolled Oriental rug. In the powder room someone had begun painting a wonderful mural of a 1920s era Spanish dancer with billowing skirts and a tightly fitted magenta bodice. In the dining room the chandelier Maddie and Kyra had so painstakingly cleaned and polished dangled over a magnificent stone pedestal dining table with a huge etched glass top. When she stepped into the kitchen and onto the incredible Spanish tile floor that Enrico's brother, Reggio, had laid two days before, she saw exactly how the room would be and knew it would be not only the show house favorite, but a huge factor in ultimately selling the house.

She imagined she could hear Bella Flora breathing a long grateful sigh of relief.

"This kitchen is going to be the ace up John Franklin's sleeve. Right up there next to the Gulf and bay views."

Avery looked up in surprise as Chase walked into the room, his words so closely mirroring her thoughts. She watched him silently, reminding herself that none of what had happened today was Chase's fault.

"I know you're probably still pissed off at Deirdre, but you did the right thing keeping her on."

Avery didn't trust herself to speak. All of her emotions were bubbling way too close to the surface.

"I realize Webster will never be running her picture in their dictionary to illustrate the word 'mother,' but houses speak to her, Avery. And she knows how to listen to them."

"And your point is?" Between Nicole's bombshell and Deirdre's behavior, it had been a truly sucky day. She'd almost let herself believe that Deirdre had come to Bella

Flora to build a relationship with her. She felt like a patsy, duped at every turn.

"Deirdre has great gifts," Chase said. "A maternal instinct just isn't one of them."

"No kidding."

He came to stand next to her. His dark hair stood up in too many directions and his cheeks and jaw were dark with stubble. His blue eyes were piercing. "Look, all I'm saying is she is who she is and you're going to have to find a way to deal with it. You're so stuck on the fact that she left you, you're completely unable to move forward. Despite everything you've been given and all the opportunities you've frittered away."

"Frittered away?" she ground out. She couldn't believe he was going to start this after the day she'd just had.

"Yep." He gave her that smug look that said he had it all figured out and she just wasn't getting it. Avery was tired of the look and the attitude. Hell, she was just tired. He had a gigantic chip on his shoulder when it came to her and it was time to knock it off.

Avery turned and stepped directly in front of him. "I've had enough of your judgments and resentments, Chase Hardin. You don't have the first idea what you're talking about, and I'm tired of feeling like I'm somehow supposed to apologize for what I've been given."

She stopped to see how he was taking it, but he still had a taunting look on his face that needed to be wiped off. "I did not get an architectural degree just to spite you. And I didn't end up in tight sweaters on national television to make a mockery of all the things you didn't get." She was building up a good head of steam. And stoking it with Nicole's and Deirdre's betrayals. "We could have enjoyed working together here if you hadn't needed to rub my nose in my 'unfair advantages' the whole time. What about your advantages?" she asked. "What about all the things you've had that I haven't?"

"Like?" His tone said she couldn't possibly come up with anything, but he was as wrong about that as he was about her.

She pressed a finger to his chest and began to tick off each point. "You had a mother who loved you and who would never have chosen to leave you." She pressed again. "You also had a wife whom you loved and who for some unknown reason actually loved you back and shared her life with you." The finger press became a poke. "Then there are Jason and Josh, who not only love but worship you." Another poke. "And a father who's still alive and whom you get to work with every"—poke—"single"—poke—"day."

They were toe to toe, finger to chest, face to, well, also chest, but she'd tilted her head back so that she could watch the emotions flit across his face. He was angry and incredulous and some other things she didn't have words for. Whether he would think about the things she'd said was uncertain, but at least he didn't laugh or interrupt.

"You want me to get over Deirdre's abandonment and her latest treachery?" She was pretty much shouting now. "Then you need to get over being resentful and pissed off at me all the time when you're the one who's had all the *real* advantages!" She kind of sputtered to a stop, unsure what was supposed to happen now that she'd had her say. Her neck hurt from craning upward and it was possible that her finger was jammed. She dropped her hand and took a step back.

"Are you finished?" His words were clipped, his tone cool.

"Yes." Her anger duly expended, she felt deflated and slightly silly. But she'd be damned if she'd apologize for speaking the truth.

"Fine!" he said. "I've gotta go."

"Good!" she replied. "Don't let me stop you."

"I won't," he said. And then he walked out the front door and slammed it behind him, leaving her and Bella Flora together again.

Nicole wiped dust from the motel room desk and placed her laptop in the center of it. The room was just off of Highway 75 and it was awfully small, unless you compared it to the pool house at Ten Beach Road, in which case it felt downright gargantuan. Its lone mattress was a bit lumpy, but at least it wasn't crammed between four other mattresses on the floor. She'd sold the last of her vintage dresses and some final accessories to a high-end designer resale shop in Tampa on her way out of town. If she were careful, the money should last her until the twenty-fifth. Tomorrow she'd leave the highway and focus on getting "lost" until then.

Idly, without admitting what she was doing, she hit the shortcut key for Bella Flora on YouTube and watched Kyra's latest post. It was titled "Trouble in Paradise" and that's exactly what it was; lots of troubled face-to-face between all the key players intercut with beauty shots of Bella Flora shown nearing completion in a really cool, time-lapse sort of way.

Nikki replayed the piece several times, watching the women she'd thought of as friends as well as herself, staggering under the weight of the task they'd undertaken. They'd survived and grown stronger. They'd helped Bella Flora become beautiful again. And then they'd crumbled under the weight of the disappointment that inevitably surfaced when one finally felt safe.

Thirty-six

A few days later Maddie lay on her mattress and watched the early morning sun filter in through the pool house blinds. On the futon beside her Kyra slept on her back, her stomach tenting the top sheet, her bare arms flung outward in complete surrender.

With Nicole and her mattress gone the tiny space felt conspicuously spacious. Her absence had blown a hole in their friendship that would be hard to repair, and although they rarely mentioned her, Maddie could sometimes hear Nikki's wry tone or sly observation in her mind.

Beyond Kyra, Deirdre slept curled on her side with her back to the rest of them, her blonde hair cradled on her silk pillowcase. Whatever personal issues might exist in Deirdre's life apparently didn't dare intrude on her sleep; Maddie had never heard her toss or turn during the night or woken to find her staring up into the ceiling. Unlike her daughter, Avery, who was a tosser and turner of the first order.

Maddie checked her cell phone, which was plugged into the wall behind her head, but there was nothing from Steve or Andrew; no response to the messages she'd left. Stretching, she turned to her right and noted Avery's empty mattress. Maddie didn't know where in Bella Flora Avery had been sleeping, but she hadn't slept in the same room as Deirdre since the intercepted phone call.

Although Maddie had been unable to get Deirdre voted "off," she felt as if they were, in fact, on some sort of survivor program—the mother/daughter version—on which your relationship might improve or implode.

The renovation of Bella Flora had proven to be not a sprint but a marathon. As they limped toward the finish line she and Kyra maintained their truce over Kyra's continued belief in Daniel Deranian's love for her. Avery and Deirdre's method of avoiding arguments was not to talk at all. Deirdre also kept her distance from Maddie since the night Maddie had told her off. Kyra thought it funny that Deirdre seemed so skittish around her big, tough mother, but Maddie knew she could have expressed her displeasure a little more diplomatically.

Maddie rose quietly and flipped on the coffeemaker. In the bathroom she washed her face and brushed her teeth, then pulled on work clothes. Taking a cup of coffee with her, she left the pool house and went out to stand on the seawall where she sipped her coffee and looked out over the pass as the sun continued its ascent over the bay.

By seven A.M. the temperatures had begun to rise. By nine it would be hot enough to suck the air right out of your lungs. Maddie was embarrassingly thankful that their painting days were over and the professional crew was only days away from completion. She turned to consider Bella Flora's bright pink castle-like walls, the slender limestone-capped bell tower rising high into the blue sky. Deirdre had said that the pink would fade to a more delicate shade over time, but for now it was the same bright hue that had been applied during Florida's Mediterranean Revival heyday to combat the Depression-era blues.

Too antsy to stand still, Maddie set down her coffee cup and took the path to the beach. The usual early morning suspects were already fishing on the jetty with their pelican and gull audience. On the beach, foot traffic was sparse, just the occasional jogger or speed walker with the more dawdling shell seekers doing their eyes-down pause, reach, and stroll. Up in the softer sand a darkly tanned older man skimmed a wand back and forth in search of dropped change. Walking at the tide line, her bare feet sluicing through the froth of warm water, Maddie breathed in the now-familiar scents and exhaled them slowly, beginning her beach mantra: Everything's all right. Everything's okay.

For a while she simply walked and breathed and tried not to think. At the Don CeSar she turned and began her walk back toward Bella Flora, but no matter how many times she breathed in and breathed out, everything did not feel all right and it most certainly didn't feel okay. Though she'd promised herself she wouldn't, Maddie speed dialed her home number and lifted the cell phone to her ear.

Andrew answered, out of breath. She gave him a moment to catch it.

"Sorry. Did I get you in the middle of something?"

"I just got back from a run and I heard the phone ringing." He breathed for a few moments.

"I've been trying to reach your father. Is he near a phone?"

"He, um, well . . . actually he's not here right now."

Maddie stopped walking. A dolphin jumped out in the Gulf and a small boy standing near the water's edge pointed and shouted for his mother. "What's going on?"

"Dad took Grandma up to North Carolina. To Aunt Emma's." Emma was Edna's sister and their relationship had always been prickly.

Maddie's feet began to move of their own volition. It had never occurred to her that if Steve found the strength to leave the house, he'd head somewhere else. Still, she felt her first real glimmer of hope. "When will they be back?" Maddie asked.

"I don't know, Mom," Andrew said, sounding about twelve. "But Grandma's house is ready to go on the market.

Dad said when he got back we'd come down and he's . . .
better than he was. Grandma got really flipped out when he
told her her house was going to have to go. But he didn't let
her talk him out of it."

Maddie thought about this as she walked. It wasn't the
home run she'd been hoping for. Steve and Andrew weren't
here. Or even on their way at the moment. But Steve was no
longer lying on the couch unable or unwilling to move. It
was an elephant bite, a definite something. For the moment
it was something to cling to.

By the time she got back to Bella Flora the painters were
working and a fleet of vans and trucks were parked at the curb.
A custom cabinet company truck had been backed into the
driveway, its rear doors open. Two men were making trips in
and out of the kitchen under Deirdre's supervision while Chase
and Robby stood in the foyer discussing the powder room,
which was too small to hold both of them at the same time.

Maddie walked through Bella Flora, delighted with all she
saw, but found no sign of Kyra. In the master bedroom, Avery
and the room's designer were mounting the room's original
wrought-iron window valances, which were now repainted
black with fabulous gold tips and bronzed bull's eyes.

When the designer was satisfied, Avery joined Maddie
on the landing where Malcolm Dyer's effigy had once hung.
"Have you seen Kyra?" Maddie asked as they stared down at
the activity below.

"Sure have," Avery said. "A big white limo came to pick
her up about twenty minutes ago. She said she'd been invited
out for brunch and would be back later." Avery smiled, and
her voice dropped to a whisper. "I took a peek when the
chauffeur opened the door for her." Avery's smile broadened.
"I'm pretty sure the person waiting in the back seat was Daniel Deranian."

Maddie had pretty much decimated what was left of her fingernails by the time the limo pulled up in front of Bella Flora

two hours later. The shiny white vehicle looked incongruous in the midst of the pickup trucks and design company vans. Everyone stopped working to watch it glide to a stop on the brick drive. The silence was complete as the driver jumped out and walked around to open the back door.

Kyra emerged first, beaming with happiness and looking quickly over her shoulder to watch Daniel Deranian emerge from the vehicle with the ease of long experience. Kyra looked like a happy, albeit pregnant, child in her white baggy capris and oversized white blouse. Daniel Deranian looked like what he was—a Hollywood megastar—tall and lithe with dark intentionally unruly hair over wide-set dark eyes. His skin was a golden brown—a testament both to California living and his Armenian ancestry—and rakishly unshaven. His white T-shirt was almost as bright as his smile and clung to a well-defined chest and abs and skimmed over low-slung jeans. He was forty, almost twenty years Kyra's senior, barely a decade younger than Maddie, but he could and did play midthirties. Everything about him shouted "look at me!" Everybody did.

Drawing a calming breath, Maddie speed walked down the stairs and pulled open the front door. Daniel followed Kyra inside and when Maddie extended her hand, he took it in his. Kyra practically levitated with happiness. She smiled a delighted "I told you so."

"Mom," she gushed. "This is Daniel Deranian. Daniel, my mom, Madeline."

He flashed perfect white teeth. The realization that his hand was softer and better manicured than hers registered briefly, but there was a personal magnetism that made this seem unimportant. It was slightly surreal to see the face that she'd seen splashed across a wide screen and in Technicolor this up close and personal. They just stood there shaking hands until she realized what she was doing and discon-nected. He smiled in amusement, but not surprise. This was a man who was used to disconcerting people, especially females. His gaze lifted to the landing where Avery still

stood in her Daisy Duke shorts and bodice-hugging T. The
flare of sexual interest in the actor's eyes was immediate and
unmistakable. Maddie had to look away from it; Kyra was
too busy smiling to notice.

"It's a beautiful house," he said to Maddie. "I've been
watching Kyra's postings on YouTube but even her video
didn't do it justice."

So he'd been watching and obviously waiting. But for
what? "Thank you. We've all fallen in love with Bella Flora.
We're hoping that someone who can appreciate her will want
to own her." Good grief, she sounded like a sales brochure.

He continued to smile at her. Maddie smiled back.

"Mom," Kyra said, still levitating with happiness. "Daniel
and I would like to talk to you about something. Can we go
outside where we can have some privacy?"

"Oh. Sure."

She turned and led them down the central hallway, keeping to the protective runners. Behind her Kyra described the
house's "before" to Daniel and stopped to show him the Casbah Lounge. They passed the arch that opened to the kitchen
and Maddie caught a glimpse of Deirdre on a stepladder
holding up two different knobs in front of a cabinet, and she
wondered whether the woman would be reporting this visit
to her contacts in Hollywood. If Deranian was worried about
being spotted, he didn't show it. Neither did he pant after
Kyra in any noticeable way.

At the pool they sat in one of the wrought-iron groupings
with a view out over the pass. Maddie tensed briefly when
a wave runner zoomed parallel to the seawall but relaxed
when it kept on going. If the paparazzi were aware of Daniel's arrival in the Tampa Bay area, they hadn't yet tracked
him this far.

"Daniel wants to take me back to California with him,"
Kyra said. "His private plane is at the Clearwater Airport."
She reached a hand out to squeeze Daniel's. Maddie hadn't
seen her happier since the Christmas morning when she got
her very first video camera.

Maddie wasn't quite sure how to respond. "Will he be divorcing his wife and marrying you first?" seemed a bit aggressive. "That's great, and what will happen to you and your child when he moves on?" seemed a tad negative. She settled for "Oh" while wishing that Steve—the old Steve—were here to help her navigate the potential minefields. Then again, Deranian had shown up just as Kyra had insisted he would. Maybe what Maddie said or didn't say wasn't all that critical; maybe Kyra was going to get her happily-ever-after after all.

"Look, I know you have to be worried about Kyra," the actor said. His delivery was smooth and perfectly sincere. If this had been a movie, she would have bought it completely. But this wasn't a movie; this was her daughter's life. "Anyway, I want you to know that I'm going to make sure that she and the baby have their own place. And a car. Well, you know Kyra will have the car, not the baby." He smiled ruefully, but earnestly, with good intention. "I'll take care of anything they need."

Maddie nodded. Kyra beamed.

"That way I can see both of them whenever my, um, schedule allows."

Kyra stopped beaming. Maddie wasn't sure whether to nod or not.

Kyra turned to Daniel. "But where will you live?" she asked, surprised.

"Why, in my house," he said as if this were obvious. "In Laurel Canyon."

"Well, why wouldn't we just live there with you?" Kyra asked. "I don't get it."

Maddie didn't want to "get it" but was afraid she did. Daniel shifted uncomfortably in his seat and for a moment he seemed at a loss, as if he'd arrived with the script memorized and now some of the lines had been changed. He turned to Maddie for help, and she felt her heart twist painfully in her chest as she watched the confusion wash over her daughter's face. Would Kyra really want her here when comprehension finally dawned?

"I'm going to let you two discuss this further on your own," Maddie said, rising. "I'll just be inside." She shot Kyra a bracing look. She had no idea what kind of look to send Daniel Deranian.

"Come on, Kyra," he said. "Let's go for a walk."

Maddie watched them head toward the path to the beach. Kyra's face was turned up to Daniel's in question, but the admiration was still there. Maddie went into the house, afraid to think about what kind of look Kyra would be wearing when they returned.

Inside she paced the central hallway dodging frantic designers, stopping for just a few minutes in the kitchen where Deirdre was supervising the cabinet and counter installation before moving into the salon where a young slim-hipped designer hung deep fuchsia curtains while his partner unfurled a brightly patterned area rug. At any other time Maddie would have savored the outstanding culmination of all their hard work—the house was practically preening under all the attention—but she couldn't seem to focus and instead moved from window to window, watching anxiously for Kyra's return.

"Are you okay?" Avery asked when she found Maddie back in the master bedroom pacing its length.

"No." Maddie pressed her forehead to the far front window and twisted in an effort to get a glimpse of the limo, which was now idling at the bottom of the driveway with the driver posted outside it. Because of the darkened windows, she couldn't tell if Kyra and Deranian were in it or still out walking on the beach. "I'm so afraid she's out there having her heart trampled all over, I can hardly breathe."

"But he came," Avery pointed out. "None of us really believed he'd show up, but he did." She smiled at Maddie. "Maybe it'll all work out."

"Maybe," Maddie said, turning away from the window to face her friend. "But I feel like there's a rock in the pit of my stomach. Daniel Deranian may play romantic heroes in his movies, but I don't think that applies to his real life."

Below, the driver moved to the rear door and swung it open. Kyra got out slowly. She took a step away from the car and stood for a moment, her shoulders set. It was only after the car had backed the rest of the way down the drive and headed toward the bay that she turned to watch it go.

Maddie watched her daughter watch the car. When it was no longer visible, Kyra turned and walked resolutely into the front garden. Maddie raced down the stairs and out the front door. She caught up with Kyra at the newly repaired fountain.

"So?" Maddie asked quietly as Kyra lifted her tear-stained face.

"So." Kyra squeezed her eyes shut, then scrubbed at the tears on her cheeks with the back of one hand. "He made me a really good offer," she said. "Considering he's not getting a divorce or ever planning to marry me."

"Aw, honey." Maddie stepped closer, wanting to wrap her arms around her daughter.

"I can go live in L.A. and see him when he feels like it. Tonja's moving back into their house. She told him it was okay." Kyra's mouth twisted in a bitter smile. Tears shimmered in her eyes. "That's the open kind of relationship they have." She sniffed. "You were right, Mom. You were right the whole time."

"No, honey, I just . . ." Maddie's voice trailed off. "It's just . . . mothers never want to see their children hurt or even disappointed." She reached out to tuck a stray lock of hair behind Kyra's ear. "I love you and I want the best for you. I hope you know that whatever you choose, I'll . . . we'll . . . always love you and stand by you."

Maddie felt her own eyes well with tears.

"He actually thought I'd jump in that stupid car and go with him," Kyra said. She looked at Maddie, her eyes too old now for her face. "What's really scary is that if I hadn't been watching you all summer, I might have."

"What do you mean?" Maddie asked.

"I've watched you deal with all the shit that's been happening. You took charge when you had to and you didn't give up on Dad; you just kept going, doing what had to be done. I didn't realize how strong you are."

The words settled over her. She hadn't thought in those terms, she'd just been plowing ahead trying to hang on. But Kyra's recognition was like a balm to her soul; one she hadn't realized she needed.

"Me, neither," Maddie said. "You don't really know what you're made of until things fall apart."

"Well, I want to be strong like you," Kyra said. "And I don't think you would have settled for being somebody's piece of ass on the side." Her gaze dropped before she looked back into Maddie's eyes. "I think I deserve better than that. And so does my baby."

She pulled out a business card from her pocket and handed it to Maddie. "He gave me his attorney's card and told me there'd be some kind of settlement for the baby. Only I have to sign something that says I'll never name him as the baby's father or give interviews or anything."

"Well, at lest he didn't try to shirk his financial responsibilities," Maddie said.

"No. Apparently this isn't the first time this has happened." Kyra's laugh was hollow. "Kind of ironic isn't it, that Tonja's trying to adopt all these third-world babies, while Daniel's just sort of running around creating his own?"

"Yeah." Maddie put her arm around Kyra and drew her into a hug. "Let's go get your video camera and get some shots of Bella Flora. I can't believe how fabulous she's looking; I know Avery's not going to want to admit it, but Deirdre's kitchen is going to be completely to die for."

Thirty-seven

On the day Tropical Storm Bernard's little sister Charlene began to form, Bella Flora's scaffolding was dismantled and hauled away, leaving her luscious pink walls glowing and unobstructed in the late afternoon sun. The next morning shortly after sunrise Avery rolled off the chaise in the master bedroom where she'd been sleeping, pulled on shorts and a T-shirt, and went into the bathroom to wash up as the first carloads of garden ladies began to arrive.

After taking a few minutes to tuck her pajamas and toiletries into the back of a closet and eradicate all signs of her occupancy, she hurried outside.

Madeline, Kyra, Deirdre, and John Franklin sat at the wrought-iron table that now anchored the loggia. Deirdre, who had kept her distance from Maddie since the recent tongue-lashing, gave Avery a raised eyebrow, which she ignored. Maddie scooted her chair over to make room and passed Avery a still-steaming cup of coffee.

Avery sipped the coffee gratefully and helped herself to a hunk of coffee cake as they watched Renée Franklin organize and deploy her troops.

John nodded at Kyra's video camera, which sat on the table within easy reach. "You know those videos of yours have caused quite a stir in real estate circles. Posting pictures and video online isn't new, but the way you've added the human element to the renovation has really built interest. I had to add on office staff just to handle the calls and emails. It would make a great television show."

Kyra looked pleased at the compliment, and Avery saw Maddie reach over to squeeze her daughter's hand. Although Daniel Deranian had apparently proven he was not the hoped-for Prince Charming, Maddie and Kyra seemed on much smoother ground.

Kyra got up to shoot video as Renée and an assistant began to fill the first of six huge containers with bright tropical blooms. "I must say you all have far exceeded my expectations."

"Why, thank you, John," Deirdre said. "It's been incredibly gratifying to see Bella Flora blossom back to life."

Avery looked at Deirdre, who'd already done her hair and makeup and gussied up in a white linen pantsuit. It was barely seven A.M. "I hope you're going to remember to thank all the 'little people' who helped make your achievement possible," Avery said.

"But of course," Deirdre said smoothly as Avery winced at how petulant she'd sounded. "No one could have done this alone. Though there are those who would have tried." She gave Avery a second eyebrow then stood regally like the Queen of freakin' England. "I'm going to go double check today's delivery schedule and then see if the mural in the living room is dry." She left, leaving a scent of gardenia in her wake and Avery feeling unvindicated.

"You know, I keep wondering where Nikki is and whether she's okay," Maddie said in an obvious effort to change the subject. "I mean maybe she was telling the truth about being a victim."

"Even if she was, she could have at least told us about the connection to Dyer," Avery said. She did not plan to admit that it just wasn't the same at Bella Flora without Nikki. "But then maybe dishonesty runs in her family."

"Like stubbornness runs in yours?" Chase had come up behind Franklin. He popped a piece of coffee cake into his mouth.

Avery snorted and sneaked a peek at Chase through her bangs. He'd never brought up the night she'd told him off, but ever since he'd been less combative. Sometimes he even listened to what she said. Once he'd actually agreed to do something her way. Which had left her feeling like she was having some sort of out-of-body experience.

Now she caught herself thinking about how his lips had felt and how much she'd liked his arms wrapped around her. She shook her head to clear it. "Do you think they'll ever catch Malcolm Dyer?" she asked. "Or figure out where he stashed all that money?"

"I sure hope so," Maddie said. "I mean it would take a while to sort everything out and return even a portion of the money, but it would be such a relief to have that to look forward to."

"I think we're going to sell Bella Flora before any of that happens," Chase said. "Don't you, John?"

The Realtor launched into an explanation of the interest they'd received to date and his plans for marketing the property. By the pool Renée Franklin was already on the second planter. She patted the bird-of-paradise into its center and then began to tuck in several poppy red geraniums and sprays of purple and yellow lantana to trail over the edge. Her straw hat bobbed up and down as she answered questions and dealt with problems presented by her minions. By working on all sides of the house at once, they hoped to be finished before the temperatures grew too hot. Tomorrow sod would be laid along the edge of the driveway and on the western side of the house.

The sound of vans and trucks arriving out front reached them and Chase popped one last bite of coffee cake in his mouth, chewing it with relish. "I'm going to do a final walk-through today and put together a punch list. Dad and I are going to take the boys camping up in the north Georgia mountains later in the week. We'll be back in time for the opening cocktail party Labor Day weekend." He smiled, pleased, and Avery's lips stretched into a smile, too.

"You've done a really great job," she said, surprising them both. "And your subs have all been first-rate."

He stilled. "You didn't just give me a compliment, did you?"

"Apparently." She felt her cheeks grow hot.

He looked around, an expression of mock desperation on his face.

"What are you doing?" Avery asked.

"I'm checking to see if hell has frozen over. But it seems pretty toasty out."

The others laughed. Avery gave him an exaggerated eye roll, but her own mood lightened.

"Anybody who'd like to come camping with us is welcome. It's probably a good fifteen degrees cooler up there right now." Chase looked right at Avery, and she could feel the heat creep up her neck to spread across her cheeks. Again. "I figure anyone who survived the pool house floor all these weeks can handle a tent."

"I wouldn't hold my breath on that one," she said, sending him a look meant to quell. "But I'll give you my remaining three hundred dollars and the keys to the Mini Cooper if you'll take Deirdre with you."

When he went off laughing to meet Enrico, Avery couldn't quite hide her own smile. It was possible that her quelling look could use some work.

On August 23, the day the house at Ten Beach Road was pronounced "done," Tropical Storm Charlene dumped rain over the Turks and Caicos and headed toward the Florida straits. On the twenty-fourth, Kyra posted her final video to YouTube. It was cut to the theme from *Rocky* and was a stunningly powerful recap of Bella Flora's renovation from the day Kyra had first arrived through that morning's formal guided tour, with comments from Chase, every Dante family artisan who'd worked on the job, and a small plug for their personal plumber, Robby.

It was hosted by Deirdre Morgan and Avery Lawson, who did *not* appear on screen together but were skillfully edited into what felt like a seamless narrative by the filmmaker herself. The last frames were of the Designer Show House Opening Soon sign and the For Sale sign being hammered in.

"You've got talent, kid," Maddie said that night as they screened the piece on the new HD set the salon's design team had tucked into a marvelous Deco reproduction armoire. The audience, which erupted into cheers and catcalls at regular intervals, included the entire Hardin clan as well as the Franklins, whose affection for each other Kyra had also managed to capture. "You need to be making movies."

Kyra rubbed her stomach and hit the rewind when the audience demanded to see the piece again. "I will," she said with a certainty that filled Maddie with pride. "I'll just be shooting newborn video for a while, first." Pushing the Play button, she added, "I'm going to need a crash course in motherhood. Do you think you could put together a syllabus?"

Madeline smiled at her daughter, thinking of the sonogram they'd seen at Kyra's last ob-gyn visit. The months until Kyra's D-day were slipping away. "Sure. Although your dad was always the calmer of the two of us." She sighed. "It's going to be hard doing this all alone, Ky," Maddie said. Just as getting through this time had been so much harder without the man who'd always been her best friend at her side.

"Have you heard anything from Dad?" Since the cessation of hostilities between them, Kyra often seemed to be on the same wavelength.

"Just a text that he was at Aunt Emma's and another apology."

"You're not really thinking about divorcing him, are you, Mom?" Kyra looked about five when she asked the question.

"How did you . . ."

"I heard Nicole and Avery talking about it one day." She looked at Maddie's face. "They didn't know I was there. But . . ."

"At the time, it seemed like the only threat that might motivate him. But it's been so long since we've spoken, I really don't know where things stand or what to do next."

"I don't blame you, Melinda," Kyra teased, using the wrong name as her grandmother so often did. "Won't Edna be upset when she finds out you've spent a whole summer with both Avery Lawson and Deirdre Morgan? Maybe we should bring her back some autographs."

Maddie smiled, relieved to be on firm footing with Kyra, even more relieved that the renovation of Bella Flora was done, each ant-sized bite thoroughly chewed and digested. Did she have the energy and strength to apply the same approach to her marriage? She now knew she could do whatever needed to be done without Steve. What she didn't know was if she'd have to.

The morning of August 25, Charlene moved out of the warm waters of the Caribbean into the even warmer and more welcoming waters of the Gulf of Mexico. The Florida Keys battened down its hatches at just about the same time that Nicole Grant battened down hers.

She'd watched Kyra's last post to YouTube more than a dozen times, cringing at the initial footage when they'd all looked so beaten and desperate, feeling almost worse at how close they'd all appeared right before she'd been booted out. It was hard not to see just how much the summer had changed them all.

When she'd left Bella Flora, she'd had no destination in mind and only the vaguest of plans for meeting up with Malcolm on her own terms. She'd zigged and zagged her way up the state of Florida always looking over her shoulder, trying to spot a tail. But if someone was following her, it wasn't Giraldi. Or else Giraldi was very, very good.

With almost ten days to kill, she'd continued north to the semirural area of Acworth, northwest of Atlanta, and stashed the Jag in the cinder block garage of an old friend of their mother's who'd never had enough money to invest with anyone, and especially not with Malcolm. After dinner and a night on a pull-out sofa that made her mattress on the floor at Bella Flora feel five-star, Nicole gave the woman the cash to pick up a car for her from Rent-A-Wreck. Nikki had spent the last week in the slightly dented beige Ford Focus holing up first at an old friend's cabin on Lake Lanier before driving east to another friend's small beach place in St. Simon's.

Yesterday she'd driven back into Florida, catching I-10 around Jacksonville and heading west to Sneads where Florida met up with the southwest corner of Georgia. Now she was ready to drive the beige rental car into the Three Rivers State Park and hike by foot to the campground on Lake Seminole, where the Chattahoochee and Flint Rivers merged.

Turning in to the park entrance, she watched her rearview mirror carefully to see if anyone had followed her, but there was no sign of movement at all—not even from white-tailed deer and gray foxes that the park's website seemed so proud of.

Afraid to trust in the absence of Giraldi, she parked at the visitors' center and went in to use the restroom, taking a good look around while she was there, but no one shouted, "Halt, FBI!" and none of the employees looked anywhere as well built or fluid as Joe. Which may have accounted for her slight flare of disappointment and the reluctance with which she left the building and proceeded on foot to the camping area where Malcolm was supposed to be waiting.

She found him at the farthest campsite very near the lake. An old canoe sat at the lake's edge with a life vest and both oars stowed neatly inside. Malcolm had set up his tent in the hollow of a Y-shaped rock wall, and was sitting under a live oak in a director's chair reading what looked like the *Wall Street Journal*. He looked up when her foot crunched loudly on a dead branch. His gaze skimmed over her, then peered beyond her, presumably to make sure she was alone.

"I hope that's not your getaway vehicle," she said with a nod toward the canoe. "I'd feel a lot better if you had that yacht you had custom built moored here. Or that race car you sponsored stashed behind one of these trees."

"Me, too," he said, folding up the paper and standing. "But at the moment, I can't even access that old dirt bike I saved all my paper route money for." He stood as she approached. She took in the rumpled Levi's and plain white T, which were a far cry from the two-thousand-dollar suit he'd been wearing the last time they met for dinner, and wondered if he'd chosen the ensemble as camouflage or out of necessity.

They hugged, but both their bodies remained stiff with tension. Nikki felt as if she were in some bad movie of the week when he ran his hands up and down her sides.

"Sorry," he said when he'd finished patting her down. "I just wanted to be sure you weren't wearing a wire or anything."

She stepped back so that she could look him in the eye. His were bloodshot and weary. He was overdue for a shave and a haircut. A bath wouldn't have hurt, either. "Funny, since I'm not the one who's been lying and stealing."

He looked surprised, and once again she wondered what he'd been expecting. "Have a seat," he said, setting up a second director's chair, keeping the one with its back to the rock face.

She sat. It was hot and humid, with the loamy smell of lake and forest, but not unbearable in the shade of the oak. For a long moment, neither of them spoke.

"I wasn't sure if you'd come," he said. "But then I figured you'd never let me down before. There's no one I trust more."

"I used to feel that way about you, too, Malcolm. Until you stole everything I had." She said it quietly, a replay of their whispered Fourth of July conversation.

"That wasn't intentional, Nik. I moved everything off-shore and spread it between the different accounts. I know exactly how much is yours. Once you start making withdrawals for me your balance comes right off the top."

"You left me high and dry. No warning, no apology, nothing to live on. You weren't the only one who made a vow to succeed as a child, Malcolm. I lost my business, my reputation, the clothes off my back . . . everything."

"But I . . ."

"You didn't care who you stole from," she said, thinking of Grace's foster children and the other charities he'd bankrupted. "Or the lives you destroyed in the process." She pictured Madeline and her family, the husband who'd lost himself along with his job and their money. "I don't know how you live with yourself. You may be living in the forest, Malcolm, but you're no Robin Hood." She narrowed her gaze, the better to see beyond the much-loved façade. "I'm ashamed of you. You're greedy and selfish and I suppose some of that is my fault. There is no justification for what you've done."

He blinked in surprise as comprehension dawned. "You're not going to help me get to my money." His tone was incredulous.

"It's not your money, Malcolm. It never was. But I am going to help you."

A slow smile of relief began to form on his lips.

"I'm going to help you turn yourself in."

The smile disappeared. He shook his head. "Not likely, Sis. If you're not on my side, you can just turn around and get the hell out of here."

"I am on your side, though I hardly understand why anymore. If you turn yourself in and hand over the account numbers, they're bound to go easier on you. You'll do some jail time and then . . ."

He stood and looked wildly around. "What have you done? Who have you been talking to?" he asked.

"I haven't been talking to anyone," she said, trying to maintain her calm. "But the FBI's been talking to me. And I don't know if you've seen the papers lately, but they're not the only ones who know I'm your sister."

"Jesus, Nik." He strode to the tent and reached inside, never taking his gaze off of her or the path behind her. When he stood he was holding a gun. "I can't fucking believe this. Where are they? Where the fuck are they hiding?"

"I didn't bring anybody," she said, her eyes on the gun. "I went out of my way to make sure of it." She stood and took a step toward him. "But I have a phone number." She thought about Giraldi and almost wished he were here.

"You are fucking crazy if you think I'm going to do that. I'm not going to jail, and I'm not ever going to be a poor nobody again." He waved the gun around for emphasis and she hoped to hell he had the safety on. This probably wasn't the time to call him on his overuse of the f-word.

"No, you'll be that thief Malcolm Dyer who came out of the gutter and stole three hundred million dollars that didn't belong to him," she said. "And you'll spend the rest of your life hiding and on the run."

"But once I access my accounts, I'll be hiding and running in style," he said. "There are all kinds of places to get lost in if you have enough money. And I do, finally."

"It's not yours, Malcolm. You need to make things right. Give it back to the people it belongs to." Like Grace's foster children. And the Singers and even the hotheaded Avery.

He shook his head, unwilling even to consider the idea. "I'm not giving back a dime, Nik. And I'm definitely not going to jail and coming out with nothing." His body went very still. His gaze skittered away. "Did you hear that?"

She listened intently for a moment, but heard nothing. This was not going at all as she'd hoped; she simply wasn't getting through. "It's just you and me, Malcolm," she said. "Just like it always was. I know why you picked this place and this date. It was a great Thanksgiving we had here. Almost like the real thing." She took a step closer, desperate to convince him. "Do you really think Mom or Dad would approve of what you've done, what you're doing now? They were poor and uneducated, and they had their weaknesses. But they weren't dishonest, Malcolm; they didn't steal."

"I'm not going to be broke, Nikki. I can't survive in prison or anywhere else without something, some kind of nest egg, to come back to."

Nicole moved another step closer. She understood the fear and dread of poverty that drove him like no one else ever would; they'd been her most powerful motivators, too. She'd come prepared to overcome his dread, even as she'd prayed that no inducement other than a rekindled conscience would be necessary. Reaching into her pocket, she pulled out a piece of paper and unfolded it, handing it to her brother. "I've signed over my third of Ten Beach Road to you. It could be worth up to a million and a half dollars if we get anywhere near the listing price. This can be your nest egg."

He eyed her and the piece of paper with suspicion. "You'd give me everything you have left to get me to turn myself in?"

She hesitated, feeling queasy, but hopeful, too, as she watched him read the printed document, which she'd signed and had notarized at a small UPS Store in Georgia. She already missed Maddie and Avery and Kyra, and the friendship that had enfolded and buoyed her. Anything that would allow them to get back even part of what had been stolen would be worthwhile. "Yep," she said. "I guess it's my way of apologizing for doing such a half-assed job of parenting."

He grimaced at the insult but didn't argue. Nor did he give the paper back. She watched him fold it one-handed and stuff it into his jean pocket. "Thanks. You see, I always have been able to count on you. You and that mile-wide soft spot of yours."

That was when Nicole finally got it. That moment in which she was forced to acknowledge that Malcolm would take the last thing she owned, her very last penny, and not blink an eye. Because he thought he was entitled to it and because nothing else mattered to him—not her love, or her sacrifices, not even their shared past. All of the things she'd cherished didn't even exist for him.

"So you'll turn yourself in?" she asked, watching his face carefully, already knowing the answer but not wanting to believe.

He didn't even pretend to think about it. "I get that you can't try to access the offshore accounts if they're aware of you," he said. "But I'm going to need some money before I can, um, even consider turning myself in. And there is one account you should be able to access without arousing suspicion."

"Oh?"

"There's an account that I kept in Mom's name. It was just something I played with when I was first starting out back in the eighties. It's got Google and Apple shares, more solid slow growers than I could have put my clients who were looking for high returns into. But it's built beautifully over the years. I was her executor. She left it to you. I, um, had someone take care of a signature card. And it was established way before my, um, difficulties."

Nikki could hardly breathe. She stared at her chipped fingernails, caked with dirt that wouldn't come out, at her rough, chapped hands. She thought about all the beautiful clothes she'd been forced to sell. "But I was supporting Mom because you said you had to plow all your profits back into your business." As Nicole should have been, except that she hadn't been able to bear watching their mother continue to struggle after all those years of doing without while Mom tried to support them.

He shrugged. "I just had a feeling I might need to keep something aside, not in my name. You know, for emergencies."

She studied her brother's face as the enormity of his betrayal sank all the way in. "It's in my name and belongs to me. But you never told me about it." He'd stolen from her like he had everyone else and then never mentioned this account, which could have saved her business and her good name. Because in his mind her money was his money.

"Yeah. But the best thing is it's right near here. I divided it up between two small banks, where no one would think to look. So you could go and make the withdrawals and bring the money to me today." He must have actually looked at her face because he added, "And of course you could take a percentage of it to tide you over until I can return the money that got mixed up in the offshore accounts."

"Gee, thanks." She looked at the still-handsome and always-beloved face and grappled with what she'd refused to see behind it. Malcolm had always been the one she'd loved most—more than her husbands, her clients, her colleagues. More even than the few people she'd let close enough to call friends. And yet she had been nothing more to him than a person he could count on, which in Malcolm's mind clearly meant to use in whatever way he saw fit.

"So, that's why you're here in this campground. Not because that Thanksgiving meant so much to you, but because the money's nearby." Her money. That he expected her to go retrieve and hand over so he could run farther and faster.

He shrugged again, not at all apologetically. He didn't know her at all. Her own brother had no idea who she was or what she was made of. And he didn't care to.

"Sure," she said with the smile that she'd practiced and perfected over the years, the easy charming one that gave no clue to what she was really thinking and that she'd never before used on Malcolm. "Give me the banks and the account numbers, and I'll go take care of it."

Thirty-eight

It had been raining for three days, a hard driving rain spewed out by an angry black sky.

They'd spent the day boarding up as many of Bella Flora's windows and French doors as they could manage, but getting plywood from the one beach hardware store had proven near impossible; the inland chain stores had also been picked clean as the western half of central Florida braced itself for the newly upgraded Charlene, which was eating up the Gulf of Mexico and growing stronger with each bite.

Madeline, Kyra, Avery, and Deirdre had darted into Bella Flora from the pool house and sat up all night in the salon watching the Weather Channel, searching for any hint that the storm might veer off its present course, which seemed to be aimed just north of them.

Maddie wanted to stay calm, but she couldn't tear her gaze from the television screen, which she'd begun to think of as the "screen of doom." Or from what she could see of the high choppy seas in the occasional spill of moonlight through the dark night and darker clouds.

Avery flipped to a local station where the TV weather

departments were making the most of the first real threat they'd had to work with this season. "Look how happy they are," she said. "They don't have to blow up a thirty percent chance of rain into a potential weather disaster. They've hit pay dirt: they've got a real one." She flipped to a competing station where an attractive redhead had to bite back her grin as she explained that Hurricane Charlene was now a Category 3 and expected to grow stronger.

"Just look at the excitement in her eyes," Kyra said. "She can hardly contain herself."

"Well, it is the opportunity of a lifetime," Deirdre said. "If Charlene hits anywhere near the Tampa Bay area and that girl acquits herself well, her career will be made." As had become habit, Deirdre sat slightly apart, not venturing too close to Avery or Maddie. With them, but not a part of them.

"Leave it to Deirdre to see the career potential in a looming disaster." Avery kept her gaze on the screen, but Maddie saw the barb hit home. Since her last exchange with her daughter, Deirdre no longer attempted to defend herself.

There was a loud beeping sound from the TV and in large letters information about evacuation and shelters opening flashed on the screen.

"We could be right in her path," Kyra said. "All the beaches are being evacuated. We really need to think about where we want to go."

"I'm not leaving Bella Flora," Avery said, getting up and beginning to pace. "Not after everything we've gone through this summer."

"I wish we could reach Chase and Jeff," Maddie said. "They could at least tell us what else to do to the house before we leave."

"Yes, well, there's no cell phone service up where they are, or TV. They may not have even heard about Charlene," Avery said.

"Even if we could reach them, it's far too late to retrofit the roof or do anything else structural. And all the workmen are busy securing their own homes," Deirdre said. "Even the

show house designers have had to leave their things in place."
She shrugged. "Charlene's bringing winds over one hundred
miles per hour, along with rain bands that can cause flooding
and spawn tornadoes. And then there's the very real threat of
a major storm surge. Bella Flora is a sitting duck."

"Not exactly an optimist, are you?" Maddie looked at the
older woman. They could have used some of Nicole's dry wit
and strategic thinking right about now.

"I'm a realist," Deirdre said. "If that storm comes ashore anywhere within a hundred-mile radius, Bella Flora is finished."

Outside the wind bent the palms almost double and the
rain pounded against the roof and the windows, insistent and
hard. "We need to secure the outdoor furniture," Avery said.
"We don't want to lose it or have it slam into the house; they
can turn into missiles. Most hotels put the outdoor furniture
into the pool. We can stash the cushions in the pool house."

They looked at each other. No one wanted to go out into
the wind and rain, which was no longer vertical but horizon-
tal. But what choice did they have?

"All right," Maddie said. "But Kyra stays here. And after
we secure the furniture we get some things together and get
the hell out of here. You know it's probably already bumper
to bumper getting off the beach." Panic rose, like bile, in her
throat. If they took too long, they could get trapped here.
They'd be even more vulnerable than the house.

Avery led the way outside. Kyra shot video of them leaving, then stood on the loggia, her back braced against the
wall, shooting their rescue mission. By the time they'd buried the last pieces in the pool and carried the cushions inside
they were soaked.

Avery arranged the mattresses against the windows of the
pool house and one of the French doors, buttressing them
with the outdoor cushions. Maddie eyed the dry clothing she
pulled out of her drawer with longing; she'd give almost anything to be dry. And safe.

"Forget it. There's no point in changing now," Deirdre
said. "We're going to be soaked again by the time we get

back to the house and then into the car. Here," she said to Avery. "Take this carryall."

"I don't need a bag," Avery said. "Because I'm *not* evacuating."

Ignoring her, Deirdre gathered Avery's things and shoved them into the carryall while Maddie packed an overnight bag for herself and Kyra. Hurrying to the refrigerator, she packed a cooler with ice and waters then filled one plastic grocery bag with bread, peanut butter, and Cheez Doodles, the only nonperishables in the cupboard. Her fingers felt clumsy as she gathered everything together; the sound of blood whooshing through her veins was almost as loud in her ears as the growing wind outside.

"Ready?" Deirdre asked her.

Maddie nodded and got a firmer grip on the overnight bag and the cooler. She handed Avery the grocery bag.

"I told you I'm not leaving." Avery reached for the bag that Deirdre had slung over her shoulder. Deirdre held on to it.

"Didn't you see all those videos about what storm surge looks like? Did you pay any attention to how many people die in the tornadoes and flooding that a storm like Charlene causes?" Maddie asked. "We can't waste any more time getting out of here. We've done what we can for Bella Flora. But it's not safe to stay."

"I don't care. You all can go. I'm staying here."

Not bothering to argue, Deirdre took hold of Avery's arm. Avery broke loose and turned toward the bathroom. If she locked herself inside, they'd lose even more time.

"Oh, no, you're not." Deirdre followed Avery and got a strong hold on her arm. Then despite Avery's attempts to free herself, she managed to half propel/half drag her out of the pool house and toward Bella Flora. It was the first completely motherly thing Maddie had seen her do.

They made it to the loggia and then the four of them muscled the door open and pushed their way into the kitchen. Even in the midst of battling the storm they knew to stay off the wood floors.

"I was afraid you would still be here!"

They looked up in surprise at the unexpected voice.

Nicole stood near the kitchen island, a pool of rainwater around her feet. Short of breath from her sprint inside, she pushed the wet hair out of her eyes and braced for their reaction to her presence.

"What are you doing here?" Avery asked. Her gaze narrowed, but her belligerence seemed automatic, not personal.

"I came to make sure you evacuated," Nicole said. "I figured if anyone would be a problem, it would be you."

"Ha!" Avery said. Her chin jerked upward, but with far less venom than Nicole had been expecting.

A small, if grudging, smile tugged at Maddie's lips and Nikki began to hope that the need to evacuate might expedite her acceptance back into the fold.

"You always were the most persuasive of us, Nikki. If you can talk some sense into her, I won't give you half the shit I was planning to the next time I saw you." Maddie's voice came out in a rush. "We need to get out of here."

Kyra stood near the loggia door filming everything. Maddie the mother hen clucked at them, intent on hurrying everyone along. Deirdre, with a determined glint in her eyes and a bag slung over her shoulder, contemplated her belligerent daughter.

Nicole stepped closer to Avery so that she could stare down at her.

"There's nothing Nikki can say that's going to change my mind," Avery said. "We don't even know whether she was in league with her brother. She . . ."

"He stole from me the same way he stole from you. Maybe my mistake was not telling you up front. I'm sorry for that."

There was a bang as something metal slammed into something solid outside.

"Listen," Nicole said. "We really need to get the hell out of here. I was the last car allowed onto the beach. There's a huge line of vehicles trying to get off."

She studied their faces and thought she saw a grudging

acceptance. No one came out and told her she was forgiven, but no one told her to go away, either.

"I'm not leaving," Avery said. "You all can go ahead, but I've worked too hard to leave Bella Flora defenseless."

"And what do you think you can do against one-hundred-mile-per-hour winds and a ten-foot storm surge?" Maddie asked. "You're being ridiculous."

"I'm not . . ."

Deirdre looked at Avery and then at the rest of them. "It might as well be me," she said cryptically. "She already hates me."

Maddie looked confused, but Nicole sensed what was coming before Deirdre even pointed and said, "Oh, my gosh, Avery. Look over there!"

Avery turned and before Nikki could offer to do it for her, Deirdre's fist shot out and connected with Avery's chin. Avery crumpled.

"Jesus!" Maddie said. Her mouth dropped open.

"Wow!" Kyra said from behind the camera.

"I can't believe you beat me to it," Nikki said as she grasped Avery under the arms and waited for Deirdre to get her ankles. "Do you have your keys out, Maddie?" she asked as Kyra finally stopped shooting in order to put her camera in its waterproof case. Maddie went to the kitchen door.

"You actually want to go in the minivan?" Maddie asked with a stab at a smile. "I don't know that I'd be leaving a classic Jaguar here in a potential hurricane."

"You'll understand when you see my current wheels," Nikki said as they waited for Maddie to aim her remote at the van's doors. "This is the first time I've fully appreciated the whole automatic sliding doors thing," she said.

"Ready?" With a final look at each other they raced out of Bella Flora and toward the van, Nicole and Deirdre carrying the inert Avery between them. As soon as Maddie got the rear door open, they slung Avery into the cargo hold.

The endless journey off the beach passed largely in intense

eyes-on-the-road-trying-to-see-through-the-driving-rain-
while-willing-themselves-forward silence. It took an hour to
reach the Don CeSar, where they followed the Bayway toward
the interstate.

Avery sputtered awake much later. Traveling at what felt
like an inch per hour, it had taken an eternity to reach the
Howard Franklin Bridge. The relative safety of Tampa lay on
the other side. Nikki turned in her seat when Avery groaned
and watched the blonde struggle to lift her head off the overnight bag they'd pillowed underneath it.

"Shit!" Avery groaned, pulling herself into a sitting position. She rubbed her jaw slowly. "What happened? Did somebody hit me?"

"We all wanted to," Nicole said. "But Deirdre got in the
first and only punch."

"Shit." The curse was almost reflective, and Nikki imagined
Avery was recalling what had happened. Kyra was turned in
the passenger seat aiming the camera at them. Avery grabbed
on to Nicole's and Deirdre's seats to pull herself upright. She
looked at Nikki. "You *are* here. I thought I had dreamed it."
She rubbed the side of her face, still regrouping. "This is a
frickin' nightmare," she said. "And as for you, Deirdre, I can't
believe you slugged me. I told you I didn't want to . . ."

"Be quiet," Deirdre said, turning to face Avery. "You were
being unreasonable. We did what we had to do."

"You always have a way of justifying yourself, don't you?"
Avery asked angrily. "You always have to be right."

"Like mother, like daughter," Nicole murmured loud enough
for both of them to hear. Before Avery or Deirdre could protest,
Maddie, whose hands were white from her death grip on the
wheel, said, "Shut up, all of you! I can barely see through this
rain, we're packed in so tightly between cars I couldn't change
lanes if I had to, and our gas is getting low. I can't take your
petty sniping on top of everything else. If you can't say something nice, just . . . shut up!" Maddie's loss of control stunned
them into a silence, which lasted for some time.

"I can't see anything from back here," Avery finally said. "Where are we?"

"We're almost in Tampa," Maddie replied, her voice still tight. "I'm going to start breathing again as soon as we get off this bridge and away from all this water."

Kyra panned the camera across their faces and out the window to capture the traffic that surrounded them.

"Kyra, please," Maddie said. Kyra put the camera away.

"Where are we headed?" Deirdre asked, staring out the windshield. Nicole noticed that she only stole glances at Avery when she thought no one was looking.

"I don't know," Maddie said. "It looks like people are continuing north on the interstate, but we don't have enough gas to get far, and I figured we'd want to be safe but in the vicinity so that we can go and check on Bella Flora as soon as we're allowed back on the beach."

There was another long silence and Nicole knew they were all thinking about the defenseless house sitting and waiting for unwelcome guest Charlene.

"Ky," Maddie said. "Plug in the GPS and go into 'points of interest.' That'll bring up a list of hotels within whatever radius we choose."

Kyra put down the camera and did as her mother asked. A few minutes later, they'd moved about an inch, and the mechanical voice said, "recalculating," in a chiding tone.

"It looks like North Dale Mabry has a ton of gas stations, restaurants, and hotels," Maddie said after Kyra had read her the list. "I don't know how hard it'll be to find a room, but we can just keep heading north on it while we look. Maybe we'll get lucky."

They didn't. In fact, by the tenth hotel Nikki was tired of jumping out and asking if they had anything available plus her patience was wearing thin. "We're in the middle of nowhere," she complained to the current desk clerk. "How can you be out of rooms?"

"Hurricane's coming. All the beaches are emptying."

He shrugged. "Can't create a room I don't have," he said reasonably.

But Nicole was all out of reasonable. They were traveling on fumes and the lines at the gas pumps were even longer than the ones wrapped around the hotels. They'd consumed what little food Maddie had managed to pack for them hours ago. They needed a place to stay.

She strode out to the car and opened Kyra's door. "Leave the camera," Nikki said. "Come with me."

She took Kyra by the arm and speed walked her into the tiny motel office. Kyra was out of breath by the time they got there, which Nikki decided could work in their favor. The more pathetic the better.

They marched up to the filthy Formica counter. The desk clerk's eyes widened slightly when he saw Kyra's stomach and noticed her labored breathing. He shook his head. "I'm real sorry," he said. "I see you've got a problem. But I don't have . . ."

"I know," Nikki said. "Any room at the inn." She let the biblical reference sink in a moment. "How about a stable? Or even the lobby area here?" She nodded to the small space with its chair and vinyl love seat. Even using the term "lobby" was a stretch. But it was dry and had places to sit. They were way beyond picky. "I know you don't want to turn a pregnant girl out in this weather." They all looked out the filthy front window to the artificial darkness and the heavy rain gushing out of it. The clerk glanced down at the computer screen.

"You must have something . . ." Nicole began.

"Well." He punched a few keys. "I do have one room. It was booked, but they didn't ask for a late arrival and they're way overdue. They've probably gotten held up by the weather."

Nicole was very careful not to move too quickly or to presume. She didn't hug the man or Kyra or pump a triumphant fist in the air. "Gosh," she said. "That would mean so much to us. Her mother's out in the van. And her, um, sister, too." And then because she couldn't resist. "Today was supposed to be her baby shower."

Kyra's eyes went very wide but fortunately the clerk was too busy typing on the keyboard to notice. Nicole elbowed the girl. "Why don't you go back to the car while I get the key and the room number?"

Kyra went.

Thirty-nine

It said a lot for how desperate they were to get out of the storm and into something resembling safety that no one complained about the room, although as far as Maddie could see it wouldn't have even qualified as a Motel 6, because six dollars would have far exceeded what it was worth.

While the others stripped out of their wet clothes, Maddie gathered all of the change she'd scraped out of the van ashtray and carried it to the motel's vending machines, where she used every bit of it to buy a dinner of three Hershey Bars, two packets of peanut butter crackers, and two cans of Coke. Back in the room, where the Weather Channel showed Charlene picking up speed and drawing inexorably closer, Maddie divvied up the meal, changed out of her still-damp clothes, and crawled into bed beside Kyra. Deirdre and Avery lay as far away from each other as they could get on the second bed. Nicole slumped on the rickety desk chair. All of them had their phones out. Maddie couldn't reach Steve or Andrew. None of them could get a signal.

Maddie lay in an odd state of fear-fueled exhaustion in the

tension-filled silence. The only one talking was the meteo-rologist and nothing he was saying was anything Maddie wanted to hear.

She lay awake worrying for a long time, wishing Steve and Andrew were here—or at least on their way—their life repaired, her family intact. She must have fallen asleep because she woke to a distant siren and Kyra's hands on her arm. "The right front quadrant of the hurricane is close to shore but hasn't hit land yet. Do you hear that siren and the beeping from the TV? There's a tornado warning in the area. They're telling everyone to go into a small interior room."

Kyra's voice caught slightly in fear, and Maddie sat up and pulled her into a hug. "I think I read once that you're sup-posed to sit in the bathtub." Kyra's voice quivered. "Should we wake everybody up?"

Groggy, the five of them filed into the bathroom. Without asking, Maddie helped Kyra into the tub, propping her up against her pillow, handing her another one to put over her head just in case though she was careful not to add in case of what. Avery was selected to crawl in with her because she was the only one with any chance of fitting.

Deirdre sat on the toilet lid while Maddie and Nicole folded their bedspreads into piles on either end of the tub then sat on them with their backs against the wall. The tiny jalousie window on the exterior wall had a big X of tape across it, which was presumably meant to stop pieces of glass from spraying into the room, but didn't prevent it from rat-tling. The sound on the TV was up as far as it would go, but Maddie could only pick out every fourth or fifth word; none of them were reassuring.

"What is it with us and bathrooms?" Nicole asked. "Have you noticed how many of them we've been stuck in together?"

Deirdre and Kyra managed smiles.

"I've noticed. I had a damned period because of it," Mad-die said, trying for another smile. "Nobody's carrying, are they? No tampons or Kotex or anything?"

"Mother!" Kyra said and for a moment her embarrassment seemed to cancel out her fear. Which felt like a victory of sorts to Madeline.

Nikki laughed and some of the tension dissipated. But Avery seemed to be looking for something to think about beside the approaching storm. "Where did you go? And why did you come back?" she asked Nicole.

Outside the wind kicked up a notch. The little window rattled more insistently. The warning beep on the TV grew louder, which seemed unnecessary; could there possibly be anyone left who didn't know a hurricane was coming?

"I'd been trying to find Malcolm for a long time." Nicole considered them all. "He contacted me on the fourth. When you asked me to leave I went to where he was."

Avery's "aha" died mid-syllable.

"I was going to talk him into turning himself in. At least that was my plan."

"And what actually happened?" Deirdre asked.

"I offered him my third of Bella Flora to turn himself in, so that you and everyone else would get at least some part of your money back," Nicole said. She shifted uncomfortably on the floor. "He took the deed I'd had drawn up, but it was pretty clear he wasn't going to turn himself in." She hesitated; their gazes were locked on her like an infrared target. "He asked me to get some cash for him that he'd managed to put in our mother's name and which apparently passed on to me."

"So you weren't really broke," Avery said.

"That money could have saved me from ruin. If I'd known anything about it. But that was the first I'd heard of it," Nikki replied. "And he only told me about it because he'd set it up so that I could access it when he couldn't. And because he assumed I'd run to the bank for him, retrieve the money, and then hand it over."

"And did you?' Deirdre asked.

Nicole looked away, which wasn't easy in such a small space crammed with so many people. "I'd always put him first no matter what he did. I guess it never occurred to him that could change. It hadn't occurred to me until that moment."

"But why?" Maddie asked, not understanding the sheer one-sidedness of it. "Why would he think that?"

"Because Malcolm and I were raised in what you'd call abject poverty. Our dad died working on the docks and our mother—she had maybe a seventh-grade education—worked two jobs to try to support Malcolm and me. One was nights at a bar. She worked days cleaning hotel rooms, although I don't think she ever worked in a hotel as nice as this."

Nicole tried to smile, but her face was stark in the bathroom's harsh lighting. Her voice matched her face. It was odd how little you could really tell about people.

"Anyway," Nikki continued when no one interrupted her. "I'm six years older than Malcolm and our mother was always working or trying to sleep enough to go back to work, so I was pretty much in charge of us. We had a pact that we'd work our way out of poverty. I put us both through college and helped fund Malcolm's first investment firm. It's crazy, but we both achieved our goals." She sighed and her shoulders sagged. "I didn't realize Malcolm built his fortune by stealing from others. I didn't know. And then when I did know, I just kept trying not to believe it. But the other day at the park, I couldn't pretend anymore. I knew I had to do something." Her eyes were bleak. "I turned him in."

"Who did you turn him in to?" Avery was still skeptical. Madeline wondered if she was going to demand a name and phone number.

"Giraldi."

"Your friend Joe?"

"My FBI agent Joe," Nikki corrected. "I called him and told him where to find Malcolm." She swallowed. "I imagine they've taken him into custody by now. I haven't seen anything on the news. I headed right for Bella Flora when I saw the hurricane warning for Pass-a-Grille."

Maddie didn't know whether Avery was as floored by Nikki's revelations as she was, but she didn't press for more detail. The blonde's gaze slid from Nicole to the rattling window where she could just make out the shadows of what might be a stand of palm trees—or some triple-headed monster—swaying madly in the wind.

The lights flickered and snapped off. The air-conditioning shuddered to a halt and the blare of the TV went off in mid-beep. It grew deadly calm outside.

No one spoke. Or moved. Until Kyra lifted her cell phone up and pressed a key creating a small glow of light. The others followed suit.

"This is when you're not supposed to go outside," Kyra whispered in the same kind of voice one might use to tell spooky stories around a campfire. "It's either the wind changing direction or maybe part of the eye passing over us. You go out thinking it's over and get trampled by the rest of the hurricane."

"I'm not going anywhere," Maddie said. "And neither is anyone else."

"I couldn't get out of this bathtub if I wanted to," Avery said. "Not without a crowbar."

"I hope Bella Flora is okay." Kyra still whispered. Maddie reached over and slipped her arm around her daughter's shoulders.

"She has to be. I refuse to believe fate, or nature, or whatever is at work could ignore how much we poured into her," Maddie said.

"Do you really think it works that way?" Deirdre asked. "That hard work is rewarded and evil gets punished? Where have you been living—in never-never land?"

Maddie flushed with anger. They were cowering in a moldy bathroom; how many other harsh realities did they have to face?

"Call it whatever you want, but where I come from we don't abandon our children."

Avery went very still and Maddie feared she'd somehow managed to offend both mother and daughter. "I'm sorry, that was . . ."

"No, don't apologize," Avery said. "I'd really like to hear what Deirdre has to say to that."

They all turned to Deirdre, who looked slightly less regal on her toilet throne. "I'll say what I've been trying to say all along," Deirdre began.

Avery's tone was taunting, but even in the muted glow of their cell phones, Maddie could see that her eyes were sad. "You mean before we found out you were just using us to get your career back on track or after? Before you exposed Kyra and us to the paparazzi and the foul-mouthed Tonja Kay or after? Before you . . ."

"That's enough!" Deirdre snapped. She stood and began to pace, but of course there was nowhere to go in the tiny and too-full space. In a certain kind of film, she'd go running out into the eye of the storm trying to outrun her daughter's censure and never be heard from again. Maddie smiled at her flight of fancy. They were jammed into a really crappy hotel bathroom in a hurricane, not a Nicholas Sparks movie.

Deirdre stopped and leaned against the bathroom wall. "I'm sorry that being here has helped my career. I know that's the worst possible insult to you, Avery. But that isn't why I came."

"Right."

"Oh, I did come because my career was in the toilet. Just like you did," she said. "But that was because there was no longer anything holding me there. I was out of excuses. I couldn't pretend I was too busy to find you and try to make amends."

If there had been anywhere else to go, Maddie would have led Kyra and Nikki out of the bathroom, but they were a captive audience. She remained still, wishing she could don Harry Potter's invisibility cloak, but she wasn't sure it mattered. Deirdre seemed far too intent on getting through to Avery to worry about them.

"Do you really think that before I came I knew about the merry band that would be assembled? Or that one of them would be a filmmaker with Internet savvy? That she'd happen to be pregnant by the husband of a Hollywood celebrity? You give me far too much credit, Avery. I'm a shitty mother, but even I am not that Machiavellian."

They sat in the near dark listening to the wind whip back up again. The trees outlined in the window no longer swayed, they jitterbugged.

"Bottom line," Deirdre continued, ignoring everything but the daughter who refused to look at her, "my career sucked. The thing I'd put before everything else had simply shriveled up and died. I heard you were in trouble and I hoped I could help enough that you'd want me around. That was my big plan."

Avery made no comment. But Maddie could feel how intently she was listening.

"I married your father because he was a wonderful man and he loved me more than anybody ever had. Certainly more than my parents did."

Deirdre's smile was rueful, her tone almost wistful. "I told him that I wasn't ready to settle down—I was barely twenty-one—and that I didn't feel the same way he did, that I wanted to go to Hollywood and have a design career. Oh, I was brutally honest.

"I told him I didn't want to be a mother; my mother was appalling at it. I didn't even know how one was supposed to behave. But he thought that the way he felt about me trumped all that. 'It'll all work out,' he said. 'I love enough for both of us.' That's what he said."

Deirdre looked down at her hands, which were clasped around her phone. For the first time since Maddie had met her she didn't look remotely "together," and it had nothing to do with the hurricane or the dim glow from their cell phones. "But it doesn't work like that. Not even when you want it to. It has to be equal. Or at least somewhere close."

She blinked back tears. "I was too young and far too messed up to handle things as I should have. And it didn't help that I got pregnant on our honeymoon. When you were born I loved you more than I'd ever loved anything. And you scared me to death. I was so afraid I'd screw everything up, that I'd screw you up."

She paused, searching Avery's face for something. All Maddie saw on it was horror and dislike.

"I stayed because you were mine and I loved you. I did my best to settle in and make things work. But I never loved your father to the exclusion of everything else, like he wanted. And I just didn't know how to be a mother."

Deirdre paused and the silence in the bathroom was in stark contrast to the howl of nature outside. Sirens blared. There was a crash of something large onto metal. None of them moved.

"Your father was born to be a parent," Deirdre said, staring into Avery's no-longer-averted eyes. "Your parent. I just got out of the way." She sighed. "And, of course, by the time I realized I'd done the absolute wrong thing and desperately wanted to beg your forgiveness, you wouldn't have anything to do with me." She paused for a moment, her voice barely more than a whisper. "I'm so sorry, Avery. I'm so very, very sorry."

Maddie drew her knees up to her chest and rested her forehead on them. She felt Deirdre's pain and Avery's deep down into her skin. Although she felt as if they'd been intruding, she was glad Kyra had heard Deirdre's story. She hoped that Avery would find it in her heart if not to forgive, then at least to forge some sort of . . . something. The reality was, they were all each other had.

Forty

A little later came what sounded—and felt—like all hell breaking loose. The wind whipped and howled and the rain pounded down. Unseen things collided. As they cowered in the bathroom, Avery's emotions kept pace with the storm. She felt as if someone had grabbed hold of everything inside her, shaken it around for a while, and then tried to wrench it out of her. Deirdre was self-centered and she had used their desperation to her advantage. But she was not completely unthinking or unfeeling and her apology had seemed stunningly sincere. The fabric of Avery's hurt and anger had been ripped into tiny shreds and brutally rearranged—still there but unrecognizable. Her last coherent thought before her eyes fluttered shut was that it was so much easier and cleaner to hate from afar.

Avery roused about five A.M. when the electricity finally flickered on. She'd fallen asleep with her knees folded up against her chest, Kyra's head on her shoulder, and her cell phone clutched in one hand. When they emerged from the bathroom a short time later, they discovered how lucky they were. The parking lot was strewn with debris. A tree on one edge had fallen across the roof of a small SUV and another had smashed into a unit at the opposite end. But Maddie's van was undamaged. All of them were rattled but unharmed.

Inside, the TV stations were filled with reports that large sections of the Tampa Bay area were without electricity and would be for some time. The beaches had been hard hit as Charlene, erratic to the end, skimmed up the west coast of Florida then skittered westward.

"Can we get back onto St. Pete Beach?" Maddie asked as they watched the images on the TV screen.

"Go to one of the local channels and see if they've got that info posted."

Maddie passed the remote to Kyra and the channel surfing, with intent, began.

"Charlene is headed toward the Mississippi coast. They think she may make landfall there."

"Jesus," Deirdre said. "That's the last thing they need up there after Katrina and the oil spill."

"They're reporting torrential rain up and down the western half of Florida," Kyra said. "Which could be impacting anyone trying to drive down from Georgia or North Carolina." She looked at her mother. "That means Dad and Andrew might have trouble getting down here."

"If they're coming," Maddie said.

"Mom, you know they'll come."

Maddie didn't comment. Avery couldn't help remembering how certain Kyra had been that Daniel Deranian would come and take her away. She'd been half right.

"That could mean the Hardins might be having trouble getting back, too," Kyra said moments after Avery had thought it.

"If Chase were here, we could maybe go by boat and take a look from the water." Avery wished he were here right now, though she wasn't about to admit it. She felt someone's gaze on her and looked up to see Deirdre watching her. Avery looked away, hoping Deirdre hadn't been able to read her thoughts.

"I can't even imagine what the bay and Gulf are like right now. I don't think I'd want to be out in a boat at the moment, even if it were possible," Maddie said.

"Have you tried to reach him?" Deirdre asked. "Or heard anything at all from the Hardins?"

Avery looked down at her phone. "No bars." She lifted it to her ear. Nothing. "Has anybody got a cell phone signal?"

No one did.

"The land line doesn't work, either." Nikki held the receiver to her ear. "No dial tone."

They looked at each other.

"I need to see Bella Flora," Avery said. "I need to make sure she's still there and intact." Her pulse quickened at the thought of the abuse that must have been heaped on her.

"Why don't we see if we can get something to eat first?" Deirdre suggested. "Now that my heart's not in my stomach anymore, it's feeling kind of empty. Hopefully by then there'll be more information."

"Deirdre's right," Maddie said, surprising them all. "Nikki, can you talk to your friend at the desk and see if there's anything close enough to walk to and where the closest gas stations are?"

"I'm on it."

A few minutes later they were at a Waffle House two streets over. Only the cook and one waitress had made it in that morning, but there was electricity and that meant food. They wolfed down their breakfasts as other customers trickled in. There was a TV mounted nearby and as they ate they learned that five people had died and twelve were unaccounted for. Reports about which beaches had been hardest hit and who did and did not have electricity continued to pour in, but those reports seemed conflicting.

A photo of Malcolm Dyer flashed on the screen for a few brief seconds along with the caption "Financial Schemer Captured," and Avery let out a whoop. They all stopped eating to watch footage of Dyer being led toward a police car in handcuffs while a knot of people wearing FBI windbreakers looked on.

Nicole's gaze remained riveted on the screen even after the images faded and were replaced by a radar map that showed Hurricane Charlene roaring toward Biloxi. Her face reflected both regret and resignation. A few moments later she turned her attention back to her plate.

Avery could hardly sit still long enough to swallow. All she wanted was to get back to Ten Beach Road and see Bella Flora for herself. But it was two days before they were allowed back across the Howard Franklin to St. Petersburg.

Avery rode shotgun and noted the things in Tampa Bay that didn't belong there—things like half-submerged cars and a hotel roof. A palm tree, apparently uprooted, floated against a piling. A power- and a sailboat sat aground, rammed up against a tree on the side of the causeway.

Traffic moved slowly, but it wasn't the agonizing inching along of evacuation. It felt as if far fewer people were returning. Avery wasn't sure if this was a good thing or a bad thing.

Traffic lights were out on Gulf Boulevard and crews from the power and phone company worked in pockets everywhere they looked. Trees were down and buildings were sorely damaged. Drifts of sand covered the asphalt, many with dark clumps mixed in.

"Is that seaweed?" Kyra asked. She'd been filming out the window since they'd first rolled onto the Howard Franklin. "Oh, my God, there're fish over there." She swung her lens toward a crosswalk where several fish lay belly up. The aroma promised many more as yet unseen.

"It kind of makes you wonder how much sand is left on the beach given how much of it is here," Deirdre said.

No one mentioned Bella Flora, though Avery knew it had to be at the forefront of all of their thoughts. Would she still be standing? Could she be, considering her precarious position at the southernmost tip of the narrow barrier island?

Just before the Don CeSar things slowed further as identification was checked and those who'd returned via the Pinellas Bayway merged into the two lanes of Pass-a-Grille Way. "Oh, my God, look at the Don." Kyra panned her camera up the stained pink façade. Two of the bell towers had broken off and fallen to the pavement. A whole section of windows was without glass. An employee was already busy sweeping the shards into piles on the sidewalk. Despite the traffic behind them, they slowed to gawk. "I can't believe it. Imagine what things would look like if Charlene had come ashore anywhere near here."

All the way down the narrow twist of road, debris cluttered their way. They gasped at the damage, which often seemed arbitrary. One minute Avery believed Bella Flora might have gotten through unscathed, the next she feared they'd find nothing waiting for them but an empty lot.

Without asking, Maddie stayed on Pass-a-Grille Way, hugging the bay rather than jogging over and paralleling the Gulf. Avery knew then that Maddie's fears mirrored her own. At the corner of Beach Road, Maddie pulled the van to a complete stop. Cottage Inn's cottages still stood, though they looked the worse for wear. Maddie and Avery considered each other. Kyra crouched forward so that she could shoot both out the windshield and over her mother's shoulder.

"Are we ready?" Maddie asked.

"I'm rolling," Kyra said as if that was all they were waiting for.

Maddie drew in a deep breath. Avery did the same.

"I'm not sure I can take this," Avery said.

"All I want to do is close my eyes and not look until someone tells me it's okay."

"That might work if you weren't driving, Maddie," Nikki said. "Not so good as things stand."

There was nervous laughter and a collective drawing of breath. "All right," Maddie said, pressing down on the gas pedal. "Here we go."

They turned onto Beach Road and headed toward number ten.

At the end of the road John Franklin's Cadillac was bellied up to the curb. The Realtor and his wife stood in front of the white garden wall in the middle of what might have been a small sandbar. Renée Franklin was crying.

"I'm not getting a good feeling about this." Maddie pulled the van to a stop and they clambered out, craning their necks, turning as one for a first glimpse of Bella Flora.

Avery was swept back to the first time she'd seen it and her partners all those months ago. The garden had looked bad then, but it was far worse now. In fact, it was decimated. Trees, plants, and bushes had been torn up by the roots and flung around; sand and seaweed were everywhere; the fabulous concrete fountain had toppled and smashed into far too many pieces to ever be put back together again.

But the front façade of the house appeared intact—chipped up and still damp, but all there. Even the windows seemed all right. Until Avery tilted her head up just a bit. And realized that from the doorway over there was no red tile, angled or otherwise. Because there was no roof for it to cling to.

"Oh, my God," she breathed. "Not the roof."

John Franklin looked helpless. Renée was in mourning. "My poor triple hibiscus," she breathed. "That lovely jasmine and frangipani. And wait until you see what's happened to the reclinada."

"This doesn't look that bad," Deirdre said. "If it's just a few sections of the roof, we can . . ."

The Realtor shook his head sadly. "This is the only exposure that doesn't face water. It gets worse."

Numb, they followed him around the west side of the house where pretty much all of the windows were either shattered or missing. Puddles of broken glass lay on the ground. There was no red tile poking over the edge of the house here, either. The western half of Bella Flora's roof had been torn off by the wind, leaving jagged pieces of the frame poking into the sky. Shards of barrel tile lay everywhere as did pile after pile of debris, some of it mundane, some of it—like the crumpled baby stroller and the volleyball poles and netting—especially troubling.

They rounded the house, their gazes glued to the battered walls. The master bedroom's wrought-iron balcony and spiral staircase hung crookedly down the back of the house, scraping against what remained of the loggia roof. Avery couldn't bear to think about what Bella Flora must look like inside with so many of her windows missing and only half of a roof to protect her from the rain and the wind. All of it—the floors and doors, the hardware, the chandeliers, the walls, everything they'd worked on and slaved over, exposed and vulnerable. Deirdre's kitchen, that work of art Avery had been unable to acknowledge, was bound to be a sodden mess. And what about the things the designers had just installed?

"Oh, my windows," Maddie groaned. "All that time re-glazing and half of them are just . . . gone."

"It'll be all right," Kyra said as she and Nikki stepped up on either side of Maddie. "We'll just move into the pool house again and . . ." She panned her camera away from the house and toward the pass. They turned with her. And saw the reclinada palm, torn out by the roots, lying across it, the roof smashed but intact. One glassless French door lay at the bottom of the filthy pool along with the outdoor furniture.

Deirdre took Avery's hand and squeezed it. "It'll be all right," she said. "It's a good strong house with great bones. As long as it's still standing, it can be fixed."

Avery removed her hand and wiped it on her pant leg, automatically lashing out. "I'm not some rich client with endless money that you can jolly along," she said. "This is not the time to bullshit."

"It's not the time to quit, either," Deirdre snapped. "It's never the time to quit."

Avery snorted.

"I can't believe this," Maddie whispered. "How could this happen now?"

"It'll be all right, Mom," Kyra said.

"I knew I should have kept my eyes closed," Maddie said. "I can't bear to look at her like this."

Avery couldn't have agreed more. She wanted to leave

right now and pretend none of it had happened. Her stomach rolled and she felt her gorge rise. Hurrying away from the group she reached a stand of sea oats and lost her breakfast. A brown pelican watched with sad eyes, making Avery feel even more pathetic.

Straightening, she stared out toward the beach and noticed that the fishing pier was gone, ripped from its concrete pilings and most likely lying at the bottom of the Gulf. The beach itself looked different; the sand oddly piled and rearranged, the walkovers smashed like matchsticks. The water was a murky green like some smoothie gone awry. Or a dirty martini with too many olives that had been both shaken and stirred.

Car doors slammed, and there were shouts. Avery looked up and saw Chase and Jeff and the boys standing frozen in front of Bella Flora. A wave of relief rushed through her and she tried to banish it, but she was embarrassingly glad to see him. The Hardins stood for a few long moments clearly taking in the damage, then headed around Bella Flora. Chase looked up and spotted her. He said something to his dad and then walked toward her.

"Are you all right?" He came directly to her and cupped the nape of her neck in his big warm hand. "You look almost as beat up as Bella Flora."

She smiled a ridiculously wobbly smile. She couldn't seem to locate their normal combative tone. "And that's saying something."

"We took the boys camping. I didn't even hear Charlene had been upgraded until late yesterday," he said. "We got back as fast as we could."

Avery nodded, not trusting herself to speak.

"I was so afraid something had happened to you." He said this quietly but with a depth of feeling that she'd never heard from him before.

Hot tears formed. She broke eye contact to look at Bella Flora. "Something did."

"Ah, Avery." He pulled her close and she buried her face in

his chest, breathing in the scent of wood smoke and pine forest. "She's a beauty, but she's just a house. She can be rebuilt."

He put both of his arms around her and held her there. "Truly maddening women like you are harder to come by." Carefully, he set her away from him and looked down into her eyes. "You're a lot of things, Avery. Many of them incredibly annoying. But you're no quitter." He smiled, and she dredged one up to match it, but he was wrong. And so was Deirdre. She didn't have the strength or the money to start over. None of them did.

Near the pool Jeff Hardin shook his head in dismay. Even John Franklin seemed subdued, leaning on his wife in a way that belied the blow they'd all taken. Maddie looked like someone had punched her in the gut. Every time any kind of vehicle could be heard she paused for a moment with a sad yet hopeful look that made Avery's heart hurt even more. Nikki looked both angry and oddly determined. Kyra hid behind her camera, moving through the rubble, documenting the damage.

Forty-one

Like their very first night on Beach Road, their last would be spent at the Cottage Inn.

They'd spent the last three days doing what they could to clean up Bella Flora. Like triage nurses in a war zone, they focused on making the bleeding stop and the patient comfortable.

The show house designers came to remove what was salvageable and prepare their insurance claims for what wasn't. The Dumpster returned to its former spot on the brick drive and filled so quickly it might have been a trick of time-lapse photography—one moment empty, the next brimming with the once-beautiful architectural details and contents of the wounded house.

Maddie, Avery, Nikki, Kyra, and Deirdre swept and mopped and wet-vacced and carried while Chase and Jeff and their crew cleared away the remains of the broken bell tower, then boarded up the missing windows and doors. Enrico and his team ripped off the damaged trussing, gathered the few whole barrel tiles, and covered Bella Flora's gaping insides with a patchwork of tarps so that she looked like some moth-eaten circus tent that had seen better days.

It seemed to Maddie that virtually everyone who had had a hand in rebuilding Bella Flora showed up at some point to help. When they left they shook Maddie's and the others' hands and offered their condolences as one might after a funeral. It seemed appropriate to Maddie because deep inside she felt as if a family member had died.

Before dawn of their last day, Maddie lay in bed searching for the strength she needed to get through the next twenty-four hours. She was no longer the Little Red Hen and she surely was not the emotional Energizer Bunny. She was tired, bone tired, and she still couldn't believe that all they had achieved had been snatched so meanly away.

She chided herself for a fool and admitted once and for all that her optimism about her marriage was as riddled with wishful thinking as her optimism for Bella Flora. Steve had not been there for his family for the last nine months, and he wasn't here now. Cell service had finally been restored, but Andrew seemed to know no more about his father's plans than Maddie, who'd heard nothing from Steve. Her calls to him had gone directly to voice mail, and after a couple of really pathetic messages she'd forced herself to stop calling. Perhaps he and his mother were now vacationing on the moon.

Too restless to stay in bed, Maddie got up and dressed quietly, careful not to wake Kyra as she tiptoed out of their cottage. Unable to face Bella Flora, she walked over to the bay and settled in to watch the sunrise, hoping for inspiration. But not even the bright ball of yellow sun ascending over the water and lightening the sky cheered her. Shoving her hands into the pockets of her shorts she walked along the sidewalk, noting the damage to the big homes on the other side of the bay, sidestepping the drifts of sand and seaweed along with the odd piles of debris that Charlene had deposited everywhere from the far curb to the center of the narrow streets.

At Eighth Avenue she noticed that Merry Pier, like the

fishing jetty on the gulf side, was gone, ripped from its pilings, most likely not for the first time. The shops were tightly closed and the restaurants unopened. One or two people passed, walking dogs or maybe, like her, not yet ready to confront their realities. She peered down the block-long streets and saw others picking through and carting away debris, throwing open windows, sweeping away the sand. She paused to marvel at a piece of plywood embedded in the trunk of a palm tree and tried not to breathe in the smell of dead fish that permeated the air. Pass-a-Grille hadn't been wiped off the map, but it wasn't exactly ready for its close-up, either.

Turning on Eleventh, Maddie walked toward the beach. For a while she stood and watched the beach cleanup under way, pained by the flattened dunes and piles of foreign debris, the scattered pieces of wood that had once been walkovers.

She headed slowly back toward Bella Flora, dragging her feet along the sidewalk, still not ready to face the house they'd nurtured and brought back to life just as she had done for them. Turning, she took one last look down the beach, knowing that if there had been a couch and a remote handy she would have availed herself of them. Just like Steve had.

Footsteps sounded on the pavement behind her. When she heard the voice she thought she might have conjured it.

"Maddie?" the voice that sounded like Steve's asked. "Is that you? Are you okay?"

She turned slowly, still thinking she was imagining things, not at all prepared for the reality of Steve.

"Maddie?"

A host of emotions bombarded her as she took in his appearance, the uncertainty on his face. She'd imagined this so many times, hoped for it, prayed for it, but now that he was here she felt not the relief and happiness she'd imagined but an unexpected wariness. And the first stirrings of anger.

With his gaze on her face, he said, "Emma's place is so far up in the mountains we had no cell service at all. And she favors *Wheel of Fortune* and *General Hospital* over the news. Then my cell phone fell out of my pocket and got run over while I was moving in my mother's things." He paused, seeming to realize that he was running on and she wasn't responding.

"Anyway, I didn't realize what was going on here until I got back to Atlanta. That was after dinnertime yesterday. We drove all night." His voice trailed off. "We went to the house and Kyra said you might be out here."

A small voice told her to cross the distance between them, to put her arms around him, to be grateful that he was finally here. But she didn't feel grateful. She'd been through so much: their dire financial situation, his breakdown, Kyra's pregnancy, the appearance of Daniel Deranian and Hurricane Charlene, and had dealt with all of them alone. Steve had been more than her husband; he'd been her best friend. Yet he'd deserted her when she'd needed him most. Could she throw herself into his arms and pretend she hadn't felt abandoned?

She didn't want to think what would have happened to her if she hadn't had Avery and Nikki. "I didn't think you were going to come at all," Maddie said. "I didn't even realize it until now, but I guess I'd given up."

"Don't say that." Steve took a step closer. "Your belief in me is what pulled me through. Your ultimatum, the thought of losing you, was what finally got me up off that damned couch. Not exactly on time, but up. Please tell me I'm not too late."

They stared at each other. She wasn't sure what he saw, but she didn't feel like the same person who'd left Atlanta in May, not even close. He looked like the "old" Steve, shaved, his hair neatly trimmed, his eyes clear and focused, his voice sad and regretful. But she couldn't see him in the same old way.

"You didn't call," she said. "You didn't answer my messages. I needed you, and you couldn't make yourself return a phone call?" Her throat clogged with all the pent-up anxiety that she'd tried so hard to beat back down. "Those ridiculous texts. They were so vague and so . . . nothing. What were those?" The anger grew hotter, like the sun overhead.

"They were the best I could do, Mad," he said. "I was afraid to promise anything I couldn't deliver. And I was so ashamed."

He looked out over the beach and then back to her. "I

didn't want to come until I had something to offer. I . . ." He gestured to the nearby bench. "Will you sit a minute and just listen?"

They sat facing each other. Although she didn't offer it, he took her hand in both of his, which was another shock. How long had it been since they'd touched in any way?

"I'm so sorry, Maddie," he said quietly, his tone painfully sincere. "I can't believe what I've put you and the kids through. It all seems like some long, horrible nightmare. I'm just so relieved to be awake."

She drew a long shuddering breath as his words sank in, sliding down into the empty places she'd been trying not to notice and hadn't yet figured out how to fill.

"When I finally got it together, thanks to your ultimatum, I knew I had to prove myself," he said. "I had to find a way to apologize that would make things okay again."

She listened numbly, unsure what was coming next.

"I promised myself I wouldn't come to you until I had a job and some way to pay off our bills. I couldn't bear not being able to take care of you all."

She shook her head. "I need a partner, Steve, not a parent. You don't have to 'take care of me.' You just have to be 'present.'" She might not have known it before she came here, but she did now.

"I know. I've seen just how strong you are. You've been amazing. But I needed to contribute. I just didn't see how I could face you again until I'd found a job." He smiled, and she saw a flash of the old confidence, the thing that had drawn her to him all those years ago.

"You have a new job?" she asked, surprised.

"Not exactly," he conceded. "But I've got a good shot at being the new territory manager for Perimeter Capital. I made the top five."

She saw a tiny pinprick of light in the dark tunnel of loss, a small ray of possibility. She swallowed. "That's great." But still she wasn't sure what came next or how exactly she should respond.

Steve raised her hand and brushed his lips across the knuckle before looking back into her eyes. "I'm sorry, too, for allowing my mother to treat you the way she did. I couldn't believe it when I realized she'd been calling you Melinda all these years." His smile turned wry. "That was, as Andrew pointed out, completely lame. Edna and I agreed that she'd work on getting it straight."

A smile found its way to her lips. "I think it had become almost habit with her. I doubt . . ."

"I took her up to North Carolina because her sister couldn't live alone anymore and neither could my mother. They'll be good for each other."

"You mean she's not just visiting?" Maddie asked.

Steve shook his head. "Maybe we can invite them both for the holidays or whatever we feel makes sense, but the move is permanent. She'll be better off up there."

Maddie smiled intentionally this time. It had taken him far longer than she had hoped or wanted, but her husband was here. He'd apologized and was doing his best to make amends. She could hold on to her anger and disappointment, or she could choose to let it go. She drew in a breath and exhaled slowly. "I love you," she said, meaning it. "But I've gotten used to relying on myself. I'm good at a lot more than I realized. Things won't be exactly like they were."

"You've always been good at a lot more than you realized," he said simply. "I can live with change. As long as we're together."

He lifted his hands to bracket her face and stared into her eyes long and hard before he kissed her. As they headed back to Ten Beach Road, she felt the pull of new beginnings and possibility. She only wished the same could be true for Bella Flora.

Admitting defeat hurt. Which was, Avery thought, sort of like saying a bullet to the heart was kind of painful. Regardless of how it felt, they just couldn't seem to find any way around it: Bella Flora was going to have to be sold "as is," assuming anyone was going to be interested in a derelict teardown on a stretch of beach that had just been pounded by a hormonal hurricane. Or they were going to have to find the money to tear her down themselves. They'd come full circle.

Avery, Deirdre, Maddie and her husband, Steve, Nikki, and Chase sat around John Franklin's conference table hashing it out, trying once again to add two and two and come up with something other than four.

"We already owe Chase everything he's put out to his subs and to purchase materials. We don't have the money," Avery said. "There's just no way." It was hard to push the words out past her disappointment, but pretending was equally painful.

"But Dyer's in custody; you're bound to get at least some portion of what your father left you," Deirdre argued. "And so will Maddie and Nikki. You could rebuild." She turned to the others looking for agreement. No one met her eye.

"That could take years, and we have no way of knowing how much anyone will be awarded," Avery said for what seemed like the millionth time. She didn't understand how this had happened, but somewhere along the way she had surrendered to the harsh realities while Deirdre seemed to have purchased her very own ticket to never-never land.

"Insurance will have to cover some of the expense, won't it?" Steve Singer asked.

Avery watched the way he took Maddie's hand and looked at her with love and relief and appreciation all sort of rolled up together. At least something seemed to be ending happily.

"But not enough and probably not anytime soon given the amount of damage Charlene did up and down the Florida coast," Maddie said. "We only had flood insurance because it was transferable. We couldn't afford wind or homeowner's policies. We're just lucky the things the designers put in for the show house were underwritten separately."

"And Bella Flora hadn't been reappraised yet," Nikki pointed out. "That was supposed to happen next week. The maximum we could collect is two hundred fifty thousand dollars." She stole a glance at her cell phone, which she'd placed on the table.

Avery drew in a deep breath; she could barely stand to think about Bella Flora's condition and their situation. Talking about it was even worse.

Nicole's phone rang.

"Sorry." She reached for the phone and looked down at the screen. "I'm sorry," she said again, standing and moving toward the door. "But I need to take this."

Nikki hurried from the conference room and went outside.

Avery could see her through the office picture window the phone to her ear, pacing back and forth out on the sidewalk. She and Maddie exchanged glances. Deirdre raised her eyebrow.

"Maybe we could try to raise the money somehow," Deirdre said. "Do a telethon, look for a wealthy backer of some kind. We know exactly what we're doing now. We could renovate much faster and more efficiently this time."

Avery felt Chase's gaze on her and looked up to meet his eyes. She knew he felt the loss of Bella Flora almost as keenly as she did. It was all so ridiculously pathetic. They had knocked one out of the park when they'd finished Bella Flora. Hurricane Charlene had thrown the baseball back at them and the umpire had called it foul.

"It's over," Avery said. "Let's just accept reality and get on with it."

Nicole came back in and took her seat. "Sorry." Her shoulders were slumped and her voice subdued.

"What's wrong?" Maddie asked. "What happened?"

"I thought I might have good news. I'd almost convinced myself I'd be charging back in here like the financial cavalry." Nicole shook her head sadly.

"What are you talking about?" Deirdre asked.

"I've been clinging to the hope that at least some portion of those accounts Malcolm kept in our mother's name—the ones I turned over to the FBI—would somehow be deemed mine and that we could use it on Bella Flora." Her smile was rueful. "But it's all going into the pot that will be divided among Malcolm's victims."

Avery didn't think she could stand it. "If you hadn't turned the accounts over, would the FBI have found them?"

"I'm not sure," Nicole said. "According to Giraldi they can't just go looking at family member's bank accounts. Not without a direct link to Malcolm."

"Jesus," Avery said. "So we might have had enough to re-renovate."

Nicole nodded, her expression glum. Avery felt even worse now, if that were possible. Like a condemned prisoner who'd been told about a possible reprieve from the governor after it had been denied.

"You did the right thing, Nikki," Maddie said. "You did."

"I know. He left so many people in such dire straits. I'm glad they'll at least get something back." Nikki looked up at them. "But I couldn't help hoping."

"So you all may see some of that money at some point," John Franklin said.

"Yes," Nikki agreed. "But not soon enough to save Bella Flora."

Avery drew yet another deep breath, though the whole breathing thing didn't seem to be particularly effective. She felt far from calm and could actually feel the hot scald of tears forming. She wanted out of here before she humiliated herself completely. "Seeing as we have a whole lot of bills and no money, I move that we authorize John to sell Bella Flora 'as is,'" Avery said, hating the tremor in her voice. She paused, trying to get herself and her voice under control. "If we receive any insurance or other monies before she sells, we'll use it to pay back Chase and tear her the rest of the way down."

As soon as she'd said the words Avery wanted to haul them back. She sat very still and concentrated on holding back her tears. The room went horribly silent.

"I second the motion," Maddie finally said.

Looking up, Avery saw Steve squeeze his wife's hand on top of the table.

"All in favor . . ." Chase said.

Avery sighed, but there was no cavalry coming and no point in prolonging the agony.

"All in favor of authorizing John to sell 'as is' and tear down if possible, say 'aye,'" Maddie managed.

Nobody was actually in favor and everybody knew it. Nobody actually said "aye," either. But the motion carried anyway.

Forty-two

On the morning of their last day on Pass-a-Grille, Nicole woke early. Like she had so many other mornings, she pulled on her running clothes, which now sported dabs of pink paint and blobs of polyurethane, and walked outside to stretch.

The sky was once again a soft powder blue, the sun pale and gentle in its initial ascent, as she stepped out onto Beach Road and headed resolutely past Bella Flora and toward the beach. Chiding her inner wussiness, she barely glanced at the battered façade, then took the path to the jetty with its pier-less pilings, picking her way around the newly formed dunes and mountains of still-damp sand.

Drawing in a breath that carried scents decidedly less attractive than the normal tang of salt, she began a slow jog, careful to keep her gaze on the pink castle-like walls of the Don CeSar, already debating whether she would turn around before she got close enough to see any indignities it might have suffered.

Her focus was so inward that it took her a few moments to notice the shadow coming up from behind to obliterate her own. At the sound of footsteps coming up beside her, she glanced over to see Joe Giraldi. He looked much as he had the first time he'd joined her on this beach: T-shirt tucked into the waistband of his running shorts, bare chest sun-kissed but not yet glistening with sweat. They ran for a time without speaking, sidestepping drifts of seaweed and dead fish, sticking to the hardest-packed sand, their shoes crunching on broken bits of shell.

"Did you come to gloat?" she finally asked, her focus still locked on the Don in the distance.

"No," he said, turning his head. Even behind the sun-glasses she could feel the intensity of his gaze. "I came to thank you. I know it couldn't have been easy. But you did a good thing."

Nicole snorted. She'd given up all the second-guessing. Malcolm had left her no choice and she couldn't, in good conscience, have kept the money from the Florida accounts. She knew that ultimately she'd done the right thing. But the fact that it was right didn't make it feel good.

She turned to study Giraldi, the beak of a nose, the strong jaw and even stronger shoulders. "So, this is good-bye then?"

"Oh, I may not disappear completely," he said. "The accoun-tants and the prosecutors take over now, but I won't be com-pletely out of the loop." He paused for a moment though there was no hesitation in his stride. "The report I filed indicates that you were working with us when you went into the park. It's not everyone who would have turned over that money."

They ran for a time in silence, reaching the Don, where workers were still clearing away debris and setting things to rights. From here it appeared the hotel had fared better than Bella Flora. It was bound to be better insured.

Without discussion they turned back, Giraldi matching his pace to hers. Questions flitted through her mind as they ran, but the answers no longer mattered. They neared the shuttered Paradise Grille, many of its tables buried under mounds of sand. The marauding seagulls would be forced to maraud elsewhere.

"Off to play Peeping Tom again?" she asked after they'd

neared the jetty and slowed to a walk. Her gaze was on his face now, but the sunglasses hid his eyes along with his thoughts.

"I always have my trench coat in the car, just in case," he said, flashing her a white-toothed smile. "But I doubt I'm going to get a shot at anything anywhere near as enjoyable as keeping tabs on you."

It was maudlin and showed her age, but "Leaving on a Jet Plane" played in Maddie's head that afternoon as she set her suitcases next to the cottage door and cleaned out the van for the drive back to Atlanta in the morning. Over and over she told herself that everything would be all right. That Steve was back, the kids were okay, their family was intact.

Still, she had to force a smile as she waved Steve and Andrew off for their guys' cookout at the Hardins', then dragged herself to Bella Flora to meet Avery and Nicole and Deirdre and Kyra for their very last sunset.

She didn't walk through Bella Flora; she simply couldn't face her gouged walls and gaping wounds, the pungent wet salt smell that didn't complement the smell of plastic tarp, the dark injured rooms with their sodden floors and plywood Band-Aids. Instead she followed the brick drive around to the back where she set out their neon-strapped aluminum beach chairs, which had been unearthed in the garage closet. Their "cocktail table" was an electrical cable spindle delivered by Hurricane Charlene and turned on its end.

From a grocery bag Maddie pulled the family-sized bag of Cheez Doodles and a foil-covered plate of the tiny hotdogs in blankets that had been a sunset staple and which Kyra now craved. Nikki arrived carrying a blender of margaritas. Kyra, her assistant, followed with her camera bag over one shoulder and a second pitcher in her hands. Avery and Deirdre brought the plastic margarita glasses, which they passed around. Bella Flora hunkered beside them dark and abandoned. After all the rain she'd absorbed she was probably not thirsty.

"Ah," Avery said when she spotted the beach chairs. "I

never really felt comfortable with all that fancy wrought iron." She cast a glance at the cushionless furniture that had been dragged out of the pool much the worse for the experience.

"No, aluminum and corrugated cardboard is definitely more your style," Nikki said automatically, but without heat.

They fell silent as they sipped their drinks and nibbled on the snacks. Their gazes were focused on the sky like strangers in an elevator watching the floor numbers go by. They'd been just those kind of strangers when they'd arrived back in May, Maddie thought. Since then they'd slept, sweated, laughed, and cried together, and of course, they'd fought with each other. They'd survived some of the worst things life could throw at them. Together.

The sun glowed golden red as it inched toward its resting place beneath the now-calm water. The concrete pilings of the fishing pier stood as silent testament to all that had been ripped away. Just as Bella Flora did.

"I can't believe it's ending like this," Avery said. "I can't believe we're leaving Bella Flora worse off than we found her."

Kyra had begun shooting after just a few sips of her non-alcoholic margarita. No one thought to ask her to stop; she'd captured and shared much worse than this final good-bye, though Maddie didn't think she'd shot anything sadder.

No one talked about where they would go in the morning or what they would do next. Maddie could feel all of them straining to stay in the moment, but it was impossible not to think about the fact that she might never see these women, who knew her in ways no one ever had, again.

"I hope to hell you're not expecting anyone to come up with anything good tonight, Maddie," Avery said, her gaze fixed on the sun, which now hovered above the Gulf, its reflected brilliance shimmering beneath it.

Deirdre drank silently, but Maddie noticed the way the designer kept studying her daughter as if recording each feature and expression for playback at a later time.

"It's not going to be easy," Maddie acknowledged. "But we're all going to have to come up with . . . something." She smiled and felt her heart twist. "We wouldn't be 'us' without our 'one good thing.'"

There was another silence as she imagined them thinking, as she was, that after tonight there wouldn't be an "us."

"I'll go first," Maddie said, pushing the thought away. "I'm incredibly glad that Steve's found himself and made it here. I'll be forever grateful for that." She raised her glass not toward the setting sun, but toward them. "But my one good thing, my best thing, is all of you."

"Shit," Avery said. "Did you really have to say that? You're going to make me cry."

Unhappiness hung over them like a blanket, warm and heavy. Nikki poured them each a final drink, but no one drank.

Avery harrumphed and swiped at her eyes. Deirdre's gaze remained on the puddle of red sun oozing into the Gulf. Leached of color, the sky turned the palest of grays.

No one spoke as the shadows continued to lengthen. Dusk settled in.

In the growing dark, Maddie tried to read the others' faces. It seemed pretty clear that no one else was going to offer their "one good thing," and Maddie didn't have the heart to force them. She set her glass down and began to gather the snacks. She felt as if she'd been about to stride over the finish line when someone stuck out a foot to trip her. Kyra reached for her camera bag, tucking the video camera into it while Avery stared morosely out over the pass.

"Well, I guess that's it then," Maddie said, standing. "We might as well call it a night."

The others stood and began to gather up the remnants of their sunset snack.

There was the ding of an incoming message, and Kyra pulled out her cell phone. She gasped in surprise and began to scroll through a message. Her eyes widened as she read it.

"What is it?" Maddie asked, thinking it might be work related. Or some sort of change of heart from Daniel Deranian.

"Oh, my God!" Kyra said, clutching at Maddie's arm. "Oh, my God!"

"Take some deep breaths and try to calm down," Deirdre said. "No one needs you hyperventilating yourself into an early labor."

There was nervous laughter, but they all looked at Kyra expectantly.

Kyra drew an exaggerated breath, then held up her cell phone, brightening the backlight so that she could read them the email. "I can't believe it. It's from Karen Crandall, head of development at Lifetime." She smiled. *"Dear Ms. Singer,"* she read. *"We've been watching your YouTube posts on the renovation at Ten Beach Road with great interest. You are a gifted filmmaker and storyteller."* Kyra's smile lit her face; she took a mock bow. *"We enjoyed not only the footage of Bella Flora being brought back to her former glory, but the chemistry—good and bad—between the people on this project, each of whom brought unique talents and perspectives to the renovation. We couldn't have cast it better ourselves and are certain our viewers will relate."*

Kyra paused as they contemplated each other. Even Bella Flora seemed to be listening.

Avery turned to Deirdre. "Wasn't Karen Crandall the person who bought your design specials for Lifetime?"

Deirdre nodded and smiled as Kyra continued. *"We would like to discuss shooting a pilot for a new series in which you would serve as producer/director and the group would select significant homes in different parts of the country to renovate."* Kyra grinned. "It ends with her cell phone number and a request that I call her as soon as possible." She peered down at the screen and then her watch. "It says she's out in California and to call anytime."

"Oh, my God," Maddie said, hugging Kyra. "That's fabulous!"

"It is," Avery agreed. "It sounds like a wonderful opportunity. What do you all think?"

"I don't know what there is to think about!" Maddie said. She couldn't seem to stop smiling. "I'm in!"

"Me, too. If you'll have me," Deirdre added, looking directly at Avery and waiting for her nod. Kyra, who had already unpacked her camera to shoot their reactions, captured their identical smiles.

"I'm in!" Avery said, clearly uncertain how to deal with Deirdre's possible role in the network's interest. "As long as there's no nodding or pointing. And none of us, under any circumstances, is ever asked to wear a sweater no matter how cold it gets."

"Damn straight," Deirdre said.

"I'm with you on that!" Maddie laughed.

There were jubilant high fives and lots of hugs, which Kyra documented from every possible angle. Until she panned the camera lens over to the battered hulk of Bella Flora.

Kyra stopped recording and slowly lowered her camera. One by one they fell silent as they regarded the house that had brought them together and whose resurrection had led to their own.

"Even if we're able to make a deal with the network, it'll take a while to come to terms. And any money's going to be pretty far down the road." Avery continued to look at the dark and silent house. "That still leaves Bella Flora on the market 'as is.'"

There was a longer silence as this unwelcome truth tempered their euphoria. How could they celebrate when Bella Flora was so bruised and battered?

"You know," Deirdre said, considering her daughter. "I wasn't blowing smoke when I told you how much easier and faster it would be to re-create what we've already done." She looked at the others. "Which would make Bella Flora a perfect choice for the pilot."

There was an even longer silence as they all absorbed Deirdre's suggestion. Maddie imagined Bella Flora perking up in the gathering dark.

"The network might go for it. And Kyra's YouTube posts have already given Bella Flora a certain following," Avery said.

"But what if they want us to start with something else?" Maddie asked.

"We might not have that kind of control," Nicole said. "And a television series isn't an opportunity that comes along every day."

"That's for sure," Kyra said. "It's pretty much a dream come true."

Deirdre nodded her agreement. "There are no guarantees here. And all we're being offered is the chance to make a pilot. The odds of a series actually happening are low."

"We'd have to stand together on this, make it a condition for moving forward," Avery said. She shot Deirdre and then Nicole a look. "No side deals or jockeying for position. We'd have to put Bella Flora's comeback before our own."

Maddie couldn't imagine wanting to do this without the others, but this was Kyra's dream. "What do you think, Ky? You made this happen and it could be the shot you've been working toward. Are you willing to take the risk?"

Slowly, Kyra nodded. "I think we owe it to Bella Flora. And to ourselves." She smiled at all of them. "I'm willing to roll the dice if you are."

Each of them nodded their agreement as Maddie's heart swelled with pride in her daughter.

"Call her back right now," Avery said. "And tell her we're all on board. But only if we can do Bella Flora first."

They sat on the edge of their chairs while Kyra punched in the numbers, the cheap straps and aluminum straining. Maddie could see the mixture of hope and fear on all of their faces. She was fairly certain no one was breathing. She knew for sure she wasn't.

"Is this Karen Crandall?" Kyra's voice wobbled slightly as her call was answered. "This is Kyra Singer. I'm the one who . . ."

She fell silent, listening carefully, her gaze on Bella Flora. The voice on the other end sounded tinny and distant in the silence, but Maddie couldn't make out what was being said. "Thank you. Yes. We're interested. In fact, we're all together right now. At Bella Flora." Kyra swallowed. "With Bella Flora."

The woman said something else and Kyra nodded, but her

expression gave nothing away. "Yes, we're all excited about the opportunity, but there's just one thing."

They listened as Kyra explained their position and waited, still barely breathing, while Kyra listened to the network head's answer.

"No," Kyra said, her expression still unreadable. "Of course. Yes. I understand."

Maddie thought it a miracle that no one had passed out from lack of oxygen by the time Kyra hung up the phone. Her hand shook as she set down the phone and reached for the camera.

"Jesus, Kyra!" Nicole said. "Forget about the damned camera. Just tell us what she said!"

"I don't think I want to hear it unless it's good news," Avery said. "I can't take any more bad."

Deirdre reached out to squeeze Avery's hand. "I could have my agent call the network. Maybe we should . . ."

"Come on, Ky," Maddie said. "Just tell us. Put us out of our misery. My heart is pounding so hard I'm afraid it's going to burst through my chest."

"Okay," Kyra said quietly. "But I want to be able to capture your reactions." She raised the camera to her eye and fiddled with the zoom. "Because I'm thinking that maybe we could use footage of this moment. You know . . ." A small smile tugged at her lips. "During the opening credits of the pilot!"

"You mean . . ." Nikki began.

". . . She agreed?" Deirdre asked.

Kyra nodded happily but didn't speak until she'd finished capturing their first gasps of joy. "Yes, she said yes!" Kyra beamed. "There's lots of details to work out, and a budget to set, but she agreed to let us redo Bella Flora for the pilot!"

"Oh, my God," Avery said. "I can't believe it." The tears she'd been holding back streamed down her face. Deirdre reached over with a napkin and dabbed at the corners of her daughter's eyes.

Nikki had turned her face, but Maddie could see the sheen of tears in the corner of her eye.

It hit home then that the miracle Maddie had been afraid to wish for had actually come true. They were going to get another chance to bring Bella Flora back to life just as she had given them back theirs. Despite her injuries, Bella Flora hunkered almost protectively behind them; she was strong deep down where it mattered most.

"To Bella Flora!" Maddie said, raising her glass. "And everything she taught us!"

"To Bella Flora!" they said in unison, clinking their plastic tumblers, then lifting them toward the house in homage before draining them in long, celebratory gulps.

The moonlight flattered Bella Flora's angles and curves and spilled out over the pass to shimmer on the water's surface as they laughed and talked.

"Just think of all the things we know now that we didn't know the first time around," Maddie said.

"Like no polyurethane in an enclosed space," Deirdre said.

"No working for bananas or dancing to the organ grinder's tune," Avery added.

"No shutting down more than one bathroom at a time," Kyra said. "Especially when pregnant women are present."

"No early bird specials or senior citizen discounts," Nicole interjected, looking at Maddie. "No matter how great the savings!"

"And absolutely, positively no renovating on a barrier island during hurricane season," Maddie added with absolute certainty. "I say we aim to start work after the holidays. Maybe my grandson or granddaughter can have a cameo."

The breeze was soft and warm on their skin, the moon's glow gentle as they talked late into the night, laying their plans, buoyed by a friendship they'd never expected on a journey they hadn't meant to take.

Readers Guide to

Ten Beach Road

DISCUSSION QUESTIONS

1. At the very start of the novel, Madeline's world is crashing down around her—an empty nest, the shocking news of her mother-in-law's accident and move, Steve's unemployment, and her daughter's pregnancy. How does this set the stage for the rest of what Madeline undergoes in the book? Do these challenges force her to become more adaptive, stronger? Do you think she did the right thing by leaving her husband and Edna behind during a complicated and emotionally volatile situation?

2. Could you relate to Madeline's frustration at the slow economy—or Steve's reluctance to act and crushing depression? What would you have done in Maddie's position? How does Maddie resist the temptation to let everything fall to pieces?

3. How does Malcolm Dyer's Ponzi scheme frame the events of the book? How does this crisis tie the characters together?

4. Which woman's struggles—Madeline's, Avery's, or Nicole's—did you identify with the most? What does Bella Flora mean to each of them, and how does this change over the course of the novel?

5. Do you think Nicole had an ethical obligation to share her information on Malcolm with the authorities? Even after he destroyed her livelihood and wiped out her life savings, why does she hesitate? What changes in Nicole's

heart about helping bring her brother to justice? What influences her decision, or trumps her protective sibling nature?

6. How would you describe Avery and Deirdre's relationship? How is it similar to that of Kyra and Maddie? How do these mother-daughter relationships evolve over the course of their stay at Bella Flora? What are the catalyst events?

7. Each woman finds herself at a breakthrough point as the renovation comes to a close, where she finds she is able to speak her deepest feelings and act more boldly. What are these moments for each, and what are the ramifications?

8. Were you shocked by Deirdre's ulterior motives and her role as the publicity leak? Did you hope that she would have a change of heart and work to reconcile with her daughter?

9. Do you think the women were right to be outraged and to exile Nicole after learning the truth about her relationship to Malcolm and her lack of disclosure? How would you have reacted? When do you think an appropriate time would have been to share this information—and how do you think it would have affected the bond the women felt?

10. Were you surprised by Daniel Deranian's sudden appearance? Do you think Kyra made the right choice? What led to her decision? How does Maddie's attitude influence this?

11. What motivated Steve's appearance at Bella Flora, his reformed behavior, and pledge to wellness? Could you have forgiven such bad behavior in a time of family crisis?

12. How do you think the second set of renovations will go at Bella Flora? How will the lessons learned over the summer set the team up?

Acknowledgments

Every book presents its own journey of discovery. Even when you think you know your setting and your characters, there are countless details that need to be researched and understood. A lot of people contributed their unique insights and experiences to *Ten Beach Road*, and I'm very grateful for their help.

This time thanks are owed to:

Pat Rossignol, whose own renovation of an incredibly special house both inspired and awed me. Thank you for sharing your experiences and your home; the champagne and encouragement were unexpected bonuses.

"Sister" Carol Lane, who made introductions and went with me on that first fabulous tour.

Marie Beth Cheezem for sharing her gorgeous home, and to the "Yes" Girls, Rhonda Sanderford and Marian Yon Maguire, for the tour of Snell Isle homes that led me to it. Thank you for answering the real estate questions that arose.

Frank T. Hurley, Jr., former neighbor, well-known Realtor and beach historian for answering both real estate and preservation questions and for helping me understand what could and couldn't happen. Your books gave me a greater understanding of Pass-a-Grille and the beach I grew up on.

Catherine Hartley, AICP, for helping me get started.

Joe Frohock, All Lines Insurance Group, for answering questions up to the last minute, especially when I realized that I simply couldn't "kill the house."

Rob Griffin and "Tito" Vargas for talking me through the intricacies and order of construction and remodeling. And to Rebecca Ritchie, who took pity on my lack of understanding and not only re-clarified but read the final draft to make sure I'd gotten it right.

Jon and Barry Wax for boating and other feedback, Jeff Brizzi for sharing his knowledge of classic cars, and Special Agent Karen Marshall for helping me keep FBI Agent Giraldi as real as possible.

Tonja Kay, whose donation to F.A.C.E.S., Families and Children Experiencing Separation, in Morgan County, Alabama, won her the right to have a character named after her. My apologies for using your lovely name on a less than loveable character.

Reneé Athey for her friendship and for helping me envision Bella Flora and her surrounding grounds and for lending me her name—accent aigu and all.

Ingrid Jacobus for her unflagging friendship and for serving as a first reader. This book probably never would have existed if it weren't for all those great breakfasts at The Seahorse and our walks on my favorite beach in the world.

And, of course, no list of thanks would be complete without Karen White, intrepid friend and critique partner, who is not afraid to tell me when something's not working. And to Susan Crandall, retreat and critique partner. It's great to have you in the mix.

I hope that my love of the real Pass-a-Grille is apparent in this story. I cartwheeled my way down its beautiful white sand beach as a child, strutted across it in a bikini as a teenager, and brought my own children to build sand castles on it as an adult. I trust those of you in the know will forgive me for altering parts of it. I've changed a few street and business names to suit the story and removed an entire condo building to make room for Bella Flora. This is, after all, a work of fiction. And although I have borrowed some names and a few occupations, the characters are imaginary and not based on or intended to represent real people in any way.

Turn the page for a preview of
Wendy Wax's novel . . .

MAGNOLIA WEDNESDAYS

Featuring Vivien Armstrong Gray, "an easy
protagonist to love; plucky, resourceful, and
witty" (*Publishers Weekly*).

Available in paperback!

Well-bred girls from good southern families are not supposed to get shot.

Vivien Armstrong Gray's mother had never come out and actually told her this, but Vivi had no doubt it belonged on the long list of unwritten, yet critically important, rules of conduct on which she'd been raised. Dictates like "Always address older women and men as ma'am and sir" and "Never ask directly for what you want if you can get it with charm, manners, or your family name." And one of Vivien's personal favorites, "Although it's perfectly fine to visit New York City on occasion in order to shop, see shows and ballets, or visit a museum, there's really no good reason to live there."

Vivien had managed to break all of those rules and quite a few others over the last forty-one years, the last fifteen of which she'd spent as an investigative reporter in that most Yankee of cities.

The night her life fell apart Vivi wasn't thinking about rules or decorum or anything much but getting the footage she needed to break a story on oil speculation and price manipulation that she'd been working on for months.

It was ten P.M. on a muggy September night when Vivien pressed herself into a doorway in a darkened corner of a Wall Street parking garage a few feet away from where a source had told her an FBI financial agent posing as a large institutional investor was going to pay off a debt-ridden commodities trader.

Crouched beside her cameraman, Marty Phelps, in the heat-soaked semidarkness, Vivien tried to ignore the flu symptoms she'd been battling all week. Eager to finally document the first in a string of long awaited arrests, she'd just noted the time—ten fifteen P.M.—when a bullet sailed past her cheek with the force of a pointy-tipped locomotive. The part of her brain that didn't freeze up in shock realized that the bullet had come from the wrong direction.

Marty swore, but she couldn't tell if it was in pain or surprise, and his video camera clattered onto the concrete floor. Loudly. Too loudly.

Two pings followed, shattering one of the overhead lights that had illuminated the area.

Heart pounding, Vivien willed her eyes to adjust to the deeper darkness, but she couldn't see Marty, or his camera, or who was shooting at them. Before she could think what to do, more bullets buzzed by like a swarm of mosquitoes after bare flesh at a barbecue. They ricocheted off concrete, pinged off steel and metal just like they do in the movies and on TV. Except that these bullets were real, and it occurred to her then that if one of them found her, she might actually die.

Afraid to move out of the doorway in which she cowered, Vivien turned and hugged the hard metal of the door. One hand reached down to test the locked knob as she pressed her face against its pock-marked surface, sucking in everything that could be sucked, trying to become one with the door, trying to become too flat, too thin, too "not there" for a bullet to find her.

Her life did not pass before her eyes. There was no highlight reel—maybe when you were over forty a full viewing would take too long?—no snippets, no "best of Vivi," no "worst of," either, which would have taken more time.

What there was was a vague sense of regret that settled over her like a shroud, making Vivi wish deeply, urgently, that she'd done better, been more. Maybes and should-haves consumed her; little bursts of clarity that seized her and shook her up and down, back and forth like a pit bull with a rag doll clenched between its teeth.

Maybe she *should* have listened to her parents. Maybe she *would* have been happier, more fulfilled, if she hadn't rebelled so completely, hadn't done that exposé on that Democratic senator who was her father's best friend and political ally, hadn't always put work before everything else. If she'd stayed home in Atlanta. Gotten married. Raised children like her younger sister, Melanie. Or gone into family politics like her older brother, Hamilton.

If regret and dismay had been bulletproof, Vivien might have walked away unscathed. But as it turned out, would'ves, should'ves, and could'ves were nowhere near as potent as Kevlar. The next thing Vivien knew, her regret was pierced by the sharp slap of a bullet entering her body, sucking the air straight out of her lungs and sending her crumpling to the ground.

Facedown on the concrete, grit filling her mouth, Vivien tried to absorb what had happened and what might happen next as a final hail of bullets flew above her head. Then something metal hit the ground followed by the thud of what she was afraid might be a body.

Her eyes squinched tightly shut, she tried to marshal her thoughts, but they skittered through her brain at random and of their own accord. At first she was aware only of a general ache. Then a sharper, clearer pain drew her attention. With what clarity her befuddled brain could cling to, she realized that the bullet had struck the only body part that hadn't fit all the way into the doorway. Modesty and good breeding should have prohibited her from naming that body part, but a decade and a half in New York City compelled her to acknowledge that the bullet was lodged in the part that she usually sat on. The part on which the sun does not shine.

The part that irate cab drivers and construction workers, who can't understand why a woman is not flattered by their attentions, are always shouting for that woman to kiss.

Despite the pain and the darkness into which her brain seemed determined to retreat, Vivi almost smiled at the thought.

There were shouts and the pounding of feet. The concrete shook beneath her, but she didn't have the mental capacity or the energy to worry about it. The sound of approaching sirens pierced the darkness—and her own personal fog—briefly. And then there was nothing.

Which at least protected her from knowing that Marty's camera was rolling when it fell. That it had somehow captured everything that happened to her—from the moment she tried to become one with the door to the moment she shrieked and grabbed her butt to the moment they found her and loaded her facedown onto the stretcher, her derriere pointing upward at the concrete roof above.

Vivien spent the night in the hospital apparently so that everyone in possession of a medical degree—or aspirations to one—could examine her rear end. The pain pills muted the pain in her posterior to a dull throb, but there didn't seem to be any medication that could eliminate her embarrassment.

When she woke up the next morning, exhausted and irritated from trying to sleep on her side as well as round-the-clock butt checks, she found a bouquet of butt-shaped balloons from the network news division sitting on her nightstand. A bouquet of flowers arranged in a butt-shaped vase sat beside it. No wonder there was a trade deficit. We seemed to be importing endless versions of buttocks.

Making the mistake of flipping on the television, she was forced to watch a replay of last night's shooting—the only footage in what they called a sting gone awry was of her—and discovered that she was one of the last human beings on the face of the earth to see it. Everyone from the morning anchors at her own network to the hosts of the other networks' morning talk shows seemed to be having a big yuck over it.

If she'd been one for dictates and rules, she would have added, "If a well-bred girl from a good southern family slips up and *does* somehow get shot, she should make sure the wound is fatal and not just humiliating."

If she'd died in that parking garage, they would have been hailing Vivi as a hero and replaying some of her best investigative moments. Instead she was a laughingstock.

Vivien swallowed back her indignation along with the contents of her stomach, which kept threatening to escape. She desperately wanted to take her rear end and go home where both of them could get some privacy.

The phone rang. She ignored it.

It was almost noon when Marty strolled into the room. He was tall and lanky with straight brown hair he was always pushing out of his eyes and a long pale face dominated by a beak of a nose. She always pictured him rolling AV equipment into a high school classroom or caressing computer keys with his long, surprisingly delicate fingers. He was a gifted photojournalist and over the last ten years had demonstrated that he would follow her anywhere to get a story and could shoot video under the most trying circumstances as he had, unfortunately, proven yet again last night.

Marty looked relaxed and well rested. But then, he hadn't taken a bullet in his butt last night. Or had people prodding and laughing at him since.

"You don't look so good," he said by way of greeting.

"You're kidding?" Vivien feigned chagrin. "And here I thought I was all bright-eyed and bushy-tailed and ready for my close-up."

He dropped down onto the bedside chair, and she envied the fact that he could sit without discomfort or forethought. If he noted the jealousy that must have flared in her eyes, he didn't comment.

"If you've brought anything shaped like a butt or with a picture of a butt on it, or are even remotely considering using the word 'butt' in this conversation, you might as well leave now," she said.

"My, my, you certainly are touchy this morning."

"Touchy?" She snorted. "You don't know the half of it."

They regarded each other for a moment while Vivien wondered if she could talk him into breaking her out of here.

"Your mother called me on my cell this morning," Marty said. "I heard from Stone, too."

About five years ago her mother, noting that Vivien had had a longer relationship with her cameraman than she'd ever had with anyone she dated and frustrated at the slowness of Vivien's responses, had started using Marty as a middleman. Stone Seymour, who actually was her boyfriend, or, as he liked to call himself, Vivien's main squeeze, used Marty to reach her, too, especially when he was on assignment in some war-smudged part of the globe from which communication was difficult and sporadic and Vivien had forgotten to clear her voice-mail box or plug in her phone.

"How in the world did he hear about this already?" Stone was CIN's senior international correspondent and the network's terrorist expert, which meant he spent great blocks of time in places so remote that even the latest technology was rendered useless.

"He was doing live shots from outside Kabul early this morning and one of the New York producers told him. And, um, I think he might have seen the, um, video on . . ." There was a long drawn out bobbing of his Adam's apple. ". . . Um, YouTube."

Her gaze moved from Marty's throat to his face, which was strangely flushed. "Did you say YouTube?"

Marty shifted uncomfortably in his chair, his long frame clearly too large for the piece of furniture just like his Adam's apple seemed too large for his throat. He looked away.

"What does YouTube have to do with me?"

Marty met her gaze, swallowed slowly and painfully again. "I hit my head when I fell and missed most of what happened after that."

She waited. As an investigative reporter, silence had always been one of her best weapons.

"But apparently the target sensed something was up from the beginning. When the undercover guy approached him to complete the transaction, he got nervous and pulled out a gun. I never expected a commodities trader to show up armed. Isn't white-collar crime supposed to be nonviolent?

"Anyway, he must have been really nervous, because the agent said the guy's hand was shaking so badly they're not even sure whether the first shot was intentional. That was the bullet that came between us and made me drop my camera."

"So how'd I get shot? What were all the rest of those bullets?"

"It just got out of control. Somebody on the FBI's side fired back—some rookie, it looks like—and then it was the shoot-out at the O.K. Corral. I don't think they even realized we were there. I sure would like to know why your contact kept that tidbit to himself."

It was Vivi's turn to look away and for her Adam's apple to feel too big for her throat. She hadn't actually notified her contact that they'd planned to be there. She'd thought they'd get better footage if no one was mugging for the camera. And she hadn't expected the commodities trader to have a gun, either.

"The target is dead," Marty continued. "And there's going to be an internal investigation. It was a real screwup. And, um, strangely enough when I dropped my camera it got wedged up against a tire, rolling. And, um, trained on you. I mean what are the odds of that happening? It's actually kind of funny, really." His voice trailed off when he saw her face. "In a bizarre sort of way."

"Yeah," Vivien said. "It's hysterical."

"So anyway, while I was out cold the FBI took my camera and watched the video to see if it would provide any clues as to what went down, who was at fault. But, um, unfortunately the only thing on the tape was . . . you."

"And?"

"And someone made a copy. And, um, posted it on YouTube."

Vivien stared at him in silence, not intentionally this time, but because she couldn't help it.

"It's been extremely popular. Phenomenally so. I think you've already had fifty thousand views in less than twenty-four hours. You've got four and a half stars."

Now Vivien's life flashed before her eyes. In Technicolor and 3-D. She watched it in painful slo-mo. Those first years in New York, alone and friendless, a southern-fried fish out of water in a sea of self-assured northern sharks.

Then came the long grueling years spent building cred-ibility, honing her interview techniques, building her con-tact base, developing her research skills. Not to mention the endless hours spent smothering her southern accent, merci-lessly shortening and clipping those lazy vowels and drawn-out syllables so that she could have been from anywhere, or nowhere, under the equally merciless tutelage of New York's most expensive voice coach.

The years of working twice as hard as any man around her. Of always putting the job, the story, the next break before anything else. Before family, before friends, before lovers. She had worked with single-minded determination until the name Vivien Gray became synonymous with "inside scoop."

All of it ground to dust by a ten-minute video of her butt.

Scooting on her side, she managed to swing her legs off the bed and lower her feet to the floor and ultimately to stand. Marty jumped up from his chair, concerned. "What are you doing? Are you allowed to get out of bed?"

"I don't know and I don't care. They've poked and prodded me since I got here. And when they weren't poking or prod-ding they were laughing. Or trying not to. One of the doctors actually told me I should have 'turned the other cheek.'"

A snort of amusement escaped Marty's lips, and she shot him a withering look. "Don't you dare laugh. Don't you dare!"

Wincing with each step, she carried her clothes into the bathroom and removed the hospital gown. Her body was bruised and battered. Her underwear and jeans had holes laced with blood where the bullet had passed through. Vivien pushed back the nausea she felt at the remembered feel of steel slamming into her flesh. Gingerly she stepped into the jeans, careful not to dislodge the dressing on her wound as she pulled them up, then tossed the underwear into the trash can.

She was about to slip an arm into the shirt she'd been wearing the night before when she noticed that it, too, had a hole in the same spot. Holding it up in front of her, she opened the bathroom door and reached out a bare arm. "Give me the T-shirt you have on under your long sleeves." She held her hand out until she felt the cotton cross her palm, then pulled it on over her head and down over her rear end.

As she walked back into the hospital room ready to bully Marty into helping her slip out of the hospital and into a cab, it occurred to her that the well-bred southern girls' code of conduct might be in need of an addendum. Because surely if such a girl should have the bad taste to not only get shot but *survive*, she'd better make damned sure her abject humiliation wasn't captured on camera, aired on national television, or uploaded to YouTube.